SAMSON AND DELILAH

Frances Edmonds is well known for her bestsellers *Another Bloody Tour* and *Cricket XXXX Cricket*, and as a broadcaster both in Britain and Australia. She is married to former England Test cricketer, Phil Edmonds, and lives in London. *Samson and Delilah* is her first novel.

Also by Frances Edmonds

ANOTHER BLOODY TOUR
CRICKET XXXX CRICKET
MEMBERS ONLY

Frances Edmonds

SAMSON
AND
DELILAH

A TALE OF VENGEANCE

PAN BOOKS
IN ASSOCIATION WITH MACMILLAN LONDON

First published 1992 by Macmillan London Limited

This edition published 1993 by Pan Books Limited
a division of Pan Macmillan Publishers Limited
Cavaye Place London SW10 9PG
and Basingstoke

in association with Macmillan London Limited
Associated companies throughout the world

ISBN 0 330 32388 1
Copyright © Frances Edmonds 1992

3 5 7 9 8 6 4

A CIP catalogue record for this book is available from
the British Library

Phototypeset by Intype, London
Printed and bound in Great Britain by
Cox & Wyman Ltd, Reading, Berkshire

ACKNOWLEDGEMENTS

I have made many friends while researching this book – all of whom have given generously of their time and advice. I would hasten to add, however, that while most of these people are acknowledged experts in their fields, any inaccuracies are a reflection neither upon their opinions nor their expertise. For their help and kindness I would like to thank:

Sam Quick (Comexim); Peter Robbins (World Gold Commission); Alan Austin (Johnson Matthey); Barry Davidson (MD Platinum, Johannesburg Consolidated Investments Co. Ltd); Salome Pouroulis and her father, Loucas Pouroulis (Golden Dumps (Pty) Ltd); Arthur Barlow, Susan van Zyl and the team at the Rustenburg platinum mine; Gordon Kaye (Jeffreys Henry); Vincent van der Bijl; my brother, Brendan Moriarty, consultant ophthalmologist, whose qualifications would fill an entire page; the much missed Penny B. Staples, now of Miami, and her cat, Ernie; my dear friend and neighbour, Irene Beard (INA Antiques); my old mate and gossip partner, Harold Winton, and his wife, Iva; Jo Foley, former editor of *Options*; my two anonymous friends in the City, Richard and most especially, John – without whose indefatigable support this book would never have been written.

Samson and Delilah is my first novel and I am therefore grateful to my publishers at Pan Macmillan for their constant encouragement. My thanks to Felicity Rubinstein – who seems to have had a hand in every deal I've ever done; to Jane Wood, my editor, who has been an enormous help and support; to Hazel Orme, for her meticulous copy-editing; to Billy Adair –

who continues to imbue me with such enthusiasm, and to all the staff for their hard work and assistance.

I am very fortunate to have Desmond Elliott as my business manager. He is quite simply the best and most understanding friend an author could ever wish for. He also makes me laugh.

On a more personal note, I would like to express my deepest gratitude to my family. They continue to be my greatest source of strength. Finally I would like to thank Liz Pullen who has lived through all the ups and downs of this book. Without her and my daughter, Alexandra, I would have been lost.

To JC
WITH THANKS

SAMSON
AND
DELILAH

PROLOGUE

London, March 1991

LILAH was never late.

Punctuality. It was almost an obsession with her, one of the less destructive legacies of a convent school education.

Sir Roger Samson glanced at his watch. Eleven thirty-five. The board meeting should have started over half an hour ago. Why on earth should she keep them waiting today of all days, the day he most needed his wife to be there, to stand shoulder to shoulder with him for all the world to see? It was so unlike her. What could possibly have happened? Seated bolt upright at the head of the large, mahogany, horseshoe-shaped table, Sir Roger stared fixedly through the window opposite. Outside, London was enjoying a glorious early spring day, a slight breeze, a gentle nip in the air, the sun shining. From the vantage point of Samson International's boardroom, the view of the Thames below was superb. It was this, more than any other consideration, that made Samson Heights the most precious piece of real estate in the City of London. A monument to his own personal success story, the imposing twenty-storey edifice of polished black granite, grey steel and silver glass was Sir Roger's pride and joy. Completed in 1985 and still the talking point of the business community, it epitomized the three most distinctive hallmarks of Samson International: adventure, new wealth and boundless optimism. With its vast airy atrium and space-age, Plexiglass elevator modules, this building said it all.

'Shall I serve coffee, Sir Roger?' asked Miss Kerwin, Samson's impeccable personal assistant. He turned to face her, his concentration temporarily disturbed. Miss Kerwin shivered involuntarily. A handsome woman of indeterminate age, Sally Kerwin was no nubile flibbertigibbet. A model of discretion and efficiency with her well-cut bob and her business-like Aquascutum suits, it was quite some time since any man had turned her head or quickened her heart. But even after ten years, there was something about Sir Roger's icy blue eyes that never failed to disturb her. Slightly flustered, Miss Kerwin affected to reorganize the sheaf of papers she was carrying.

'Would you, please, Miss Kerwin,' replied Sir Roger who, despite his studiously averted gaze, was all too well aware of the mounting tension in the room.

If the pressure was getting to him, it was impossible to see. No tell-tale flicker of emotion animated those handsome features. No give-away signs of anxiety. If ever a man was built to cope with stress, it was 'ir Roger Samson. At forty-three he was in peak physical condition, still managing to maintain the physique of a modern pentathlete and the stamina of a long-distance runner. 'Nothing in life comes easy,' he would laugh when complimented on his fitness by half-envious colleagues. And he did indeed fight hard to preserve that powerful, sinewy body. Whatever his business commitments, he still found time to work out daily in the Samsons' private gymnasium. The results were impressive.

Sir Roger scanned the room, desperately trying to read the mood of his board. Ten men. And Lilah. He needn't worry about Lilah, of course. She was his wife. But ten men. It was difficult, under the circumstances, to be absolutely sure. Although he had done everything in his power to maintain control, it still meant ten individuals to be bribed, convinced or otherwise 'fixed'. For the first time in a long while, Sir Roger Samson felt a slight twinge of disquiet. Friends or foes – which way would they split? It would be a close call, but in the end he would win. He had to.

'No, thank you, Miss Kerwin, no coffee for me.' Roger recognized the unmistakably patrician tones of his friend, Charles Watson-Smith.

That's at least one in my camp, he thought, drawing up a

mental tally of those directors he could trust. And one worth having, too. Roger felt immediately heartened. Unlike the majority of the Samson International board, the Hon. Charles Watson-Smith came without a price-tag. His approval could not be bought. The thought had always comforted Roger. If he, of all people, could not 'fix' Charles, then the chances were that no one else could either. What a refreshing change, mused Roger, to deal with genuine respectability.

Respectability. In the lexicon of Samson's mind, the concept was a vague one. But whatever it meant, Charles, the second son of an English baronet, was its personification for Roger. At sixty-six, he was still a fine-looking man with a high, intelligent forehead, greying temples and a fine, chiselled profile. Over six feet five inches tall, his back remained ramrod straight from youthful, long-gone days in the Guards. The Hon. Charles Watson-Smith was a classic of his type. Whatever the situation, he could always be guaranteed to look and act the part: a pillar of the Establishment and a fully paid-up member of the British aristocracy.

Roger tried to catch his eye but Charles was miles away, engrossed in the massive Kandinsky on the wall behind Roger. More of a Turner man himself, Charles had spent many an hour in tedious board meetings trying to understand this brash and difficult work. Even after years of effort, he still found it ugly and reckless. His brow furrowed in frustration. Despite his age, he was sufficiently open-minded to learn about any-thing. But this was totally alien to him. There was nothing here he could relate to. For someone like Charles, a man of patterns and traditions, it was all too arbitrary. If there was one thing he could not abide in any area of his life, it was this sort of confusion. It was hardly surprising that much of the last twelve months had been absolute hell for him.

Roger smiled to himself. After so many years, he believed he could read his friend like a book. Coming through loud and clear, the message on Charles's face was one of perplexity. Roger assumed the obvious, attributing such a degree of puzzlement to the painting alone. Why not? After all, it had much the same effect on most people. That was just the way Roger wanted it. That was precisely why this particular abstract had been hung there in the first place. It disturbed people. It bothered them. It diverted their attention away from much of what was being said and done. That was precisely the point.

For a brief moment, Sir Roger Samson felt utterly weary. Throughout his life, he had been adept at spreading confusion among the opposition. As chairman and chief executive officer of Samson International, confusion had been an essential part of his operation. But, in earlier days, the opposing forces were finite in number and more clearly defined. Now almost everyone was potential opposition. Particularly his fellow board members.

'Yes, please, Miss Kerwin.' Roger found no difficulty in distinguishing the deep, guttural inflection of Rijnhard van Polen's voice. 'Did you ever hear a Dutchman refusing a cup of coffee?'

Miss Kerwin returned van Polen's broad smile. 'Just black, isn't it, Mr van Polen?' she enquired, as if she didn't already know. 'No milk or sugar.' Van Polen's smile broadened even further. Like every other board member, he knew that even his most trivial idiosyncracies had long ago been consigned to this lady's extraordinary memory. He nodded, helping himself to two chocolate biscuits in the process. A sweet tooth was his only weakness. Rijnhard van Polen would never be slim.

Sir Roger stared across the room at the stocky, late middle-aged banker and wondered how he was going to play it. Well respected in the Netherlands for his remarkable business acumen, Rijnhard was still something of an unknown quantity within Samson International. His promotion to finance director could not have happened at a more sensitive period. But bad things never happen at good times and for the last year or so Samson International seemed to have done nothing but lurch from crisis to crisis. At least Rijnhard's appointment has stopped the rot, reflected Roger who, in a matter of months, had quite taken to the round, friendly Dutchman. At least he's managed to restore some semblance of confidence in the company. Lord knows, we're all very grateful for that. But how thorough is he? And how much has he managed to find out?

For all his amiable bonhomie, Rijnhard was a difficult one to read. In the past, Roger Samson had always managed to cover his tracks well. But precisely what did Rijnhard know?

Not enough to be dangerous, he decided. He hadn't had the time. Besides, hadn't Lilah assured him that Rijnhard could be trusted to do the right thing? And where people were concerned, Lilah was never wrong. Somewhat cheered, Roger dropped van Polen's name from his mental list of foes.

Unaware of the chairman's attention, Rijnhard continued his study of Roger's enigmatic Klein. A birthday present from Lilah, this bizarre canvas of wild splodges was typical of her. A joke, she always maintained, purchased because it reminded her of her husband's eyes: so very blue and impossible to fathom.

Rijnhard sipped his coffee slowly. What a waste of £1 million. A man of straightforward Calvinist stock, he had no time for waste and even less for enigma. Things were either right or wrong. It was as simple as that. In the end, it was all a question of clarity, that most basic precept of good accounting. Once everything was transparent, it was easy to distinguish good from bad.

Sir Roger looked again at his wrist-watch, a 1935 platinum Patek Philippe, another Sotherby's find for Lilah. Midday. Despite the imperturbable exterior, Roger was beginning to feel impatient. Without thinking, he began to wind his watch. Why had he never told his wife how much the wretched thing aggravated him? For the first four decades of his life he had managed quite happily without one. All those years in the South African *veldt*, he had known instinctively what time it was. But now he was lost without a watch. It had become a necessity. Roger hated that. He loathed dependence of any kind. It made him feel insecure, and consequently nervous.

'Miss Kerwin.' If there was the slightest hint of irritation in Sir Roger Samson's voice, only his PA would have discerned it. She scurried over, still carrying the coffee pot. 'Would you please telephone Lady Samson and tell her that the entire board has been kept waiting for over an hour.'

'Of course,' replied Miss Kerwin, acutely aware of the situation. Swiftly she replenished the insistent Sir Howard Anderson's cup before retreating to her office. The atmosphere in the boardroom was oppressive. Miss Kerwin was beginning to feel quite ill.

Safe in the seclusion of her own sanctuary, the carefully

maintained façade disintegrated. No sooner had Miss Kerwin closed the door than her lip began to quiver. Samson International was part of her life. *Part?* Who was she kidding? For a middle-aged spinster with no family and few friends, Samson International *was* her life. The company had become her pride and joy. She identified with it completely. Like an only child, its successes and achievements had been hers. Yet suddenly this adored only child had gone completely off the rails. What on earth had gone wrong?

Miss Kerwin recalled the same boardroom two years ago. It was another glorious spring day. What a party she had organized to surprise Sir Roger on his return from Buckingham Palace! No fuss, he had insisted all along, and business as usual. But neither Lilah nor Miss Kerwin was going to let him get away with that. It wasn't every day of the week a man received his knighthood for services to British industry. Miss Kerwin's lips began to tremble once more. That Samson International should have come to this. Pulling herself together, she dialled the Samson household.

Back in the boardroom, Roger's mind was racing. His assistant was not alone in wondering how things could have gone so dramatically wrong. First those damning revelations (God knows from where – Roger's office and the boardroom were checked every day for electronic bugs) and the inevitable slump in Samson International's share price. Then that appalling slew of so-called investigative journalists. Cheeky young pups. Not one of them capable of recognizing a deal if it hit them in the face let alone having the guts to close one. Next that bloody Dutch company's shenanigans and the threat of a full-scale Stock Exchange investigation. And then, just when he needed him most, George Hamish rushed suddenly into hospital with a massive coronary, dead before he even reached St Bart's. Roger still felt the loss acutely. Over the years George had been very useful. Very useful indeed.

'Lady Samson gone AWOL?' Roger was suddenly aware of the grotesque figure of Sir Howard Anderson towering behind his chair.

'Looks like it,' replied Roger lightly, determined to keep his unease in check. How he despised this former cabinet minister. The man oozed insincerity. But while some politicians succeeded in being charmingly insincere, Sir Howard could manage only the insincerity. His single other talent, as far as Roger could ascertain, was having once been in the right place at the right time. It had been fortunate for Roger that Sir Howard's lack of ability and principle were matched by a quite unfortunate greed. A horse-mad wife and a demanding mistress, combined with the very modest salary of a British cabinet minister – Sir Howard had been easy prey. The promise of a lucrative directorship on retirement and the former Secretary of State had been totally convinced of the pressing nature of Samson International's case. London needed more hotels and office space. Hotels and offices needed planning consent. Sir Howard and Roger Samson had soon seen eye to eye.

Today, once again, the chairman of Samson International needed Sir Howard's help. Roger looked at the flabby, dissolute face and smiled. What an incorrigible slob, he thought. Not all the talent in Savile Row could hide that hideous obesity. Sir Howard returned the smile, his usual smirk honed to perfection over the years on appalling constituents and their snivelling brats. The two men understood one another perfectly. Despite everything, they were bound together by something deeper than trust. Theirs was the bond of mutual apprehension. So long as Roger could pay Sir Howard's price, he knew he was one of his.

'Sir Roger,' said Miss Kerwin, returning slightly red-eyed to the boardroom, 'I'm afraid I haven't been able to speak to Lady Samson. But the housekeeper assures me that she'll be over here soon. Mrs Owen says your wife hasn't been herself this morning. Apparently she couldn't eat her breakfast and has just been sitting in her dressing room since you left for the office. She's given instructions not to be disturbed by anyone, not even you. But a few minutes ago she asked for the car to be brought round, which must be a good sign, I suppose.'

'Not pregnant again, is she?' asked Sir Howard breezily. Heavens, the man was crass!

'Not that I'm aware,' snapped Roger, momentarily losing his cool. Oh, God. He hoped Lilah had not sunk back into one of her depressions. Losing that baby had wrought such havoc on her. It did seem very odd. Lilah had appeared perfectly fine when he'd left at seven. She was still in bed, of course, but already wide awake, reading her usual array of papers: *The Times*, *Le Monde*, *El Pais* . . . Roger often wondered how she managed to find the time.

'Goodbye, Roger,' she had called cheerily as he left for Samson Heights. 'I'm sure to see you around.'

Roger had laughed. It seemed like one of Lilah's little jokes. After all, she knew they would be together at the board meeting and afterwards at the shareholders' annual general meeting. He recalled thinking to himself that she seemed to be in a positive frame of mind. So what on earth was she playing at?

'I say, Roger,' said Christopher Grafton quizzically, 'I don't suppose you could give us Lilah's estimated time of arrival? I was hoping to nip away for a spot of lunch before the AGM.'

Deep in his own thoughts, Roger had hardly been consciously aware of Christopher's presence in the room. He was such an ephemeral character, with that embarrassing little cocaine habit of his. Roger did not dislike him – he did not possess enough personality to generate strong emotion – but he certainly had no time for him. For all the benefits of Eton and Oxford and a multi-million-pound inheritance, Grafton had developed into nothing but a hopeless degenerate. How many times had Roger been obliged to use his contacts and influence to keep the idiot's name out of the gutter press? When he wasn't smashing Ferraris and screwing actresses he was doing dope, popping pills or dropping fortunes at the gaming tables. Nowadays, the only mention under 'Clubs' in Christopher Grafton's *Who's Who* entry was Les Ambassadeurs.

'For God's sake, Christopher,' snapped Roger, discernibly tetchy by this stage, 'this isn't a bloody cocktail party. Don't you read the papers? Haven't you been following what's been happening to this company of late? Do you realize what the share price is today? Yet there you are, asking me to sort it all out in half an hour so that you can keep your lunch appointment . . .'

Christopher looked contrite, like a schoolboy caught smoking behind the bicycle shed. It hardly seemed credible that Samson was only eight years his senior. He always made Christopher feel like an adolescent. But Christopher admired him more than any other man he could think of. Roger was a doer. And, hell, who else could have bailed him out as often as he had? Christopher owed him and they both knew it. Roger marked down Christopher Grafton as one more man in his camp.

Standing in her dressing room, Lady Samson stared at her reflection in the large Louis XV looking glass. Four months away from her thirty-first birthday, she looked not a day over twenty. 'The luck of the Irish,' she would giggle whenever beauticians marvelled at that smooth, creamy skin.

Five feet ten inches tall, Lilah Samson was unusually striking. Even as a child, her mane of auburn hair and vibrant emerald green eyes had set neighbours' tongues wagging.

'When that Delilah Dooley grows up,' old Mrs Curzon would say to her husband, Sid, 'she'll be one of those models. You just mark my words. Thousands of pounds she'll be earning.'

But Mr and Mrs Dooley, Irish immigrants to London in 1958, had no intention of filling their lovely daughter's head with such superficial nonsense. For them, education was the answer, the stepping stone to a bright future. Off she was sent at an early age to be taught by the nuns at the local convent school. And Lilah had not let them down. Oh no, Miss Delilah Dooley had done well for herself. Remarkably well, indeed.

Tears pricked hard behind Lilah's eyes as she thought of her dear, departed parents. Yes, she'd come a long way from that terraced house in Islington. Too far, perhaps, and, for the last few years, mostly in the wrong direction. Lilah straightened her shoulders. It was time to put things in order. It was time—
A gentle knock on the bedroom door interrupted her train of thought. It was Mrs Owen to tell her that Eamonn was waiting in the drive.

'Thanks, Mrs Owen,' smiled Lilah. 'Could you please tell him I'll be out in five minutes.'

Mrs Owen nodded and went off to tell the chauffeur. Lilah resumed her inspection in the mirror. A trifle pale, she thought, stroking her cheek dispassionately. All the same, she knew she was looking good. She had decided to leave her long hair loose, just sweeping her shoulders. Recently she had taken to wearing it in a chic French pleat, but this morning she wanted it to look the way it was the day she met Roger Samson.

Red. She had decided on a simple red dress in soft jersey. Cunningly cut, with a high neck and long sleeves, it hung perfectly on her slender body. Hemmed just below the knee, the dress still managed to do justice to Lilah's long, shapely legs.

No important jewellery today, she decided, just the small, antique emerald ring she always wore on the ring finger of her right hand. Lilah checked her sheer black stockings and her low-heeled black patent shoes. *Le rouge et le noir*, she thought, staring at her own reflection. How apposite. *Le rouge et le noir*. Despite the slight pallor, she had opted for little make-up. Today it was unnecessary. For the first time in what felt like years, Lilah was feeling strong. It had all been terribly difficult, of course, but at last Lilah knew she was right.

'Good morning, Eamonn,' said Lilah, as the chauffeur helped her into the back of the black BMW. With its personalized number plate SI 2 (SI 1 was Roger's of course), the car had been Roger's latest Christmas present to his wife. 'And how are you today?'

'Fine, thank you, Lady Samson,' replied Eamonn. 'And yourself?'

'Not so bad,' said Lilah, unconsciously picking up on Eamonn's soft Cork brogue. 'And how is Mrs O'Reilly's back?'

'Grand, just grand since you sent her to that acupuncturist fellah of yours,' said Eamonn enthusiastically. 'In fact, Lady Samson, she'll be after writing you a letter to tell you thank you and all. Says she's never felt so good since she was a young girl in Ballineen. But now she's wondering if you'll be wanting back the tickets for Lourdes?'

Lilah laughed out loud. 'Of course not, Eamonn,' she spluttered. 'Tell Mrs O'Reilly to go to Lourdes with my blessing. I bought the tickets for her and your daughter. And,' Lilah caught Eamonn's eye, 'to give you a break from the pair of them. But ask her to bring me back a bottle of holy water, will you? Tell her I've got a few problems not even the acupuncturist can cure.'

Eamonn closed the car door. 'Are you comfortable, Lady Samson?' he enquired. 'You're looking wonderful today, if you don't mind my saying, but at the same time, in a peculiar sort of way, you're looking awful banjaxed.'

Lilah smiled again. Trust an Irishman from Cork to see straight through her. To Lilah, Eamonn O'Reilly was worth his weight in gold, though Roger never used him, said he chattered too much. But Lilah loved Eamonn's quaint Irish mannerisms and his down-to-earth approach. She was used to it, after all. It was the way she'd been brought up.

'As comfortable as can be expected, thanks,' said Lilah. 'Now, Eamonn, it's ten past twelve and I'm running rather late. Could you please take me to Samson Heights.'

The computer screen flickered in the corner of the boardroom. Mike Patterson studied it carefully. The TOPIC system, he had been told, was a direct link into the London Stock Exchange. Any information on any share – price, movement, buying, selling – all at the touch of a button. Such things fascinated Mike. He was eager to learn. How else did a man with no formal education, an ex-shop steward of the Amalgamated Hotel Workers Confederation, become a director of a company like Samson International? Mike Patterson felt justifiably proud of himself. He realized, of course, that his directorship had been Lady Samson's idea. Lovely lady. He would always remember the day they had met, almost three years ago, during the annual wage bargaining. He was negotiating on behalf of the staff at Samson International Hotels. And she was representing management. Of course, she had not been 'Lady' Samson then, simply 'Mrs'. But still, Mike reckoned he had a fair idea of what the boss's wife would be like. 'Just call me Lilah,' Mrs Samson had said, as soon as they had been formally introduced, 'and I'll call you Mike. It cuts out all the crap, don't you think?' Mike could have dropped dead on the spot. The son of a Yorkshire miner, he'd been a union man all his life. At fifty-five, he was known as one of the toughest negotiators in the country. In his time, he had broken men as hard as Sir Roger Samson. But never had Mike Patterson been so utterly disarmed by any employer as by Roger Samson's wife.

Since that day, industrial relations at Samson International Hotels had improved beyond all recognition. Not that Lilah Samson didn't know how to stand her ground. By God, she did. But, somehow, with Lilah, everyone came away from the table thinking he'd got what he wanted. With Roger, on the contrary, people always ended up feeling flattened, which only led to further discontent.

That woman sure has a touch of genius, thought Mike warmly, idly calling up Samson International's latest share prices on TOPIC. I bet she'll be giving it everything she's got to convince the AGM today. Strange, though, considering how important this was. Today was the first time Mike had ever known Lilah to be late.

At the other end of the boardroom, Sir Roger Samson was drawing up his final balance sheet. All things considered, he was feeling fairly confident. Lilah, Charles, Sir Howard, Christopher and a dozen others who 'owed' him, they were all his. And, with a bit of luck, Lilah would swing the rest. Roger eyed Mike Patterson warily. That was certainly one he couldn't rely on, with his self-righteous, socialist ideals. Why Lilah had insisted on having him on the board Roger would never know. She'd spent too much time on the continent, of course. All these trendy European ideas she'd imbibed about industrial democracy and worker participation. Roger had no time for any of it. But Lilah had made a point of principle and, in the end, he'd let her have her way. To be fair, since Mike Patterson's appointment, the UK Samson International Hotels had been more profitable, Still, one worker on the board was more than enough. Before you knew where you were, they'd be insisting on equal numbers of women!

'Morning, Sir Roger,' called Mike, aware of the chairman's steely gaze. 'Lilah busy down at Harrods? Doing a leveraged buy-out, is she? I wouldn't be surprised.'

How it irritated Roger, Lilah's indiscriminate capacity for friendship. Of course, on occasion, it served his purposes well. But that Lilah should be on first-name terms with a man like

Patterson! Why did she allow it? After all, these people didn't count. 'Good morning, Mr Patterson,' replied Roger coldly. With a curious irony, Mike was the only board member Roger ever addressed by his surname. 'I take it you're well briefed?'

'Never better,' said Mike, ignoring Samson's patronizing tone. 'Just waiting to hear what your good lady has to say. I think we can all trust her.'

Roger caught the none-too-subtle implication of the remark – that Patterson wouldn't trust Roger as far as he could throw him. But, as he had hoped, the few remaining waverers would fall in behind Lilah.

Lilah's car drew up outside Samson Heights. Twelve thirty, precisely.

'Shall I wait for you here, Lady Samson?' asked Eamonn.

'No, thanks,' replied Lilah. 'But could you be waiting for me at the Samson International, Park Lane, as from three o'clock?'

'Of course, Lady Samson.' Eamonn helped Lilah out of the car. She'd been silent during the journey, just staring out of the window. No, thought Eamonn, despite appearances, herself is somehow not herself at all.

Lilah walked up the sweep of steps and strode into the building.

'Good morning, Lady Samson,' said Clive, the doorman, respectfully touching his cap. 'Shall I advise the board of your arrival?'

'No thank you, Clive,' replied Lilah. 'And don't worry about finding an escort for me either. I know how to make my own way up.'

Heads turned as Lady Samson crossed the atrium and made her way to the special lift reserved exclusively for the board-room on the twentieth floor. There were only two buttons on the control panel. 'G' for ground floor and '20'. Lilah pressed '20'. With barely a sound, the large, transparent module ascended smoothly to the twentieth floor.

Twelve thirty-three. By now, everyone in the boardroom was beginning to feel restless. In the corner, Christopher Grafton

13

stubbed out another cigarette, his twentieth this morning. Still seated at the table, Charles Watson-Smith appeared to be doodling on one of the large green leather-covered writing pads. Rijnhard van Polen had joined Mike Patterson over by the computer. The two men were now locked in earnest conversation about the peculiarities of vertical unions. For want of anything better to do, Sir Howard Anderson was eavesdropping shamelessly. But whatever Sir Howard knew about vertical unions, it had nothing to do with wage-bargaining.

Without warning, the two panelled doors of the boardroom were flung wide open. A curious hush descended as Lady Samson appeared on the threshold. She looked at her husband, but made no move towards him.

'Well, darling,' said Roger, visibly relieved, 'better late than never.' He got up to go and kiss his wife. Then, suddenly, something stopped him.

That look on Lilah's face.

PART I

1981–7

CHAPTER ONE

London, Spring 1981

'Do you mind if I use the phone?'

Roger Samson, sipping fresh orange juice while studying a detailed real estate plan of Manhattan, looked up and nodded. 'Go ahead,' he replied, instinctively moving his black crocodile briefcase from the chair nearest the phone cubicle. He returned to his documents.

'It's made all the difference, hasn't it?' continued his assailant, full of the frequent-traveller banter which so irritated Roger. 'I used to fly this route regularly in the early seventies,' he went on good-naturedly, 'even before they introduced Concorde. But that was in the good old days – before the shit hit the fan.'

'I beg your pardon?' replied Roger, not quite catching the man's drift.

'The good old days in the seventies. The days of the property boom here in England. I'm sorry.' Somewhat embarrassed by Roger's laconic responses, the stranger tried swiftly to retrieve the situation. 'I assumed from those,' he glanced at the plans on Roger's lap, 'that you were a property man yourself.'

'And you'd be right,' replied Roger, taking a sudden interest in this large, overweight man with his unhealthy ruddy complexion. It was part of Roger's private philosophy: the most useful information often came from the most unexpected sources. 'Roger Samson,' he said, decidedly more amenable.

'Property is one of my interests – along with a couple of other things.'

'George Hamish,' replied the man, putting out his hand. 'I'm in computers now. Bloody awful business. But a bloke's got to do something for a living. After the 'seventy-three property crash, I had to go and be "recycled". They should've just buried me there and then. Since they kicked me out of real estate, I've been like a fish out of water.'

'Really?' Roger's face gave nothing away. But he'd heard tell of George Hamish. Everyone in the property business had. A legend in his own lunch-time, so his detractors said. Or the most brilliant property man never to make a billion, according to the rest.

'Yes.' George shuffled nervously in his seat. No matter how many planes he had taken in his life, he still hated flying with a passion. It was good to have someone to talk to in the departure lounge, someone to take his mind off the trip. 'Yes,' he continued, surreptitiously checking his fly buttons, 'I was finance director at London & Hong Kong Properties. Loved every minute of it. That's before they went belly-up. But then again, in those days, everyone was going broke.'

Roger nodded pleasantly. It took time and patience to get where you wanted. Of course, he had heard the stories of that era – studied the details, even. Triumph Investment Trust, Keyser Ullmann, Slater Walker, First National Finance Corporation – much bigger punters than London & Hong Kong – Roger knew how all of them had eventually come a cropper.

'I suppose that was all a bit before your time,' continued George, unintentionally patronizing. Roger said nothing. George certainly looked old enough to be his father. No one would have guessed that the difference between them was as little as seven or eight years. 'But I can tell you, it was such amazing fun while it lasted.' George smiled happily to himself at the memory.

'Would you care for a drink?' asked Roger. It was forty-five minutes to boarding and he had plenty of work to do. All the same, George could be a mine of useful information.

'Champagne, please,' replied George, his telephone call quite forgotten. Already he could feel stirrings of the old enthusiasm. Nothing excited him so much as the property business. Nothing pleased him more than recounting tales of boom and bust in the seventies. Roger returned with a glass of champagne for George and a tumbler of orange juice for himself. Roger never drank alcohol either before or during a flight. However tedious the journey, he prided himself on never feeling jet-lagged by the end of it. He would emerge, rested and uncrumpled at his destination, raring to do business.

George Hamish had no such qualms. Wining and dining at other people's expense had become an integral part of his life. An accountant by profession, he had learned his trade during the sixties at Touche Ross of London. With his flair for figures and his ability for lateral thinking, George rose quickly through the ranks of the company. Everyone in the City soon agreed. When it came to reading a balance sheet or spotting an under-valued asset, George Hamish was in a league of his own. It was this which first brought him to the attention of Sir Ralph Morgan, chairman of London & Hong Kong Properties. On the eve of the 'sixty-nine property boom, Sir Ralph had George appointed to the board as finance director.

'Thanks,' said George, taking a huge swig of champagne. Roger noticed the clock in the departure lounge. It was not yet ten in the morning. What kind of shape would George be in by the time he reached New York?

By now the flow was unstoppable. 'In those days,' George went on, 'you could mint your own money if you had the right combination of balls and chutzpah. I can still remember the look on Jim Slater's face the day he flogged Granite House to the Singapore Monetary Authority. They coughed up £22.4 million for it! Only a few months before, Slater Walker had picked it up for nine. Over thirteen million pounds profit – and we're talking nineteen seventy-three values – even Jim was staggered.'

Roger nodded his continued interest. Such stories were part of the folklore, but never before had he heard them recounted with so much passion.

'But then, about three years later,' resumed George, the sudden rush of excitement leaving him slightly out of breath,

19

'there was Jim claiming to be a "minus millionaire". And there was Slater Walker being bailed out by the Bank of England for a hundred million.'

'They must have been fascinating times,' prodded Roger, as if George needed the slightest encouragement.

'I'll say. Christ, it was madness. We were all riding a wave. Then suddenly – snap, crackle, pop – whichever way you want to look at it – we lost millions overnight.'

Noticing George's empty glass, Roger went over to the bar to fill it.

'Thanks,' said George. 'Got a taste for this stuff on the Euro-junkets we used to have. What a time! God, were we desperate to wave the flag in Europe! Even newly floated companies felt they hadn't arrived until they'd bought something *sur le continent*. Prices went berserk. And the parties out there! God, you should have seen those parties.'

'But surely,' interrupted Roger, uninterested in George's list of remembered booze-ups and turning the conversation back to business, 'you must have known that the bubble had to burst?'

'Of course,' replied George, 'but it's like being on a winning streak at roulette. You always think you'll call it a day after the next deal. But then it's after the next one. And then—'

'And then?'

'And then, well, suddenly it's all too late. You've lost the lot. I could see the crash coming. It was impossible to ignore the signs. But, somehow, most of us just did.'

'But if you could see the early warning signals, why didn't you bail out in time?'

'Easier said than done,' said George, by now scanning the departure lounge for a passing stewardess. Roger got the message. Returning to the bar, he refilled George's glass once more. 'Oh, and a few of those little smoked salmon sandwiches while you're there,' shouted George. He was beginning to feel quite peckish.

'Here you are,' said Roger, a plan already beginning to hatch in his mind. 'You were saying, bailing out at the right time was easier said than done.'

'Sure,' said George, stuffing a sandwich into his mouth. 'For the simple reason that we couldn't stop doing business because we were nothing but middle-men. Oh, yes, the press called us property tycoons. It sounded very grand. But in the end, if you looked at it, we produced absolutely nothing. We were just parasites on the industry.'

'Come now, George,' said Roger, very matter-of-fact. He had no time for bad attacks of guilt. Guilt was such a waste of time. 'You know that's nonsense. Besides, why denigrate the good old middle-man? It's the middle-man who makes the business world go round. What you were doing was merely acting as honest brokers.'

George's face brightened. He could warm to a man who found excuses for him. All these years, George had borne the lonely burden of his guilt – the guilt of fortunes made and lost overnight. But now he had served his time for what happened almost a decade ago. He had paid the price for being too rich too quick. Now George was dying of terminal boredom. He hated his job as finance director of BJM Computers. It was an excellent position, accepted not because George wanted it, but because he had a wife, two children and a mortgage on the Esher house. Sure, the salary was generous, far more than he needed to keep body and soul together, which in George's seventeen-stone case meant plenty. But the job was dull and monotonous. Where was the thrill of microchips? Where was the buzz in baud modems? No wonder George had hit the booze.

'British Airways Concorde flight 002 to New York is now ready for boarding.' The homogenized voice of the British Airways stewardess echoed around the departure lounge. 'Will passengers please ensure that they take all hand baggage and personal items with them.'

'George,' said Roger, the plan now definitively formulated in his head, 'how would you like to be in the property business again?'

'In London the time is right again,' replied George, his eyes brightening perceptibly. 'For anyone with capital and time to wait – say five or six years – I'd say there are fortunes to be made.'

'On the right properties.'

'Of course. But nowadays I don't know anyone who's prepared to gamble. Besides, what new breed of high-flyer is

21

likely to take a chance with a clapped-out old has-been like me?'

'My breed,' said Roger decisively. George almost dropped his glass.

'George, I know what you're saying is right. I know that now is the time to be buying in London. But I need your expertise. I need a man like you to recognize the pitfalls, to tell me when to buy and sell, to teach me the ins and outs of the system. You're right. I never lived through the seventies crash. I was abroad,' Roger paused, 'involved in other things.' He handed George an embossed visiting card. 'Why don't you come and talk to me when you're back in London? There could well be a place for a man of your talents on the board of Samson International.'

George Hamish felt an irrepressible tingle running the length of his spine. It was just like the good old days. A snap decision. That was what was required of him now. He could not have this Roger Samson chap thinking he was some kind of prevaricating fuddy-duddy. And as for BJM, they could stuff their dreadful job and their new user-friendly number-cruncher. Let the lot of them go to hell! George Hamish was rolling again.

'You don't have to decide anything right now,' said Roger, trying to read George's slightly sozzled expression. 'Think about it if you like. Check out my credentials when you get back to London. Then give me a call in a week or so.'

'Thanks,' said George, 'but I've already made up my mind. I'd be delighted to come onto your board, but only on condition.' George felt obliged to make some semblance of negotiation.

'Yes?' replied Roger, smiling. The ploy was so incandescently obvious.

'On condition,' continued George, 'that I join as finance director.'

'Done,' said Roger, shaking George firmly by the hand. 'Together, George, we're going to make a packet.'

'Will all remaining passengers please board Concorde now.'

Collecting their briefcases, Roger and George left the calm grey coolness of the lounge for the effortless efficiency of the sleek, silver-white bird. Roger was feeling good. At last he was getting his team together. Now the only person he really needed was Charles Watson-Smith. He'd be dealing with that this evening.

Slightly squashed in his not over-generous seat, George Hamish was ecstatic. By the time Concorde touched down at J. F. Kennedy airport, he'd worked his way through Concorde's excellent choice of wines by way of celebration.

CHAPTER TWO

New York, spring 1981

THE Hon. Charles Watson-Smith hated shopping anywhere, but particularly in New York. London he could just about cope with. A few familiar places and faces (Turnbull & Asser for shirts; Savile Row for suits; Lobbs for shoes, and the wonderful Miss M in the cosmetics department of Fortnum & Mason to organize Christmas and birthday gifts for his female staff) and the whole ghastly business was done. Even so, shopping was still an alien concept to a man like Charles. Born in 1925, the second son of the much-loved if somewhat eccentric Lord Windesmere, Charles belonged to an age of customer accounts and home deliveries. Cash and plastic credit cards – it all seemed so unnecessarily sordid to him, so lacking in good faith and good taste. In Charles's world, you signed. In its clubs, in its stores, with its tradesmen, a scribbled signature was all that was required. Trust, thought Charles, wandering around New York's elegant Bergdorf Goodman, that was what business used to be about – the days when a man's word was his bond and his handshake a contract. It was all so different now.

'Good morning, sir.' A chirpy voice interrupted Charles's reverie. 'How may I help you?' Charles looked up startled. How long had he been standing there at the counter, staring at the bright arrangements of pure silk scarves?

'I'm sorry, I was miles away. I'm looking for a few presents to take back to London. Something for my secretary and my

24

housekeeper.' Charles smiled wanly at the expertly made-up assistant. 'What would you suggest?'

'The new Hermès range has just come in,' said the assistant. 'Beautiful scarves, all of them. Would you care to take a look?'

'Not really,' said Charles. 'Would you please choose two for me? And, if you'd be so good, I'd like them gift-wrapped.'

'Certainly, sir,' said the assistant, selecting her two favourite designs. A sudden pained shadow crossed Charles's face. 'Is everything all right, sir?' she added, concerned, for he looked very pale.

'Oh, it's nothing,' replied Charles quickly. 'I suppose I'm still tired from my flight over here. Only just arrived.'

The assistant looked relieved as Charles made a brave attempt to laugh it off. How could he possibly explain to anyone this excruciating sense of loss? Even now, everything he did still reminded him of Lydia. Buying presents, indeed! What a monumental waste of time. And yet it was merely one of the million little tasks that Lydia had always accomplished so cheerfully on his behalf. Of course, Charles had staff to look after him, to see to all his practical needs. But no amount of staff, however efficient, could ever compensate for the loss of his wife. Who else but Lydia, for instance, knew his little idiosyncrasies: his penchant for Floris soap and Vetiver de Guerlain aftershave? Who else but Lydia could make his commuting between a large estate in Scotland, an eight-bedroomed house in London and a duplex apartment on West 57th Street so painless? Lydia had been the love and joy of his life. Without her, Charles could hardly see the point of carrying on.

Absent-mindedly, he paid for his purchases. Four hours to kill before dinner with this chap, Roger Samson. Charles had never met the man before and none of his own contacts knew much about him. But whoever he was, he was certainly persistent. His lines of credit were good – that at least was beyond doubt. So why not sell out? Charles no longer had any interest in hanging onto those warehouses in Manhattan. If Samson came up with a reasonable offer, he might as well offload them. He was certainly never going to develop the sites now, he no longer had the heart for it – for anything. All he really yearned for was some peace and tranquillity. Peace. A thought crossed Charles's mind. Leaving the department store, he began the brisk walk along Fifth Avenue to his favourite New York refuge.

The receptionist at the Carlyle gave Roger Samson her most welcoming smile.

'Your usual suite, I think, Mr Samson,' she said, handing the key to the bell-hop who waited discreetly in attendance.

'Yes,' replied Roger, returning the smile.

'And I see from the computer, sir, that you have dinner for two booked in the Carlyle restaurant at eight o'clock. Will there be any special requirements?' The question seemed redundant. Roger Samson had the aura of someone whose every requirement was met spontaneously.

'No, thank you.' Roger picked up the briefcase which rarely left his side. 'But, by the way, my dinner guest this evening will be Mr Charles Watson-Smith. He'll be meeting me here in Bemelmans bar at half past seven. When he arrives, I'd be grateful if someone could just show him up to the bar. I'll be in my usual place – as far away as possible from the piano.'

'Of course, Mr Samson,' said the receptionist, carefully making a note of the request. 'I hope you enjoy your short stay with us.'

Roger smiled. That would depend, to a large extent, on the Hon. Charles Watson-Smith.

Ensconced in his magnificent Mark Hampton suite, Roger spent the next two hours poring over his plans. The deal was perfectly obvious. London aside, Manhattan was clearly the place to be in property. He had to have those sites. And more than the sites themselves, he had to have Charles Watson-Smith as a member of his team. Money was all very well but alone it was not sufficient. What Roger needed now was the respectability of *old* money and all it implied. Later on none of this would matter so much. Even in England, after the first few hundred million, new money had a strange way of appearing very old. But for the moment, Roger wanted Charles with his name, his kudos and his contacts. The Hon. Charles

Watson-Smith would be his direct link into society's old-boy network.

A little tired after his ridiculously early start, Roger resisted the temptation of a quiet nap in the king-size bed. Instead he made his way to the Carlyle's fitness centre, exercising strenuously for over an hour. As he worked out, his lean, muscular body drew admiring glances from women and envy from men, but Roger seemed oblivious to them. Unlike so many other fitness fanatics, he did not exercise to attract attention, nor merely to achieve a body beautiful. For Roger, fitness meant control. At one time in his life, it had also meant survival.

Refreshed, he returned to his suite and ordered iced tea on the terrace. What a glorious hotel, he thought. It was like travelling in a time warp. Down below, the hullabaloo of Madison Avenue seemed light-years away. Slowly Roger sipped his tea. Yes, he was feeling strong, in the perfect frame of mind to negotiate a deal. Now it was essential to maintain this state of mental and physical well-being. To do this, he knew precisely how he would spend the rest of the afternoon.

As soon as he arrived, Charles knew he had made a mistake. Housed in its glorious *beaux-arts* mansion, the Frick Collection held too many bitter-sweet memories of happier days. Lydia particularly had loved it. She said it reminded her of a private home and only wished such a home were hers. Charles also loved the house but for different reasons. With its Constables, Gainsboroughs and Turners, the Frick reminded him of a little piece of old England in the very heart of New York. He paused for a time, trying to absorb the serenity of the indoor court with its tranquil fountain. But everything hurt too much. He would take one last look at his favourite masterpiece before returning home to his large and now desperately empty apartment.

It was precisely as he remembered it – Renoir's *Mother and Children*. In his childhood, Charles had learned to love this charming painting. During the early days of their marriage, before Lydia discovered her infertility, they would study the

27

work for ages. Lydia, laughing, maintained that she would make an equally gracious mother. Instead of two daughters, however, she said she yearned for sons, at least five of them, and each the spitting image of his father. Charles would pretend to be horrified, arguing that he could never cope with such strong male competition for the attentions of his wife. No, he would smile, he wanted two daughters, the very image of their mother. But unlike Renoir, he had maintained, kissing his wife on the lips in full view of the security guard, he would never allow his precious trio to walk unaccompanied through the park.

He knew it was quite unreasonable, but Charles was angry to find another man studying *his* picture. Reliving all these memories was hurting him even more, but perhaps he needed the pain in order to feel alive. Feeling anything, even grief, was better than this numb emptiness.

The other man stood motionless, staring at the canvas. Despite himself, Charles could not avoid an appreciative glance at the tall, elegant figure. It was not so much the man's good looks which caught Charles's attention. Handsome himself despite his age, Charles rarely registered another man's physical attributes. But this man's whole being radiated vitality and force, strength and control. It also radiated something far more disturbing. Charles recognized it from his days in the Guards. It was what soldiers generally referred to as the 'killer instinct'. There they stood, two complete strangers in a museum, oddly drawn together by the attraction of one picture. Charles wondered what was going through the man's mind. As he turned to leave, the man caught Charles's gaze. 'Good afternoon,' he ventured politely. Both the accent and the salutation seemed peculiarly English.

'Good afternoon,' replied Charles automatically. Charles watched him as he made his exit. For some reason, he felt strangely shaken. Charles could not say precisely why, but it was something in the man's eyes.

It was seven twenty-five and Roger Samson sat waiting for his guest.

'Your usual, Mr Samson?' asked the waiter, his slight hips

swaying snake-like to the strains of 'Unforgettable'. The pianist, the celebrated Barbara Carroll, was as ever in sparkling form.

'Yes, please,' replied Roger. It was such a relief to know that in Bemelmans bar the malt whisky would not arrive adulterated with water and half a dozen ice-cubes.

'Mr Samson, your guest, sir.' A deferential young man escorted Charles to Roger's table. Charles looked vaguely surprised.

'I think we've already met,' he said.

'The Frick,' replied Roger, standing up to welcome Charles.

'Your drink, Mr Samson,' said the waiter, placing a double whisky on the table. 'Something for you, sir?'

'Make mine a malt whisky, too,' replied Charles. 'No ice or water.'

Roger laughed. 'We seem to have more than one thing in common. Let's hope we can add to the list.' Charles suppressed a smile. This man Samson was certainly no time-waster. Twenty-five years ago, Charles had possessed the same kind of drive.

'No doubt,' he replied, deliberately non-committal. There was no point in giving away his hand too soon. Suddenly, Charles began to sense the old thrill of negotiation. For the first time in months, he was almost enjoying himself.

'Are you often in New York?' asked Roger, aware of the subtle implications of Charles's vague response. Steady on. He must not be too brash with a man like Watson-Smith. This one needed time. But in the end, Roger knew, Charles would take the bait. After all, he had studied every detail of his prey. What Charles needed more than anything now was an interest in his life.

'Not so often since . . .' Charles flinched involuntarily, 'since my wife died.'

'I'm sorry.' Roger paused for a moment. 'It's almost a year ago, isn't it?'

'Just over,' replied Charles. 'But I keep myself very busy, you know.'

The statement seemed designed to convince Charles himself.

'Fund-raising for the Cure Cancer Campaign?'

Charles smiled again. This man Samson had certainly done

his homework. 'Mainly. Last year, we raised over five million.'

'And business?'

'I'm lucky to be a wealthy man,' replied Charles, suddenly subdued, 'with no dependants. Since . . . Well, of late, business seems to have taken a back seat in my life.'

'So who handles the day-to-day running of your company?' asked Roger as the waiter arrived with Charles's drink.

'W&S? Why W&S could almost run itself. I'm fortunate, I suppose. It's my own private company. I couldn't bear having to explain myself constantly to a bunch of rapacious shareholders.'

'All the same, that's what I'm aiming for with Samson International. I'm going to need a full listing on the Stock Exchange to raise the kind of money I'm looking for.'

'Good ideas will always find funding,' replied Charles, raising his glass. 'Here's to good ideas.'

Roger nodded politely. Neither did it hurt, he thought, to have been to school with all the people who held the purse strings. 'And your property portfolio?' he continued. 'Who manages that?'

'Oh, I suppose I keep a weather eye on things,' said Charles vaguely. 'How about you?' Suddenly he had grown tired of this cross-examination. 'How long have you been interested in the property business?'

It went against Roger's grain to talk about himself. But even the best poker player, on occasion, was obliged to show his hand. 'I'm a complete and utter novice,' he replied disarmingly. 'My background is in mining – precious metals, mainly.'

'Gold?'

'No, platinum. There's more money to be made in platinum.'

'Really?' said Charles intrigued. 'I believe they find the stuff in the USSR and South Africa.'

'Mostly.'

'So you were mining in South Africa?'

'Yes. In fact, that's where I was born.' Already Roger had decided on his tactics. He would give the impression of being frank, of divulging information, just enough to make himself and his story plausible.

'Extraordinary,' murmured Charles, 'not a trace of an accent.'

Roger laughed again, a charming self-deprecating laugh. 'My mother was English. When I was a child, she forced me to listen to the World Service on the radio. She said she didn't want me growing up sounding like some Yarpie.'

By now, even Charles was smiling. 'Well, between them the World Service and the mining business seem to have been good to you.'

'We all know success is one per cent inspiration and ninety-nine per cent perspiration. Hard work combined with an ability to delegate and the flair to communicate. I believe that these are three of the four requirements for anyone who's going places.'

'And the fourth?' asked Charles.

'The fourth,' said Roger, his eyes fixed, his mouth drawn into a tight line, 'is the most important of all. It's having the guts to gamble the lot whenever the stakes are sufficiently high.'

Charles felt a strange sensation, the sort of feeling he first experienced half-way down the Cresta run. The hairs on the nape of his neck prickled against his pristine starched collar. The cold fingers of fear, perhaps, or the sheer buzz of adrenaline, Charles could not discern. Neither did he know whether he liked or even trusted this man, Roger Samson. But one thing was certain. For the first time in his remarkably conventional life and for no logical reason he could explain, Charles Watson-Smith was gearing up to take a flyer.

'Mr Samson.' The waiter appeared as if from nowhere. 'Your table's ready, sir.'

'Thanks. Charles, time for dinner?'

Charles nodded. It was fascinating to experience – this man's strange amalgam of business brusqueness and personal charm. It was, Roger knew, a combination which never failed.

One shared Châteaubriand and a bottle of '53 Musigny later, he had virtually snared his prey.

'You see, Charles,' continued Roger, lazily inhaling his antique Hine cognac, 'if Samson International were to build apartment blocks on your warehouse sites, we could make a fortune. We'd offer them freehold, of course, rather than creating a co-operative to sell on a leasehold basis. Everyone else has done that. But if we do it my way, we could get the highest price per square foot ever seen in New York.'

'For a South African platinum miner,' said Charles, by now both mellow and mesmerized, 'you seem to be thoroughly *au fait* with property values everywhere.'

'I'm sorry,' laughed Roger. 'In my list of basic requirements, I forgot to mention homework.'

Charles swirled the deep-golden liquid in the bottom of his glass. It was a long time since he had felt so well, so energized, so interested in anything. Or, for that matter, anybody. 'And my site on Manhattan's east side, near the United Nations headquarters. Would you turn that into an apartment block too?'

'I want that to be something very special,' replied Roger. For the first time an emotion vaguely akin to excitement animated those disturbingly expressionless eyes. 'That will be the jewel in Samson International's New York crown.'

'What do you have in mind?'

'A seventy-storey hotel,' said Roger decisively. 'Samson Tower, with its own sweeping drive and extensive private gardens – it will be a landmark.'

'To guts and optimism?' said Charles, his eyes twinkling.

'To guts and optimism,' returned Roger, raising his glass.

Charles looked at Roger hard and straight. Suddenly he knew what it was about Samson that made him so unnerving. Other men made promises hedged with provisos. This man talked in absolute certainties. When Roger Samson talked of success, Charles knew he was going to achieve it.

On the next table, Harold and Claudia Weiss were toasting the success of their only daughter, Sophie, with a bottle of '75 Krug. It was not every day a woman was taken on by the prestigious investment bank of Horneffer & Salzmann.

CHAPTER THREE

Cambridge, June 1981

THE Trinity Ball, thought Lilah, her fingers playing in the water, had been the most wonderful of all May Balls. Not that she and Jonathan had been aware of the boisterous good humour and occasional bad behaviour which always hallmarked the event. As everyone in the college knew, they were far too besotted with one another ever to notice what anyone else was up to. 'Trinity Couple of the Year' they had been voted earlier that week by an unofficial and very drunken delegation from the Junior Common Room. Grace, Lilah's devoted bedder, had been most impressed by the silver-painted beer bottle awarded with the title. Yes, that nice surgeon Mr Morton and that lovely Miss Dooley, they seemed made for one another.

Reclining exhausted in the bottom of the punt, Lilah smiled up at Jonathan as slowly, rhythmically, he guided the shallow vessel along a strangely quiet Cam. Most of the revellers were still enjoying the copious post-Ball breakfast now being served in the marquee. But Lilah and Jonathan had other plans. Avoiding the inevitable rush, they had left the Ball at four o'clock and started punting up to Grantchester in the time-honoured tradition.

'It's so beautiful here at this time of the morning,' sighed Lilah. 'Don't you just wish it could go on for ever and ever?'

Jonathan made as if to say something but then thought better of it. No, he could not tell her now. Not with the dawn mists still playing in wisps above the river. Not with the muffled sounds of tipsy madrigal singers hanging in patches along the Backs. Not with Lilah looking up at him so irresistibly.

'Oh dear,' he mumbled vaguely, 'you seem to have torn your dress.'

'So I have,' said Lilah, inspecting the damage to her green silk Traina Norell gown. What a shame. She must have caught it as they were pulling the punt over the rollers near the Garden House Hotel. 'Never mind,' she continued, 'it's not the end of the world. It's only a bargain I picked up for a tenner at the OXFAM shop.'

'Trust you,' laughed Jonathan. 'In a dress which costs a tenner you still manage to look a million dollars.' Standing perfectly erect, the sleeves of his dress shirt rolled up, Jonathan continued expertly to manipulate the punt pole.

Yes, thought Lilah sadly, taking in his ascetic good looks and kind brown eyes, it was going to be difficult. Better leave it until later, when they were both safely back at college.

'Penny for your thoughts?' asked Jonathan.

'I was just thinking that you're not half bad yourself.'

Jonathan blew her a kiss. 'Shall we go home?'

'Later.' She smiled up at him. 'Actually, you're looking a bit knackered. Do you want me to have a go?'

'Not on your life!' replied Jonathan, mock-horrified. 'The last time you were in charge, we almost ended up demolishing a bridge.' It was true and she knew it. The Mathematical Bridge at Queen's had never been the same since. Nevertheless, it seemed right to be aggrieved.

'How dare you?' Lilah filled her shoe with water and threw it at him. He saw it coming and ducked. By now he was used to her. Jonathan looked suddenly subdued. Was it really three whole years since he had walked into Trinity dining hall and found her sitting there, marvelling at the vast windows of heraldic glass and the hammerbeam roof? It seemed like only yesterday. 'Do you remember when we met? You'd just arrived and you were so gung-ho about the place.'

'How could I ever forget?' Lilah smiled. 'And when you told me you were an *eye surgeon* and gave supervisions at the college, I was so impressed I could hardly speak.'

'Hardly speak! That'll be the day. I couldn't get a word in

edgeways. You kept wittering on about how happy you were to be there. How proud your parents were. How, when you were at school in the convent, you told all the nuns that you wanted to go to Trinity. And now here you were, sitting in the very place where scholars like Dryden, Tennyson, Wittgenstein and Newton had sat.'

'Don't be such a rat. You knew how flustered I was. I always get flustered when I'm talking to older men.'

Jonathan laughed. That was egregious nonsense, even by Lilah's standards.

'You little madam. I'm only eight years older—'

'Don't interrupt. And when I get flustered, I always talk a lot.'

'You must be constantly flustered.'

'Do you want another shoeful?'

Jonathan ducked again as Lilah dipped her evening slipper into the river. 'Anyway, I can't help it. When you're the fifth child in a family, you have to talk a lot or else everyone forgets you're there.'

'I can't ever see that happening to you.' The damp green silk had moulded itself to Lilah's body. As the punt moved along, slicing through the water, Jonathan thought once more of turning for home.

'It's all right for you.' When Lilah had a bee in her bonnet, there was no stopping her. 'You're an only one. No wonder you can afford to be so quiet and contemplative.'

Jonathan smiled at her. She couldn't help it. It was the Irish in her. She loved to pick an argument.

'Then it's a good job opposites attract.' He was determined not to spoil the moment's peace before he made love to her and faced the inevitable storm that would follow his news. Suddenly Lilah felt ashamed of herself. She was only being awkward because she was feeling so dreadfully guilty.

'I'm sorry,' she whispered. 'We've had such a wonderful time. I don't want to spoil it, really I don't. I . . . oh, God . . . Jonathan!' Lilah scrambled to her feet in a desperate attempt to catch him. But it was too late. The pole had become stuck in the mud at the bottom of the river. Still hanging onto it, Jonathan was now immobilized a mere six inches above the water. As the punt was projected forward, he gradually

slid down the pole into the cold glaucous water of the Cam.
'Grab the bloody paddle,' he shouted. 'It's freezing in here.'

'I'm coming,' yelled Lilah, hoicking up her ball-gown and
paddling furiously towards him. 'Let that be a lesson to you.
Now we'll see who can handle a punt.'

It made things so much easier, mused Andrea Blackwell, to
wake up next to a man you actually recognized.

Instinctively, she disentangled herself from the embrace of
the warm, sleeping figure beside her. Outside, the bells of
Trinity College chapel reverberated loudly around Great Court.
What a hangover! The sound of bells was nothing compared
to the little men with large pneumatic drills currently excavating their way through her skull. She reached out from under
the duvet, blindly fumbling for the mug of mineral water she
half remembered leaving beside her bed. Empty! A whole pint
pot! Andrea groaned. God, she must have been loaded last
night, to drink so much water and still feel so lousy. The mug.
Andrea made a mental note. All these little 'loans' would have
to be returned to the college bar before she finally came down.

In the cobbled courtyard below, teams of men were noisily
clearing away the debris from the previous night's May Ball.
Up at Cambridge, May Balls were held in June which, if you
thought about it with a hangover, made about as much sense
as anything else in this place of arcane and archaic tradition.
Andrea thought she had better get up. There was far too much
to do to waste time moping all day in bed. Suddenly a strong
oarsman's arm reached out to stop her. 'Surely the party's not
over yet?' William Stanton buried his face sleepily in the tousled mass of Andrea's long blonde hair.

'I've got a headache,' protested Andrea feebly, the nipples
of her small firm breasts responding immediately to William's
expert caress. He laughed, massaging her abdomen, insistently
moving downwards to that warm soft mound of pleasure.

Andrea moaned as she felt his sex hard beside her. The
paracetamol could wait. Andrea put the hangover on hold as
she started to run her fingers through William's thick, dark
hair. She, too, was adept at teasing. Already she could feel
herself deliciously moist, but there was no point in hurrying

things. To travel hopefully, as Andrea had discovered with many other, less practised undergraduate performers, was often better than to arrive.

Andrea began to kiss William's lean, muscular torso, honed over months of rigorous diet, punishing circuits and gruelling team-work. None of it had helped in the Boat Race, however. Oxford had still beaten Cambridge by more lengths than William would ever care to remember. But at least all that training had not gone entirely to waste. When it came to physical stamina, either in boats or in bed, William Stanton left most men behind.

But right now William was in no mood for playing games. As far as he was concerned, strategy and pacing were for the river, not for the bedroom. Foreplay was like training: necessary up to a point but no substitute for the real thing. His tongue began insistently to probe her secret, most intimate places. Andrea could feel the urgency of his lust and her soft, wanton little body throbbed in response. She was aching, no longer in control, her juices flowing. She begged greedily for more, playing with herself now, feeling his tongue and her fingers entwined together.

'Miss Blackwell, Miss Blackwell.' There was a clattering sound of metal buckets being deposited in the sitting room. Andrea recognized the high-pitched, East Anglian whine of Grace, the bedder. She winced.

'Miss Blackwell,' continued Grace, 'it's well past lunch-time, you know. I've done all the other rooms on this staircase, I have. Left you and Miss Dooley till last. Thought you might want a lie-in after the Ball. But I've got to get my work done. Miss Blackwell,' Grace screeched above the noise of the Hoover. 'Are you still asleep? Today I really must clean that bedroom of yours. There'll be conference people using this place the day after tomorrow, you know.'

William Stanton groaned in the excruciating frustration of certainty denied. What a bloody shambles! In all his years as an oarsman, he had never before been quite so put off his stroke.

'It's OK, Grace,' shouted Andrea, a trifle hysterically, the mood of illicit lasciviousness now destroyed. She scanned the room, hunting for her dressing gown. She must get up immediately and encourage Grace to leave. What a hassle! Of all the bedders in Trinity, why did she and Lilah have to end up with this one? Most of them, despite the promise of their title, refused to make beds – refused to do much, in fact, except the most rudimentary cleaning, and even less of that for the women undergraduates. The young gentlemen, now that was a different matter. There wasn't a single bedder in Cambridge didn't want to mother every one of them. But like the rest of the world, Cambridge bedders expected women to fend for themselves. Grace, however, had turned out to be an exception. Perhaps it was the tea and fruit cake with which Lilah plied her, or the way Lilah never failed to ask after Grace's young son, Tom, and his scout group. Whatever the reason, the Misses Dooley and Blackwell had the neatest, cleanest rooms in Trinity.

At that moment, however, Andrea needed Grace with her vacuum cleaner and her obsessively sanitizing attentions like a hole in the head. It wasn't as if Grace was going to say or do anything about the presence of a man in her bed. No, it was a bit late for that. Besides, since the college had gone co-ed in the late 1970s, rules on that score had been virtually ignored if not abolished. By now, Grace had seen it all, or most of it. All the same, Andrea did not want the bedder to catch her here with William. She could not quite explain it, but she could not bear the look that would cloud Grace's lined and leathery face. A look of disapproval and disgust, all encapsulated in one sideways glance which said, simply, 'another one'.

'Miss Blackwell, Miss Blackwell,' resumed Grace, her piercing voice like a bad attack of tinnitus. 'Miss Dooley's bed has not been slept in.'

'Not back from the Ball yet,' shouted Andrea. 'Probably gone punting up to Grantchester.'

'Ah yes,' replied Grace fondly. 'Gone with that nice young man of hers.' It did Grace's large heart good, it did, to think of her favourite undergraduate having such a good time. All the same, she was sorry that Miss Dooley was not there for their usual chat. Grace mainlined on gossip, but so far this morning none of the students Grace 'did for' had come up with the goods. The vast majority were positively comatose.

A few were still out punting. And one or two were noisily throwing up in the bathrooms on the second- and third-floor landings. Grace was determined to find some excuse, however spurious, for a chat. 'Shall I throw out that pile of Sunday colour supplements in the study, or do you want to keep them?'

Andrea realized that there was no way out. Grace was never going to leave those rooms until she had managed to button-hole someone. At last, Andrea located her dressing gown, a white towelling number liberated from an hotel room after a particularly tacky one-night stand in Paris.

William Stanton's eyes followed her as, unsteadily, she made her way across the room to retrieve it. Good grief, he thought watching in amazement as she groped hopelessly around, she's still completely smashed.

'Coming, Grace, coming,' shouted Andrea. 'Just give me a few minutes, will you. I'll be with you in a tick.'

'Right ho, Miss Blackwell,' replied Grace, happy at last to have drawn some response. 'I'll put the kettle on for you, shall I?' Without waiting for a reply, Grace pottered off to the gyp room nearby. She would extract the highlights of the event from Andrea over a cup of Miss Dooley's Lapsang Souchong.

Andrea started to pick up the clothes strewn across the floor. What a shame! The blue taffeta gown, hired for her by William, looked a complete write-off. She tried hard to remember how it had come to be so water-stained. Vague recollections of rowing hearties combined with the Great Court canopied foun-tain swam uneasily around her head.

'Get up, will you, William,' ordered Andrea briskly. 'If you get dressed now, you can be out of here before the dreaded Grace claps eyes on you.'

William Stanton looked stunned. He was not used to young women telling him or wanting him to leave in a hurry. 'Come off it, Andrea,' he retorted, irritated by the sudden change in tone. 'What does it matter if the old bat catches me here? They're hardly going to rusticate you now, you know. Besides,' he patted the warm bed next to him invitingly, 'you and I have unfinished business to attend to.'

'Sorry,' replied Andrea, tossing a dampish dinner suit across the room in his direction, 'but it's time for you to be off. I'm going down tomorrow and I've still got an awful lot to do.'

'Hang on a minute,' said William, angry now, 'precisely what are you trying to tell me? Is this your way of saying, "Thanks very much, it's been nice knowing you. Now will you please fuck off?" '

Andrea looked at him in surprise. 'What on earth has got into you? We had an arrangement, didn't we? You needed a partner for May Week. Well, now May Week's been and gone.'

William could hardly believe his ears. Over the seven days and nights he had known her, Andrea had proved intelligent and amusing company for the non-stop swirl of balls and parties. 'But, Andrea, you can't just call it a day like that.' She had to be joking. Could this be the same woman who, over the last week, had made love to him passionately, frenetically and in every conceivable position?

Andrea was getting aggravated. Why didn't this bloke just get up and go? She really did have a lot to do. 'Come off it, William. We had a deal. Surely a banker's son, of all people should understand that?' Andrea's lip curled as she spoke. A merchant bank, a sizeable chunk of Sussex and most of the Kenyan coffee crop – it was all right for men like William Stanton. They had other people to do everything for them.

'You little bitch!' By now William was feeling both furious and degraded. 'I'm sorry, I hadn't understood. So with you, sex is nothing but a traded commodity?'

Andrea continued to tidy her belongings. With a hangover, who needed this crap? 'Look, William,' she said, barely bothering to look up. 'Perhaps Lilah should have told you when she introduced us, but I've never been one for the financial ramifications of feminism. I've never felt equality means paying fifty-fifty. All I know is I had something you wanted. So why shouldn't you pay for it? Simple as that, really.'

William hopped out of bed and hurriedly pulled on his clothes. She was right. Their time together had been nothing but a deal. Now the whole episode made him want to retch.

'Goodbye, Andrea,' he said, as he opened the bedroom door to leave. Andrea continued to tidy. 'Just one more thing,' he added. His voice was cold with anger. 'Make sure your path never crosses mine.' He slammed the door behind him. A

40

bishop leaving a brothel could not have exited more swiftly than William Stanton. Clattering down the staircase, he bumped into Lilah and Jonathan and almost sent them flying.

'Hello,' Lilah half-yawned. 'My word, William, you look as if you're in a hurry.'

Seeing Lilah made William feel better. Like Lilah a modern linguist, he had spent the last three years lusting after her during their French literature supervisions.

'And you two look as if you've been in for a swim.' Both Lilah and Jonathan were dripping all over the grey stone staircase.

'We'd better get a move on,' urged Jonathan. 'Otherwise, Lilah, you're going to end up with pneumonia.'

'Oh, I'll be all right,' she replied, brightly. 'I'm sure there's time to say goodbye to my old supervision sparring partner here.'

'I'll miss our little sessions together,' said William, grinning at her.

'So, now, I suppose you're off to the family firm?'

'Afraid so,' replied William. 'Someone's got to keep coining the boodle. How about you? Research, I suppose. New and incisive insights into the lesser-known works of Théophile de Gautier.'

'Get lost, Stanton. Actually I've decided—' Lilah caught herself in mid-sentence. 'I've decided that the fusty world of academe is not for me after all. I'll be trying my hand at something else.'

William kissed her on the cheek. 'Good luck. Look after her, Jonathan.' William started down the stairs again. 'You're a very lucky man. Lilah, if ever you need a merchant banker, remember to give me a shout.'

CHAPTER FOUR

WILLIAM STANTON shaded his eyes from the bright summer sunlight as he emerged into Great Court.

'Good morning, Professor,' he shouted to Professor Legrand, an ancient and arthritic don hobbling slowly across the college lawn. At Cambridge, only dons had this right of passage. Professor Legrand ventured no response. Immured in a sixteenth-century world of his own, he seemed completely unaware of everything around him.

'Hello down there,' hailed a voice. Squinting up into the early morning sunshine, William recognized Hugo Newsom wafting a half-empty bottle of Bollinger and hanging out of a second-floor casement window. 'Fancy one in the bar?'

'I don't think I could face it.'

'Come on,' shouted Hugo, himself still plastered from the previous night's festivities. 'Hair of the dog?' He swayed perilously above on the sill.

'OK, then. Anything to stop you falling out of that bloody window.' The fresh air and sunshine were having a salutary effect on William. A few drinks with Hugo might further improve his spirits. William had known Hugo since the day they arrived in Cambridge. Somewhat effete for William's rowing cronies, Hugo still ranked as his closest friend. During their first year, the two men had shared cold and miserable rooms in Trinity's Whewell's Court. It made for a lasting bond. Hugo trundled down the stairs and into the courtyard.

'Let's go and get Lilah,' he slurred, as they staggered along the cobbled path which led to Trinity bar.

'No point,' said William. 'I've just seen her and Morton – soaked to the skin the pair of them, about to hit the sack.'

'How did it go with Andrea last night?' Hugo's face looked as if he had been sucking lemons.

'Don't let's talk about it. What a bitch.'

'Bizarre, isn't it?' said Hugo, tumbling into the bar. 'That's always been my impression. But old Lilah can see no wrong in her.'

The barman moved across to take their order.

'Hello, Harry. Make that two pints of Greene King, will you? And have one for yourself.'

'It's weird,' agreed William, once the beers had arrived. 'Who'll ever understand the female mind?'

'Not my problem, dearie,' said Hugo, pursing his lips. William burst out laughing. 'But I've had so much fun acting opposite Lilah, if I were into women, I'd have fallen for her myself.'

'Join the club,' said William, by now supping his beer quite enthusiastically. 'God, I've fancied her something rotten ever since our first supervision. How can anyone that sexy be so bloody clever? Another one, Hugo?'

Decidedly glassy-eyed, Hugo nodded eagerly. 'Those legs . . .' he burbled.

'I'll say,' agreed William, his eyes now rotating independently like Catherine wheels. 'You should've seen old Legrand in supervisions. Poor chap hardly ever registered I was in the room. Just as well, really.'

Hugo laughed, a loud, drunken laugh. 'D'you think you've done enough to scrape through your finals?'

'Just about. I reckon I've managed a third.'

'A third? Thank goodness you're only going into banking.'

'Absolutely. And Daddy's bank at that. What about you? The stage?'

'Too dicey. No, I'm taking the job at Sotheby's. Fine porcelain department.'

William burped.

'Think I'd better go and visit the porcelain myself. Another round, please, Harry. Looks like it's going to be one of those days.'

The bedroom was stifling. Lilah opened the casement window which gave onto Great Court. Thank goodness, she thought. At least by now the workmen had finished clearing up around her set of rooms and that part of the college had resumed its normal, monastic tranquillity.

'Jonathan.'

'Lilah.' Lying close together on the narrow, college bed, Jonathan stroked Lilah's hair. Nuzzling against his chest, she wished she could feel the usual glow of security and peace.

'Lilah,' said Jonathan, starting again. 'There's something I've been meaning to say to you. I suppose I should have mentioned it earlier. But I didn't want to distract you. Not in the middle of your finals.' His arms around her shoulders, he drew her to him more closely still and gently kissed the top of her head.

'Don't tell me,' Lilah was disconcerted by the tone of his voice. 'You're pregnant.'

For once Jonathan was in no mood for her little jokes.

'Lilah, I'm no longer happy in Cambridge.' He paused. It would be all right so long as she made no attempt to look up at him. 'To tell the truth, I'm bored with working in England.'

Lilah said nothing, but he could feel her body freeze.

'I can't help it,' he soldiered on, increasingly uneasy. 'I'm frustrated here. I feel I could be doing so much more.' He stopped. 'Lilah?'

'But you're a wonderful doctor,' she blurted out at last. 'Everybody knows that. Nobody could be more caring than you. Nobody could work harder. Nobody . . .'

'I'm afraid that's not the point. The point is there's so much to be done elsewhere. The Third World is screaming out for people like me to go and help.'

'But, Jonathan,' protested Lilah, seeing the writing all to clearly on the wall, 'there's so much to be done here as well.' Her voice trailed off. She understood Jonathan too well. Deep down, she knew his mind had already been made up. It was futile to argue. He had never been a man for easy options. Affluence and security formed no part of his career plan. Jonathan was an idealist. She had always known that. It was the reason she had fallen in love with him in the first place. But now his wretched idealism was about to tear them apart. 'So where are you off to?' she asked brusquely.

'South Africa.'

Lilah raised her eyebrows. '*South* Africa?'

'It's not what you think. I'm not trading Harley Street for the blue-rinse mob of Houghton.'

'Then where?'

'You won't have heard of it. It's a place called Meroto, a black township not far from Johannesburg.'

'Well, congratulations,' said Lilah. 'A black township named Meroto. I don't suppose a bit of warning might have been in order?'

'Believe me, darling,' said Jonathan, taking her hand in his and raising it to his lips, 'I had no idea myself until recently.'

'So what's the rush?' Lilah fought to choke back the tears. 'How did it happen so suddenly?'

Jonathan tried to kiss the tips of her fingers. Angrily, she withdrew her hand.

'About a month ago, I came across a South African ophthalmologist at a conference. After I'd delivered my paper, he asked me why Western do-gooders are all so concerned about eye care in "black" Africa while the blacks in so-called "white" South Africa rarely get a look in.'

Lilah smiled at the inadvertent pun. Grasping the opening, Jonathan leaned across to kiss her cheek and resumed stroking her tangled hair.

'Then, afterwards, during the coffee break, he told me about this hospital in Meroto. Apparently it's impossible to get a decent ophthalmic surgeon to go and operate there. The black doctors prepared to go just don't have the necessary expertise or qualifications. And what white surgeon is going to work in a place like that for next to nothing?'

'Except a fool like you.' Lilah could hear Jonathan's heart pounding anxiously.

'Yes, darling. That's about the top and bottom of it. Except a fool like me.'

Despite her hostility, Lilah was intrigued. 'Who'll be funding you?' Usually Jonathan was so vague about details such as money.

'Trust you to think of the practical side.' He laughed. 'I'm almost afraid to say.'

'Don't tell me!' Lilah found it impossible to stay angry with him for very long. 'Drug barons' conscience money?'

'Not quite that bad. But almost.'

'Good grief.' By now, even Lilah was laughing. 'Not the Mafia? You're not going to be laundering Mafia money through Meroto?'

'Do cut it out.' Jonathan was relieved to see her sense of humour had returned. 'I'll be funded by the Christian Sight-Savers Mission.'

Lilah looked incredulous. Jonathan was an out and out atheist – a Protestant atheist she had always joked.

'What? Jonathan, you bloody hypocrite! That crowd are arch Bible-bashers. Next you'll be telling me you're a born-again Christian.'

'Not a chance. I told them right from the beginning I was a non-believer.'

'That must have gone down a storm. What an interview! It must have sounded like Jack Nicholson running for Pope.'

Jonathan smiled wryly. 'I must admit, they weren't exactly over the moon about it. But in the end, they knew they had to accept my conditions. I told them it was either me or Lassie on a skateboard.' They both burst out laughing.

'You're a one-off.' Lilah's eyes filled with tears again. How could she bear to let him go? If only she could bring herself to share his enthusiasm for this project.

'It'll be hard work,' he continued. 'At least a five-year programme, probably more. The conditions are rough and the political situation – well, I don't have to tell you. There's always a chance of getting caught in the cross-fire. But, Lilah,' Jonathan retrieved a small antique emerald ring from the depths of his breast pocket, 'what I'm trying to say is, I know it isn't much to offer, but will you marry me?'

Her mind still reeling, Lilah stared at her own reflection, liquid in Jonathan's dark brown eyes. Idealists! Why were they

were so easy to love and so impossible to live with? 'Jonathan,'
she began, a strange empty feeling clawing its way into the
pit of her stomach. Suddenly this was no longer a joke. A
dozen conflicting emotions raced around in her head.

'Jonathan.' She could hardly get the words out. 'You know
it would never work.'

'But, Lilah . . .'

'No, just think about it. What could I possibly do in a place
like Meroto?'

Jonathan looked taken aback. 'Well, I must say, I hadn't
really thought about it. I suppose you could always teach.'

'Sure.' Immediately Lilah's apprehension had turned to sarcasm. 'And tell me what precisely? Goethe? Dante? Or how
about a nice course of lectures on Racine? That'd go down
really well with the good folk of Meroto.'

'Don't be so negative. Lots of women—' Jonathan knew he'd
made a mistake.

'But I'm not lots of women!' yelled Lilah. 'I haven't killed
myself learning all these languages just to go and throw everything away in some God-forsaken backwater. You've found
yourself a vocation. Well, bully for you. But I'm too young,
you know, to start playing Mother Teresa yet.'

'And far too beautiful.' Jonathan had not meant it to sound
like a gibe. Immediately he realized he should have gauged
Lilah's flashpoint more accurately. Now he could see her brist-
ling, ready for a fight. 'Lilah, listen, I wasn't—'

'No, you just bloody well listen. I'll tell you why I can't go
and live with you in Meroto.' Disengaging herself from his
arms, she jumped out of bed and stormed around the bedroom. 'It's because of you, Jonathan. Because of who you are
and the way you think.'

'What do you mean?'

'You know it yourself!' Lilah was distraught. Fear, love and
misery – it was a highly inflammable combination. 'Ever since
I've known you, you've gone on and on about the hosts of
hopeless do-gooders who turn up in developing countries,
offering no more than bleeding hearts and guilty consciences.'

'But that's not what I—'

'Let me finish. It's true, you know how you despise them,

47

locked in the comfort of their international development agencies with occasional sorties into the Third World for some genuine "hands-on" experience.'

'But you, Lilah, you're not—'

'You were talking about them only the other day – all those useless jerks with their degrees in social and developmental sciences.' By now the tears were streaming down Lilah's face.

'I still believe that. Developing countries need doers not talkers.'

'But don't you see? If I went to Meroto I'd be nothing more than one of these bleeding-heart liberals you so despise. I'm not a doctor or a farmer or an engineer. I'm a bloody linguist, for Chrissake. What possible use could I be out there?'

'You could be my support—'

'Oh, Jesus. Wouldn't you bloody well know it? Underneath the right-on image beats the good old "macho" heart. I can be *your* support, can I? Get lost, Jonathan. What about my fucking career?'

'Lilah, please. Honestly, I didn't mean—'

'No, thank God these things are coming out now. Before it's too late. And to think I wanted to marry you . . .' Suddenly Lilah collapsed back on to the bed, sobbing into her pillow.

'Come on, Lilah.' Jonathan moved towards her and tenderly touched her cheek. 'Now you can see why I didn't mention it before. But you've just *admitted* you want to marry me. So what's the problem? I'm sure we can work it out.'

'I don't see how.'

Jonathan felt his heart would break as he watched her shoulders, heaving with misery.

'Not now you've decided to go and do your Albert Schweitzer number in the middle of nowhere.'

'Lilah, for God's sake—'

'Listen, why don't you? Now I've got something to say. It only came up last week and I'd been wondering how to go about it.' Lilah tried to control her tears. 'It wasn't my idea to begin with. But Professor Legrand has this old friend in Geneva . . . at the United Nations . . . the sort of person you can't abide—'

'Don't put words into—'

'I'm not putting words into your mouth. You do loathe

them. Perhaps I ought to start saying *us* not them. Because, Jonathan, the United Nations has offered me a job as a conference interpreter.'

It was Jonathan's turn to look shocked. This was totally unexpected. Now he was losing the woman he loved. That had never been part of his plan.

'Great, just great,' he said sarcastically. 'So you bite my head off for going to Meroto but you're off to Geneva in any event.'

'It's not the same,' said Lilah, sitting up straight on the bed. 'Geneva we could have coped with. I could have commuted. Lots of people do.' She burst into tears again. Jonathan put his arms around her. This time she made no move to shake them off.

'Let's try to be sensible about this,' he said, feeling anything but. 'We don't have to make any decisions now. If we give it some time, I'm sure things will fall into place.'

Lilah shook her head miserably. Oh God, why did she have to be so uncompromising? Why couldn't she just give in and follow the man she loved into the South African bush?

Jonathan found his handkerchief and gently wiped away her tears. 'Here,' he said, retrieving the small box from where it had fallen beside the bed. 'I still want you to have this ring.'

'But, Jonathan, I can't promise . . .'

'Please. It belonged to my mother and to her mother before her. Please, Lilah, I want you to wear it. That would make me very happy.'

Still battling to stifle the tears, Lilah nodded her assent. Jonathan placed the small antique emerald on the third finger of her elegant right hand.

'And I'm hoping,' he touched her cheek, 'that one day I can transfer it.' Through her tears, Lilah smiled up at him as, slowly, he began to unbutton the glass buttons down the front of her ball-gown.

'I love you,' she murmured, as the green silk dress slipped silently onto the floor.

'And I love you too,' he whispered and tenderly kissed her breasts.

*

The next day, their last together up at Cambridge, Lilah and Andrea met for lunch in hall. There was little doubt that Andrea would have preferred the Eros, a cheap and cheerful restaurant much frequented by impecunious undergraduates – not so much for the menu, which was interesting and varied, but for the very fanciable Greek waiter with whom Andrea loved to flirt. For once in their relationship, however, Lilah was determined to have her way. The great dining hall of Trinity College held so many happy memories. How often had she dined at High Table with Jonathan – it was one of the many privileges associated with his teaching at the college – and stared, entranced, as the flickering candelabra cast their shadows all over the Jacobean gallery? It was hardly surprising that the place had come to mean so much to her; she had to bid it one last farewell.

'Jonathan working?' asked Andrea, sitting down opposite her friend at one of the long wooden trestle tables.

'Yes, he's up at Addenbrooke's, operating.' Lilah looked across at Andrea's plate. A few pieces of lettuce and a tomato. 'Are you sure that's going to be enough?'

'Of course not. I'll be ravenous in half an hour. But I've got to lose some weight before I start getting interviews.' Andrea cast an envious eyes over Lilah's lunch – a hamburger, double beans and chips. 'I don't know how you do it.'

Lilah smiled good-naturedly. It was true. She ate like a horse and stayed as slim as a pencil. 'Just one of those things,' she said, emptying two sachets of tomato sauce over her chips. 'Talking about interviews, have you heard anything?'

'About that job at the *Courier*? No, nothing yet.' Andrea stared morosely at her lettuce leaves. How long could she keep this up?

'Come on,' said Lilah, encouragingly. 'You're bound to get the job. You've got first-rate ability.'

'And, no doubt, a third-rate degree.'

'Oh, do buck up, Andrea. Which tabloid newspaper is going to give a hoot about that? At least you read English. You've got to be in with a chance.'

'I hope so. But the competition is very stiff. Honestly, I'd do anything to get that job.' Lilah waved to Hugo and William as they came into the hall.

'How did it go with William?'

'He was OK,' replied Andrea. 'Useful for May Week, anyhow.'

'Will you be seeing him again?' It was one of Lilah's theories. All that Andrea really needed was a good man to calm her down.

Andrea speared her tomato. 'What's the point? Men like William Stanton don't end up marrying girls like me.' Andrea shuddered as she thought of Grimford in Essex and the poky council house she had once called home.

'Don't be silly. You're bright and clever and funny—'

'Oh, Lilah, do grow up,' snapped Andrea. 'You still believe love conquers all, don't you? Anyone would think you'd spent the last three years studying Mills and Boon.'

Lilah started to laugh. She knew most of her friends disapproved of Andrea. An awful little tart, Jonathan had once called her. But they didn't really know her. She *was* bright. And she *was* clever. And she *was* funny. All this bed-hopping, Lilah had convinced herself, was just a passing phase.

'Well, let me tell you something about rich young men,' continued Andrea. 'And God knows, I've known enough of them. They'll screw you till you're black and blue and string you along till you're past it. Then they'll bugger off and marry some nice Sloane with a cookery diploma and an IQ to match her Alice band.'

Lilah burst out laughing. 'Andrea! You really are the limit! How could the *Courier* possibly turn you down? You'd make a brilliant gossip columnist.'

Andrea's cornflower-blue eyes twinkled with mischief. 'That's the plan. If you can't be one of the beautiful people, at least you can slag them off.'

A cloud crossed Lilah's face. 'You don't mean that.'

'Try me. Anyway, I haven't got the job yet, more's the pity. They're not interviewing for some time. You don't know how lucky you are, Lilah. All fixed up already.'

'It isn't going to be easy,' said Lilah, suddenly subdued. 'Me in Geneva and Jonathan in Meroto.' Andrea tried in vain to look sympathetic. She had never cared for Jonathan – far too earnest for her taste. Off to the wilds of South Africa, indeed. If she was Lilah she'd give him the heave-ho right now. A bloke near at hand had to be worth two in the Transvaal bush.

'I'm sure you'll figure something out.' Andrea noticed the ring on Lilah's right hand but decided to say nothing.

'I hope so. We talked about it most of yesterday. If I stayed two years at the UN, I could get myself elected to the International Association of Conference Interpreters. After that, if I started working on a freelance basis, I could spend more time with Jonathan.'

'Very neat,' said Andrea.

Lilah was so enthusiastic she mistook the sarcasm for support. She felt suddenly embarrassed. 'Oh, I'm sorry. Here am I rabbiting on about my job and my bloke and you haven't got either yet.' Lilah bit her tongue. She hadn't meant it to sound like that. Deftly she changed the subject. 'Will you be coming back for graduation?'

'No.'

Lilah looked taken aback. 'But don't your parents want to come?'

'Yes,' said Andrea. 'But I've told them not to. I couldn't bear it. They're such unbelievable oicks.'

Lilah shook her head in disbelief. How could anyone talk like that about her father and mother? Lilah's parents had both died in a car crash during her second year. Thank God for her brothers and Jonathan. She did not know how she would have coped without them. Jonathan, in particular, had counselled and supported her through her very darkest moments. It was this tragedy more than anything else which had taught her how much she loved and needed him.

'How can you be so cruel?' she asked.

'Easy,' replied Andrea bitterly. 'At Grimford Comprehensive they give you lessons in it. I suppose lover-boy will be tipping up to see you graduate – *summa cum laude* no doubt.'

'Yes, Jonathan will be there,' said Lilah quietly. 'And then we'll have a few months together before . . .' Suddenly, all her well-laid plans no longer seemed to be making sense. Andrea looked on, almost content, as Lilah's expression turned to one of desolation.

CHAPTER FIVE

Meroto, South Africa, November 1981

IT WAS only 7 o'clock in the morning, but a long queue was waiting as Jonathan arrived for his clinic. Already the strong summer sunshine was beating down on the corrugated tin roof of the Christian Sight-Savers Mission Hospital. As the day wore on, the heat inside the building would gradually become unbearable, but no one complained. The people of Meroto had far worse hardships to contend with than the minor niggle of temperature extremes.

During his first two months in Meroto, there had been days when Jonathan felt like throwing in the towel, but somehow the placid and stoical fortitude of his patients gave him the strength to continue. If necessary, they would wait for him for hours, grateful for the tepid respite provided by a few desultory electric fans. Even those could not be relied on for permanent relief. The hospital's private generator was notoriously erratic.

From the outside, the hospital was quite unremarkable. Most buildings in the township, apart from the pullulating sprawl of instant shanty housing, were pretty much the same. A dozen heavy stones pinned the roof to a square grey cinder-brick structure. It was a miracle how such makeshift arrangements withstood the violence of the Transvaal's bitter hailstorms. Jonathan walked down the noisy, crowded corridor and along to his consulting room. Already Sister Ndaba was at work, busily clerking patients.

'Good morning, Dr Morton,' she smiled. Sister Ndaba thought the sun rose and set with her clever new English surgeon.

'Good morning, Sister. Looks like we're in for another busy day.' Sister Ndaba nodded as she handed Jonathan his white coat. 'Thanks,' he said, pulling it on as he walked into his consulting room.

Within two minutes, he was seated behind his rickety old desk. 'OK,' he shouted to Sister Ndaba, struggling to maintain order in the waiting room. 'Let battle commence.'

Credo Sekese was twenty-five years old. Wiry and of medium height, he had the fine, somewhat angular features of the Xhosa tribe to which he belonged.

'Sit down, Credo,' said Jonathan, glancing at the brief details Sister Ndaba had taken. 'Tell me, when did this accident occur?'

'About two weeks ago, Doctor.'

'Two weeks ago! Why didn't you come to see me sooner?'

'Impossible. If I don't work, I don't get paid. And I'm working down the mine every day except Sunday.'

Jonathan started to examine Credo's right eye which was still badly inflamed. 'How did it happen?'

'It all happened very quick. I'm drilling at the working-face and suddenly there's a sharp pain in my eye. I stop drilling and I crawl over to the gang leader. He looks, but he cannot find anything. So he says, "Go back to work, Credo. You must finish drilling the holes. We have to be out of the mine in one hour so that the blasting can begin. If there are no holes, where can we put the charges?" So I go back to work like he says. I finish my job.'

Jonathan was shining a light into Credo's eye. 'And if you'd come and seen me before, you'd have lost a day's pay?' By now, Jonathan was making notes. 'Isn't there a trade union you can complain to?' He could see the muscles stiffen in Credo's neck.

'No. The mine belongs to a company called Metallinc. They do not allow unions.' Credo gave a hollow laugh. 'That is why you never see us, Doctor. That is why we men are never sick.'

Jonathan looked up quizzically. 'But you did manage to come in today.'

'I am number one machine boy in our gang.' Credo's voice was expressionless. This was simply a matter of fact. 'Last month, we mine the most ore and we get the biggest bonus. So yesterday I am coming up in the lift with the *baas* and he say, "Credo, you better go see that *kaffirboetie* doctor about that eye of your." ' Jonathan stared at Credo but the Xhosa's face gave nothing away. *Kaffirboetie* – lover of blacks. In Afrikaans, the expression was never anything but pejorative.

'I see,' said Jonathan, equally impassive. 'Well, Credo, I'm afraid you've developed an infection. You'd better put these drops in three times a day.' He gave Credo a bottle of anti-biotics which he took with a nod of gratitude. 'If we were in England,' continued Jonathan, 'I wouldn't allow you underground until that infection had cleared up.'

'England must be a wonderful country,' said Credo, standing up to leave. 'I dream one day of visiting my hero in London.'

'Oh, yes,' replied Jonathan casually, rinsing his hands in the washbasin. 'Who's that?'

'Karl Marx.'

Jonathan spun around and stared aghast at his patient. This was foolhardy talk. Suspected Communist sympathies, like complicity with the banned African National Congress party, could land Credo in jail. Jonathan was alarmed. 'You should be careful who you say that to.'

'I am.'

'Then why say it to me?'

'Because I trust you, Doctor.'

Jonathan was touched. 'All the same,' he said, 'for your own sake, you'd better keep those opinions to yourself.'

He watched as Credo closed the consulting-room door behind him. He could not pinpoint precisely what it was but there was a strange energy about this man, something essentially strong and vital. Whatever it was, thought Jonathan, Credo Sekese was no ordinary machine boy.

It was well past noon when Sister Ndaba ushered the last patient into Jonathan's consulting room. Hell, it was hot. With a bit of luck there would be time for a quick shower and a sandwich before he started the afternoon's operating list. It had been the usual hectic clinic. In the space of one morning, Jonathan had diagnosed conditions most Western doctors would never see. Of course, patients came to Jonathan suffering from eye complaints. But it was impossible to ignore the instances of kwashiorkor, a life-threatening protein deficiency, and the starvation condition of marasmus, both of which were endemic among the children of Meroto. Jonathan sighed. He was tough, always had been. At Winchester, he had excelled in long-distance running and martial arts, sports which encouraged stamina, self-reliance and a degree of masochism. But the mental strain of his task in Meroto seemed unbearable at times and being alone did not help. If only Lilah were there with him! Jonathan felt in his pocket for her latest letter. Earlier that morning he had devoured its contents – lots of good-natured gossip about the international conference circuit and her busy life in Geneva. Jonathan felt a sudden twinge of jealousy and anger. How on earth could Lilah even begin to understand about his work in Meroto? He watched the ancient metal sterilizer bubbling away by the washbasin and attempted to conjure up her face. The whole picture eluded him, so he tried concentrating on one feature at a time: her eyes, hair, lips, laugh – the very feel of her.

'Doctor.' Sister Ndaba's voice broke into his thoughts. 'This is Nora Shiburi. She's too frightened to talk to you. She's been sitting in the clinic all morning just crying over that baby.'

'Thank you, Sister.'

Sister Ndaba made to leave.

'No, don't go,' he added. 'Perhaps Mrs Shiburi would feel better if you stayed here with us. Now then, Nora, what seems to be the problem?'

The young woman, still crying, hugged a small ragged parcel close to her chest. The parcel had neither the strength nor the energy to wail out loud. It merely whimpered pathetically.

'Come now, I'm not going to hurt your baby. Is it a little boy or a little girl?'

'A boy.'

'And what's his name?'

'Abram.'

'And how old is Abram?'

'Nearly one year old.' The woman choked back the tears. 'The baby is blind, Doctor. And it's all my fault. I'm a very wicked woman.'

Jonathan placed one arm around the woman's thin shoulders. 'I'm sure you're not. Now you just tell me what happened.'

Nora took a deep gulp of breath, mopping her eyes with her shawl. 'When the baby is born, Doctor, I am so very happy. He is no trouble at all. Then the mother of the baby-father come to visit me.'

Jonathan knew enough about life in the township not to ask embarrassing questions about the woman's marital status. Odds were that the 'baby-father' would not be Nora's legal husband.

'Was she pleased to see the baby?'

'No,' sobbed Nora helplessly, 'she was not happy at all. She say I am a very bad mother. She say, "Look. This baby has sticky eye. What are you doing about it?" '

'And what were you doing about it?'

'I am doing what my cousin tell me to do,' said Nora. 'My cousin bring her baby here to see you. He has the same problem as my baby. You give her magic water to put in the baby's eye. Very soon, the sticky eye go away.'

'There is no magic water,' said Jonathan, perhaps for the hundredth time that week, 'only antibiotics. But why didn't you come to me for some of the same antibiotics?'

'My cousin have some magic water left,' wept Nora. 'She give it to me and I put it in baby's eye. Soon the sticky eye is not so bad. But then the mother of baby-father come and she say I must take baby to *sangoma*.'

Oh, God. Obviously that bastard Moses Obateo had been at it again. Would these people never learn? During his few months in the township, Jonathan had seen many victims irretrievably injured by the local witch-doctor's evil handiwork. The superstitions of ancient folklore ran deep in the community. The influence of the *sangoma* was both pervasive and pernicious. Jonathan clenched his fist in anger. As if there weren't enough problems on his plate already. Now medicine in the township had become a battle of prestige – a head-on confrontation between Jonathan's white magic and the *sangoma*'s black *mhuti*.

'And then what?' asked Jonathan, already afraid of the answer.

'The *sangoma* is very angry when I tell him of your magic water. He throw it away when I show him. He look at the baby and say he has a special potion. I take it home and put it in baby's eye like he tell me.'

Sister Ndaba handed Jonathan an old beer bottle full of brownish liquid. Jonathan uncorked the bottle and sniffed the familiar, foul-smelling recipe. Just as he had feared. The same terrifying concoction of human urine, tree bark and household bleach that he had encountered on previous occasions.

'That evil fucking bastard,' muttered Jonathan under his breath. He had yet to meet his shadowy adversary. But if ever he did, Jonathan feared he might strangle the man. 'So for how long did you apply the potion?'

'Three weeks, four weeks, I don't know. But then I get very frightened. It seem to me that baby is not seeing me at all. So I go back to *sangoma* and he say my baby is now blind. He say baby go blind because I am very bad woman. He say my ancestors are wicked people. They steal cattle a long time ago. For this I and baby are now being punished.' Nora Shiburi stifled a sob.

The poor woman, thought Jonathan. She looked no more than a child herself. 'Let me examine the baby.'

Gently Sister Ndaba removed the child from Nora's shaking arms. The results of the examination were a foregone conclusion. The tiny mite just lay there, passively whimpering in the nurse's arms as Jonathan observed the dry, scarred, corneal tissue of his sightless eyes. In England, Jonathan would have tried to perform a corneal graft, but here, with only the most basic technology at his disposal, such an operation was out of the question.

'Nora,' said Jonathan, gently restoring Abram to his mother, 'listen to me. The *sangoma* is a very evil man. It was the potion he gave you which made your baby blind. Believe me, it has nothing to do with you or your ancestors.'

'But, Doctor,' said Nora, a faint glimmer of hope illuminating her face, 'can you make my baby see again?'

'I'm afraid not, Nora.' Jonathan sighed. 'Not right now.'

'Perhaps some time,' insisted Nora, 'when the baby is bigger?'

'Perhaps,' said Jonathan, trying hard to sound convincing, 'when the baby is a lot bigger.' Nora Shiburi stifled a sob. The white doctor's magic was not so strong, after all. It was as she had feared. Nothing could be done.

Dejected, Jonathan watched as Nora rose to leave. In one swift movement of her shawl, she attached the small human parcel to the security of her own slight body. It was a long journey home, in the heat of the day, along the red dirt road – doubly long and painful now in her hopelessness and pain.

'Moses Obateo,' shouted Jonathan, after he had ushered Nora out. Angrily he smashed the wall with his fist. 'So help me, I'd like to wring that bastard's neck.'

Approximately six miles away, in the canteen kitchen of the Meroto platinum mine, Jojo Matwetwe was sullenly grilling a steak. Steak! Jojo could not remember the last time she had eaten a piece of meat, let alone a steak. Other kitchen workers would steal the leftovers and take them home to their ravenous children. But Jojo had none. After the fatal mining accident two years before, she did not even have a husband. It had been no one's fault, of course. At least, that was the conclusion of the official report: 'Darius Matwetwe, rock-drill operator, was buried by a rockfall at the working face on November 5 1979. The rockfall could not have been foreseen. It was due exclusively to the fractured nature of the ground.'

Jojo could still remember every word of the document. Cold, clinical, matter-of-fact. A man had died, been cleared away, and production had continued. That was the way things were down the Meroto mine. There had been no talk of compensation for the widow. Just the offer of a job in the white administrators' canteen. The steak spat and sizzled noisily. A good fourteen ounces in weight, she knew half of it would be returned uneaten. But let the others fight for the crumbs from the white man's table. Jojo was far too proud to scavenge.

As a child, Jojo Matwetwe had never known a father – not that there was any shame attached to illegitimacy in a place like Meroto. No, the problem was her colour. Even in her mid-twenties, the mental scars she bore were as livid as ever. Jojo could still remember the cruel taunts of her classmates in the Holy Rosary convent. Of course, the nuns had done everything in their power to protect the child from her tormentors. In catechism lessons, Mother Benigna would spend hours explaining that each and every one of them was created in God's own image and likeness, all of them equal in the eyes of the Lord. But even at the age of seven, Jojo knew Mother Benigna was lying. She had to be. If all children were made in God's image and likeness, why should she be so different from all the rest? With her light brown skin and her extraordinary blue eyes, she knew there had to be something wrong with her.

'Jojo, how long is that steak going to be? The *baas* said rare, you know.'

Jojo nodded at Sam, the supervisor. How she despised him, the sort of black who grovelled to the whites and then, in the security of the kitchen, called them every name under the sun.

'Coming,' replied Jojo, completely unconcerned. It was her own little piece of subversion for the day. If the *baas* wanted his steak rare, she would ensure it was over-done. That way, some black comrade was guaranteed to get the whole thing when it was sent back.

'You got to change your attitude, you know,' said Sam.

How Jojo hated it when he adopted that soft, patronizing tone. She felt like throwing the carving knife at him.

'The security police, they are keeping an eye on you,' he continued. 'Captain van Staden have his spies everywhere. In the kitchen, down the mine, in the hostels, everywhere. Yesterday, I hear him talking to the site manager. He say, "That Matwetwe woman, she is *te wit*." '

Jojo laughed, a hollow cynical laugh. Too white – too uppity for a *kaffir*. And to think she'd always believed her problem was she wasn't white enough! 'Thanks for telling me,' she growled. Sam might be a coward, but at least he fancied Jojo too much to split on her. All around there were others she could not be so sure of. Yet, despite the dangers, she had to keep preaching the message. She had to convince more comrades to join the FAP. The Freedom for the African People movement was now their major hope. 'Security forces,' she spat. 'Why don't they spend their time making sure things are more secure down the mine?'

'Sssh,' said Sam, petrified that someone in the kitchen might overhear her. 'Look, Jojo, all of us were sorry about Darius. But if Captain van Staden's spies hear you talking like that, you get sacked from here right away. Then what you going to do?'

Jojo shrugged.

'Please, Jojo,' pleaded Sam, 'be careful. They take your work permit away. They take your pass. Who knows, maybe they even send you to some homeland hundreds of miles away.'

'OK,' said Jojo, producing a carbonized steak from under the grill.

Kenny pulled a face. 'I'm begging you, for your own sake. Do another one. And this time make sure you do it right. Today there are important visitors from London at the mine. If the site manager see a steak like that . . .'

'Oh, all right,' conceded Jojo gracelessly. She knew what Sam said was true. Her ostentatious awkwardness might get her dismissed before her real work had even started. It went against her temperament, but she could not afford to let Credo and the FAP down. For them she must button her lip and lower her eyes, at least for the time being.

CHAPTER SIX

November, 1981

SWEATING in his cream overalls and green wellington boots, George Hamish was wishing he had not polished off that second bottle of Nederburg Riesling the previous evening. Looking decidedly more sprightly, despite his fifty-six years, Charles Watson-Smith hopped enthusiastically into the orange metal cage that was about to transport the small group underground.

'Come on,' said Charles, slapping George encouragingly on the back. 'There's nothing to worry about. I'm sure Roger wouldn't risk losing his two most supportive directors.'

Roger Samson was attaching the heavy power-pack to the belt around George's generous waist. 'There you are,' he said. 'Yes, it's perfectly safe. Now try your lamp.'

Hands trembling, George flashed his lamp around the corners of the cage. 'Seems fine now,' he said, 'but what if the power fails?'

'It won't,' said Roger. 'And even if it does, you'll have Piet and me down there with you.'

George looked up at the comforting bulk of the Meroto site manager, Piet van der Hoorn.

'Stick with us,' said Piet, his deep voice reverberating around the cage. 'Roger and I have been going down mines for as long as anyone can remember. He knows more about mining than the rest of us put together. So he should. He had the best teacher in South Africa.'

Charles was intrigued. 'You're full of surprises, Roger. I'd assumed your interest was more on the financial side.'

Roger shot Piet a sideways look.

'He's too modest,' Piet went on proudly. 'I don't suppose you folk ever heard talk of Simon Weiss. Now that was the man who taught Roger—'

'I think we're ready to go down now, aren't we?' interrupted Roger brusquely. He closed the heavy metal gate with a resounding clang and pushed the button on the control panel. Slowly the cage descended, leaving the Transvaal morning sun shining brightly above them.

'Now, George,' said Piet, as the cage cranked and whirred down the shaft, 'you'll be happy to hear the Merensky Reef is close to the surface here. We'll be going to a depth of about eight hundred and fifty metres.'

'What!' George's cheeks were flushed with a combination of hangover and apprehension. 'When you told me "not too far down" last night, I thought you meant ten or twenty metres.'

Roger laughed. 'Just be grateful we're not mining for gold. Then you really would be talking deep. Eight hundred and fifty metres is nothing.'

Piet was used to visitors. 'Today, we'll be going down one of the Meroto mine's second generation of vertical shafts. The first generation were simple incline shafts but we've completely exhausted those now.'

'I'd never realized platinum was so accessible,' said Charles.

Piet smiled. 'It is around here. When Simon Weiss located this strike, the platinum was outcropping at the surface.'

'I suppose that's what you call striking it lucky,' muttered George, who wished he'd been visiting in those days.

Piet nodded. 'Yes, but we're doubly lucky. Around here, we're considered a real fluke mine. We're getting around eighteen grams of platinoid metals from every ton of ore we mine.'

'Compared to?' Charles wanted to know.

'In the mining business, we're all very secretive about our figures,' replied Piet, 'but up the road at Rustenburg, for instance, I reckon they're getting between five to ten grams per ton.'

George whistled.

'Yes,' enthused Piet, 'our stuff is beautiful, the best.' He might have been talking about a woman.

Roger's face remained immobile, his lips a hard line in the half light. He had not expected this. Of course, he'd wanted his directors to see the Meroto operation, but this thirst for detail had come as a complete surprise. If only Piet would do as he was told – provide no more information than was absolutely necessary.

Suddenly the cage stopped. Roger pulled open the door and the group exited into a dimly lit tunnel.

'It's about a twenty-minute walk to the working face,' said Roger. George stifled a groan.

'Take my arm,' said Piet. Respected by the entire workforce for his courage, this giant of an Afrikaner generated confidence. In the last accident at Meroto, an unexpected rockfall, he had dug out three drill-operators with his own bare hands. The fourth, Darius Matwetwe, he had been unable to save. But such incidents, unfortunately, would always occur in the mines. As Simon Weiss used to say, you had to include human life in the price of any mineral.

'Thanks,' said George, bravely. 'Luckily, it's not as hot as I'd expected.'

'Heat is a major problem down any platinum mine,' explained Piet. 'But we've installed refrigeration and a chilled water system. It's done wonders for productivity.'

Slowly, the four men continued on their way down the tunnel. Charles was taking in every aspect of the mine. Piet was surprised and pleased by the Englishman's enthusiasm.

'Look here,' he said, shining his lamp along the wall. 'Do you see? This is a typical cross-section of Merensky Reef.'

George and Charles stopped, both struck by the beauty of the rock. White, silver, black and grey – it shimmered in the lamp-light.

'Some silver and gold in there. But we cover all our mining costs from the copper and nickel we extract. The platinoid metals are pure profit – the icing on the cake. In fact, Simon Weiss used to say—'

Roger interrupted him sharply. 'In fact, we're doing so well here, I'm thinking of expanding.'

'In what direction?' asked Charles.

'We need our own refinery. I'll have to organize a rights offer to fund it.'

'How much do you need to raise?' Figures never failed to interest George.

'Over a hundred million rand,' replied Roger. 'That's what we'll need to have a refinery on stream by nineteen eighty-five.'

George felt slightly nervous. How could anyone be sure that the demand for platinum would justify that kind of investment? Of course, you had to take a long-term view. Back in the forties, no one was too interested in platinum. Then in the fifties, the petrochemical industry started using it in their industrial processes. Later, in the sixties, the Japanese started buying heavily for their domestic jewellery industry. And then, in the seventies, the American automobile industry had starting fitting anti-pollutant catalysts in their cars. Now the car industry was the largest consumer of platinum in the world. George had read all about it before his trip to Meroto. All the same, he would like to know more about market trends before agreeing to such an investment.

The tunnel had opened out as they reached the face. The sound of drilling was deafening. The combination of noise and sudden heat made George feel quite dizzy. He looked at Piet. 'I'm terribly sorry about this,' he had to shout, 'but would you mind taking me back to the surface?'

'Of course.'

'Take it easy, now,' said Charles, already scrambling up beside a rockdrill-operator to see what he was up to.

Roger climbed up beside him. 'You see,' Roger was shrieking above the din, 'this is where the machine boys bore the holes. Then we charge the holes with Anfex explosive and clear the mine. When we're sure everyone is out, we detonate the Anfex. Then we let things die down for a few hours before the next shift comes on to dig out the ore.'

Later, as they made their way back down to the tunnel, Charles continued to probe. 'Remind me, Roger, how long has this mine of yours been in operation?'

Roger's eyes were cold. 'Since nineteen seventy-five.'

'And exporting?'

'Since then, naturally.'

'And repatriating the profits?'

Roger's face remained impassive. 'I've always continued to reinvest in Meroto.'

'That isn't the answer to my question.'

Suddenly Roger smiled disarmingly. 'I've been selling platinum to the United States, Germany, Japan and the UK since nineteen seventy-five. I don't suppose the South African government would be too thrilled if they found out. But there's no point in hiding it from you, Charles. Most of the early proceeds were invested in London's Docklands.'

Charles grinned like a chief investigator who had just uncovered the murderer. At last he had solved the enigma, the mystery of Samson's early wealth. He brushed the dust from his overalls. 'I was wondering how you managed it. Now, about those Docklands sites. There's a chap in government by the name of Howard Anderson. Clever as a bag of monkeys, believe me, but he might prove very helpful all the same.'

Roger smiled graciously. The Hon. Charles Watson-Smith had just dug as far as anyone was likely to dig, and had still come up with nothing.

'Sorry for all the fuss.' George and Piet were getting dry after a long cool shower. In one gulp, Piet downed a pint of water from the jug waiting in the changing room. Being underground was such a dehydrating business.

'Don't mention it. I hope you learned a few things.'

By now, George was feeling decidedly more human. 'Oh, I did. Although, I thought Roger seemed to clam up whenever you mentioned this character, Simon Weiss.'

'My fault,' said Piet. 'Sometimes, I forget. Simon was like a father to Roger. He was an extraordinary man, you know, a German Jew, escaped to South Africa just before the war.'

'And how did he and Roger become so close?'

'Simon had no family. Or, at least, if he did, he never mentioned it. Almost from the first day Roger arrived here, back in nineteen seventy, Simon treated him like a son. When he died, Roger didn't speak for weeks.'

'Was it a mining accident?'

'No. Natural causes. The postmortem showed he'd had a massive coronary just before his car swerved off the road. It was after this that the rest of us realized just how much Roger had meant to him.'

'Really? How so?' Doing up his trousers, George noticed the waistband seemed to be getting tighter.

'Because when Simon acquired the mineral rights to Meroto in nineteen seventy-one, he'd had them put in Roger's name. He kept the land rights for himself. But with a mine, land rights don't really matter. It's the mineral rights that count.'

George puffed a bit as he laced up his shoes.

'Mind you,' continued Piet, 'it's fair to say that without Roger, Simon would never have been able to mine Meroto. Originally both the land and mineral rights belonged to an old Afrikaner called Erasmus de Jongh. A nasty piece of work. He'd been a leading light in the Ossewa-Brandwag – the Ox-Wagon sentinels. Then Roger suggested he should go and negotiate instead of Simon. He was sure he could convince de Jongh.'

'And the old boy never rumbled him?'

'Why should he? Roger's surname was Samson. Erasmus never associated him with Simon Weiss.'

'So he just sold the rights to Roger there and then?'

'Oh, no.' Piet knotted his tie in the mirror. 'It wasn't that simple. God, I've never seen Roger so drunk. He was still ill in bed three days later!'

George was feeling fonder of Roger by the minute. 'Roger – drunk?'

'All in a good cause. At first, apparently, the old man refused even to discuss the matter. But then Roger produced a can of *mampoer* . . .'

'*Mampoer?*'

'An old voortrekker brew made from apricots, wild berries, the fruit of prickly pear cactus – just about anything you can lay your hands on.'

'Sounds as if it'd knock your socks off,' said George approvingly.

'It's the most vicious homemade hooch you can imagine. Anyway, between them, Roger and de Jongh polished off a gallon of the stuff. I'm surprised the session didn't kill the old boy. He was already in his eighties. By the time Roger had finished with him, he signed the documents without even reading them.'

'Good for Roger.'

Piet laughed. 'That's just what Simon said. From that day on he let Roger do all his negotiating. Simon always hated that kind of aggravation. He was too generous to strike a hard bargain with anyone. That was always Roger's strength.'

'And after that?'

'Well, Simon had already done a lot of the preliminary work, studying maps, doing feasibility studies, that sort of thing. But as soon as de Jongh signed the documents, Simon bonded his house and farm – everything he owned – to pay him. Then he began to start work in earnest at Meroto.' Piet was combing his thick, greying hair.

'We spent months trenching to locate the outcrops. Then we started drilling our boreholes. I can still remember the day we sent our ore samples off to Johannesburg to be assayed. The look on Simon's face when the results came back.' Piet smiled at the memory of his friend. 'After that we continued prospecting. But by late 'seventy-two, Simon was seriously strapped for cash. I don't know how he did it, but somehow he kept persuading the bank to support him. Over the next three years they continued to extend his credit. And then, just as everything looked as if he was going to be fine . . .' Piet sat down heavily on the bench next to George.

'I'm sorry, Piet. I didn't mean to pry.'

'No, it's OK. It was such a shock, that's all. I was away in Durban, visiting my sister, when it happened. And Roger was in New York on business. Simon was all ready to float the company, Metallinc, on the Johannesburg Stock Exchange. He was so confident. The feasibility study he'd commissioned was even better than he'd expected. So off he sets to Jo'burg one morning to see his stockbroker and a couple of merchant bankers. And on the way back . . .' Piet's voice faltered but he swiftly pulled himself together. 'Roger continued with the flotation, of course. It was a great success. He said it was what Simon would have wanted.'

George nodded slowly. For the first time in the months he had known Roger, things seemed to make some sort of sense.

*

When Roger waved goodbye to Charles and George that evening at Jan Smuts International Airport, he had good reason to smile to himself. Their visit to the Meroto platinum mine had been a complete success.

CHAPTER SEVEN

London, December 1981

As USUAL, Andrea Blackwell got what she wanted. In this case, the job. Of course, the competition for cub reporter on the *Courier* had been extraordinarily fierce but Andrea always enjoyed that sort of personal contest. It made success so much sweeter, to have been confronted with rivals and to know you had licked them. It gave her a physical thrill. Like the moment of sexual climax, it made her feel more secure. Getting one over on people and screwing them, it was all of a piece. Jobs, sex, fellow human beings, for Andrea they were nothing but rungs on the ladder out of Grimford.

Andrea knew she would get the position just as soon as she met the editor. Balding, fat and forty-five, Freddie Higgins had also come up the hard way. He had started out in the newspaper business at the age of sixteen, dealing with everything from 'Dog Lost' ads to the Women's Institute Best Fruitcake Prize for his local rag. By the time he reached forty, Freddie was editor of the *Courier*, now Fleet Street's most successful tabloid. If circulation had tripled during the five years of his editorship, it was not difficult to understand why. Neither the truth nor professional ethics were ever allowed to interfere with a good story – by no means a new recipe for success on the Street of Shame but, as everyone in the game agreed, Freddie's editorial genius was in a class of its own. His lies, his libels and his lewdness were so much better than all the rest.

'Sit down, love,' he said, his hand temporarily covering the telephone mouthpiece, as Andrea was ushered into his office. 'I'm just finishing off this call.'

Andrea looked around, assimilating every detail of the decidedly grubby room. Half-empty polystyrene teacups littered Higgins's desk and the heavy onyx ashtray overflowed with untipped cigarette butts. The floor around the editor's large, swivel chair was littered with torn and crumpled-up pieces of paper. A grease-spattered McDonald's carton, oddly bright red and white among the predominantly grey detritus, peeped out from the heaving wastepaper basket, an empty bottle of Johnnie Walker whisky balanced precariously on top. Along with the bus depot in Grimford, this was one of the least inspiring places Andrea had ever seen.

For the occasion, Andrea had worn her best (and shortest) black Escada skirt. Reeking of Estée Lauder's Youth Dew, her eyelashes rigid with mascara, she was already feeling confident. Andrea knew all about balding, middle-aged men and their faltering male egos. The buttons on Freddie's blue striped polyester shirt strained around the midriff as he exhaled heavily. Andrea was glad she'd thought to apply a double dose of frosted fuschia lip gloss.

'Good morning, then,' said Freddie, replacing the receiver and taking in the black-stockinged expanse of Andrea's plumpish legs. Other women, reared on a calorie-controlled diet of Jerry Halls and Shakira Caines, could never understand it. While they starved to look sexy, men everywhere seemed to go for Andrea's decidedly fleshy look. Pretty though she was, particularly with her long blonde hair hanging loose around her shoulders, she did not have star quality. Perhaps that was why so many men fancied her. Andrea always looked available.

'How do you do,' replied Andrea, turning the full force of her blue eyes on the editor from beneath a slightly overgrown fringe.

Freddie shifted in his chair.

Good, she thought instinctively. She was creating the desired effect.

'So you're here about the job on the gossip column?' Freddie turned the pages of her meticulously typed life history.

'Interesting CV, love. Very interesting. An English degree from Cambridge – my word, aren't we posh?' Freddie's voice dripped sarcasm. Carelessly, he dropped the CV on his desk. 'Look here, love – what's your name again?' He glanced at her notes. 'Andrea. Right, Andrea, I'm a very busy man. I haven't got time to wade through crap like this. All I really need to know, love, is what can you actually *do*?'

'*Do*?' repeated Andrea, smiling sweetly. 'I can't *do* anything. That's why I'm here for the job. I was hoping you could teach me.' Freddie smirked. He was not at all unimpressed by this young lady's perfect gall. Known as Fleet Street's biggest bully-boy, Freddie Higgins had been known to reduce union leaders to tears. In general, people did not stand up to him, especially not young female employees. Freddie stared at Andrea in studied disbelief. He found her insolence exciting.

'So tell me, love, what do you think you could offer the *Courier* in return?' Freddie's eyes followed Andrea as slowly, deliberately, she crossed and uncrossed her legs.

'A new approach.'

Freddie affected to look puzzled. 'You what?'

'A new approach. I've been reading your paper over the last few weeks—'

'Only the last few weeks? I'm gutted. Too down-market, are we, for clever dicks from Cambridge?'

Wisely, Andrea refused to take the bait. 'And it seems to me that the present column has lost its way completely. I'm sure old Bosworth produced decent stuff to start with. But that must have been years ago.'

'Ten, actually,' replied Freddie, tapping a leaky blue biro on his notepad. He was really enjoying himself. 'Now let me tell you something, love. Humphrey Bosworth's got contacts in places where other columnists don't even know there's places.' Freddie beamed. He was proud of his way with words. Andrea forced a smile. 'Are you telling me that's useless too?'

'Yes,' replied Andrea. 'As soon as any journalist becomes too familiar with his subjects he stops being objective.'

'So you're telling me that Bosworth's past his prime and the column needs spicing up a bit?'

'Spicing up a bit? I think it needs a radical dose of salts. If you're going to call a column a gossip column, then it's got to carry genuinely meaty gossip. Who cares whether Princess Michael of Kent has flogged the family silver? What I want to know is why she flogged it and who she spent the loot on.'

Freddie was hugely impressed. For some time now he'd been thinking the same about Bosworth's palsy-walsy pieces. And here was this kid, barely out of college, saying exactly what he felt. How come no one else had ever had the guts to say it?

'So who do you reckon could come up with the goods?'

'Me,' said Andrea decisively.

Freddie laughed out loud. 'And what do you suppose good old Bosworth is going to say about that?'

Leaning back on her chair, her arms extended, Andrea yawned. Underneath her white satin blouse, Freddie could discern the shape of a half-cup bra, struggling to contain the fullness of her breasts. 'Not my problem,' she replied lazily. 'More the editor's, I'd have thought. Christ, it's hot in here.'

Freddie needed no encouragement. 'Fancy a beaker?'

'And how,' she replied enthusiastically.

He picked up the phone. 'Vera,' said Freddie. 'I'm off for the rest of the day – conducting interviews. Any problems, just give Tony a bell.'

Happily, the two Australian air hostesses who shared Andrea's Earls Court digs were abroad for the week. After a few bottles of moderately indifferent Beaujolais at El Vino's, she invited Freddie back to her flat for coffee.

'I don't drink coffee,' he replied, stroking Andrea's black-stocking-covered knee in the taxi. 'But I'll come anyway.'

It was the least arousing sex Andrea had ever had, like making love to a hyperventilating hippo. But it was worth it. At least by the end of the evening, Andrea knew she had the job. Six months later, after a fearful row with his editor, Humphrey Bosworth resigned in a fit of pique. With barely half a year's experience on the *Courier*, Andrea was running Fleet Street's most popular gossip column.

CHAPTER EIGHT

Geneva, July 1982

LESS THAN a year after arriving in Geneva, Lilah had established herself as one of the brightest young conference interpreters in the United Nations. Even old hands in the interpreting profession, men and women who could still remember the first time simultaneous interpretation had been used at the Nuremberg trials, were impressed. Madame Bessmertny, a Jewish-Russian *émigrée* considered the doyenne of the interpreting technique and rarely heard to utter anything about colleagues other than the most sublimely turned insults, graciously pronounced Lilah a born interpreter. When Lilah interpreted from Russian, she did not merely *interpret* Russian. She *became* Russian. She raged with the speaker, cried with him, argued with him, threatened with him. Like the brilliant actress she was, she quite simply assumed his part.

Not that Lilah found life at the United Nations easy. Every evening, she would return from the Palais des Nations to her *pied-à-terre* in the rue de Moillebeau feeling as if her brains had been puréed in the Magimix. Although there were always at least two interpreters working side by side in each language booth, for a beginner it was enormously stressful to spend hours listening to more or less hysterical delegates, trying simultaneously to make linguistic silk purses out of syntactic sows' ears.

It had been a particularly hard day in the interpreting booth. A Spaniard with a speech defect reading legal texts at a thousand words a minute had done little to improve Lilah's temper. The French delegation, as usual, had been thoroughly awkward and obnoxious. And the Russians had been acting up, making ridiculous complaints about the interpretation, in an effort to play for time. It was an old ploy and familiar to everyone, but it drove Lilah to distraction.

'If it happens once more,' she said, angrily stuffing documents into her briefcase at the end of the day, 'I'll strangle that bastard Kiriloff.'

'Calm down,' laughed her colleague, Ken. 'Let's go and have a drink.'

'No, thanks,' said Lilah, 'there'll be too many people in the bar I want to thump. Besides, I'm expecting a friend from London. I've told the *concierge* to let her in but I'd rather shoot off all the same.'

Ken started collecting the broken pencils Lilah had snapped in sheer frustration during the course of the afternoon. 'Go and enjoy yourself,' he said. 'You deserve it. I'll see you tomorrow morning.'

Andrea had already made herself at home with a large gin and tonic and the latest copy of *Vogue* magazine. Dumping her briefcase in the hall, Lilah rushed into the sitting room and fondly embraced her friend. 'Gosh,' she enthused, 'you're looking well.'

Andrea straightened a crease in her new silk dress and, eyeing Lilah's elegant linen suit, elected to say nothing.

'What a day!' sighed Lilah, pouring herself a long, cool drink and collapsing onto the sofa.

Andrea fanned herself with the magazine. 'Is Geneva always so hot in summer? I don't think I could bear it.'

The slightest hint of a breeze wafted in through the open window.

Lilah nodded. 'I can stand the weather. It's the locals. They're all so bloody xenophobic.'

'And how many locals do you meet down at the United Nations?'

Lilah laughed. 'OK,' she conceded. 'I'm just feeling a bit homesick – a bit rootless, that's all.'

'I thought that was what being international was all about.'

'Thanks Andrea! I knew I could rely on your sympathy. No, I suppose the real problem is I'm missing Jonathan.'

Andrea stifled a groan. Why was Lilah such a sentimental fool? With all the nice rootless men knocking around in Geneva, why hadn't she off-loaded that bore Morton yet? 'How's he getting on?' she asked.

Lilah perked up immediately. 'From his letters it sounds as if life is a bit rough. He's desperately overworked. It'll be ages before he gets to visit my flat in London.'

'You've bought a flat?' Andrea felt an even greater surge of envy. Christ, these international civil servants didn't half rake it in! Despite her recent raise, as editor of the *Courier*'s gossip column Andrea was still unable to contemplate a place of her own.

'It's only tiny – in Notting Hill Gate – but I love it. You remember Hugo Newsom from Trinity? He found it for me.'

Andrea continued to sip her drink. 'How do you suppose our surgeon friend is going to take that? Doesn't sound like you're moving in a Meroto direction now, does it?'

Lilah said nothing, just stared mournfully into her glass. Eventually Andrea broke the silence. 'Get real, why don't you, Lilah?' she said. 'You've got a brilliant career mapped out for yourself. OK – so Jonathan Morton wants to be a hero, a sturdy banister on the rickety stairway of life. But that's not for you. Where's the fun in hopeless causes?'

Lilah was feeling tired. For once she couldn't muster the conviction to argue with her friend. 'I'm going to Meroto for August,' she said lamely. 'With a bit of time together, I'm sure we'll manage to sort something out.'

'Whatever you say.' Andrea could not help sounding cynical. 'Look,' she continued brightly. It was good to see Lilah brought down a peg or two. 'I haven't come all this way just to see you looking miserable.' She started to laugh. 'Actually, you'll die when you hear the real reason I'm here. A little whisper about a minor British royal and a Swiss multi-millionaire.'

'You've come to interview them?'

'Oh, Lilah, darling, don't be so thick. This is strictly naughty nooky. I've come to catch them at it. Wonderful stuff. I never did like that arrogant bitch.'

In spite of herself, Lilah couldn't help laughing. 'You are the giddy limit!'

Andrea laughed again. 'It's so easy when you're being paid.' She stood up to leave. 'Come on, I want you to take me to the most expensive restaurant in Geneva. It's on the *Courier*.'

Lilah got up from the sofa. 'Wonderful. Then you can tell me how you landed the job.'

Looking in the mirror, Andrea applied some lipstick. 'that won't take long. It was a push-over. I just waved my legs at the editor. Actually, I'm still waving them.'

CHAPTER NINE

Meroto, August 1982

LILAH watched as dawn broke crimson and gold over Johannesburg's barren hinterland.

'Ladies and gentlemen, would you please fasten your seat belts and refrain from smoking until safely inside the terminal building.'

Lilah removed the unopened paperback from her lap and stuffed it into her hand baggage. She had not slept a wink during the entire twelve-hour journey, but neither had she felt the urge to read, eat or watch the in-flight movie. All night long she had simply stared out of the window, thinking about Jonathan.

She felt her stomach lurch as the plane began its descent towards Jan Smuts Airport. The plane alone was not to blame. The prospect of seeing Jonathan again was making her feel giddy. Fidgeting around in her handbag, she pulled out a wedge of dog-eared correspondence. Written in barely legible medico-scrawl, it formed an exhaustive account of Jonathan's life in the hospital. Lilah flicked through the pile. Jonathan's missives might end passionately enough, but they were, for the most part, descriptions of problems at work. She picked a letter at random and started to reread. It was one of the earlier ones, full of details about vitamin A deficiency in Meroto and the supplement programme he was determined to set up. She shuffled the pages back into a tidy bundle. Angry diatribes about shortages of sedatives, clean sheets and disposable surgical gloves – they were not what you'd call conventional love-letters.

By the time the plane landed, Lilah was so nervous she forgot to ask the Immigration Officer not to stamp her passport. What a nuisance. A South African stamp would guarantee aggravation if she travelled to a black African or Caribbean country. She walked through into the baggage hall and waited for what seemed like hours. Why did your bags always arrive last whenever you were in a hurry? Eventually the luggage appeared on the carousel and Lilah hoisted hers onto a trolley. Hell! It just had to be one of those with independently minded wheels. Lilah zig-zagged past Customs and into the arrival hall. She looked but could not see Jonathan in the sea of waiting faces. Her heart sank. He had probably been held up by an emergency. Perhaps she should hire a car. But how on earth was she going to find her own way to Meroto?

'Give you a lift, miss?'

Lilah jumped at the sound of the familiar voice. She turned to find him standing there, slim and slightly tanned in faded jeans and a navy blue Guernsey sweater. The tears of joy welled up in her eyes.

'Jonathan. I didn't see you. I thought you'd been held up. I was going . . .' But already she was in his arms, her face pressed so hard against his chest it was almost impossible to breathe. Smiling, Jonathan tilted her chin upwards and bent to kiss her lips. It felt good – so warm and safe – as if she had just come home. When at last she opened her eyes, the butterflies in her stomach had flown.

'The Range Rover's outside,' said Jonathan, picking up her luggage.

'Range Rover? I thought you were supposed to be on your uppers.'

'I am. The car was a gift from some anonymous benefactor. If only whoever it was had asked me first, I'd gladly have swapped the bloody thing for a year's supply of hypodermic needles.'

Lilah smiled as she thought of the three silk ties she had bought him at the duty-free shop. Whatever had she been thinking of?

*

It was a cold, wintry day in Meroto and the overpowering smell of paraffin heaters working overtime made Lilah want to retch. Dropping with fatigue despite her excitement, she rubbed her eyes as, proudly, Jonathan showed her around the hospital. The drive from the airport had taken three hours. For the difference between the city and this place, it might have been three centuries.

The waiting room was full – as usual, a predominance of old people, women and children. Outside, a group of women appeared to have set up camp.

'What are they cooking?' asked Lilah, peering out of the window at the array of old zinc pots bubbling away on the fire.

'Corn mealie-meal,' replied Jonathan. 'It's the staple diet – calorific and filling but vitamin deficient.'

Feeling increasingly awkward in the simple yet expensive trouser suit she was wearing, Lilah looked at her feet. 'I wish I could do more to help.'

'You could,' he replied pointedly.

She said nothing but, turning her attention to the white distempered walls, continued on down the corridor.

By nine o'clock that evening, Lilah was exhausted.

'Time for bed?' asked Jonathan, draining the remains of his cognac – one of Lilah's more welcome gifts.

'Yes, please,' she said, nestling closer to him on the sofa. Standing up, Jonathan lifted her in his arms and carried her into the bedroom. Within seconds they were lying naked together on his hard, spartan bed.

'Still tired?' Lightly, he ran his hand up her thigh.

'Not as tired as all that.' To prove it, she rolled over and started to kiss his nipples. Jonathan arched his back. It had been so long, so desperately long, already he could feel a hard-on. Lilah gave a slight gasp as she felt two fingers, strong yet gentle, penetrate her. Gently, he withdrew them and began to rub her clitoris until it throbbed with pressure. Warm and moist, Lilah moved to sit astride him. He closed his eyes as she guided him into her. Then, clenching his buttocks hard, he started to thrust. Lilah groaned as he moved rhythmically back and forth. Then suddenly she could feel him coming with strong, hot jets inside her. Within seconds, she too had climaxed, her whole body quivering with pleasure. For what seemed like ages, they lay there silently in one another's arms.

'I've missed you, darling,' said Jonathan.

'Me too,' replied Lilah. 'I didn't realize how much.'

Over the next three weeks Lilah saw rather too much of Jonathan's basic bachelor house and decidedly too little of him. It was impossible to plan even the simplest of arrangements. At the hospital by seven, he usually worked straight through his lunch break. More often than not, it would be ten at night before he staggered home, too exhausted to do much more than tumble into bed and sleep. The previous weekend, their projected trip to the Kruger National Park had been cancelled when an emergency case was admitted into hospital. Jonathan apologized profusely and, of course, Lilah had understood. But as her holiday drew to a close, she was growing increasingly concerned. This would be the reality of married life with Jonathan. Had she come to Meroto with such a future seriously in mind?

It was her last day in the township. Determined to end her stay on a high note, Lilah had decided to cook Jonathan his favourite dinner. She borrowed the Range Rover and spent the morning shopping for groceries in Johannesburg. Humming happily to herself, she drove back along the newly asphalted highway. A large joint of beef, carrots, onions, sprouts, potatoes, fruit, wine, flowers, candles – she was going to make her last night in Meroto a memorable one. It was a bright clear day, cool, but not a cloud in the sky. Even the dry brown scrub by the side of the road cried out for a good dose of rain. Lilah turned the car down the narrow red dirt track which linked the highway to the township of Meroto. Like walking into a dream, she mused. The optimism and opulence of Johannesburg's silver glass skyscrapers belonged to another world.

Lilah unpacked the car and carried the groceries into the kitchen. Poor Jonathan, he'd been very busy. So far, there had been no real opportunity to discuss where their relationship was going. Tonight she would ensure that things were put to rights.

Lilah set to, cleaning Jonathan's ancient oven. Congealed fat, carbonized crumbs – it looked as if it had not been used for ages. No wonder he had lost so much weight. Lilah rubbed away with the scouring powder. Yes, tonight they would find a solution.

On Jonathan's instructions, Sister Ndaba had pared down the afternoon's operating list to a minimum. Nevertheless, it was going on seven before he had finished in theatre. Still washing his hands, he heard Sister's footsteps racing back down the corridor.

'Doctor,' she said breathlessly as she opened the door, 'you got to come quick. The *sangoma* is here with his mother. I tell him to come back tomorrow. But he said no, he must see you right now.'

'Moses Obateo!' sighed Jonathan. 'Of all nights, he has to choose this one!'

Sister Ndaba's eyes were wide with anxiety. 'If you don't see him people will say you are frightened of him. They will say his magic is more powerful than yours. Then no one will come to this hospital.'

'Don't worry, Sister. I've every intention of seeing the evil little bastard. It's high time everyone in this township realized what a con-man he really is.'

There was absolute silence in the recovery ward. Jonathan paused for a second as he saw the bizarre figure of the *sangoma* standing motionless in the middle of the room. Tall, thin and ascetic, Moses Obateo looked like a scarecrow in his long, black overcoat. A fur headband did little to restrain his mass of fuzzy grey hair. A large, knitting-needle-shaped bone stood vertically up from the back of his head. Jonathan stared at his adversary with interest. If he had not been so bloody dangerous, he might have been quite a joke.

'You are the white doctor?' asked the *sangoma*, expressionless. Jonathan nodded. The *sangoma* pointed to a small, wizened creature sitting quietly in the corner.

'My mother has gone blind in her right eye. Can your magic make her see again?'

Jonathan went over to where the old lady was sitting. 'A cataract,' he said, after a brief examination. 'I'll operate tomorrow.'

'Now!' insisted the *sangoma*, turning to face his audience. There were reasons for his pitching up at the most populated ward in the hospital. 'Or maybe the white doctor is afraid.' The tension in the room was palpable.

Jonathan knew he had no option. He spoke calmly to Sister Ndaba. 'Take the patient to theatre, will you please, Sister? I'll be operating on her immediately.'

Back at the house, Lilah was putting the finishing touches to dinner. It was wonderful what a few flowers and candles could do for a room. The smell of roast beef permeated the place – the solid, sensible, comforting smell of family gatherings and English Sundays. The batter for the Yorkshire pudding had stood quite long enough. Looking at her watch, Lilah decided to put it into the oven. Yes, that beef was cooking nicely. By eight o'clock it would be done just right, pink and juicy in the middle, the way she knew Jonathan liked it.

Lilah opened a bottle of wine and poured herself a glass. Idly she rifled through Jonathan's eclectic selection of tapes: *The Best of the Beatles, The Best of James Taylor, The Best of . . .* – yes, that just about summed up his attitude to everything except medicine. Interested but not fanatic. Lilah removed *The Best of James Taylor* from its box and placed it on the tape deck.

Pleasantly relaxed after a long, hot shower, she lounged on the sofa listening to the music and surveying her handiwork. It had taken her most of the day to achieve, but she was pleased with the results. Still not back yet. Surely, tonight of all nights, Jonathan would manage to slip away early?

> You just call out my name,
> And you know wherever I am,
> I'll come runnin'
> To see you again . . .

The wine and music were fine, just fine. Now what she really needed was her man. Restless, Lilah started making coronets out of the red paper napkins she had purchased that morning in Joey's. It was no use. They looked more like crash-landed DC-10s. Irritated, she threw them into the waste basket and replaced them with two more. Calm down, she told herself. He was bound to be home soon. Briskly, Lilah walked into the kitchen and put the vegetables on to boil.

> You got a friend, oh darlin' yeah,
> You got a friend.

It was the second time she had played the same tape. A tear trickled into the carrots which by now were almost done. Pouring herself another glass of wine, Lilah wandered back to the table and replaced a guttering candle.

Jonathan patted the old woman's hand as she lay passively on the table. 'It's all right,' he said soothingly. 'Just trust me.' The woman managed a smile as Sister Ndaba swabbed around her eye with iodine. Quickly, Jonathan froze the woman's facial nerve with local anaesthetic before anaesthetizing her eye.

'What is magic potion?' asked Moses Obateo, staring suspiciously at the syringe full of Lignocaine. Irritated, Jonathan remembered the *sangoma*'s presence in the room.

'Please be quiet,' he ordered. 'I must have silence and no interruption.' Anxious for his mother, the *sangoma* retreated to the far end of the theatre.

Taking the stainless steel speculum from Sister, Jonathan gently prised the woman's eyelids apart. A superior rectus suture – that would stop the eye from moving. Jonathan took a deep breath. He was ready to start the operation.

Gloomily, he surveyed his assortment of instruments. Not even a diamond knife! How ironic. Only a few miles away, De Beers were pulling diamonds out of the ground by the sackful. But here he was, with nothing but razor blades with which to operate. The *sangoma* moved closer to the table. Jonathan cut into the conjunctiva and peeled the flap of membrane downwards. Meanwhile, Sister Ndaba was heating a metal probe in a paraffin flame. It was primitive. But in Meroto, that was all Jonathan had to cauterize the blood vessels.

The witch doctor stood rooted to the spot as the white doctor went about his work. Expertly, Jonathan made an incision between the clear and white parts of the woman's eye. He clenched his teeth. Now came the most difficult part – the actual removal of the lens.

'Is the cryoprobe ready, Sister?' She handed Jonathan the instrument. It had a small metal ball frozen at one end. Slowly, Jonathan opened the incision and applied the cryoprobe to the lens. Suddenly an image crossed his mind. An expulsive haemorrhage – it had been the most traumatic moment of his life – vitreous and retina spewing uncontrollably out of his patient's eye. There had been nothing he could do. Jonathan gripped the probe, attached by now to the old lady's lens. He started moving it from side to side, gradually pulling the lens away.

Then suddenly the whole theatre was plunged into darkness. Oh God, no, not again. The hospital generator had failed.

The lights went out while Lilah was struggling to turn the oven down. Thank God she had bought the candles. At least she was not sitting alone in the dark. She groped her way back out of the kitchen and picked up the 'Trinity Couple of the Year' silver-painted beer bottle now serving as a candlestick. Where the hell was that corkscrew? The floral arrangement teetered as she banged into the table. Opening the second bottle of wine, she poured herself a glass. Jonathan had better come soon. The roast beef was already well done and the Yorkshire pudding had peaked. The vegetables – well, Jonathan never did like his vegetables *al dente* but now they were virtually mashed. Taking a large slug of wine, Lilah kicked off her shoes and put her feet up on the sofa.

Jonathan was still manipulating the cryoprobe back and forth in the dark. By now he was working by instinct. If he stopped, the lens might dislocate and that would be curtains for his future in Meroto.

'Sister,' murmured Jonathan, 'there's a torch in my office. Would you fetch it?'

Cowering in the corner, the *sangoma* had started to chant – a low, moaning, monotonous wail. Jonathan could cheerfully have slugged him.

Slowly, he continued to prise the lens away. Then, suddenly, it was out. By now the beads of sweat were dripping from Jonathan's face. It seemed like an eternity before Sister Ndaba returned with the torch. He nodded gratefully. Enough light, thank goodness, to sew the old lady's eye up again.

'My mother can see?' asked the *sangoma*, trembling, when Jonathan appeared to have finished. Jonathan nodded. Tomorrow he'd fit her up with spectacles and she'd be as right as rain. It was not the ideal solution. In England, he'd have fitted an intra-ocular lens. But here that was out of the question. The old woman grasped Jonathan's hand in silent gratitude. Sister Ndaba flashed Jonathan a knowing smile. Somehow Moses Obateo seemed to have shrunk by half.

Slumped exhausted in a chair, Jonathan woke with a start as the lights came back on. Jumping to his feet, he snatched his jacket and ran the half-mile journey home. It was already well past midnight. Bursting through the door, he found Lilah asleep on the sofa. On the table stood a large joint of beef, burnt to a cinder. The Yorkshire pudding was more brown and shrivelled than the average Key West widow. And the vegetables had been boiled to slush. Jonathan knelt down by the side of the sofa.

'Lilah, darling, please, wake up.'

Blearily, Lilah opened her eyes. After a bottle and a half of wine, she had fallen asleep quite drunk.

'Lilah, I'm so sorry.' Jonathan looked around at the detritus of dinner. 'I'll make it up to you, I promise.'

Refusing to look at him, Lilah turned her head to face the back of the sofa. 'It doesn't matter,' she said, mouthing her words with difficulty. 'Nothing matters except Dr Morton and his patients.'

'Please, Lilah, I can see you've gone to a lot of trouble.' Putting his arms around her, he kissed the crown of her head. Angrily, she pulled away. 'But you must understand,' he continued. 'It was the witch doctor's mother. I had to operate. I'd have lost all credibility if I didn't. Please, Lilah, turn around and look at me.' She shook her head. Jonathan could hear she was crying.

'Look, sweetheart. I know you're angry. I don't blame you. Let me make some coffee and we can talk about it.'

'Sod the coffee. And sod the talk. It's a bit late for both. I'm sick to death of patients and Meroto and this entire holier-than-thou bloody shooting match.'

Now it was Jonathan's turn to be angry. 'Grow up, Lilah. You're acting like a spoilt brat. You have to expect this sort of thing when you're living with me.' That was a big mistake and he knew it.

'Well, thank God I'm not,' she shouted. 'This has been the most boring holiday I've ever had in my life.'

'Yes, I suppose you must have missed your flashy friends and your posh restaurants and your expensive boutiques.'

'You bastard. You know that's not fair. I've missed you – that's what I've missed. I came here to spend some time with you and I've hardly seen you at all.' She burst into tears.

Jonathan felt like kicking himself. She was right, of course. Looking after the human race was a very selfish business. 'I'm sorry, darling. I know I've neglected you. Come on, let's go to bed. I want to make love to you.'

Lilah turned to face him. 'Oh, yes, a session in the sack and it's all sweetness and light. Why don't you grow up, Jonathan? Grow up and fuck off.' The tears were rolling down her cheeks.

'Please.' Jonathan tried to touch her arm.

'Leave me alone. Tonight I'll sleep here on the sofa. Just to remind me what a riot I'd have had if I'd been daft enough to marry you.'

Jonathan shook his head. He knew there was no point arguing with her when she was in one of these moods. Reluctantly, he retreated to his bedroom and fell, exhausted and depressed, into bed.

Stretched out on the sofa, Lilah lay awake feeling miserable and lonely. It was hopeless – a classic case of the irresistible force and the immovable object. Result – intense heat. Now, as the effects of the wine were starting to wear off, she wished she had not been quite so quick with her tongue. Dear Jonathan! He must be under enormous pressure. She did not want to leave like this.

'Jonathan?'

Still wide awake, he could see her standing in the doorway. 'Yes?'

'I'm sorry.'

In an instant he was out of bed and holding her in his arms. 'No, darling, it was all my fault.' He kissed her on the mouth and felt the thrill of her responding. He watched as, swiftly, she undressed and stood before him naked.

'You're beautiful,' he murmured, unable to take his eyes off her. He reached for her hand and led her to the bed. Tenderly he began to kiss her lips and throat before moving down to tongue her nipples. Lilah trembled with anticipation. Cupping his balls in the palm of her hand, she started to stroke his erection. Then, opening her legs wide, she urged his cock towards her soft silky bush. Jonathan groaned as he entered her warm, creamy body. She tilted her pelvis towards him so he could penetrate more deeply. They came together, almost at once. It was the most delicious orgasm Lilah had ever enjoyed, painful in its intensity, exquisite in its irony. They were one, she and Jonathan, always would be, separated only by youth and its absurd requirement to achieve.

'We'll find a way of making it work,' said Jonathan, encircling her with his arms. It was something he felt he had to say.

'Sure we will.' But Lilah's voice was muffled and her cheek wet against the pillow.

CHAPTER TEN

London, November 1982

ANOTHER gold-edged, embossed invitation to a charity lunch at the Savoy. After almost a year at the *Courier*, Andrea Blackwell was becoming quite blasé about such things. It had all been very exciting to begin with, a seemingly endless whirl of champagne, society and gossip. For a brittle, bright journalist like Andrea, it had proved an exceedingly rich seam to mine, a seam she had delighted in exploiting relentlessly. Her new-look column had created quite a hullabaloo with its quick, iconoclastic wit and its scalpel-sharp observations. But as far as the newspaper's circulation was concerned, the results of her new, no-holds-barred approach were impressive. The *Courier*'s mailbag had never been so full. Whether people loved her or loathed her, Andrea and her often vicious little column remained compulsive reading.

'Will you be going, then, Miss Blackwell?' asked Paula Dickens, the middle-aged secretary Andrea had inherited from her dislodged predecessor, Humphrey Bosworth. Paula was a quiet, motherly type who wore large comfortable Laura Ashley print frocks. Her prize possession was the lovingly framed photograph she kept on her desk of her granddaughter presenting a bouquet to the Queen Mother on her birthday. An out and out royalist, in her view – and that of her adored Mr Bosworth – the royal family were above reproach. She hated what Andrea was doing to dear Humphrey's old column. ('Can Prince "Randy" Andy really be as thick as his aunty's ankles?'

– that, by way of example, was today's lead story.) Paula Dickens was ashamed to be associated with such unkind and often downright malicious drivel. On the other hand, she was a widow. She had a mortgage and a pension plan to consider. Working for Andrea Blackwell was uncongenial to say the least, but it was necessary.

'Yes, I think I will. The Cure Cancer Campaign Christmas lunch, isn't it?'

Paula nodded enthusiastically. 'I'm so glad you're going to give them a plug. They do so much good work, you know. I think the *Courier* should give them as much support as possible.'

'For goodness sake,' snapped Andrea. 'Do you honestly think the people who toss up to these bashes are really interested in what the charity is doing? Half of them will be there to gawp at the Princess of Wales and the other half because it's tax deductible.'

Paula stared at Andrea with a mixture of disgust and disbelief, but Andrea was oblivious. 'I'm only going because I want to meet the committee chairman, Charles Watson-Smith. I'm not even particularly interested in him, but I want to pick his brains about this character, Roger Samson.'

Paula bit her tongue. 'I searched the library as you asked.' She was determined not to lose her temper. That would have been so unseemly. 'But there's precious little on Roger Samson.'

'Quite the mystery man, isn't he? Arrives in London from nowhere, already loaded, and since then he's been doing deals and buying up property as if there was no tomorrow. Fascinating. I'd love to get some dirt on him.'

Thin-lipped, Paula handed over the slim sheaf of press-cuttings to Andrea. What *was* the paper coming to? A journalist of Humphrey Bosworth's standards never talked like that.

'Thanks,' said Andrea offhandedly. 'Oh, and coffee, please, Paula. Black, no sugar. And when you've done that . . .' Andrea could hardly be bothered to glance up from her cuttings, 'get Watson-Smith's secretary on the phone. Give her some sort of spiel. You know the sort of thing: I'm so impressed with the work of the charity I'm dying to interview Watson-Smith.'

Paula moved to leave.

'When I've got him going on that,' continued Andrea, 'I'll nail him on Roger Samson.'

Paula closed the office door quietly behind her and grimaced. For the thousandth time that week she felt her own integrity horribly compromised.

As usual, Anton Edelmann, the Savoy's legendary *maître chef de cuisine*, had somehow managed to excel himself. Of the four hundred and fifty people who sat down to the Cure Cancer Campaign's sumptuous fund-raising lunch, not one of them was anything other than impressed. For an hour and a half they ploughed their way through a truly gastronomic menu of Quenelle de Truite Saumonée Cardinal, Coeur de Filet de Boeuf Pique Rôti à la Perigourdine, finished off with La Tulipe des Fraises et Framboises Glacée Madame Melba. The guest of honour, HRH The Princess of Wales, looked radiant in a cream wool Catherine Walker suit. From the corner of her eye she could see the table specifically reserved for members of the press. Mischievously the Princess smiled. Every one of them was straining to establish the quantities on her plate (were all these stories of eating disorders really true?) and to lip-read her conversation with her pop idol Phil Collins.

Andrea loved the Savoy's Lancaster Room. With crystal chandeliers, Wedgwood blue and ivory walls, mirrored panelling and cloud effect ceiling, it made an ideal setting for such gala events.

'More wine, madam?' The waiter was hovering from hack to hack.

'Yes, please,' said Andrea. To hell with the diet. The waiter poured Andrea a fourth glass of a Burgundy far better than she was used to.

'And how is darling Freddie managing nowadays at the *Courier*?' asked Lulu Waters, senior feature writer for *Social Whirl* magazine. 'Is it still bonk your way to your own by-line down there?'

The assembled hacks started studying the ceiling's *trompe l'oeil* clouds with renewed interest. Apart from Neil Waite, royal correspondent of the *Globe*, who clearly fancied her, not one of them cared two hoots for Andrea. The kind of stuff she was writing nowadays was queering everybody's pitch. She was just the sort of journalist who made people nervous about talking to the press. And that made life difficult for everyone. It was not so much that Andrea refused to play by the rules of the game. She simply seemed unaware that there were any rules at all. It was great to see Lulu putting the Kurt Geiger boot in.

'Miss Blackwell, I do hope I'm not interrupting anything. Charles Watson-Smith, chairman of the appeal committee.' Charles held out his hand. 'My secretary tells me that you're particularly interested in the work of our charity. I understand you'd like to interview me.'

Ignoring the congregation of smirking journalists, Andrea beamed up at him. 'Yes, please. I know you're awfully busy. But if you could possibly spare me a minute?'

Charles returned her smile. 'Now the guest of honour has left, I'm entirely at your disposal. I'm afraid I've never read your newspaper – the *Courier* isn't it? – I'm a *Times* man myself. But I'll do what I can to help. The more people know about us the better, don't you think?'

'Of course,' replied Andrea earnestly. She was beginning to feel quite giddy. She had not expected this man, by now almost in his sixties, to be so amazingly attractive. 'Is there anywhere else we can talk?' she added, looking up and giving Charles the full benefit of her entirely innocent eyes. 'It's still very noisy in here.'

'We could go to the Parlour Room,' replied Charles. 'The committee were using it before lunch. There may even be some literature on the campaign still floating around in there.' With the easy courtesy born of countless generations of unimpeachable breeding, Charles helped Andrea from her seat. The rest of the table stared, dumbfounded, as the Hon. Charles Watson-Smith escorted Andrea from the room.

'And so, my dear,' said Charles, glancing at his watch, 'what more can I tell you?' He was now running late for an appointment with his stockbrokers in the City.

If any other man had referred to her as 'my dear', Andrea

would have given him a mouthful. But with Charles, it was different, in no way patronizing, in fact, thought Andrea wistfully, really rather nice. 'I think I have all the facts and figures about the campaign,' she said, extracting a second biro from her capacious black imitation leather bag. 'Now, if you wouldn't mind, just a few personal details. How did you become so involved with this charity?'

'My wife, Lydia, died of cancer,' replied Charles simply.

'I'm sorry.' To her surprise, Andrea felt moved.

'Thank you. I'm still trying to get over it.'

'And before that,' continued Andrea, taking in the high, intelligent forehead and kind, doleful eyes, 'did you concern yourself much with charities?'

'Of course. Though not quite so actively. One has to do something with one's money, I suppose. You see, we had no children.' It was ridiculous. This girl was young enough to be his daughter. And yet right from the beginning, Charles had felt oddly drawn to her. She seemed so young and vulnerable.

'Do you think you'd view things differently if you did have children?'

'I'm sorry?'

At last Andrea was ready to make her move. 'I mean, would you, for example, be doing deals with unknown playboys like Roger Samson?'

'My dear,' smiled Charles indulgently, 'he may be unknown. For all I know, he may also be a playboy. But at least with Roger Samson I know I've backed a winner. Now, I'm awfully sorry. I'm afraid I have to dash. About the campaign. Do you have all the documentation you need?'

More than enough, thought Andrea. He had illustrated his comments with a plethora of reports, projects and medical prognoses. 'I'm very grateful for all your help,' she said. 'I think it's so important for journalists to get their facts straight.' Andrea was glad Lulu Waters was not within earshot.

'Yes,' said Charles quietly, 'especially for something like this. People's lives depend on it.'

Andrea started collecting her things. This Charles Watson-Smith was certainly a good-looking man. And so rich and well connected. She was overcome by the old familiar wave of envy and frustration. It was all so bloody unfair. Her mind returned to Cambridge days, to the effortless superiority that wealth and connections conferred on the William Stantons of life. It was all a matter of family. With a father like Charles Watson-Smith, what could she herself have been? Standing up, Andrea glanced at the tall attractive figure waiting courteously in attendance. Then suddenly it occurred to her. With a *husband* like Charles Watson-Smith, what could she not still be?

Andrea put on her sweetest little-girl-lost look. 'I'd like to send you a copy of my piece before it goes to press. Just to ensure that I've made no mistakes. I'm only just finding my feet in journalism, you know.' Andrea lowered her eyes demurely, affecting to stare at the floor. Charles looked down on the small figure with its tousled crown of shiny blonde hair. That was it! It had been bothering him throughout the entire interview. And only now had it struck him. Of course, Renoir's little girls had dark eyes. But that sweet, vulnerable face, the hair, the slightly plump, childlike figure – why hadn't he realized it before? Andrea was the very image of the younger girl in Renoir's *Mother and Children*. Charles looked at Andrea with a feeling of overwhelming sadness. This woman might have been the daughter he and Lydia never had. A thought suddenly crossed his mind. It was a silly idea, of course, but on the other hand, why not? At worst, all she could do was turn him down.

'I'm so sorry I have to rush away like this, Miss Blackwell. I'd like to make amends. Would you have dinner with me this evening?'

Andrea's eyes shone brightly. 'I'd love to.'

Charles smiled. 'Good. I'll have my secretary call you later this afternoon with the details.'

Andrea Blackwell waltzed out of the Savoy with a definite spring in her step. And so, for that matter, did the Hon. Charles Watson-Smith.

Perhaps, thought Paula Dickens charitably, Miss Blackwell was not so bad after all. Certainly, the piece she had written that afternoon on the work of the Cure Cancer Campaign was as well researched and sensitive an article as Paula had ever read.

'Miss Blackwell,' she said, popping her head round Andrea's office door before going home for the evening, 'I just wanted to congratulate you on today's piece for the column. I think you've done something you can really be proud of.'

Stupid old bat, thought Andrea. How can people be so naïve?

'Thanks,' said Andrea. 'Yes, it really is a worthwhile cause. As you were saying only this morning, they deserve the *Courier*'s support.'

Paula beamed. 'I'm off now,' she said. 'Is there anything else you need before I go?'

'No thanks, Paula. Have a good evening.'

'Thanks. Oh, did you find the details for dinner I left on your desk?'

'Yes,' smiled Andrea. 'I've got them here.'

'Have a lovely time, then.' Paula closed the door. For the first time since Andrea Blackwell had taken over the column, Paula Dickens left the office a vaguely contented woman.

The phone on Andrea's desk rang loudly.

'Andrea, it's Freddie here. I've just read your piece, and I want to know what the hell you think you're playing at.'

'I beg your pardon?'

'It's crap,' shouted Freddie, 'C-R-A-P. What do you think the *Courier* is? The *British* bloody *Medical Journal*? Do you honestly think your average punter wants a gossip column full of malignant myeloma coming between him and his early morning cornflakes?'

'It's the duty of every newspaper to keep people informed on such problems,' replied Andrea.

'Don't give me such complete and utter bullshit!' His voice rose alarmingly. 'Since when did you give a tinker's about "keeping people informed on such problems"? What else do we have here? "The Hon. Charles Watson-Smith, his personal desire equalled only by his burning desire to help others." Fuck me, Andrea, it's worse than Bosworth at his most arse-licking. What's going on? Are you screwing this Watson-Smith bloke?' All his professional life Freddie Higgins had been a gut journalist. In matters such as these, he knew his initial instincts were never, ever wrong.

'No, I am not.' At least, she added to herself, not yet.

'I'm going to spike this piece. And you're going to stay here until you have rewritten this entire thing.'

'If you change so much as one single comma,' said Andrea, icily, 'you can take my resignation as read.' There was a pause.

'Andrea, love,' Freddie sounded shocked by her threat, 'it's not worth a fight. Just a few more cracks at the assembled glitterati and a bit less of the Dr Miriam Stoppard stuff and the piece would be OK.'

'Not one single comma,' repeated Andrea.

'Well, perhaps if we cut the bull about Watson-Smith being such a superstar—'

'I've told you. Not one single comma.'

'All right.' By now Freddie was trying desperately to retrieve the upper hand. 'I'll let it pass this once. But everyone loves your column the way it is. We don't want it turning into the sort of tosh these other brown-nosers churn out.'

Andrea said nothing. If she played her cards right, she wouldn't be writing for Freddie Higgins or his sordid little rag much longer. At the other end of the telephone, Freddie could sense there was something wrong. 'Andrea, sweetheart, I think you've been overdoing it of late. How about a few jars at El Vino's?'

'No, thanks,' replied Andrea archly. 'Actually, this evening I'm having dinner at Claridge's.' She slammed down the phone. Angrily, Freddie grabbed his jacket from the back of his chair. It was bad enough losing the best gossip columnist the *Courier* had ever had, but losing the best lay in Fleet Street at the same time . . . Christ, he needed a drink.

CHAPTER ELEVEN

London, spring 1983

ROGER SAMSON awoke screaming in his Regent's Park mansion. Seated bolt upright in his antique, mahogany tester bed, sweat streamed down his body.

'Roger, what is it?' Simonetta Bonino was awake in an instant, her violet eyes wide with fear and amazement. Who would ever have thought Roger Samson would be a man prone to recurrent nightmares? It was the second time that month that this had happened and yet Simonetta dared not say anything nor voice the question even now on the tip of her tongue. Without a word, Roger got up and walked across to his *en suite* bathroom. Simonetta watched him as he went. He would never talk about it and always came up with some spurious excuse. But were those dreams related to that band of ugly, whitish weals still evident on Roger's back?

He showered and returned to bed. He seemed calmer now, in command – the familiar Roger Samson.

'Roger, please, if there's something worrying you, talk to me about it.'

'It's nothing, Simonetta. Just pressure of business, that's all.'

But Simonetta was nobody's fool. She had known more than enough men in her life to recognize when one was lying. Business was not the problem, she was convinced. Stress was the drug that kept men like Roger Samson on the ball. But if Roger was frightened of something, those cold, blue eyes refused to admit it. Neither did he need to answer her question. Brusquely, he pulled her towards him, diverting her gaze, gripping her close to his chest. Gulping for breath, Simonetta could hear his heart still palpitating. How she loved him like this, when he was, for a few moments at least, vulnerable. Overwhelmed with tenderness, she responded, slowly massaging the tight, tense muscles of his neck. His body was warm, his skin soft against her fingers. Desperate to please, Simonetta went down on him to taste the softest skin of all. But there Roger stopped her, suddenly taking control. Soon his face was buried in her pubic mound, his tongue, warm and slippery inside her. He entered her, kissing her face, her neck, her nipples, her breasts. Somewhere among the myriad sensations, she could feel Roger's nails, digging deep, bruising the flesh of her buttocks. Simonetta gasped as the pain bit, her whole being tingling with excitement at this fusion of sensuality and suffering. It was always the same with Roger. Simonetta shuddered as she came, clinging to him, yearning for him to say something, anything, some small word of affection or endearment. But Roger said nothing. He followed her swiftly – a huge heave of physical release, an exorcism, Simonetta often imagined, of terrors unspoken and tears unspilled.

She lay on the bed quite still, exhausted. Twenty-five years old and one of the world's most highly paid models, Simonetta Bonino was no stranger to sex without love. It was the price she had paid for her meteoric career. At eighteen she was already the darling of the Paris catwalk. Now she was being hailed in every gossip column as Roger Samson's beautiful mistress.

Mistress? More like a part-time bedfellow. Simonetta had few illusions about her status in Roger's life. However much she reached out to him, tacitly asked to be allowed to love him, she was met with the most charming of blank walls. She knew Roger Samson did not want her as the woman to share his life. That she could cope with. What really hurt was the complete exclusion. Roger never treated her as a friend or confidante, just an extremely beautiful and desirable accessory, to be flaunted or put away as occasion might demand. She did not even feel like a lover, simply someone to have sex with. With Roger Samson, making love had nothing to do with either affection or companionship – it was quite simply a matter of dominance and release.

Deep down, Simonetta knew it was a hopeless situation. But at a conscious level, she stubbornly refused to admit it to herself. In the six months she had known Roger Samson, she had lost over fourteen pounds and now her booking agent was beginning to feel anxious. ('Too skinny, darling. You know, whatever they say, it is possible to look too skinny.') The agent was right. This relationship was draining her. But still Simonetta clung on, against all her friends' advice. No one could really understand it. Of course, it did her modelling career no harm to be seen at all the right places, escorted by Roger Samson. But there was another reason as well, a motive more serious and ultimately far more damaging. Simonetta actually loved him.

Roger looked at the digital alarm clock by the side of his head. 'Half past five. Time to get going. The chauffeur can take you home now, OK, Simonetta? Sorry I have to race, but I have an important meeting this morning.'

Simonetta knew the drill by now. No clothes, no cosmetics, not even a toothbrush must be left at Roger's house. Roger wanted no evidence, however slight, of intimacy or intrusion into his life.

'Don't you ever sleep more than four hours a night?' asked Simonetta wearily. Thank God she had no modelling assignment booked today. Now she just felt like going home and crashing out until late that afternoon. They'd been dancing at Annabel's until one o'clock that morning.

'Sleep's a waste of time,' said Roger, already up and half-way to the bathroom. 'It's just a loser's habit.'

When Simonetta talked about this, her therapist had reckoned otherwise. Insomnia, Dr Pfeiffer told her, was simply a sign of profound insecurity.

Simonetta rolled out of bed and dressed quickly. Already she felt unwelcome, a hassle – like the morning after's empty bottles. She would leave as soon as possible and bath later, in peace and tranquillity, when she reached her Hampstead home.

'Is Mark waiting outside?' she called. No response. Roger could not hear her for the force of his power shower. Quietly she left the bedroom, making her way along the corridor and down the impressive staircase. The chauffeur was indeed waiting outside and, after a brief 'Good morning,' whisked Simonetta away through the park in Roger's dark blue Corniche.

Looking a bit rough, thought Mark as he studied Simonetta's tired eyes in the rear-view mirror. He felt sorry for the girl. Sure, she was doing well out of Roger Samson. Mark himself had delivered flowers from Moyses Stevens and enough parcels from Asprey's to know just how generous his boss could be. But then again, Simonetta wasn't the only woman currently benefiting from Roger's material largesse. Not by a very long chalk.

'Thanks,' said Simonetta, as the chauffeur helped her from the car. 'You're up very early for me.'

Mark could not resist a smile. 'No trouble at all, Miss Bonino. I'm on call anyway from five thirty every morning. That's the way Mr Samson likes it.'

Dropping with nervous exhaustion, Simonetta let herself into her small Flask Walk home. Immediately she went to the phone and dialled the by now familiar number. It was, of course, far too early and the answering machine was still switched on. Simonetta listened to the recorded message and waited for the tone.

'Dr Pfeiffer,' her voice listless, 'it's Simonetta Bonino here. About five forty-five on Wednesday morning. I'm feeling rather down. Could I please make an appointment to see you this afternoon?'

Roger Samson was feeling on top of the world. A quick shower on awakening, a fast twenty-minute jog around Regent's Park, a gruelling thirty-minute circuit followed by another swift shower and he was ready to take on all comers.

'Whitehall, please, Mark,' said Roger, hopping into the back of the car. 'Department of Integrated Planning.'

If only London could always be this peaceful, thought Mark, as the car swept down an empty Regent's Street, through Piccadilly, round Trafalgar Square and into a silent Whitehall. Inside the car was equally quiet. Early on in his job, Mark had learned never to speak to his passenger unless first invited. Roger Samson, he soon realized, was not a man to waste his time on idle conversation about the vagaries of the English weather or the dreadful state of London's traffic. More often than not, a journey, however long, would pass without Roger's even saying a word to his chauffeur. Sometimes he was busy on the car telephone, or dealing with incoming faxes. More often than not, he was studying the copious contents of his bulging briefcase. But whatever he was doing, thought Mark admiringly, there was not one moment in Roger Samson's life that ever ticked by wasted.

The car pulled up smoothly outside the Department of Integrated Planning. 'Thanks, Mark,' said Roger, as the chauffeur opened the door. If Roger was never intimate with employees, mused Mark, at least he was always polite. 'I'll see you back here in an hour.'

Roger strode into the anonymous-looking building, still eerily empty at this time of the morning. Of course, the Secretary of State himself, Howard Anderson, was often there by 7.30 a.m. But, as his personal private secretary had once admitted loudly in Annie's Bar, never for anything other than 'Anderson's most personal public business'.

The security officer at reception recognized Roger immediately. Sometimes, after all, it helped to be the toast of London's gossip columns. 'Good morning, sir,' he said. 'I've been advised to expect you. I'll inform the Secretary of State's office that you've just arrived. If you could just take the lift to the fifth floor, someone will meet you there.'

The man watched as Roger disappeared into the lift. Christ Almighty! The crocodile briefcase alone must have been worth three months of a security officer's salary. Not to mention the gear! He would have had a coronary if he'd known the price of Roger's Alan Flusser suit. All the same, he thought, without the slightest trace of envy, a physique like that deserved a good tailor to show it to full advantage.

No detail of Roger Samson's appearance was lost on the Secretary of State for Integrated Planning. All his life, Howard Anderson had maintained a keen eye for other people's affluence and, in an understated yet undeniable way, Roger Samson was affluence personified.

'Good morning, Roger,' said the Secretary of State with the gratuitous familiarity Roger associated with American chat-show hosts.

'Good morning, Minister. It's good of you to see me at such short notice.'

'A pleasure, my dear chap,' enthused Anderson. 'Any friend of Watson-Smith's is a friend of mine.'

Friend! thought Roger, quietly amused. True, Charles Watson-Smith had organized this meeting. But all along he had been at pains to warn Roger that Anderson was a totally unprincipled shit.

'I wouldn't touch a man like that with a barge pole,' he said. 'Can't even tell the truth about his age or education in his *Who's Who* entry. Sort of chap who makes me wonder what's become of the Tory party.'

Roger had not been dismayed to hear Charles's appraisal of Howard Anderson. He sounded just the sort of politician Roger could do business with. Besides, it was often preferable to deal with people you neither liked nor trusted. It made going for the jugular so much easier, should the necessity ever arise.

Roger smiled at the politician's large degenerate face. That private detective had come up with some interesting insights into the Secretary of State's more dubious proclivities. How on earth he had discovered Anderson's penchant for sado-masochism was anybody's guess, but perhaps it explained the mistress Anderson kept in Holland Park. Roger could not see the formidable Mrs Anderson (all brogues, tweeds and twin-sets if her photos were anything to go by) putting up with any sort of deviant nonsense. 'I believe your wife and Charles's were great friends for many years.'

Anderson nodded. 'The girls were at Roedean together. Serena and I were both devastated when Lydia passed away. Terrible tragedy.' He did his best to look suitably grief-stricken. 'Mind you, I do think Charles has improved tremendously since he threw in his lot with you.'

'I hope so,' said Roger. 'He's only a non-executive director, but I do feel our operation has given him an interest.'

'Very modest of you,' the Secretary of State guffawed loudly. 'I'll say it's given him an interest. Nowadays, Samson International is giving us all an interest.'

'We do our best. And we're lucky to have a PM who believes that the country's economy depends on the prosperity of companies like ours.'

The Secretary of State nodded his ostentatious agreement. What utter bollocks! he thought, cynically recalling the details of the latest multinational transfer-pricing scandal. 'It's entrepreneurs like you who are the nation's wealth creators,' he went on. 'Miserable politicians like me, we merely try to create the conditions to allow companies like yours to flourish.'

Roger continued to smile politely. God, the man was such a blatant hypocrite. How dare a twerp like Howard Anderson pontificate to him about wealth creation? The detective's report had been nothing if not exhaustive. A small-town estate agent, Anderson could barely afford to keep his clapped-out Jaguar on the road until he married money. Even after his promotion to Secretary of State, he was certainly not what civil servants referred to as a high-flyer. His political peer group had been nothing but a hot-bed of mediocrity. The odd thing was, thought Roger ruefully, that far from impeding their progress up the greasy pole, their careers had all managed to flourish because of it.

'That's the very reason I'm here, Minister. As you know, Samson International's main interest remains property development.'

'Fascinating business,' interrupted Anderson, preening himself in his large, leather armchair. 'I'm a property man myself.'

Pompous prat! thought Roger. As if flogging forty-thousand-pound semis made anyone a property man. 'Indeed, so you'll be as pleased as I am that the City of London is planning to expand. It has to. Soon there's going to be a desperate shortage of decent office accommodation, hence our interest in developing London's Docklands.'

'An inspirational project,' enthused Howard who, in his capacity as Secretary of State for Integrated Planning, had spent many an hour down by the Thames, visiting this controversial programme of regeneration. 'Just goes to show what can be done with the right amalgam of private investment and public money.'

Howard Anderson could not open his mouth without sounding like a party political broadcast. Already Roger loathed him. It was neither the man's greed nor his corruption that he found so contemptible. Heaven forbid. No, more than anything it was the hypocrisy and, perhaps even worse, the cowardice. Despite all his mumbo-jumbo about a society geared for entrepreneurs, Anderson himself was not a risk-taker. Behind the rhetoric, Roger knew there was nothing of substance, just a bent politician. Howard Anderson had never built an empire or swung a deal. He had never created a real job or generated one penny of real wealth. In fact, his entire public life had been devoted to nothing but feathering his own sordid little nest while exhorting the rest of the country to 'get off its butt'.

Swiftly Roger moved to the crux of the matter. 'The problem is, Minister, that sometimes things seem to move – how shall I put it? – a little too slowly for a company like ours.'

'Slowly?' The Secretary of State raised an eyebrow.

'Minister, you must know the sort of thing. Problems with planning officers over building permissions. Aggravation from the Homes Before Hotels lobby. Resistance from the locals.'

Howard Anderson nodded dolefully.

'I do assure you,' continued Roger, 'that Samson International is as socially and environmentally aware as any major company but . . .' there was the slightest of pauses, 'I can't help wondering whether the long-term returns are really worth the current hassle.'

'I see.' The Secretary of State started to make notes in the back of his diary. Momentarily he glanced up, staring Roger straight in the eye. Unflinching, Roger returned his gaze. It was obvious. Already they understood one another completely.

'I believe,' continued Roger, 'that this government hopes to attract over two billion pounds of private investment before nineteen eighty-seven. I'd like to think of Samson International as a major contributor to that inflow.'

'Where else is Samson International hoping to invest?'

'We're currently planning a chain of luxury hotels throughout Europe and the United States. Building has already started in Paris and New York. But I'd dearly love to see the Samson International flagship hotel here, in Park Lane.'

'Difficult,' mused Howard, chewing the cap of his fountain pen. 'Very difficult at the moment. But not impossible. And how do you see your company funding such massive undertakings?'

'As your old friend Charles Watson-Smith keeps telling me, Minister, good ideas will always find funding. Myself, I'm not quite such a *laissez-aller* optimist.'

'No?'

Roger flicked an imperceptible speck of dust from his sleeve. 'No, Minister. I believe you have to plan your funding carefully. It's been some time now since I owned a hundred per cent of Samson International. I hated losing control. But I needed to bring in outside shareholders to strengthen the balance sheet. It was the only way I could operate on the scale that interests me.'

'So that explains your involvement with Charles.'

'To a large extent,' replied Roger, almost truthfully. Charles's major contribution to Samson International could not be gauged in pounds or dollars. He conferred class. He opened doors. Today was a small example. 'And I must say,' he continued, 'that the banks are currently falling over themselves to lend.'

'Happy sign of the times,' smiled the Secretary of State. God, these politicians never missed a trick. 'But banks are conservative by nature. I suppose they also want to see you in good institutional company.'

'Naturally,' said Roger. 'They seem impressed with our ability to take over other companies and – let's say – rationalize their structures.'

Howard Anderson smiled. Everyone knew about Samson International and its hit squad of management experts, 'the SS' as they were called in the City for the ruthlessness of their methods. It was hardly surprising that redundant executives all over the country still blanched at the mention of Roger Samson's name. He glanced at his watch. 'Roger, I'm afraid I have a briefing session with my permanent secretary.' The Secretary of State tore the two back pages out of his diary and handed them to Roger. 'I've written down a few names of people I'm sure you'll find amenable. The sort of chaps,' he gave a little cough, 'who understand how the world really works.'

Carefully Roger placed the list of names in his briefcase. 'I'm extremely grateful for your help, Minister. Extremely.' None of the names on that list was going to come cheap. But Roger could deal with that. If things worked out as planned, there was going to be plenty there for everyone. He recalled the details of the detective's report: the Secretary of State's penchant for Lafitte, Lagondas and ladies of dubious repute. For men like Howard Anderson, he realized, plenty would just about be sufficient.

'Oh, and by the way,' added Roger, on the point of leaving, 'for your information, Minister, I intend to take Samson International public within the next twenty-four months.'

'How very interesting,' said Anderson, scribbling down another note in the back of his diary. 'A full listing on the London Stock Exchange by nineteen eighty-five.'

'If everything goes according to plan.'

Shaking Roger's hand, Howard stared pointedly at the crocodile briefcase. 'I'm sure,' he said, 'that everything now will.'

Mark was already waiting as Roger emerged from the building.

'Samson Heights, please,' instructed Roger, jumping into the back of the car. 'I just want to see how the building work is progressing down there.'

It was a matter of paramount importance to Roger. He wanted this great black granite edifice finished before Samson International became a public company. The offices in Baker Street would have to do until then. But now the burgeoning Samson International empire deserved a monument worthy of its achievement.

CHAPTER TWELVE

Summer, 1983

THE Cork and Bottle near Leicester Square had to be one of London's busiest wine bars. Owned by a New Zealander with a flair for good food and reasonably priced wine, it was a favourite early evening haunt for London's theatre-goers. During the day it was equally packed, often with a fair sprinkling of friendly Antipodean visitors. It was a great meeting place for a drink and a laugh and just about the last place on earth Lilah would have chosen for a quiet heart-to-heart.

Balancing a bottle of wine and two large plates of salade Niçoise, Andrea fought her way back to where Lilah was sitting. Four other people, complete strangers, had parked themselves around the table while Andrea had been getting the food.

'What a scrum!' she gasped, sitting down and pouring Lilah a glass of wine.

Lilah nodded. 'Worse than UN delegates on a junket. Don't you think we should go somewhere quieter? I mean if you've got something you really want to talk about.'

'Oh, no, it's OK,' replied Andrea brightly. 'I like it here.'

Irritated, Lilah sipped her wine. Whatever the problem, it was obvious that Andrea had already made up her mind. Now she was merely looking for a sounding board for her decision. Well, let her choose her own time.

'I've been reading your column recently,' said Lilah. Nowadays she bought the *Courier* whenever she was back in

London, which was not half as often as she wished. Idly, she speared an anchovy. What on earth was she doing with her life? Originally, the whole idea of resigning from the United Nations was to spend more time with Jonathan. But after her trip to Meroto, their relationship seemed to be on hold. Now she was compensating by throwing herself into her work. Not that that was difficult. With her extraordinary array of languages, she was heavily in demand on the freelance interpreting circuit. Andrea and her problems! Over the last four weeks, Lilah had been in six different capitals and as many hotel beds. She could have done with a day to herself.

'And what do you think?' asked Andrea. Lilah seemed miles away. 'About the column?'

Lilah forced a smile. Now she was here, she might as well make an effort. 'Much less aggressive,' she said, approvingly. 'I'd say, from your writing, that you're far more contented.'

'I wish I could say the same for the editor. Old Freddie keeps doing his nut. Says it's beginning to look like Jennifer's Diary.'

Lilah looked contrite. 'Is that what's on your mind?'

Andrea shook her head. 'Christ, no! I can still twist Freddie round my little finger. Well, at least for the time being. He thinks I'm just going through a phase. He's bet the assistant editor I'll be back to my good old backstabbing ways before you can say flick-knife.'

'Honestly,' laughed Lilah, picking up a juicy black olive with her fingers, 'to listen to you talk, anybody'd think you were genuinely wicked. I always reckon you're just striving for effect.'

Andrea pushed the green beans around her plate. 'Tell that to Charles's old cronies. They think I'm a real viper in the bosom. That's why I've had to tone down my stuff. I don't want them upsetting him.'

Lilah felt a genuine warmth towards her friend. 'That's nice,' she said. 'And I must say I think he's worth it. He's a lovely man and he seems to be making you happy.'

Andrea refilled their empty glasses. 'That's what I wanted to talk to you about. Do you realize Charles has been taking me out for over six months?'

Lilah could not resist the obvious. 'Must be some sort of record for you.'

'Not the only bloody record, I can tell you. He hasn't even taken me to bed yet. And, God knows, it isn't as if I haven't tried.'

The man sitting next to Andrea pricked up his ears.

'Do you know, he hasn't slept with anyone since his wife died? He even told me that when they were married, he was never once unfaithful to her.'

'Looks like you've got yourself a paragon.'

Impatiently, Andrea tossed her hair. 'Oh, yes. Very honourable. Very Coldstream. A peck on the cheek after dinner and another night alone in the sack.'

By now, the man had given up even pretending to converse with his girlfriend.

'How do I move this bloke along?'

Lilah looked amazed. 'Andrea, *you*'re asking *me*?'

'Yes, I am. I'm only used to screwing blokes like Freddie Higgins. I'm not sure how to deal with a decent man like Charles. How do I get him to propose? I can't keep on turning out this tripe for the *Courier* indefinitely. Sooner or later Freddie is bound to blow his top. Besides,' Andrea took a gulp of wine, 'I'm bored with journalism. It's time for me to move on. I've been thinking about public relations. But I can't make the move without Charles's financial backing.'

Lilah gazed hard at her friend. 'Do you love him?'

Andrea shrugged. 'Oh, I'm very fond of him,' she replied breezily. 'He's very kind, very generous. He's the first man I've ever met who makes me feel secure.'

Lilah looked disturbed. 'Isn't that enough for the time being?'

'No,' replied Andrea crisply. 'It's no good *feeling* secure. Now I want to *be* secure. If only I could get Charles to set me up with a PR company, I know I'd make a success of it.'

'Have you suggested it to him?'

'Good grief, no. Not yet. It might sound pushy.' Lilah couldn't help thinking that her friend from Grimford had learned a trick or two. 'So what do you intend to do?'

Andrea smiled her cutest, most cunning little smile. 'He's invited me up to his estate in Scotland. There's only going to be the two of us. I'm sure I'll think of something.'

*

The eighteen-inch granite walls of the square-built Georgian mansion ensured that Charles's bedroom was always cold, even now at the height of summer.

'I'm sorry,' he said anxiously, as Andrea rolled over onto her side of the bed in a gesture of sheer frustration. 'This has never happened to me before. I'm afraid I don't know what to do.'

That afternoon, while they had been out walking on the estate, an hour's drive from the heart of Inverness, Charles had at last plucked up the courage to tell Andrea he loved her, and then surprised himself by asking her to marry him. Naturally she had accepted. In fact, she'd felt like pinching herself. At last, she thought, she was home and dry.

Andrea said nothing, just continued to shiver under the starched linen sheets and the pile of pure wool blankets. Lovingly, Charles pulled the massive patchwork quilt from off the floor and smoothed it across the bed. It had been a present to him from Lydia on their third wedding anniversary. God knows how long it had taken her to make it – years, probably. Gently Charles stroked this masterpiece of patience and needlework. More than anything he possessed, this was the ultimate testimony of Lydia's unfailing devotion. Tonight, however, it offered him no solace. It even seemed to exacerbate the problem. To be in Lydia's bed with another woman – somehow it didn't seem right at all.

'Forget it,' said Andrea, pulling the blankets up around her ears. 'I want to go to sleep.' What a fiasco, she thought angrily. Never happened to him? It had never happened to her either! Not with any one of scores of men. God knows, it wasn't as if she hadn't tried. On the contrary, she had tried every trick in her extremely comprehensive book to encourage his erection. But the harder she tried, the less hard he became.

Charles looked across at the small figure huddled up on the other side of the bed and wondered if he felt like reaching out to her or not. Although he would never admit it, especially not to himself, he had been disturbed, shocked even, by Andrea's all too obvious expertise. As he'd watched her, greedily sucking his unwilling cock, he knew that what he'd felt was bordering on distaste. Her childlike innocence, the very quality that had attracted him to her in the first place, had evaporated as she tormented, teased and even offered to fetch the riding crop she'd noticed hanging in his wardrobe.

'I'm sure it'll work out in time,' continued Charles apologetically. 'It's just, I suppose, I . . .'

'I said forget it,' said Andrea impatiently. By this stage, her reserves of sympathy were utterly depleted. Sex was important to her. Apart from anything, it was the best way she knew of cementing her relationship with this man. All the same, perhaps her knowledge of his problem would bind him to her even more securely. Suddenly Andrea smiled to herself. After all, that was what really mattered.

Relenting, she rolled back towards Charles and snuggled up against him. He held her in his arms, tentatively running his fingers through her hair. Andrea could feel his cheeks, warm with tears and almost – but only almost – felt ashamed.

'I'll go and seek professional advice,' he murmured. 'There must be . . .'

Andrea raised herself up on one elbow and put her finger to his lips. 'It'll get better,' she said softly. 'Believe me, Charles, I'm going to see to that.'

'I'm so happy for you,' enthused Paula Dickens when Andrea finally arrived. Never a demon for punctuality, Andrea had recently taken to tipping up at the *Courier* at any time that suited her. This morning it was half past ten before she wafted in on a cloud of Joy de Patou.

'Thanks,' replied Andrea, flashing her large sapphire and diamond engagement ring. 'That's sweet of you.' She tried to raise a smile. Women like Paula Dickens – they were all such pathetic sentimentalists. Babies, weddings, royalty, soap operas, anything in that line of twaddle would reduce them to tears in seconds. Immediately Andrea started to busy herself about her desk. Memos, messages, invitations, the daily bouquet of red roses from Charles, there was always so much to be done.

Paula hovered for a minute. 'I know it's nothing to do with me. But I do think you're very lucky. Mr Watson-Smith is such a fine man. He's had a wonderful effect on you.'

You can say that again, mused Andrea, hanging the jacket

of her navy and white Chanel suit on a coat-hanger. For a moment, her thoughts turned to her mother, Brenda, with her fluorescent fuchsia frocks and mango blouses. The weekly outing to the bowling alley, the annual fortnight on the Costa del Sol and the bottle of Marks & Spencer's pink champagne on 'special occasions' – Brenda thought herself a lucky woman. Andrea winced. There was no doubt about it. Money, loads of it, certainly did make all the difference. She brushed an imaginary blonde hair off the collar of her jacket. How sweet of Charles to hire a personal dresser. Goodness knows what that week's shopping expedition must have cost. Not that she would ever know, of course. Her accounts at Chanel, Hermès, Jourdan and Yves St Laurent were simply forwarded to him. Andrea smiled the same, myopic smile that had so captivated Charles. And why shouldn't she smile? It was pointless to keep playing the angry young woman when your fiancé had just bought you a Porsche.

'Paula, would you be an absolute angel and get me a cup of coffee? I'm dropping. We were at Le Boulestin till two this morning.'

'Of course.' Paula hummed happily as she closed the office door behind her. Nothing Miss Blackwell asked was too much trouble nowadays.

Sitting in his office, Freddie Higgins was fuming. David Burgess, the *Courier*'s legal advisor, surveyed the editor with alarm though this was not the first time he'd witnessed the fall-out of Freddie's Vesuvian temper.

'Freddie,' said David calmly, 'I'm afraid you can't sack your top columnist simply because she's got engaged. We'll have the Equal Opportunities Commission down on us like a ton of bricks. She'll have every right to take us to the cleaners for unfair dismissal.'

'First of all,' shouted Freddie, incandescent, 'if you're supposed to be such a clever bloody lawyer, you'd better start getting your facts straight. Number one. Andrea Blackwell is not my top columnist.'

'But, Freddie, you said—'

'No, you just listen to what I said. I said she *was* my top columnist. She was a fantastic bloody gossip columnist before she met this Watson-Smith bloke. Since then, she's been writing absolute bollocks. Listen to this!' Freddie brandished a copy of the previous day's *Courier*. ' "Hugo Newsom, formerly of Sotheby's, now Britain's latest style guru. More witty than Valentino, more innovative than Conran, more daring then Stefanidis . . ." – it goes on in the same vein for an entire page. That's the third time in six months she's given this bloke a plug. She's not writing a gossip column. She's giving away free bloody advertising space.'

'In that case,' resumed David, 'why didn't you call her in before and warn her? Why did you decide to wait until the day her engagement was announced before you tried to sack her?'

Freddie looked suddenly deflated. 'I know it sounds ridiculous, but I kept hoping that this business with Watson-Smith was just a fling. I didn't want to lose her.'

'As a columnist . . . or was there something more to your relationship?'

'Don't play silly buggers with me,' bellowed Freddie, instantly on the attack again. 'Everybody on the staff here knows there was more to it than that!'

'Believe me, Freddie, I'm on your side,' said David soothingly. 'But I need this information if I'm going to stop you making a complete fool of yourself. I have to question you the way any lawyer would. And I don't mind telling you that if you sack her now, it will be made to look like the revenge of a spurned and spiteful lover. The rest of Fleet Street would have a field day at your expense.'

Freddie tried hard to look contrite. 'Look, sunshine, I know you're trying to give me the best advice, but I just can't allow her to get away with it. That woman has already managed to make me look a fool – the way she wormed her way into poor old Bosworth's job, telling me it was time to put some bite in the column.'

David coughed. Poor old Bosworth, indeed. Bosworth's job at the *Courier* had been his whole life, a life swiftly discarded for a bit of skirt. It was a bit late for the likes of Freddie Higgins to start having twinges of conscience now.

'Which, you agree, she did.'

'Yes, she did. And, by God, it worked while she was doing it. But then she latches on to this sprig of the aristocracy and starts using my newspaper to ingratiate herself with his set. All this flannel about the beautiful people, I should have known she was up to something. For the last six months, her copy has been nothing but a bloody mating call. Fuck me, and to think she used to despise these people!'

'Calm down, now, Freddie. She can't have had it planned from the outset. And if even she had, I'm not entirely sure you can dismiss her on the grounds of gradual non-malice aforethought.'

'Don't pay fucking barristers with me,' yelled Freddie. 'You're not down at the Wig and Pen with all your clever-dick mates now, you know. This woman has taken me for a ride. Now I want her out. And I want you to give me some good goddamn reason to get her out.'

Freddie was still wheezing from his outburst when the phone rang. 'Vera,' he shouted, lifting up the receiver, 'I thought I told you I was taking no calls.'

'Yes, sir. I know that. But it's Miss Blackwell on the line. She says it's very important.'

'OK,' said Freddie, still steaming. 'As it happens, there are a few things I very much want to say to her.'

A slight click, a few ersatz bars of 'We shall overcome' and the call had been transferred.

'Hello, Freddie,' said Andrea brightly, 'I just thought I'd give you a buzz to let you know that I've decided to resign from the paper. Two months' notice either side, isn't it? I believe those are the terms of my contract.'

'Two months? You can bloody well leave immediately, you ungrateful bitch. I thought you were my ally in the class war. Now I know you're nothing but a scheming little traitor.'

'I'm sorry you've decided to take it like that,' said Andrea sweetly. It was incredible – Freddie could have sworn she'd been taking elocution lessons. 'In that case I'll have my things out of here by the end of the morning. Goodbye, Freddie. Oh, and by the way, thanks for everything. It's all been terribly, really terribly useful.'

David poured Freddie a stiff Scotch from the drinks cupboard. The editor looked as if he were about to burst a blood vessel. 'Are you all right?' asked David.

'Fine, just fine,' murmured Freddie, downing the whisky in one and immediately pouring himself another. 'But mark my words. I know her sort. Sooner or later, she's bound to stick her head above the parapet. And when she does, I'll be there, waiting for her. Believe me, if it takes the next twenty years, I'll get Miss Andrea Blackwell.'

CHAPTER THIRTEEN

Meroto, December 1983

SATURDAY night, and it was standing-room only in Gloria Moloko's malodorous shebeen. Flushed with their week's wages, many of Meroto's mineworkers congregated at this, the most popular of the township's illegal drinking places. The oblivion produced by alcohol – for a few brief hours at least – made life seem almost bearable. Some of the regulars, inmates of the local mine's men-only hostels, were in search of female company. Fortunately for them, Meroto's 'madam', Constance Tshabalala, was happy to provide for their needs. In the hostels, many of the men were separated from their families and homelands for a year at a time and homosexuality was rife. Constance knew all about AIDS – the 'slimming sickness' – and how it was transmitted. She had heard from her cousin, Sister Ndaba, at the Christian Sight-Savers Mission Hospital, that the extent of the disease had now reached epidemic proportions. Like most small-scale entrepreneurs, Constance was prudent by nature. She had asked Sister Ndaba to provide some basic diagrams and at regular intervals she would lecture her girls on the dangers of disease and the benefits of 'protection'. God only knew how much of it was sinking in.

There were, of course, legal drinking establishments in the township, but they just didn't have the atmosphere of Gloria's, celebrated for the warmth of its welcome and its easy camaraderie. Yet a more unprepossessing establishment it was difficult to imagine. The shebeen was a lean-to arrangement, knocked up quickly out of corrugated iron and attached to Gloria's own shanty home. The door was missing, still badly shattered from the last police raid. Such wanton damage angered Gloria even more than the hefty fine. But what incensed her most of all was the confiscation of her liquor. If only the police poured the stuff down the drain she wouldn't have minded so much. But somehow that same confiscated liquor always found its way back to the government-run liquor store where Gloria had bought it in the first place. It was a source of bitter humour in the shebeen. Credo Sekese, one of Gloria's favourites, had dubbed it 'the government recycling programme'. In England, he said, the government had also implemented a bottle recycling scheme, but there, he added to general hilarity, at least the people were allowed to drink the contents first.

It had been a long hard week in the Meroto platinum mine and beer sales in Gloria's shebeen were high. Lion, Castle, Black Label – what did it matter what it was called so long as it was cold, wet and in plentiful supply? An ancient record player boomed out over some hastily rigged loudspeakers. 'No woman, no cry,' wailed Bob Marley plaintively, 'No woman, no cry.' As usual, a group of people clustered around Credo. Articulate and intelligent, he always seemed to attract the younger, more restive elements of the establishment.

'This is our liberty,' he laughed, sardonically toasting the audience with his half-empty glass of Lion lager, 'this is our freedom.'

'Yes,' replied an oddly well-educated voice, 'the liberty to drink ourselves senseless. And the freedom to extend our bondage by wasting our hard-earned money on liquor.'

Jojo Matwetwe. It was hardly surprising that, in her increasingly embittered case, the seeds of the FAP cause should have fallen on fertile ground. Sometimes even Credo Sekese, the leader of the Meroto FAP cell, found her hardline attitude alarming. Throughout the misery of her childhood, Jojo had felt the rejection of both black and white alike. But now the FAP seemed to have given her resentment a more positive outlet.

'Neither blacks nor whites are wicked,' Credo would constantly reiterate at the FAP's secret meetings. 'Only the system which alienates them from one another.'

Hungry for solace from any source, Jojo Matwetwe lapped up her mentor's words. She knew what he was trying to do was dangerous. The members of the Metallinc security force were all trained to spot potential troublemakers. If discovered, Credo's efforts to establish a union at the platinum mine were bound to be viewed as left-wing subversion. Nevertheless, in the mine's white canteen where she worked, Jojo was constantly expounding the FAP philosophy to any black workmate who dared listen. At the same time, covertly in the hostels and every Saturday night at the shebeen, Credo Sekese was also busy recruiting new members to the FAP cause. 'There is always strength in numbers,' he explained to Jojo. 'That is why we must wait until we are sure we have the majority behind us. Then and only then can we really act effectively.'

Credo noticed his comrade's empty glass. 'Let me buy you a drink.'

'Thanks,' replied Jojo, no flicker of a smile. 'I'll have a Coke, please.'

At least this was progress. Credo had known Jojo over two years before she agreed to accept a drink from him or, indeed, from any man. Alcohol, of course, was out of the question. As far as Jojo was concerned, booze created far more problems that it ever solved. No comrade could see hope with a hangover.

'A Coke and a Lion, please,' ordered Credo, catching Gloria's ever-watchful eye.

'Sure,' replied Gloria. 'I hope you and your friend there are not causing me no worries.' As a shebeen queen, Gloria had developed a sixth sense for potential aggravation. She was fond of Credo, with his sharp tongue and his easy charm. But that Jojo Matwetwe bothered her no end. There was trouble written all over that woman's surly half-breed face.

'Worries?' laughed Credo. 'Come on, Gloria. You of all people should be used to plenty of them.'

'Illegal drinking, that's one thing,' said Gloria, seriously. 'The police come. They break up my place a bit. They fine me. They steal my liquor and then they go away. I leave things cool down for a few weeks. Then I go down the liquor store and buy my own liquor back again. That is OK. That is the system. But you, Credo, what you are doing is different. They could send you to prison, you know. That's why I worry for you.'

'Don't,' said Credo, comically mimicking an Afrikaans accent. 'After all, like the *baas* say, "Credo is my number one machine boy." Credo is a wonderful worker. Credo don't give anyone trouble.'

He returned to his group of young admirers.

'I've done the printing,' said Jojo, extracting a large batch of leaflets from her frayed green canvas satchel.

Credo admired his comrade's handiwork. 'How ever did you manage this?'

'Easy,' said Jojo, determined not to show her pleasure at the compliment. 'I "borrowed" the key to the site manager's office. On Wednesdays there is never anyone there between midday and one o'clock. That's when the manager calls his weekly meeting. So I just let myself in and used the photo-copier.'

Credo smiled. For all her sullenness, Jojo was still his most useful ally in the movement. She was clever, and the nuns at the Holy Rosary convent had given her a thorough education. In any other country, Jojo would have been destined for higher things than the banality of canteen work.

'How many people do you think we can expect at our meeting?' asked Credo.

'It depends how many of these leaflets we circulate,' replied Jojo.

A sudden screech of brakes could be heard outside. Gloria Moloko froze.

'Quick,' said Credo, stuffing the leaflets back into Jojo's canvas bag, 'it's a police raid. We'd better hide all these.'

'There's no way out of here,' said Jojo, nimbly fastening the buckles of her bulging satchel. 'Let's hope they don't search the place. I don't want Gloria to be in more trouble than she already is. I'll just go and sit over there in the corner, near that stack of chairs. That way I can keep the satchel hidden underneath me.'

The assembled company fell silent as half a dozen burly policemen burst into the room.

'Gloria Moloko?' enquired Captain de Kock, instinctively fingering the holster in which his revolver was housed.

'That's me,' said Gloria, stepping forward calmly. She had been through this charade so many times before.

'Gloria Moloko,' continued Captain de Kock in deep, guttural tones, 'according to the register at the liquor shop, you've been buying up large quantities of beer and spirits. We believe you're running an illegal drinking establishment. We've come to confiscate your liquor and to close you down. Since this is not your first offence, you'll also be fined an amount of two thousand rand.'

The drinkers in the shebeen groaned in collective sympathy at Gloria's bad luck. Two thousand rand – a small fortune. It would take most of them at least six months to earn such a sum. Gloria said nothing. In her experience it was pointless to argue with the police. Just so long as there was no trouble, that was all that really mattered. Captain de Kock looked around him in ill-concealed disgust. Of course, orders were orders. But this was not real police work. If these kaffirs wanted to drink themselves senseless, why should anyone try to stop them? At least drunken kaffirs were easy to control. They were not *tsotsis* or hoodlums. Rounding up real agitators, now that was what Captain de Kock called proper police work. In his frustration he kicked a crate of empty beer bottles. One fell out and broke, sending splinters of glass shooting across the floor. None of the shebeen regulars moved a muscle. A couple of the policemen shuffled uncomfortably, embarrassed at such a puerile display of petulance.

'What are you looking at?' he shouted, suddenly aware of a pair of penetrating blue eyes staring at him from the other side of the room. Credo Sekese began to sweat. Trust Jojo to attract attention to herself. Unwavering, Jojo continued to stare at the captain.

'You, over there in the corner, I asked you, what are you looking at?'

Stubbornly, Jojo refused to avert her gaze. Captain de Kock felt his blood begin to boil. He was, after all, a *ware* Afrikaner, a true Afrikaner. How dare any half-breed kaffir stare at him like this? It was an insult to himself and to the entire Afrikaner *volk*. Why, even this woman's existence was an affront to everything he held dear. A half-breed, by God, the despicable product of *bloedvermenging*, illicit sex across the colour line. Conceived in sin and in direct contravention of the Immorality Act, such creatures had no place in Captain de Kock's neatly segregated universe of black and white.

But that look! It was more than Captain de Kock could bear. Hate he was used to, he saw that all the time. But this was something far more disturbing. Never in his life had he encountered such an expression of outright arrogance and insubordination. Suddenly, deep inside him, Captain de Kock felt something snap. This kaffir had to be taught her place. Here she was, this half-breed, refusing to answer him, making him look a fool. The whole thing was intolerable.

'You,' he shouted at Jojo, 'you come over here!'

Credo felt his stomach turn. 'Look, *baas*,' he intervened, desperately trying to save her, 'she is very simple. She doesn't understand what you say.'

'Get out of my way,' said Captain de Kock, roughly brushing Credo aside. 'I can tell the difference between stupidity and subversion.' Gloria hung onto Credo's arm.

'Don't interfere,' she whispered, petrified. 'They're all armed.'

Heavily, Captain de Kock walked over to where Jojo was still sitting. 'Stand up, you impudent half-breed kaffir. Stand up when I speak to you.' Credo felt an odd amalgam of pride and nausea. It was difficult not to admire his comrade's fool-hardy behaviour. But on the other hand, he could not help feeling sick at the very thought of what was bound to happen to her. Jojo stared, unrepentant, at the captain.

'*Voetsek*,' she said simply.

Credo groaned under his breath. Only Jojo would tell a captain of the South African Police Force to fuck off. The veins in Captain de Kock's neck stood out like a bull's in a lather. Even in the murky half-light of the shebeen, Credo could discern them, palpitating wildly. The ensuing crack rent the silence like the report of a gun. Captain de Kock rubbed the knuckles of his fist in sadistic satisfaction. Gloria began to sob. Blood gushed down Jojo's straight, Caucasian nose and onto her lap. Her eyelid, violently red, was already closing over. Jojo stared sullenly at her tormentor. Credo shook himself free from Gloria's terrified grip and made to grab the captain. He was not quick enough. Before he could do anything, two of the policemen lurched at him, pinning him tightly against the bar.

'Stand up,' shrieked Captain de Kock, pulling himself up to his full height and towering menacingly over Jojo. 'I'm warning you, kaffir. Stand up when I tell you.'

Jojo tilted her bloodied head and continued to stare at the man. Slowly, painfully, her mouth contorted by the swelling already visible in her face, she began to sing. The words, though distorted, were unmistakable. 'Nkosi Sikelel'i-Afrika' – 'God Bless Africa' – the anthem of black liberation.

'Stop it,' yelled Captain de Kock at the top of his voice. 'Stop it!'

There followed the appalling, hollow sound of fist on forehead. The whole shebeen moaned as Jojo slumped sideways, bringing the adjacent stack of chairs crashing heavily down on top of her.

'My God,' cried Gloria, rushing over to disengage the now silent, twitching body. The mood in the shebeen had turned. An old, shaky voice took up the hymn and soon the whole corrugated-iron structure was reverberating to the strains of 'Nkosi Sikelel'i-Afrika.'

'Let's get out of here,' whispered Private Fonteijn to his superior. A huge tank of a man, Private Fonteijn had never been afraid of physical danger. But he was a changed man since the Soweto riots of 1976. Nowadays, the idea of pointless bloodshed simply filled him with revulsion. This confrontation with the woman, why, it had all been downright stupid.

Captain de Kock was beginning to feel risible. Such a ridiculous loss of self-control. He knew he had diminished himself in his own men's estimation. 'Fucking kaffirs,' he said, trying hard to retrieve his dignity by assuming command of the situation. 'Men, remove all the alcohol from this place and put it on the van. You . . .' Gloria Moloko looked up from the semiconscious woman. 'You come down to the station tomorrow and pay your fine.'

Gloria said nothing, simply continued to bathe Jojo's bruised and swollen face with the old, beer-soaked sponge from behind the bar. Captain de Kock turned on his heel.

122

'And you,' he said to Credo, now kneeling beside Jojo's limp and lifeless figure, 'you just make sure I never see that friend of yours again.'

Credo shot the captain a look of deepest contempt. *'Siyabiza igazi wetho,'* he muttered in Xhosa under his breath.

Jojo opened her left eye and, seeing Credo, painfully managed a smile. 'Yes, Credo,' she whispered, 'spilled blood calls for vengeance.' She passed out again.

It was long past midnight when Jonathan Morton was awoken by loud, persistent banging on his door. Half dazed, he fumbled for the switch by the side of his bed. Good, he thought, as the table lamp buzzed on. At least the hospital's generator was working that evening.

'I'm coming, I'm coming,' he called, as he stumbled across the sitting room. 'Who is it?'

'It's me, Doctor,' replied an agitated voice. 'Credo Sekese. Please hurry. This is an emergency.' Jonathan unbolted the door.

'Please, Doctor,' begged Credo, staggering under the weight of a semi-conscious figure, 'please help us. My friend, Jojo, has been badly beaten up.'

'Come in.' Jonathan opened the door wide and helped Credo carry the woman into his sitting room. 'Let's put her over here on the sofa.' He went into the kitchen and returned with three tumblers. 'Here,' he said, dispensing three large measures of brandy. 'Credo, you drink that. Can you hear me, Jojo?'

Jojo tried to nod her head.

'Good,' said Jonathan, 'then try and take a few sips of this.'

'Jojo never touches alcohol,' interrupted Credo, downing his own drink in one swift nervous gulp.

'It's OK,' said Jonathan, 'she's in a state of shock. A drop of spirits won't hurt her.' Slowly, Jojo began to sip the brandy.

'When she's finished that,' said Jonathan, deciding on reflection to forgo his own drink, 'I think we'd better get her across to the hospital. I'd like to examine her more thoroughly there. But from what I can see, I'm afraid I'm going to have to operate.'

*

The lacerations were even worse than Jonathan had expected. He washed the dark, congealed blood from Jojo's tired, battered face. Credo coughed nervously as he paced up and down the consulting room.

'Not broken,' said Jonathan, examining the bridge of Jojo's nose. 'It's badly swollen but we'll have that back to normal in no time.'

Jojo lay still on the examination couch. Never before had she felt so utterly petrified. She was going to end up blind, of that she was totally convinced. It was strange that Credo, of all people, should put so much faith in this man, Dr Morton. Jojo herself remained resolutely cynical. Why should any white man give a damn what happened to her?

'Can you see out of this?' asked Jonathan, carefully examining his patient's left eye. Surprised, he noted its remarkable blue.

'Yes,' Jojo murmured. Credo moved to hold her hand. Jonathan could see him trembling.

'This may look a bit of a mess,' said Jonathan, trying to calm Credo's nerves, 'especially with that patch of blood seeping under the conjunctiva. But actually I'm not too concerned about it. It's what we call a vitreous haemorrhage. It looks nasty, but it should clear itself up within a couple of weeks. Now then, Jojo, how about your right eye? Can you see anything at all out of that?'

'No,' replied Jojo tonelessly.

It was hardly surprising. Jojo's eyelid was so badly bruised it was now completely swollen over.

'Credo,' said Jonathan, 'would you mind giving me some help?' Credo stared in disbelief as the surgeon opened two paper-clips at right angles. True, it was not quite what the boys at the Moorfields were used to. 'The joys of Third World medicine,' he joked, trying to diffuse the mounting tension. Credo watched as carefully, with the rounded ends of the clips, Jonathan prised open Jojo's horribly livid eye.

'Here, Credo,' said Jonathan, 'hold these paper-clips in place for me, will you, while I examine this more carefully.'

It was precisely as he had feared. Jojo's eye was completely soft, the cornea indented inwards, as deflated as a punctured football.

'I'm afraid this right eye is perforated. Hell, whoever that bastard policeman was, he must have given this poor girl some beating. I'm going to have to operate.' It would be touch and go, of that he was well aware. But at least from experience he knew where the perforation would be – just behind the limbus where the cornea joined the sclera. Jojo lay deathly quiet on the couch.

'You will save her sight, won't you, Doctor?' asked Credo anxiously. 'You've got to.'

'I'll do my best. Come on, let's move her into the operating theatre.'

'Dr Morton,' said Jojo weakly, as the two men lifted her onto the nearby trolley.

'Yes?'

'Thank you.'

Jonathan put his hand on Jojo's quivering arm. She was certainly a strange case, this one. Apart from the odd perfunctory yes and no, these were the first words she had spoken to him. Poor brave woman, thought Jonathan. Of course, it was difficult to tell with all the swelling, blood and bruising – but was that a single tear he saw trickling down his patient's beautiful, battered face?

CHAPTER FOURTEEN

New York, spring 1984

THIS evening was a rare exception. It was seldom that Sophie Weiss reached home before midnight. Work had become so time-consuming that a social life seemed increasingly out of the question. Sophie's mother, Claudia, fretted constantly over her only child's physical and mental well-being. ('Nearly twenty-four already, and still no regular boyfriend!') But what could be done about her? It wasn't so much that platinum dealing at Horneffer & Salzmann, one of New York's most prestigious investment banks, was relentlessly frantic. In fact, most dealers left the office at 2.30 p.m. when the European markets closed. But for a dynamic, ambitious woman such as Sophie, there was always so much else to be tied up at the end of the business day. Background reading to be assimilated, charts to be studied, forecasts to be analysed, political and industrial developments to be considered – the data was never-ending. But hard work had never bothered Sophie. Like her financier father, Harold, a German-Jewish *émigré* to the United States, she loved challenge with an absolute passion, and the more demanding it was the better.

'Good evening, Miss Weiss,' said Arnold, the concierge at Sophie's Sutton Place apartment block. 'There was a large parcel delivered for you this morning. I reckon it's from your mom.'

Sophie smiled. Dear old Arnold couldn't help himself. He

was a compulsive nosy parker. 'Thanks, Arnold,' she said. 'Yes, I was expecting it. A whole bunch of old family photos and letters. Mom was clearing out the attic the other day and found them in a suitcase. Oh, by the way, have there been any enquiries about the cat?'

Arnold shook his head. 'No, and it's been over a month now. Sure seems like no one wants to claim the little fella. I guess you've got yourself a family.'

'I guess I have,' said Sophie, sounding pretty happy about it. 'Thanks for all your trouble, Arnold. See you tomorrow morning.'

Reclining like some decadent aristocrat on Sophie's off-white sofa, the beautiful Blue Burmese turned his head languidly as his new mistress opened the door. With one swift and surprisingly energetic bound he was in Sophie's arms, purring contentedly, his glinting golden eyes the repository of many an untold feline story.

'Hi, Ernie,' said Sophie, stroking the cat's luxuriant blue-grey coat. 'What's the news today?'

Ernie continued to purr, a low, conspiratorial hum. That cat was a mystery. How on earth he had ever arrived on Sophie's tenth-floor balcony was a conundrum not even the omniscient Arnold could fathom. He had just pitched up one evening and it was love at first sight. Of course, Sophie had tried everything to locate his rightful owner. But, apart from a few cranks and crackpots, no genuine candidate had answered her ad. So now Ernie, she reckoned, was rightfully and legally hers. She buried her face in her new friend's silky, sleek fur.

'OK, Ernie, what's it to be for supper?' Sophie carried the cat into the kitchen and opened the fridge door. 'Chicken and mayo on rye toast dry?'

Ernie nestled affectionately against the translucent olive skin of Sophie's long, slim neck. Hell, thought Sophie, this cat was better company than any man. At least with Ernie she now had regular dinner dates.

Idly Sophie flicked through the lastest copy of *Time* magazine as she and Ernie tucked into their identical chicken suppers. On the cover was a photo of this thrusting new entrepreneur, Roger Samson, the guy everyone on Wall Street was talking about. What a specimen, thought Sophie. Pity about that tiny bump on the otherwise perfect nose. Looked like someone had slugged him once upon a time.

'Britain's Latest Transatlantic Buccaneer' ran the cover page headline. Sophie turned to the article inside. She had heard quite a bit about Roger Samson. He sure seemed to be building himself one giant of an empire: everything from hotels to haulage, from mining to marketing and from communications to commodities. 'I do not care for the expression "asset-stripping",' Samson was quoted as saying. 'I'd rather talk in terms of judicious "unbundling". Of course, property development is my main interest. But Samson International has also found that the time is ripe for buying up tired old companies with strong market positions, selling off key assets which don't conform to our overall plans, and ensuring that the remaining parts are managed with efficiency.'

'And when Roger Samson talks efficiency,' continued the article, 'it's wise to insert the adjective "ruthless". Whenever Samson International does a company takeover, it's like McDonald's moving in on the New York Yacht Club.'

Sophie munched away thoughtfully. This Samson character had gotten things hopping in the City of London and, since his incredible Manhattan deal, on Wall Street as well. He and his company, Samson International, would certainly be worth tracking. Fascinated, Sophie read on.

'Life?' Samson had responded to the interviewer's final question. 'Life is nothing but an exercise in expectations management.'

'Oh, please!' exclaimed Sophie loudly. 'What a *kepler* on this guy's shoulders!'

Ernie was still miaowing his total agreement when the phone in the living room rang.

'Hi, honey.'

'Hi, Mom. Thanks for the parcel. I haven't had time to open it yet. But I'll start sorting it out this evening. How's the weather over there in Palm Beach?'

'Wonderful, honey, wonderful. You should come visit more often. I worry about you, you know.' It was always the same old story.

'But, Mom. I was with you only three weeks ago. And I'm

coming again next month. Things are very busy at work.'

'Work, work, work. Just like your father. Are you eating OK, honey?'

'Sure, Mom.'

'You know, at your age you really ought to be having a little more fun. Are you seeing anybody at the moment?'

'Only Ernie.' Sophie could hear her mother brighten perceptibly. 'You remember, Mom, Ernie, my stray cat.'

The disappointment in Claudia's voice was audible all the way from Florida. 'Ernie. What kinda name is that for a cat?'

'Not so bad. When he arrived here, the poor little fella had a strangulated hernia. That's why I called him Ernie.'

Claudia sighed deeply. 'Some name, some relationship! What about that nice boy, Stephen, you were seeing?'

'I decided to call that off. He wanted a deeper commitment. And I'm too busy to make a real go of things at the moment.' What was it, wondered Sophie, about all Jewish mothers? Until you hit a certain age, no one was good enough. After that, suddenly just about anyone with strong hands would do. Sophie could almost feel her mother shaking her head in desperation.

'Well, anyway, like I say, you ought to loosen up a bit. You want a word with Dad?'

'Hi, Dad.'

'Hi, Sophie. Are you OK, baby? Is there anything you want? You only gotta say the word.' Harold Weiss spoke with the confidence of a man whose daughter had never asked him for a nickel. Even at Yale, where other rich kids never stopped demanding cars, holidays, orthodontic bridge-work, nose jobs and the odd silicone implant from their parents, Sophie had made do happily with her relatively modest allowance. Harold was inordinately proud of his only daughter. For many years he and Claudia had tried in vain for children. By the time Sophie arrived they had all but given up hope. But Sophie had been worth waiting for. Oh, yes, thought Harold Weiss fondly, his daughter Sophie had turned out just as good as any son.

Now retired from a hugely successful career in finance, Harold Weiss was finding it difficult to come to terms with the strain of relaxation. All his life he had worked hard and had positively thrived on the tension. Twenty years old when first he arrived in New York, Harold had been a penniless refugee from Hitler's Nazi Germany. Leaving behind a profitable family banking business, he and his only brother, Simon, had managed to escape Nazi persecution in 1935. Simon, five years older than Harold and a mining engineer by profession, had decided to try his luck prospecting in South Africa. But for Harold, steeped in the Weiss family's banking tradition, New York seemed the place for him, a haven of endless financial opportunity.

'Thanks, Dad. But I'm fine. My bonus this month was god-damn outrageous.'

Harold smiled happily to himself. 'You deserve it. Everyone knows my baby's the brightest dealer in the business. Sophie, you want to stick with platinum?'

'Yes, Dad. At least for the time being. You know precious metals have always fascinated me. Platinum in particular. We've got some interesting developments at the moment.'

'Yes, honey. I was reading a survey in *Business Weekly* the other day. Looks like the Europeans will soon be following us with catalytic-converter legislation.'

'They sure will. The market's a bit slow at the moment. But with the Japanese jewellery business and the petrochemical boys, demand must be on the up and up in the long term.'

Harold loved such conversations with his daughter. She certainly had the Weiss financial brain working regular over-time inside that pretty bright-eyed little head. Recently she had been asked to write a piece on her commodity for the *New York Times*. Harold had been so proud he had pinned it to the wall of his den. Every day he would reread how platinum stocks, unlike gold, were always kept low. According to Sophie, the producers preferred it that way. They wanted to maintain control by keeping supply and demand in balance. Considering that platinum was a strategic as well as a precious metal, that was particularly important. The key automobile and petrochemical industries would grind to a halt without sufficient supplies. Not, Sophie had explained, that there was any problem in that department for the moment. South Africa was quite happily delivering 80 per cent of the West's overall platinum requirement. The USSR, of course, were also pro-ducers. But their suppliers were nowhere near as reliable as the South Africans. Besides, Sophie had argued, South African ore was far superior to the Soviet stuff. South African ore yielded 70 per cent platinum and 20 per cent palladium while the USSR ore produced 70 per cent palladium and 20 per cent platinum. South Africa, she therefore concluded, was by far the major producer and refiner of the kind of platinum the West really needed. Harold smiled as he recalled the article. 'Your uncle Simon would be proud of you, baby,' he said, immediately sorry that he had touched on a raw nerve.

Perhaps it was because his daughter was an only child. Or perhaps it was something to do with the peripatetic history of the Jewish people. But whatever it was, even as a little girl Sophie had developed a tremendous sense of the importance of family. Over the years, her father's only brother, Uncle Simon, had assumed an almost mythical dimension in her mind. Sophie loved to picture him, a brave and solitary figure, trekking off into the South African *veldt* to stake his mining claim. Over time, the two brothers had lost touch with one another. But Sophie had seen old photos of Uncle Simon and he still played a vivid part in her imagination. Who knows? Perhaps in some strange way, Uncle Simon and his mineral prospecting had even influenced Sophie's choice of career. She sighed. 'I hope so. I sure do put a lot of hours into my subject. Dad,' she paused, 'do you ever suppose Uncle Simon is still alive?'

'I've no idea, sweetheart, really no idea. It must be over ten years since we heard from him. It was impossible for me to keep track of him always lost in some god-forsaken spot, looking for that elusive major strike.'

'I wish we knew what happened to him. Those things seem kinda important to me.' Sophie's voice trailed off. 'Dad, I'm going to spend the rest of the evening sorting through Mom's old collection of photos and letters. You know, you and Mom aren't getting any younger. And I want to understand all I can about my family before the evidence disappears.'

'You're a good girl, Sophie,' said Harold. 'We love you very much.'

'And I love you too, Dad. I'll call you at the weekend.'

Sophie returned to the kitchen where her mother's parcel had been dumped unceremoniously on the table. Only then did she notice Ernie, hissing angrily in the corner. What was with that lunatic cat? Shreds of *Time*'s cover page lay scattered all over the floor. In the space of a five-minute telephone conversation, Ernie had torn Roger Samson's handsome face into a hundred tiny pieces.

By midnight the carpet in Sophie's living room was covered with piles of photographs and letters. Ernie, having twice been ordered not to meddle, was singularly unimpressed. As a recently adopted orphan, he felt he still deserved his new mistress's undivided attention. But Sophie was engrossed in the accumulated memorabilia. Sorting through her mother's parcel was like travelling in a time machine. Meticulous as ever, she had spent hours organizing the photos into some sort of chronological order and now she was busily sticking them into a large maroon-leather album.

Yes, thought Sophie contentedly, this at last was a *real* family album. Here was a picture of the two brothers, Harold and Simon Weiss, taken beside Berlin's Brandenburg Gate in 1925. How handsome Uncle Simon was, a lad of fifteen, taller and more strongly built than her father. Then there was Harold on his own, quite an impressive young man by now, laughing and pointing at the Empire State Building. Here was one of Harold and Claudia on their wedding day – her mother looked ravishing, thought Sophie. And another of Claudia in hospital, cuddling a new-born baby. ('21 September 1960,' Harold had written on the back, 'the day our beautiful little Sophie finally arrived.')

But the photos that most interested Sophie were those taken in South Africa. Pictures of Uncle Simon, proudly wielding a shovel in remote and empty scrublands. Increasingly intrigued, Sophie searched for the last photo ever received from her uncle. The shot showed Uncle Simon silhouetted against a threateningly gloomy sky. It was marked 'Meroto, 1970'.

Meroto . . . Meroto. Now what had she been reading about Meroto just lately? She must be tired. Her brain did not usually take so long to retrieve any item of information. Of course, that was it! The Metallinc company report. Sophie rifled through her briefcase. Perhaps she still had a copy in there. Yes, here it was. 'Platinum production over the last ten years has been increasing steadily,' she read. 'Metallinc now has the capital investment necessary to start building its own refinery. The refinery should be completed by the end of 1985. By that stage, Metallinc hopes to have increased its annual production of platinum from five hundred kilos to seven hundred and fifty kilos in the form of good delivery metal.'

Sprawled out, idly watching his mistress's endeavours, Ernie decided to miaow his discontent more loudly.

'All right, Ernie,' said Sophie, stretching, 'I guess it's time for bed.' Already one o'clock in the morning. Sophie hadn't even noticed the hours slipping by. But what an extraordinary coincidence! Tonight it was too late, but tomorrow she would resume her research even more intensively. Of course, it was only a hunch but, as every dealer at Horneffer & Salzmann would readily concede, Sophie Weiss's hunches were usually correct. Perhaps a thorough reading of Uncle Simon's letters would shed further light on the matter. Somehow Uncle Simon and Metallinc just had to be connected.

Grey, solid, imposing and impregnable, Wall Street's Horneffer & Salzmann looked every inch the prestigious investment bank it was. Originally constructed in 1865, the squadron of massive, Ionic columns still appeared to be standing guard on the bank, defying anything – war, recession, scandal – to interrupt its enormously successful operation. Sophie climbed the polished granite steps, stopping momentarily at the top to despair over the current chairman's taste in art. There, dominating the impressive, neo-classical hall, was hung some execrable collage of nuts, bolts and springs, somewhat cynically entitled *Progress*. It made Sophie cross. Not that she had anything against modern art, on the contrary. But why spend money on some unknown Texan when Horneffer & Salzmann could have invested in a wonderful Noguchi or Dubuffet sculpture like some of their competitors?

Sophie made her way to the dealing room on the fifteenth floor. Though trading in palladium only started at 8.20 a.m., and platinum ten minutes later, the place was already humming by seven o'clock. Sitting down at the platinum desk, Sophie switched on her Reuters screen and immediately began to scan the news pages. No radical political developments overnight in the United States. Nothing to write home about in Hong Kong or Tokyo either. South Africa – same old story. Zurich – Sophie could not help but smile. When was the last time anything dramatic had ever happened in Zurich? And London – well, London was still awaiting the prosperity of Mrs Thatcher's promised land.

Next Sophie called up the exchange rates. US dollar steady. German D-Mark strong. Sterling still a bit shaky. Yen decidedly good. Sophie tapped a few brief notes into her personal computer. Naturally, she'd be operating most of the day in US dollars but occasionally another dealer might want a quotation in a different currency.

Background homework done, now it was time to start the real business of the day. Sophie called up the latest trading figures. Interminable columns of digits, displayed luminescent green against black, they were designed to look user-friendly. Just as well, reckoned Sophie, her eyes still tired from their previous evening's exertions, since she'd be staring at them all day.

It was second nature to Sophie. Expertly she started scanning the screen for the usual pointers: the last trade, the high and low of the day, the volume traded. She tapped a few more keys on her personal computer and ran her regression analysis. Before 'early morning prayers', as the daily dealing room meeting was called, she hoped to have found a reasonable trend fit.

There was little enough time to think in peace before the non-stop crossfire started. Sophie called up London's Fix. The eight market-making Members of London's Platinum and Palladium Market fixed the platinum price twice daily, first at 9.45 a.m. and again at 2 p.m. The most recent fixing price had been at 9.45 London time.

'Three hundred and fifty-four dollars per troy ounce,' noted Sophie. Nothing startling there. With a few hiccups in late '82 and early '83, platinum prices had been declining steadily since the artificially high levels of 1980.

'Seen the London Fix, Sophie?' shouted Arthur, from an adjacent desk.

'Sure,' said Sophie, 'and I don't think the price has bottomed out yet.'

'Me neither. D'you get the bumf on the new miracle anti-cancer drug? Based on carbo-platin, they tell me. Still a few problems with the second generation, though.'

Sophie nodded. 'Far too many side-effects,' she agreed. 'But the pharmaceutical industry is hoping the third generation will be a major breakthrough in the treatment of ovarian and testicular cancer.'

'Oh, please, Sophie, honey. Not on an empty stomach. I was drinking at Gino's till two this morning.'

Sophie laughed. 'Just you keep an eye on it, Arthur. If that baby comes off, the pharmaceutical boys'll be buying platinum at any price.'

'Hi, Sophie.'

'Hi, Bud. How's my favourite chartist?'

Bud Hollingway flushed to the very roots of his flaming red hair. If only he could summon up the courage to ask this woman out. But Sophie, for all her matiness, was such an alarming prospect. Second in command in the dealing room (and, as everybody knew, far more effective than her boss, the chairman's son-in-law), Sophie's rise in Horneffer & Salzmann had been positively meteoric. Today she was still the only female dealer on the trading desk – no mean achievement. It had been old Mr Salzmann's most fervently held belief that no woman was sufficently hard or decisive to make a good mar-ket-maker. In the case of Miss Sophie Weiss, however, it had taken the septuagenarian banker precisely six months to con-cede that there were exceptions to his rule.

'Fine thanks, Sophie. You want any info?' If only Sophie ever looked as if she wanted anything else from him.

'Please, Bud. I reckon things are still moving down. But, you know, the boss doesn't trust anything as ridiculous as female intuition.'

Bud laughed. Last year, Sophie's ridiculous female intuition had netted the platinum desk over $20 million in profit.

'So perhaps before this morning's meeting,' continued

Sophie, 'you could print me out a chart – one of your "double tops" and "head and shoulders" masterpieces – just so I can prove to the bastard I'm not out on such a limb.'

'Sure thing, Sophie,' said Bud, ecstatic to be of service. 'I've just been writing my annual report for the chairman. My own view is that platinum prices will reach rock bottom by the end of the first quarter of nineteen eighty-five. After that, the price will follow economic recovery in the West and greater industrial activity. I predict a steady increase in prices through 'eighty-five and 'eighty-six.'

Sophie smiled at the young man's obvious enthusiasm. It was great to have this guy on her team. If nothing else, Bud's crystal-ball-gazing genius supported Sophie's own basic instincts.

'And as for predictions beyond 'eighty-six,' teased Sophie, 'I suppose we may as well consult the tarot cards.'

Bud was desperate to share her joke. 'They're about as good as anything else,' he agreed. 'Let's face it, you can do all the charting and plotting you want, but in the end the platinum market, like any other market, is fraught with exogenous variables.' Bud immediately bit his tongue. Why, when he wanted to impress, did he end up sounding such a jerk?

As usual, the morning meeting led by Earl Shallit, the chairman's son-in-law, was over within ten minutes. Despite appearances, the horn-rimmed spectacles, the earnest expression, the compulsive note-taking, Earl was not a particularly competent man. He did, however, have one sterling quality: he had the wits to recognize ability in other people. Earl may well have been head of the dealing room, but no one failed to notice his constant deference to Sophie.

'Good morning, everybody,' said Earl, blinking his owlish eyes. There were a dozen precious-metals dealers at Horneffer & Salzmann: four on the general platinum desk, four on gold, and four on silver. 'Perhaps this morning, briefly, you'd all like to hear RJ's report.' The bank's in-house economist, R. J. Stone, bore an uncanny resemblance to Cuba's Fidel Castro. He also gave longer and marginally more boring speeches.

'Earl,' said Sophie, who had sat through quite enough of RJ's lectures on the economic ramifications of the OPEC oil-price hike, 'I'm sure RJ has some fascinating observations to share with us, but I feel that too much would be lost in an oral presentation. Don't you think it would be better if we were given the written report to study in more depth?'

'You're right,' agreed Earl, nodding vigorously. 'And I'm sure RJ would feel happier if his ideas were properly digested.'

RJ sniffed. He was not at all happy. Especially not at the very audible sigh of relief which greeted Sophie's suggestion.

'OK,' continued Earl, 'let's kick off with you, Sophie. And thanks, incidentally, for the copy of Bud's chart. I'm sure it'll come in very useful for the futures market. But next year, next month, next week, heck, even tomorrow is a helluva long way off.'

The assembled company laughed politely.

'So, Sophie, how are you calling it today?'

'Today, I reckon we should be trading platinum from a short position.' Sophie turned to Arthur, Drew and Martin, her colleagues on the desk. 'You agree, boys?' The team all nodded sagely. If Sophie said short, it was short. If Sophie said long, it was long. If Sophie had said, 'Hide under the desk like the Swiss if the going gets rough' (not that she was ever likely to), the boys would have done precisely that. Sophie possessed what everyone called 'the feel'.

'Everyone seems happy with that,' said Earl. 'Thanks, Sophie. Have a good morning's dealing.'

The telephone was already ringing as Sophie returned to her desk. From now until the European markets closed at 2.30 p.m. New York time the calls would be relentless: calls from customers trying to manage their price risk to platinum; calls from clients wanting to buy the physical, the actual metal, for immediate delivery; calls to and from other market professionals to sound out what was going on in the Street. And, of course, calls to Horneffer & Salzmann's brokers at NYMEX, the New York Mercantile Exchange, where the futures market traded. Sophie picked up the receiver. Today, just like any other day, there would be hundreds of calls like this.

'Hi, Sophie, Dick here. What are you calling it?'

'Hi, Dick. Three fifty-four at five.'

'Three fifty-four at five? OK, let me have a thousand ounces at three fifty-five.' One thousand ounces of platinum at three hundred and fifty-five dollars an ounce – Sophie made a careful note of the transaction in the sales column of her dealer sheet.

'Fine, Dick. See you later.'

'Thanks, Sophie. Bye for now.'

'Hi, Sophie, Hal here. How are you making it?'

'Hi, Hal, four at five.'

'Let me be sure on that one, Sophie. What's the big number?'

'Fifty.'

'OK, Sophie, I'll sell you five hundred ounces at three fifty-four.'

'OK, Hal. It's a deal. See you tomorrow.' Again, Sophie marked down the transaction on her sheet. Five hundred ounces of platinum purchased at three hundred and fifty-four dollars an ounce. Of course, the team policy today was to go short and sell. But as a market-maker, Sophie was always obliged to quote anyone a price. This morning, at $355, she was prepared to sell. At $354, she was obliged to buy. Of course, no one could ever know for sure what the market was going to do. During the course of the day, she and the boys would be constantly reviewing their policy and their prices.

'G'day, Sophie, Grant here.'

'Grant, is this business or bullshit? I'm a busy woman.'

'Language, Miss Weiss, language. Every one of these calls is taped, you realize.'

'Don't be so cheeky, you upstart Aussie,' said Sophie, trying hard to sound annoyed. 'Of course I do. And time-coded as well. Which means that you've just wasted sixty seconds dealing time for Horneffer & Salzmann.'

'Come, come, now, Sophie. This is a professional call, you know. Am I or am I not the New York Mercantile Exchange's number one trader?'

'You, Grant Foster,' said Sophie, endeavouring to keep her voice down, 'you are nothing but the New York Mercantile Exchange's ace bloody hoodlum. Apart from that,' she continued, trying and failing miserably to sound school-marmish, 'you really shouldn't be phoning me like this. I don't deal direct with traders, you know that. Horneffer & Salzmann's business at NYMEX is always conducted through the proper channels, via its usual brokers.'

'OK, Sophie, if that's the way you want it. Shall I tell my boss to give you a bell and ask you out for a pizza on my behalf? You're right, Sophie, darling. It's sound business practice. Let's bring in as many middlemen as possible.'

'Are you out of your bloody tree?' screeched Sophie. If Ricky di Virgilio ever got to hear that one his traders was after her, she'd be in for a terrible ribbing.

'Quite possibily,' said Grant. Oh, how he loved to wind Sophie up. Okker Aussie versus New York Jewish, it was such good sport. 'Me old ma always used to say I was a few chocolates short of the full box.'

At the next desk, Sophie could see her colleague, Drew, gesticulating wildly. 'Sophie, please. Can you cover me ten thousand ounces?

'Ten thousand ounces!' shouted Sophie, hardly bothering to shield the mouthpiece of her telephone. 'What the hell have you been playing at all morning? OK, I'll do my best.'

She returned to Grant. 'Look, Grant, I've got to go.'

'You don't seem to understand,' he replied, amused. God, it drove Sophie crazy to hear this guy laughing down the other end of the phone. 'I'm going to keep on pestering you for a date until you say yes. How about tonight?'

'OK, OK,' said Sophie, desperate to get him off the line.

'Shall I give you a ring when things have quietened down, say three o'clock, and we can take it from there?'

'Sure, yeah, anything,' said Sophie, trying to sound blasé and slamming down the phone.

At the other end of the line, Grant Foster smiled broadly to himself. 'She'll be right,' he said to no one in particular and, merrily whistling Stevie Wonder's song 'I Just Called To Say I Love You', returned to the trading pit.

If Sophie's heart was pounding, it had nothing to do with the stress of the morning's dealing. Why on earth had she agreed to go out with this lunatic Aussie character? From all that Sophie had been able to ascertain, he looked, behaved and sounded like nothing but monumental trouble. She could always get out of the date, of course, tell him she had to stay in the office until ten or eleven that evening to deal with the Tokyo calls. After all, it wasn't a lie. She often did. But that, Sophie realized, would only defer the issue. A man like Grant Foster was never going to take no for a definitive answer.

Without even realizing, Sophie started doodling in the margin of her dealing sheet. It was extraordinary. Under strain, she always came up with the same old doodles, sharply pointed Stars of David. Symbols of deep-seated aggression, one analyst had told her. Symbols of a deep-seated yearning for love and peace, said the next. It was at that point that Sophie gave up on analysis. For $300 an hour, she reckoned, who needed this kind of additional confusion?

Confusion. Despite her hard head in business, Sophie often felt confused. Perhaps that was why she took such refuge in work. Figures, at least, you could trust. They never lied or let you down. They did not discriminate against you if you were a woman or Jewish or both. Figures were neither macho nor anti-Semitic. Figures were never snobs.

But confusion, Sophie realized, was nothing but a smokescreen. What, she wondered, was the real issue she was so afraid to address? Perhaps, she conceded nervously, Grant Foster was right. Perhaps at that cocktail party, over those dry martinis in the Windows on the World restaurant, he had correctly deciphered the signals in her large, almond-shaped eyes. Suddenly, despite the air-conditioning, Sophie felt uncomfortably hot, a trifle dizzy even. It was hard to admit it, even to herself. But Sophie knew what the basic problem was. The basic problem was that she fancied this man like mad. Sophie traced another star. The turmoil of an emotional commitment? That was the last thing an ambitious young businesswoman needed in her life.

'Finished with your dealing sheet, Sophie?' asked Rose. Every half-hour or so throughout the course of the morning, Rose collected the sheets and ran them through the computer. The computer then printed out a contract for each transaction and settlement would be made within two working days. Considering the millions, sometimes even billions of dollars at stake, there were remarkably few mistakes. If ever a dispute arose, however, it could always be settled by reference to the recorded telephone conversations.

'Yes, thanks, Rose,' said Sophie, tearing off her sheet and handing it to the secretary.

'Thanks for bailing me out, Sophie,' shouted Drew, tidying his papers.

'Don't mention it, Drew. I'm not having you or anyone screwing up the desk's bonuses.' Sophie could never take a straight thank-you, as Drew was well aware.

'How did we end the day?'

'Slightly short,' said Sophie, 'which is fine. The price is falling. Are you off now?'

'Sure, Sophie. You want to come with us for a late lunch? The boys and I are thinking of having a bite at the Hors d'Oeuvrerie.'

Sophie shook her head. 'No, thanks all the same, Drew. I've still got some work to do here.'

'OK. Have a good afternoon. Bye, Sophie.'

'Bye, Drew. Bye, Martin. Don't drink too much tonight, Arthur. You know, the way you're going, you'll be all burned out by thirty.'

'Thirty? I'll consider myself a failure if I'm not all washed up by twenty-five.' The boys tumbled out of the office with the usual back-slapping and banter. It was so much easier for men, thought Sophie. Men were natural team players.

'Here's a cup of coffee.'

'Thanks, Rose,' said Sophie.

'You want a sandwich, honey?' Rose never stopped worrying about Sophie's erratic eating habits. Five years younger than Sophie, she had somehow assumed the role of mothering her boss. More than any other employee in the dealing room, Rose knew just how hard Sophie worked. Even a cursory glance at the dealing sheets showed that. On the platinum desk, Sophie did more business than the other three dealers put together.

'Would you? That'd be great.'

'Pastrami on rye, like always?'

'Please. And get one for yourself.' Sophie extracted a ten-dollar bill from her wallet and returned to her paperwork. The bumf was never-ending. She turned to the large stack of company reports still sitting in her in tray. Perhaps her mother was right, after all. Perhaps she should let up a little, have a bit more fun. Sure, she was making a fortune. But sometimes life seemed nothing but work punctuated by the odd chicken or pastrami sandwich.

The phone rang on the dot of three o'clock.

'G'day, Sophie. It's the toast of Kalgoorlie here.'

'Hi, Grant.' Sophie could not suppress a smile. That summed Grant Foster up. Trust him to choose a mining town famed exclusively for gold and brothels.

'I take it, darling, that this evening is still on? You wouldn't want me putting it around that the pride of Horneffer & Salzmann has reneged on a deal?'

'No, I wouldn't,' snapped Sophie, again trying to sound annoyed. 'But I swear, Grant, if you continue to call me "darling", I'll put the word out around NYMEX that you've started to lose your edge.'

'Jeez, Sophie, are we organizing a bloody date or an outbreak of hostilities?'

'I'm sorry,' said Sophie, relenting. God, why was she being so ridiculously awkward? She was worse than an adolescent at her first high school ball. 'I'd love to come out with you this evening, Grant, but first I've got a pile of reading to do this afternoon. And before I go off razzling with you, I've got to go home and feed my cat.'

'Christ, Sophie. Sounds like you lead a fairly hectic social life.'

'Go take a hike, Foster!'

'That's the kind of talk I like. Tell you what, Sophie. I'll come round and fetch you from the office at six. Then I'll take you home to see the tiger. After that, you can decide where you want to go and eat. You name the place. I've had a very good month.'

'D'you think I'd be seen dead in that bloody contraption of yours?' snapped Sophie and immediately felt ashamed. God, why couldn't she just level with the guy. Grant's bright yellow 'ute' had nothing to do with it. In fact, she thought it was hysterical. But the truth of the matter was, her apartment was such a mess. Old letters and photographs all over the floor. And then there was Ernie. Since his operation there had been a few unfortunate accidents. Particularly on the off-white sofa.

'Don't go insulting Mathilda,' said Grant, pretending to be offended. 'She's the best utility truck in New York. Come on, Sophie, loosen up. I'm only trying to be helpful.'

There was something about his voice, so friendly and unpretentious, that struck a chord with Sophie. He was right. Why was she being so goddamn prissy? 'I'm sorry, Grant,' she said, 'I know you are. But my apartment is such a shambles at the moment. I was up most of last night sorting through some old family photos, trying to trace my long-lost uncle Simon. Everything's still all over the place.'

'A long-lost uncle Simon?' Grant whistled. 'I like the sound of him. I've got a long-lost uncle Simon myself. He went walkabouts after he won the Queensland state lotto and was never seen again.'

'How terrible!'

'Not for him, Sophie,' chuckled Grant. 'You never met my aunt Sharleen.'

'You're insufferable.' Sophie relented. 'OK, you can come so long as you promise to close your eyes while I feed the cat. And I must warn you that Ernie, the cat, has not been – how shall I say? – very well recently. It's just possible he's not been very well again today.'

'Sophie, d'you honestly think a bloke who's sheared sheep and branded cattle is going to worry about a bit of cat crap on the carpet? I'll clean it up myself, if it bothers you, darling. I always find a drop of Hunter Valley Chardonnay works wonders on biological stains.'

By now Sophie had even forgiven Grant the 'darling'. 'I'll tell you what,' she said. 'I guess now I think about it, I am kind of worried about Ernie. How would you feel if I organized a take-home Chinese and we can eat tonight at my apartment?'

'I see,' said Grant. 'So first of all the place is such a shithouse, I'm not allowed to see it. Then all of a sudden it's so fair dinkum, I'm invited around for dinner.'

'Language, Mr Foster,' said Sophie, recalling their earlier conversation and trying to mimick Grant's Australian accent. 'Every one of these calls is taped, you realize.' Both of them dissolved into laughter.

'I'll drop by for you at six,' said Grant, his voice suddenly subdued. 'Believe me, Sophie, I'm really looking forward to this evening.'

When Rose returned with the sandwiches, she was surprised to find Sophie painting her nails.

'That's a pretty colour,' said Rose, picking up the bottle of Dior's Rouge Explosif.

'Yes,' said Sophie. 'I bought it over six months ago and it's been sitting in my desk drawer ever since. Somehow I just never got around to putting it on. I reckon it's high time I gave it an airing.'

Rose stared at Sophie. In the last fifteen minutes she seemed to have undergone a major transformation. She was always pretty, of course, with those bright almond eyes and that olive skin. But right now she looked positively ravishing. 'Here's your sandwich,' said Rose, depositing a large brown paper bag on the top of Sophie's in tray. 'And your change.'

'Thanks.'

Sophie finished her nails, ate her sandwich and returned to her mound of documents. Sitting back in her chair, she put her feet up on the desk and continued to read about Metallinc.

CHAPTER FIFTEEN

London, Summer 1984

IT WAS a sultry June evening in London's Covent Garden. Already the Royal Opera House was boiling.

'I do so love it here,' enthused Andrea, her eyes shining. Smiling, Charles helped his fiancée to her seat in their grand circle box. Carefully, Andrea arranged the folds of her mauve silk Emmanuelle gown. Off the shoulder and with a deeply plunging neckline, it showed her small shapely breasts to full advantage. She had worn it especially to impress Roger Samson.

'You're looking exceptionally pretty this evening,' said Charles. He felt proud of his protégée, a little as Professor Higgins must have felt about Eliza Doolittle. Andrea was such a willing learner, so young and malleable. And so very clever. In the end, people would see how wrong they had been to misjudge her. After all, it was not her fault she had never had the privileges of wealth and position. Eventually they would understand, as he had understood, that she had been sucked, despite herself, into the sleazy tabloid game. Thank goodness that was all behind her now.

'Thank you, darling,' replied Andrea, looking up. 'What time are you expecting Roger?'

'Oh, any time now. I told him to arrive about a quarter of an hour before the curtain.'

There was a knock at the door and an elderly waitress came

bustling in with a champagne bucket. 'Put it over there, would you?' ordered Andrea abruptly.

'Yes, please,' said Charles, slightly embarrassed. Dear girl. It was her youth, of course. But sometimes – Charles was sure she didn't mean it – she could sound so offhand.

Roger arrived with Simonetta just as the waitress was leaving the box. Andrea caught her breath. God, the photographs did not even start to do him justice. Roger Samson was the most attractive man she had ever seen.

'Charles, how wonderful to see you,' said Roger, shaking Charles warmly by the hand.

'And you, Roger.' Charles kissed Simonetta on the cheek. 'I'm so glad you both could make it. Roger, you're such a difficult man to pin down nowadays. Come. This is Andrea Blackwell, the woman I'm going to marry.'

Even with her back now turned to the audience, Andrea was aware of the hundreds of pairs of eyes suddenly trained upon the box. She felt a sudden wave of envy. Yes, Andrea was certainly pretty. But Simonetta in her simple black Azzedine Alaïa dress, with its high neck and scooped out back, was in a completely different league.

'Hi,' said Simonetta, automatically kissing Andrea on both cheeks. It was a classic society kiss – no lip contact, just a gentle brushing of makeup bases.

Christ, thought Andrea, catching a glimpse of Simonetta's spine. You could see every single vertebra. And those shoulder blades? They were so sharp, they looked as if you could carve a joint of beef with them. Anorexic, decided Andrea smugly. Fabulous on the catwalk, but far too skinny in the flesh. 'How do you do,' she replied primly. Simonetta's unfocused gaze wandered off to the champagne bucket. Andrea's eyes kept on her. She had interviewed too many pop stars and sportsmen in her time not to recognize the symptoms. Unless she was very much mistaken, Simonetta Bonino was already well away on the recreational pharmaceuticals. Andrea felt a sudden frisson as Roger touched her arm.

'You're a very lucky man, Charles,' said Roger, his extraordinary blue eyes boring deep into Andrea's, amused yet impossibly distant. Andrea giggled nervously, her recently acquired composure completely destroyed. Those high, sculpted cheekbones, that arrogant, handsome face – Roger Samson positively radiated sexual energy. No wonder his girlfriend was as high as a kite. A man like Roger Samson would be impossible to hold. He must be making her very miserable.

'Yes, I know,' said Charles, dispensing champagne. 'Come, we have so many things to celebrate tonight. Here's to my forthcoming wedding. To Samson International's successful flotation. To Simonetta's latest contract with Nec Plus Ultra cosmetics. And to W&S Communications, a subsidiary of my own W&S, and my future wife's new public relations company.'

They all joined him in the toast.

'Tell me more,' said Roger, never once taking his eyes off Andrea. 'How long has W&S Communications been in operation?'

'Oh, for a few months now,' replied Charles, happy that Roger was taking an interest in Andrea's business. 'It took us some time to get the right team together. But I already owned the offices so that was no problem. And we have the chairman. All we need now are a few high-profile clients to help us on our way.'

'Did you ever get the feeling that you were being targeted?' laughed Roger.

'Got it in one, old chap,' said Charles quietly. Roger knew that he owed Charles in a score of ways: Samson International would never have been where it was today without Charles's help and contacts. Why shouldn't Roger do him a favour?

'As it happens,' said Roger, suddenly more serious, 'we have about four PR companies working for us at the moment and I can't say that I'm over the moon about any of them. All the same, I think W&S will need some time before it's in a position to deal with a company of Samson International's scope.'

'I'm well aware of that,' said Charles.

How interesting, thought Andrea, fanning herself with a programme. So this was how real business was conducted. At the opera, in the club, on the golf course, at the cricket match – one minute it was idle gossip, the next minute a deal had been struck.

'But we're not talking specialized financial public relations at the moment,' he continued. 'W&S may or may not decide to go into that area of the market. But there are still fields, far more nebulous fields, where a fledgling PR company might stretch its wings and learn to fly.'

'Do you know?' said Roger brightly. 'I think I have just the thing.'

'Yes?' interrupted Andrea, annoyed now at being marginalized in the conversation. It was all right for Simonetta. By the look of her, her mind was already floating somewhere in the stratosphere. But these men were talking about W&S Communications which, after all, was *her* company. Of course, Charles was doing his best to get her started – for which she was very grateful. But in future, vowed Andrea, no man was ever going to talk over *her* head!

'Yes,' replied Roger, immediately turning his attention to the small petulant figure staring up at him. 'I need someone to deal with my own personal PR.'

Andrea nodded vigorously. 'I see,' she said.

'Yes,' said Roger, laughing. 'I need to be protected from columnists like you.'

'Come now,' said Charles defensively. 'I'm sure Andrea never wrote anything deliberately unkind or unfair about anyone in her life.'

Poor old Charles, thought Roger, he really must be in love. Even so, he wouldn't talk like that if he'd ever read the *Courier* when Andrea was still at her vitriolic best.

'Of course not,' he conceded. 'All the same, I do think the best poachers often make the best gamekeepers. I don't know if you can possibly understand, Andrea, but I'm tired of being quizzed and hassled about details of my private life, my family and my past.' Roger knew he'd hit the mark. It was always as well to come armed with a little prior research. Andrea Blackwell, of all people, would understand just how inconvenient antecedents could be.

'I take your point,' agreed Andrea demurely. 'But, of course, when you're a figure of public interest, it's almost impossible to stop journalists asking difficult questions.'

'Oh, the gentlemen of the press must be allowed to ask all the awkward questions they wish,' replied Roger, smiling his disturbingly flint-eyed smile. 'But they must be helped to end up with all the right answers. The answers, that is, that *I* want them to have.'

'I'm not sure I understand,' said Charles, taking his seat next to Andrea.

'Of course you do,' said Roger. 'Media manipulation by any other name. Happens all the time. Look at Mrs Thatcher, the image-creation job the PR boys have done on her. OK, Andrea, if you think you can manage it, I'd like that to be your first assignment for Samson International. I want you to organize *my* media image for *me*.'

'But the Prime Minister always says that it's issues not personalities that count,' interrupted Charles, loyally.

'Absolutely,' agreed Roger, sitting down with Simonetta. 'That's precisely what I believe myself. And that's why I want the media to concentrate on Samson International the company, not on Roger Samson the man. After all, I'm just a businessman, working for my shareholders, not a pop star flirting with my fans.'

'Really?' said Simonetta, suddenly roused from her reverie. 'If you ask me, it sounds as if there's something about yourself you want to hide.'

Charles and Andrea laughed politely. Roger smiled as well, a forced, humourless smile revealing his perfect teeth. Simonetta felt a sudden draught down the entire length of her spine. She had seen that look before and she knew precisely what it meant. Roger never forgave anyone anything, especially not indiscretion.

'I think they're about to start,' said Charles, making himself comfortable. 'I must say, Simonetta, I'm a great admirer of your fellow countryman, Puccini.'

'So am I,' replied Simonetta, grateful for Charles's good manners, 'and of all his operas, *La Bohème* has always been my favourite.'

Poverty and garrets, thought Andrea dismissively. Only people who could afford the opera enjoyed watching that sort of existence depicted on stage. Gradually, Andrea's attention began to wander. What a wonderful profile that Roger Samson had, classic – apart from that interesting bump on the nose. Probably something to do with a woman, mused Andrea idly.

'Che gelida manina' – 'Your tiny hand is frozen' – oh, no,

thought Andrea, still sipping her champagne, as if it wasn't bad enough being poor. Now the heroine, Mimi, has to be terminally consumptive as well! In the darkness of the box, Andrea was aware of Charles attempting to hold her hand. Andrea grimaced. Why did he always have to be so sentimental and sloppy? It wouldn't matter so much if he could get it up in bed. But Charles's problem in that department was getting, if anything, worse. Swiftly Andrea picked up her opera glasses and studied the set.

Roger Samson smiled. Not one move was lost on him. Poor Charles. He was far too honest and decent to see through a woman like Andrea. Roger studied her dispassionately, much as he would appraise a horse. She was pretty. She was sexy. And from what he could ascertain, she was certainly bright and ambitious. Yes, it was a lethal combination – for a man of Charles's beliefs and standards, possibly the ultimate draught of hemlock. What was it George Hamish had said to Roger only the other day? 'When an older man marries a much younger wife, he's generally a goner in business.' Already Charles was doing stupid things to impress his future wife, and she was making demands and diverting far too much of his attention.

'Mi chiamano Mimi' – Andrea was becoming progressively more irritated. Why couldn't Charles stop trying to maul her? God, it would be a different story if she were lucky enough to find Roger Samson's hand in her lap. Andrea caught Roger's eye as the lights in the box went up for the interval. She blushed immediately. That bastard must have been watching her thoughout the entire act! Roger smiled a knowing smile. Oh, yes, he understood Andrea Blackwell all right. It was as if he'd known her for ever. It was not often in life one came across a totally kindred spirit.

'I'm sorry,' Simonetta was weeping loudly as the final curtain fell, 'but I can't help it. It's so very, very sad.'

'Yes, my dear, I know,' said Charles, handing Simonetta a large white handkerchief. Tragic enough in its own right, *La Bohème* had acquired additional emotional overtones since

Lydia's untimely death. Charles struggled to master his feelings.

'Right, then,' said Andrea brightly, 'enough weeping and gnashing of teeth. Who'd like some more champagne?' Roger looked at her in amusement. Apart from his and Andrea's, there wasn't a dry eye in the entire Royal Opera House.

'Andrea, my dear,' said Charles, disappointment written all over his face, 'didn't you enjoy it?'

'Yes, of course I did,' replied Andrea breezily. 'It was fine. Although I must say, I did prefer *Così Fan Tutte* the other week.'

'Yes, I can see that you would,' said Roger pointedly. Dangerous liaisons and infidelity, that seemed far more the style of a woman like Andrea.

'Here you are, Charles,' blustered Andrea, turning scarlet once again, 'here's a glass for you. Oh, come now, Simonetta. Your mascara is running all over your face. You wouldn't want the *paparazzi* to catch you looking like that, would you? It'd do the Nec Plus Ultra smear-proof mascara claims no good whatsoever.'

Charles would not have looked more astounded if the Royal Box had just collapsed. 'Andrea, please. Simonetta is upset. Here my dear, here's another handkerchief. I've always said they ought to provide a box of tissues free with every ticket to *La Bohème*.'

'Heaven preserve us from hysterical Italians,' said Andrea under her breath.

'Where are we having dinner?' asked Roger.

'I believe Charles has booked us a table at Le Gavroche,' replied Andrea. God, if only she were having a quiet *tête-à-tête* supper with Roger Samson, now that would be something worth getting worked up about.

'Excellent,' said Roger, draining the remains of his champagne, 'I have my car waiting outside.'

'Yes, so is ours,' said Charles. Simonetta had noted Roger's choice of pronoun.

'Good. We'll see you there. I'm looking forward to progressing my relationship with W&S Communications.'

A slow, self-satisfied smile spread over Andrea's face. She

might have been from Grimford, Essex, but no come-on, however playful, was ever wasted on her.

Down in the foyer, Hugo Newsom had been separated from his companion in the crush. 'Lilah,' he shouted above the exiting mass, 'I'm sorry, it's impossible to get over there. I'll see you outside in the street.'

'Fine,' replied Lilah, looking ravishing in a long red silk gown. Coming slowly down the stairs, Roger Samson suddenly caught sight of this tall, elegant woman, who seemed to be head and shoulders above the crowd. Now that, he said to himself appreciatively, is one exceedingly beautiful lady.

PART II

1987–90

CHAPTER SIXTEEN

Summer 1987

'WHY don't you run along and find Naomi?' suggested the boy's mother wearily. She had seemed so tired of late. Perhaps it had something to do with that strange lump that seemed to be growing in her tummy. 'She should be back from church by now. I'm sure she'll find something interesting for you to do.'

He clattered down the stairs and out into the blinding sunshine. The house boasted a large sprawling garden, about three acres in all and a source of constant wonderment to him. The long, rainless Transvaal winters would leave it brown and dusty, but then the spring and summer would come and bring a mass of shapes and colours. His mother was an avid gardener and already he had learned the names of the trees by heart. He loved the wistaria tree near the stoop, and the old weeping wattle, with its delicate yellow flowers and its off-white sapwood. Sometimes he would collect the bright red fruits of the sourplum tree which his mother made into delicious jelly or jam. Often he would climb the wild mango trees to pick golden-yellow fruits before they fell.

He tore himself a whippy stick from the spineless monkey tree and ambled on his way, noisily thrashing the ground as he walked. Naomi was always warning him to take this basic precaution. Once she had almost stumbled on a poisonous green mamba, asleep in the garden, and had come screaming into the kitchen. Since then she had shown him tiger snakes and chameleons and told him to beware. Occasionally, if she had time during her busy working day, she would recount tales of sidewinder snakes and barking geckos, of springbok, bushbuck, kudu and wildebeest. Open-mouthed and silent, he would gladly have listened to her for days on end.

The servants' quarters were situated at the far end of the garden, well out of sight of the main house. He could hear the screams as he entered the compound. He ran over to Naomi's hut from where the noise appeared to be coming, and stopped cold in his tracks. Above the din he could hear his father's voice, shouting angrily, 'Come here, you little black bitch.'

The boy's blood froze. How he hoped his father wasn't beating Naomi. He'd seen the keloid scar tissue left on Tom the gardener's back from the thrashing the boy's father had once given him with his rhinoceros-hide *sjambok*. Shivering in the sunshine, he recalled how his mother had screamed, begging her husband for pity's sake to stop. But it only seemed to make things worse.

'No, *baas*, no. Please. It's not right.'

He crept silently over to the hut. Balancing precariously on an empty crate, he peered in through the window. Through the red dust and grime he could see Naomi, her Sunday-best pinafore dress torn from shoulder to hip, her white cotton blouse gaping open to reveal her firm round teenage breasts. His father lunged, catching her by her corn-beaded hair, and throwing her roughly to the ground. 'Wait till I get hold of you, you little whore. You know you want it. You want nothing else, you wicked black fornicating devils. Come here, I'll teach you a lesson.'

Naomi rolled over under the table. 'No, *baas*, please. You know it's wrong. It's a sin.'

He watched as his father grabbed Naomi by the neck and dragged her roughly from under the table. There was a hollow thud as her head smashed against the table leg. Blood poured from the gaping wound in her temple. He felt he wanted to be sick.

'You little whore. You dare talk to me about sin. There can be no sin against you people. You don't exist like we exist in the eyes of the Lord. You're no better than the beasts of burden that plough the field. I can do what I like with you.'

He stood there, rooted to the spot. He had heard his father rage like this before. His mother said it was something to do with the war, but what she would never explain.

His father started to unbuckle the belt of his trousers. Oh, no, he *was* going to beat her after all. He could hardly bear to look. Then his father did something quite extraordinary. He kicked off his shoes and removed his trousers and underpants together. Next his father pulled off his shirt and stood there completely naked. What was that angry red thing, pointing up to his belly button? Naomi screamed even louder. His father seized her dress and blouse and brutally tore them from her shoulders.

'No, *baas*,' she cried hysterically, 'I'm only sixteen. I never been with a man before.' Wildly she lashed out, tearing into the side of his father's face.

'Then you better start getting used to it,' he shouted, pinning Naomi's bare shoulders against the floor.

'Please, no, I'll tell the madam.'

There was a crack as his father brought the flat of his hand down heavily against Naomi's jaw. 'You fucking bitch. You dare to do any such thing and I'll beat you till you're raw. I'll show you who's master around here.'

Suddenly he felt horribly dizzy. Roughly his father pulled Naomi's panties down to her ankles. Raising himself on his elbows, he started pushing himself into the darkness between Naomi's shaking legs. She screamed out in pain. Surely he must be killing her? What should he do? Naomi was crying out loud, blood and tears running down her face. His father was still pushing himself into her, harder and faster, making a slap-slap sound. Then suddenly his father shuddered violently and collapsed lifeless and heavy on top of Naomi. Please, please let him be dead. Please let him stop hurting Naomi.

Naomi looked up from her tormentor and saw the boy peering in through the window. 'Please, *kleinbaas*, little master, go away!' she shouted tearfully and immediately regretted it.

'Come here!' yelled his father, jumping up suddenly and reaching for his trousers. But already he was off into the *veldt*, as fast as he could run. He was far too frightened to return home. His heart felt as if it might explode as on he ran and ran. But still he could hear his father's voice, angrily calling after him, 'Roger! Roger! Come here, you little bastard!'

He awoke with a start.

'Roger, Roger, what is it? Please, please wake up. You're having another of your nightmares.' Simonetta wiped the beads of sweat from Roger's tense and corrugated forehead.

'Don't ever do that,' snapped Roger, pushing her away. Simonetta flinched. 'How often do I have to tell you? I'm perfectly all right. There's absolutely nothing wrong with me. I'm just concerned about the planning permission for the Samson International Hotel in Tokyo, that's all. Negotiations are far more long drawn out than I'd imagined.'

Yes, thought Simonetta, and the bribes far more expensive. She had heard all about Japanese politicians from Fujiko, her masseuse. 'Of course,' she said soothingly. How she wished he would confide in her, tell her what was really going on in that handsome head of his.

'You're leaving for Paris today, aren't you?' asked Roger, deftly changing the subject.

'Yes, on the three forty-five flight this afternoon. I'll be there all week for the couture collections.'

Roger nodded vaguely. He seemed in a world of his own. Simonetta sighed. She was finding it increasingly difficult to communicate with him on even the most superficial of levels.

'Then I'm sure you have a lot of packing to do,' replied Roger, abruptly jumping out of bed. 'Perhaps you'd like to get started.'

'But Roger! It's only five o'clock!'

'Don't worry. I'll drive you home myself.' Roger headed for his bathroom, giving her no chance to protest. Anyway, experience had shown her that there was absolutely no point in arguing with him. Her position in his life was precarious enough already. Slowly she rolled out of bed and started looking for her handbag. She was nothing more to Roger Samson than an enviable accessory. There she was, alongside his Hermès ties, his Alan Flusser suits and his Turnbull & Asser shirts. Beautiful, yes – expensive, certainly – but for a man like Roger, totally and instantly replaceable.

Simonetta opened her handbag and searched for the small,

round silver box Fujiko had bought in Mexico. Sleepily she struggled to open it with her long, immaculate nails. A few flecks of the fine white powder spilled onto Roger's dark green carpet. Quickly, she rubbed them into the pile with the ball of her foot. Cocaine. For Simonetta it was just like Roger Samson. A dangerous addiction, and one that – try as she might – she could not summon the will to conquer.

The road from Regent's Park to Hampstead was completely deserted. Roger's face was expressionless as they drove silently along in his brand new Ferrari Testarossa. It was with obvious relief that he deposited Simonetta outside her quaint Flask Walk home.

'Cup of coffee?' she asked as Roger helped her out of the car.

'No, thanks.' He brushed her cheek with the barest of kisses. 'I think I'll go straight to the office. There's a lot going on at the moment.'

'Shall I ring you tonight from Paris?'

'No, don't bother. I don't know what time I'll be home – probably very late.'

'I'll be at the Samson International as usual. Perhaps you could give me a call there – you know, to wish me luck before the show.'

'Sure.' From the tone of his voice, Simonetta knew he wouldn't.

'*Va bene*. See you when I'm back, then.'

Already Roger was fastening his seat belt. As the car roared off, he could see Simonetta in the rear-view mirror, still standing on the pavement like an oddly affluent waif. She was becoming too demanding and dependent, he thought, far too much of a liability. Then there was that silly little habit of hers. It was like George Hamish and his booze. Roger despised that sort of weakness. But George was his finance director and, at least for the time being, extremely useful. Simonetta was a different proposition. A woman whose face was her fortune would always be a depreciating asset. Yes, mused Roger clinically, Simonetta had served her purpose. She had helped attract the sort of publicity he'd wanted at the time. But now he was no longer a hustler. He was chairman of a major public company. Simonetta was no longer part of the squeaky-clean image he wanted to project. She would cut up rough, he expected. But he could deal with that. Now it really was time for her to go.

Roger turned on his stereo and inserted a Tina Turner cassette.

> What's love got to do, got to do with it?
> What's love but a second-hand emotion?

The traffic lights at Swiss Cottage seemed to be stuck on red for ages. Roger tapped impatiently on the steering wheel. He must get into his office and start working, writing, phoning – anything. Anything to blot out the memories. Anything to stop the nightmares crowding in again.

> What's love got to do, got to do with it?
> Who needs a heart when a heart can be broken?

The lights turned green as Roger, already in first, put his foot down on the accelerator. Action, power, money, business, they all helped. But sometimes even they were not enough to obliterate the past. The early-morning sunshine dazzled him as he raced through Regent's Park.

It was then that it finally hit him, he could no longer fend it off. Ensconced in the black leather upholstery, he felt the same old nagging pain beginning to spread through the small of his back. Desperately, Roger clung onto the steering wheel for support. But the vision was too strong, too pressing. It refused to go away.

The small boy lay prostrate and motionless, face down in the dust, his back a raw and bloody mess where the *sjambok* had torn savagely into the flesh. It was swelteringly hot, and already the flies had started to settle in the wounds, further adding to the child's torment. Standing over him, his father was still raving violently. 'You little bastard, I'll teach you to run away from home! I'll teach you to go telling tales to your mother!'

The boy was no longer listening to him. The pain was so

unbearable he thought he was going to die. Vaguely, from her room in the house, he could hear his mother crying, 'Please, please, for the love of God, stop it!' And out of the corner of his eye, he could see his nanny, Naomi, cowering terrified behind a beech tree. It was then that the boy lost consciousness.

The next thing he knew he was in his bedroom, his mother and Naomi both sobbing over his bed. He wished the pair of them would leave him alone in his agony and humiliation. Women – where were they when you really needed them? They were such pathetic, unreliable and ineffectual creatures. Let them all go to hell!

'Roger, darling, can you hear me?' The boy glanced up from his pillow. What a look! It was like a stiletto through his mother's heart. Gone that childlike sparkle, the glow of trust and love. She sank to her knees. 'Oh, God, Roger, what has he done to you?' Something, she knew, had been beaten to death. The light had gone out. Never before had the woman seen eyes like that. Piercing, bright and icy blue, they were chillingly devoid of feeling.

CHAPTER SEVENTEEN

London, Summer 1987

GEORGE HAMISH should have been a happy man. The flotation
of Samson International on the London Stock Exchange had
been an enormous success. As finance director of the company,
he had every right to bask in much of the reflected glory.
George took a long, slow draw on yet another nine-inch Davidoff cigar. The trouble was, he wasn't feeling any of these
emotions. If anything, he was feeling distinctly ill at ease. The
last few years at Samson International had been tremendously
exciting, far more exciting than those heady days of the early
seventies at London & Hong Kong Properties, but George
could not go on while these niggling doubts assailed him.
There were things that even smoke and alcohol could not
suppress for ever.

Sitting in his luxurious new office on the twentieth floor of
Samson Heights, George considered a Scotch. No, he decided,
it was only ten o'clock in the morning and, besides, he would
need all his wits about him to pin Roger down. Wearily he
dialled the number.

'Good morning, the chairman's office.' George recognized
the familiar voice of the unimpeachable Miss Kerwin.

'Good morning, Miss Kerwin. George Hamish here. Is the
chairman in? I'd like to see him on a matter of some urgency.'

Sally Kerwin was fond of George. Despite his little drinking
problem, he was one of the old school, invariably polite to her
even in his cups. 'Yes, Mr Hamish, Mr Samson is in. He's

been at his desk since seven thirty this morning. If you can just hold on, I'll ask when he can see you.'

George took another long draw on his cigar, idly watching the rings of smoke dispersing into the air. Up in a puff of smoke – what a wonderfully apposite image for what he was about to do. Had he come this far with Samson International to jeopardize everything now?

Miss Kerwin was back on the line. 'Hello. Mr Hamish? Mr Samson can see you immediately.'

Roger stood up behind his desk and greeted George with a handshake. 'Come,' he said affably, 'let's sit over there on the sofas. More comfortable, don't you think? Coffee?'

'No, thanks,' said George. There was too much to get off his chest. He didn't want any unnecessary interruptions.

'And how are Madeleine and the children? Chloë happy to be going to Benenden? And I suppose by now Peter must have settled down at Winchester?'

'Fine, they're all fine,' replied George tonelessly. Yes, you had to give him credit for that. Roger always made the right noises.

'Share price up again this morning,' said Roger, smiling. 'I must say, George, you're doing a wonderful job. So what can I do for you? Miss Kerwin implied you had something on your mind.'

George took a deep breath. 'I've loved it here at Samson International,' he started uneasily, 'and, believe me, Roger, I'll always be very grateful for the opportunities you've given me. Whatever happens, I do assure you, you can rely on my complete support and integrity.' George fumbled awkwardly for another cigar. Roger's smile did not waver.

'I'm happy to hear that, George. Yes, we've come a long way together, you and I. And there are still higher peaks to conquer.'

George coughed nervously. He could prevaricate no longer. 'It's about Metallinc, our mining subsidiary,' he finally blurted out. 'I was doing a bit of ferreting around, and I discovered that Metallinc has been exporting platinum to the United Kingdom, the United States and Germany since the early seventies.'

'Yes,' said Roger, icily charming. 'I've never made any secret about that. You know as well as I do that I used the cash generated by the Meroto mine to buy and develop our Dock-lands sites. Mind you, without your help and expertise, I'd probably never have taken the gamble.'

George could feel Roger ever so deftly slithering away. Thank God he had not had a drink this morning. This was going to be a difficult one. 'Yes,' he agreed, slightly irritated, 'I'm aware of all that. Of course I know that some of the Metallinc cash was used on Docklands. But not all of it. In fact, quite a substantial amount – I have the precise figures in my office – has never been accounted for.'

'I see,' said Roger, standing up deliberately and walking over to the window. 'Odd, isn't it, George, that not one of the swarms of auditors in here during the flotation managed to pick that up?'

George puffed uncomfortably on his cigar. 'Oh, come on, Roger,' he wheezed. He could already feel the palpitations. 'You know as well as I do that any finance director worth his salt can camouflage the odd hundred thousand pounds – or even the odd million – when it's absolutely necessary.'

'Of course,' replied Roger, staring out over the Thames.

'Besides,' continued George breathlessly, 'it wasn't as if I had to lie outright to anybody. Property profits have so far outstripped earnings from minerals and mining that Metallinc has now been virtually relegated to a footnote in the accounts. Nobody even queried it.'

'So why not let sleeping dogs lie?' Roger still had his back to George.

'Because that's not the only thing that's worrying me.'

'Oh?' A sharp note had entered Roger's voice. George felt embarrassed.

'I was in the Reform the other night,' he continued, 'having a drink with an old friend.'

'Really, you surprise me.'

George ignored the obvious sarcasm. 'According to him, the rumour's going around in the City that Samson International's planning permissions have been helped along by systematic bribery and corruption.'

'Well, you would have to know more about that than I do, wouldn't you? After all, you are the finance director. And the money for all these backhanders must have come from somewhere in the company.'

'But I never—'

'Who can ever prove or disprove anything? Your word against mine. Perhaps you were too drunk to notice what you may or may not have done. And what was it you just said, very interesting I thought, something about any finance director worth his salt being able to camouflage the odd hundred thousand pounds, or even the odd million, if absolutely necessary? Claims like that wouldn't look too good if ever they came out in public, now would they?' George looked stunned. Arguing with Roger was like trying to box Marquess of Queensbury rules with an adversary wielding a flick-knife.

'Are you trying to blackmail me?'

'Blackmail you?' said Roger, turning to face George and flashing him his most dazzling smile. 'Why, George, we're old friends. We made this company together. We wouldn't want to go spoiling anything now, would we? Not when everything is going so incredibly well – for all of us.'

George bowed his head in utter fatigue. What had he got himself into?

'Now then,' continued Roger smoothly, 'I realize you've been operating under the most terrible strain for the last few months. And I do think you're in desperate need of a break. So why don't you take Madeleine and the kids off for a holiday, somewhere nice and warm? The rest will do you good. And in the meantime, before you go, do tell me if there's anything else that's bothering you. If not, I really must be getting back to work.' Roger walked back to his desk and, ignoring George, started to read some papers.

George felt the palpitations beating louder and louder. Pinning Roger down was like trying to catch a flash of lightning with your bare hands – dangerous even to contemplate and disastrous if you succeeded. 'Yes, there is something else,' he shouted angrily, his strict Scottish Presbyterian upbringing finally bubbling to the surface. 'My friend at the Reform tells me that the Samson International Hotel in Park Lane is involved in organized upmarket prostitution.'

'Dear me, George,' laughed Roger superciliously, 'you really are consorting with the most dubious company.'

'For God's sake, Roger, the man's a QC.'

'Tut tut. You can't trust anyone nowadays.'

'Stop it!' shouted George, lurching towards Roger's desk. 'Stop dodging the bloody issue. I can't stand it any more. Tell me, is it or is it not true?' Suddenly George felt dizzy. Heavily, he sank into the green leather armchair by Roger's desk.

'Come now,' said Roger solicitously, getting up to pour George a tumbler of mineral water. 'Calm down. You're making yourself ill. Now please drink this.'

George sipped it slowly. 'It's no good, Roger. I can't go on like this. I must know everything that's going on in this company.'

'Oh, must you, now?' replied Roger, on the attack once more. 'We've been working together for four, almost five years now, and suddenly you need to know everything that's going on. For God's sake, George, grow up, will you? How the hell do you suppose Samson International has achieved all it has achieved in such a short space of time?'

'But I had no—'

'No. You had no idea. So long as you had your massive fucking salary and your unlimited expense account you weren't too interested in anything else.'

'That's not—'

'No, now you let me finish. When I met you, you were going absolutely nowhere.'

'Yes, but—'

'Yes, but nothing. You were grateful for the opportunity to get back into the property business. Do you remember, you were wondering what kind of high-flyer would take a chance with a clapped-out old has-been like you? Your words, as I recall, old boy, not mine.'

'And I never let you down. I've worked myself to a standstill for Samson International.'

'And I'd be the first to admit it,' said Roger soothingly.

George continued to sip his water. God, talk about the hard and soft approach. One minute you were being beaten senseless, the next you were being offered one of your favourite cigarettes. George had seen it work with other people on countless previous occasions. It was this state of constant tension, never knowing what was going to happen next, that eventually wore them down. George sighed chestily. Already, he was feeling punch-drunk.

Roger poured him another tumbler of water, 'Yes,' he continued smoothly, 'and so far we've done extremely well together as a team.'

'I know. That's why I must—'

Suddenly Roger became impatient. 'George!' he shouted angrily, slamming his fist down hard on the desk, 'I didn't want to have to spell this out to you, but you leave me with no option. There's all the difference in the world between spotting the deals and having the balls to do them. The world is full of details-men like you. If it comes to the crunch, you're all dispensable – every single bloody one of you. It's men like me who make companies like Samson International happen.'

George stared into his water, totally destroyed. Roger was right. After all, it was men with guts who created empires, not pusillanimous pen-pushers like himself.

Roger smiled emolliently. 'How old are you?'

'Forty-seven,' said George quietly.

'Not a good time of life to be thinking of moving on, now, is it?'

'No, Roger, I wasn't thinking of—'

'No, I'm sure you weren't. I assume you're happy with your salary here. A hundred and fifty thousand a year – not bad really, is it?'

'I've never comp—'

'And your interest in Samson International – five per cent, isn't it, since we went public? Not an inconsiderable shareholding, you know, for someone who's never staked a penny of his own money in the company.'

'But I always intended—'

'I know, George. I know everything. I know, for instance, that almost five years ago, Charles Watson-Smith put ten million pounds' worth of property into Samson International in return for five per cent of the company. Precisely what you have, George. And he took a *gamble* on me, George, a *gamble*. When in your life did you ever stick your neck out?'

Probably only now, thought George miserably, in coming

to see you. And what a bloody disaster that turned out to be!'

'Roger, you mustn't think that I'm not grateful—'

'Then what else am I supposed to think? Believe me, George, if you want out of Samson International, please feel free. I own forty-two percent of the company, and if you want to sell your stock, I'll be only too pleased to take it off your hands. But God knows, everyone else seems happy enough with the way I'm managing this bloody company. They're all hanging onto their Samson International shares, waiting for our next move. And I'll tell you something, George, with or without you on board, there'll be no shortage of next moves!'

George Hamish felt like a drink, a real drink, not another tumblerful of that disgusting designer water. How had he painted himself into such a ridiculous corner? Or had Roger put him there? He couldn't quite remember.

'I'm sorry,' he muttered, his huge frame still heaving alarmingly in the armchair. 'I think you're right, Roger. I've been under a lot of stress just recently. Maybe I should take a break. I'm more tired than I realized.'

'Of course,' said Roger – such a calm, concerned voice. 'There's always my place in Cap Ferrat, if you're interested. The South of France is so wonderful at this time of year, don't you think? The house is lovely – quiet, secluded and the staff are totally discreet.'

'Thanks,' mumbled George, struggling to get up. His audience with the chairman now seemed to be concluded. 'I'll have to discuss it with Madeleine and the kids. But I may well take you up on that.'

'Excellent,' said Roger, again returning to his documents. 'Well, I'm glad that's all sorted out then. Oh, and, George . . .'

About to leave the office, George Hamish turned.

'Yes?'

'If ever there's anything else that's bothering you, don't hesitate to come and see me.' George closed the oak-panelled door behind him and walked slowly down the corridor. That evening, he reflected gloomily, he would have dinner at the Samson International, Park Lane. Upmarket prostitution indeed! Why had it made him feel so bad? The girls on the game were only selling their bodies. He had just sold his soul.

CHAPTER EIGHTEEN

'WELL, I must say,' said Roger, standing up and smiling as Andrea waltzed into his office, 'married life does seem to be agreeing with you.'

Andrea beamed. She had taken hours deciding what to wear for this meeting, and was now looking very smart and businesslike in an immaculately cut fine wool suit. 'Thanks,' she said, moving swiftly across the room to plant a kiss on his cheek. 'And success seems to be agreeing with you.'

Roger ushered her towards a seat near the window. 'How's Charles? I haven't seen him since the last board meeting.'

Andrea shrugged her shoulders. 'He's fine, I suppose,' she said. If you don't count his fucking impotence, she thought. 'Mind you, I do wish he'd stop complaining that I never seem to be at home.'

'That's what I hear. W&S Communications seems to be expanding by the minute.'

Andrea lowered her eyes demurely. It was one of her best-rehearsed ploys. 'Well, if it is, it's thanks to you. How can I ever repay you for the publicity contract on the hotels?'

'Easy. By doing as good a job on them as you've already done on me.'

There was a quiet knock on the door and Miss Kerwin entered with coffee.

'Ah, Miss Kerwin,' said Roger, 'yes, just leave the tray over there please. And no more interruptions.'

She closed the door behind her, but not without first noticing Andrea's patronizing smirk. 'It's gratifying to have such a satisfied customer,' continued Andrea. 'Mind you, I'm not saying it's been easy. There are always people who want to pry into areas of your life you'd rather keep private. That's why we've been bending over backwards to steer them in other directions.'

'Your idea of Samson International sponsored sporting events was inspired,' he said, handing Andrea a cup of coffee. 'How's the projected golf tournament at Gleneagles shaping up?'

'I'm still negotiating with IMG. But if we can agree on money, I'll be able to deliver most of the big names – Watson, Faldo, Nicklaus – all star attractions. Ballesteros, of course, is always a separate deal. God, I'm praying it'll work out. The publicity would be brilliant. Especially with you a scratch golfer.'

'Just the sort of publicity I like.'

Desperate to impress, Andrea searched for a slick PR slogan, 'Publicity without information,' she proffered, 'image without insight.'

Roger's features froze. 'That's right,' he said sharply. 'That's what you're paid to fix.'

Immediately Andrea knew she had gone too far. 'I'm sorry,' she said quickly. 'I didn't mean to sound offensive. I was only trying—'

'Forget it,' said Roger dismissively. 'Now what about Samson International's charity contributions? Is it generally felt we're doing enough?'

Andrea looked at Roger quizzically. He was all smiles again.

'You're right,' he said, amused, 'I don't need to play games with you. What I mean is, is our generosity being noted in all the right places?'

'Well, your contribution to the Conservative Party—'

'How often do I have to remind you? Samson International's contribution to the Conservative Party has nothing to do with charity. That, I do assure you, is an absolute necessity.' No man had ever made Andrea feel quite so awkward and uncomfortable.

'Your patronage of Covent Garden has been widely

remarked upon,' she mumbled. 'I've put the cuttings in your file.'

'Yes, I've read them. Very good.'

'And your contributions to OXFAM, Children in Need, Shelter—'

'What a brilliant idea that was! Our help for the homeless certainly took the wind out of the trendy lefties' sails. Actually, I thought that piece on Samson International in the *New Statesman* was almost complimentary.'

'And then, there was your extremely generous donation to the Cure Cancer Campaign. That was very well received. Charles is still cock-a-hoop over it.'

Roger noticed how Andrea's skirt had somehow ridden a further three inches up her leg. Charles had influence everywhere, it seemed, except over his young and upwardly mobile wife. She handed Roger a piece of paper. 'Here's the complete list of Samson International's contributions to UK charities to date. Three million last year. Four million committed for the current year. No one can say you're not a caring capitalist.'

'Everything from ante-natal screening to sporting facilities for underprivileged ethnic minorities,' said Roger, scanning the list. 'You've done a very clever job.'

Andrea beamed with pleasure. 'I know what journalists are like,' she continued. 'One day someone's bound to run a story on Samson International's massive investments in racehorses, or art, or company houses. And when that day comes, I'll be ready for them. I'll hit them all so hard with this list, they'll be calling you Father Christmas.'

'God, you're tough. If you go on like this I'll have to start considering you for the company's financial PR as well.'

It was the chance Andrea had been waiting for. 'Piece of cake. Let's face it, the City editors already think you're God. Mind you, that's no thanks to the piss-artists who've been doing the job so far.'

'Be fair,' countered Roger. 'Millions of pounds have been added to our market value by the euphoric support of the City pages.'

Andrea tossed her hair. 'Sure, but they were all stories that wrote themselves. I bet none of them was actually planted. How many financial PR firms do you have working for you?'

'Four.'

'Right. And what do the brave boys do all day apart from hanging around in Harry's Bar knocking back Bellinis and gassing to one another?'

Roger was impressed by her vehemence. 'You honestly think you're ready to handle that side of the business?'

'Try me. Sack those coke-toting layabouts and give me a chance. You won't regret it. I'll take a third of what you're paying them and do a ten times better job.'

'Aren't you doing well enough for yourself already? And you have a rich and doting husband. What more do you want?'

If only you knew, thought Andrea. She stared him straight in the eye. 'Of course I want more. I'd have thought that you, of all people, would understand that.'

Roger nodded slowly, returned the stare. His initial impression had been dead right. They were kindred spirits.

'It's a deal, then?' ventured Andrea.

'Not so fast. I'll offer you one fifth of what I'm currently paying the brave boys.'

'A quarter. And you can take it from me, you'll also be saving yourself a couple of hundred thousand a year in ludicrous expenses.'

'Done. You strike a hard bargain, Andrea. I'm almost starting to pity Mark McCormack.'

By this stage, Andrea's skirt had risen to almost panty level. She leaned back in her chair. 'Well, now that's all sorted out, is there anything – anything else at all I can do for you?'

The implication was obvious. Roger stood up swiftly and moved over to his desk. The games were over. Clever, manipulative, ruthless and certainly attractive, this little vixen was not going to spoil his relationship with Charles. That association, after all, was the very basis of Samson International's success, something no woman could ever be allowed to jeopardize. Roger began to flick through a file. 'Yes,' he said pointedly. 'You can start liaising with our US public relations people on the list of American charities we might support.'

Andrea got the message. 'Starting with the Met?' she asked, surreptitiously pulling down her skirt.

Roger shrugged. 'I leave all that entirely up to you. My

business is creating the money, not spending it. Oh, and, Andrea, before you go . . .'

Aware that she'd made a tactical error, Andrea got up to leave. 'Yes?'

'I don't know if you can help me out on this. But I'm convening a meeting on the twentieth of August.'

'Samson International negotiations?'

'Not entirely. Just a group of like-minded entrepreneurs trying to put a few things together.'

'How can I help?'

'Well, there's a bit of a language problem. I need someone to interpret for us – mainly Russian and Japanese. Perhaps some French as well. Someone of the utmost discretion.'

Andrea smiled beatifically. Aha! A chance to retrieve herself. 'You know, Roger,' she said, picking up her briefcase and resuming her businesslike look, 'you really are a lucky man to have me on the payroll. As it happens, I know the only woman in London who fits the bill precisely. Give me a few days to track her down. I'll see if she's free to do it.'

CHAPTER NINETEEN

LILAH groaned as she saw the heap of mail waiting for her in the entrance hall. Six weeks – it was far too long a stretch to be away from home, but nowadays such stints were common. Still, it was almost August and the frenetic activity of the international conference circuit was slowing down for the summer recess. Lilah was looking forward to a well-earned holiday. Somewhere, anywhere, it didn't really matter. Just a warm, sandy beach where she could stretch out naked and think about nothing at all for a while.

She opened the door and wearily dragged her two heavy suitcases into her Ladbroke Square flat. It was odd. Nowadays her life seemed both busy and empty. Work alone could never obliterate her loneliness and longing for Jonathan. She walked into the sitting room and her face brightened at once.

'Hugo!' she exclaimed, delighted. 'It must be Hugo.' Awash with a riot of long-stemmed red roses, the whole room bore his hallmark. Looking down at the coffee table, Lilah found a card propped up against a large Val St Lambert crystal vase. Lilah smiled. He was so very naughty, it must have cost a fortune. She'd have to threaten, weakly of course, to take her keys away from him. 'Welcome home, Lilah,' ran the message. 'Have been dementedly busy. So much to gossip about. Call me when you touch base. All my love, Hugo.'

Lilah smiled. What a friend and neighbour! Despite his recent publicity and massive contracts, success had not spoiled Hugo in the slightest. How could it? As he was at pains to point out to anyone who cared to listen, he was already thoroughly ruined before it arrived.

She wandered into the kitchen to make a cup of tea. Perhaps there was some of that appalling skimmed milk powder still hanging around somewhere. Opening the fridge, Lilah could hardly believe her eyes. No wonder Hugo was doing so well in the interior design business. Such attention to detail! It had been filled, courtesy of Mr Christian's, the local delicatessen, with all her favourite things. Lilah shook her head in amusement. There they were, all the little treats she could have happily killed for last week in Moscow. Wodges of Dolcelatte and farmhouse Cheddar cheese; small individual parcels of Parma ham and Milanese salami; a packet of homemade gnocchi with a carton of Nico's famous sauce; a loaf of wonderful Italian bread made with olive oil; milk and butter and, of course, the statutory bottle of pink champagne. That was Hugo's real genius. He was almost as good as a wife.

'The hell with it!' said Lilah, kicking off her shoes, and reaching for the pink. She would celebrate being home and drink to her friendship with Hugo! At least that was one relationship that had never caused her pain.

She brought the bottle back into the sitting room and slumped down into her favourite armchair. Slowly, she started sifting her mail into two distinct piles. Official correspondence – bills, contracts, importune communications from the Inland Revenue – she would deal with all those tomorrow. Or possibly the next day. Lilah yawned as the pile grew ominously larger. Or whenever. Anything personal she would save till later to read in the bath. A Republic of South Africa stamp – she felt the same old joyous flutter as she recognized the handwriting. A nice newsy letter from Jonathan by the look of it. It seemed ages since she'd heard from him. They'd seen one another over six months ago when he was on a flying visit to London to lobby some charity or other. Their meeting had not been a conspicuous success. He was so preoccupied, she so frustrated that they'd ended up rowing again. Their letters had grown scarcer since then. Lilah looked wistfully at the envelope. Absence, work and distance were turning the lovers into pen-pals.

Lilah poured herself another glass of champagne. Already she was feeling better – sufficiently revived, in fact, to deal with the myriad of messages accumulated on her answering-machine. She never rang it from abroad. If something was urgent, she always reckoned, there was no way you could deal with it from a hotel room in Tokyo or Delhi. And if it was not, then it could wait until you returned home. As Hugo maintained, machines were there to serve us, not to rule our lives.

Pen and memo pad ready on her lap, Lilah turned on the tape. Nothing extraordinary for the first two or three minutes, just the usual litany of job offers: an IMF conference in Bangkok; an UNCTAD meeting in Brazzaville; another session of the CSCE in Helsinki; an offer for the next World Economic Summit. Lilah noted down the dates and return telephone numbers. God, it was difficult to turn things down, but perhaps she should reduce her commitments next season. Her work schedule was getting out of control. Lilah sighed and took another sip of pink. The tape seemed to drone on interminably.

'Hi, Lilah, Andrea here. Twenty-first of July. Which reminds me, it's your birthday next week, isn't it? It's high time I invited you to lunch. Sorry I haven't been in touch for such ages, but I've been so busy, I've hardly had time to breathe.'

Join the club, thought Lilah, cheered by Andrea's bright and breezy tone.

'Listen.' Unconsciously, Lilah vetted with an expert linguist's ear. Still sexy, she concluded, but decidedly de-Essexy. My word. We had come up in the world. 'Could you possibly do me a favour? A client of mine, *an extremely important client*, needs an interpreter. Small meeting, very hush-hush, the twentieth of August. Russian and Japanese, possibly some French. Feel free to name your own fee. Anyway, give me a call when you get back. Bye for now.' Andrea's voice clicked off.

The twentieth of August, thought Lilah despondently. So much for her holiday plans. And yet how could she let her old friend down? She knew she'd have to do it. The fact was, no one else could.

It was still early afternoon but with a combination of champagne, jet-lag and fatigue (six major conferences in six different
capitals in the space of six weeks), it was hardly surprising
that Lilah felt ready for bed. She made a half-hearted stab at
unpacking her clothes as she ran water for a bath. In the end
she gave up, leaving things scattered haphazardly across the
floor. What was the hurry? After all, there was no one else in
the flat to be disturbed or annoyed by her untidiness. Surreptitiously, the sense of loneliness had returned. Adding a few
drops of Guerlain's Heure Bleue essence, she quickly hopped
into the bath. Shoulders immersed under the water, she
reached for Jonathan's letter and eagerly tore open the
envelope.

Suddenly the water in the bath tub seemed to grow cold.
No, this was precisely not what she wanted to hear from
Jonathan right now – page after page of praise for his helper
at the hospital. It was not the first time Jonathan had mentioned this woman Jojo, but he seemed to be growing increasingly fond of her. Lilah knew she was being unreasonable.
What right had she to feel any claim over him? Not that there
was any suggestion of a sexual relationship – at least, not yet.
But that was not the point. Lilah was a Leo. Passionate and
possessive, loyal and jealous, it was both the best and worst
astrological sign. Lilah started to sob. Why not? Why sniffle
silently into a sponge when you'd just lost your best friend?
No, who was she kidding? He was much more than that.
Numb now, despite a top-up of boiling water, she got out of
the bath and tried to rub herself warm with a towel. Jojo
Matwetwe: the name went round and round in her head until
she thought she was going to scream. Wearily she slumped
into bed. She'd been killing herself with work to camouflage
her feelings, all she could think of was how much Jonathan
still meant to her. Lilah thumped her pillow hard. Jojo bloody
Matwetwe. Suddenly, Lilah felt a strange taste in her mouth.
The bitter tang of jealousy perhaps? Or perhaps of misery and
loss.

The day of her lunch appointment with Andrea, Lilah tried
hard to snap out of her lingering depression. It was her

birthday, after all, and she was determined not to allow anything to get her down today.

'Lilah, darling,' gushed Andrea as she waltzed into Monsieur Thompson's a full thirty minutes late, 'how wonderful to see you.'

Already thoroughly irritated, Lilah still did her best to smile.

'Sorry to be so late,' continued Andrea, expertly scanning the lunchtime congregation as she sat down. A former cabinet minister, a famous playwright and an aristocratic lady biographer, Andrea graced them all with the perfect PR smile. 'You know how it is,' she went on loudly, 'I was tied up on a conference call between LA, New York and Tokyo. Couldn't get them off the line. How are you keeping, darling? I must say you're looking a little tired.'

By now, Lilah wanted to hit her.

'Ma chère Lilah,' interrupted Dominique, the Lyonnais patron, kissing Lilah on both cheeks, 'they tell me it's your birthday. Please, Michèle, a bottle of champagne for Madame. On the house.'

Lilah felt immediately better. Dominique was such a star. No wonder Monsieur Thompson's was one of Notting Hill Gate's favourite culinary haunts. 'Merci, Dominique.'

'Enchantée de faire ta connaissance,' said Andrea, miffed at being ignored. Oh God, thought Lilah, shuddering. Thank God Dominique was a friend. No lady should tutoyer a gentleman she had only just met. It was considered such execrable form.

'How do you do?' replied Dominique pointedly. 'I'll go and fetch the menus.'

'So, then,' resumed Andrea, completely oblivious to the subtext, 'tell me all about you. Have you heard from what's his name?'

'You mean Jonathan?' Lilah was wondering whether this birthday lunch had been such a good idea. 'Yes, we're still in touch. Still good friends, you know.' The two women studied the menu.

'Just a small salad for me,' said Andrea loudly to the waitress. 'We've been invited to dinner at Kensington Palace this evening.' Andrea glanced around to ensure that everyone in the restaurant was suitably impressed.

178

God, thought Lilah, was she always so vulgar?

'I'll have the *table d'hôte*,' said Lilah.

Andrea looked enviously at her friend. No, despite every-thing, things had not really changed. Andrea bit her lip. If eyes were focused on their table, she realized, they were still trained on Lilah.

The lunch was no pleasure at all. Had Lilah been less tired or in a better frame of mind, she might have found Andrea's performance amusing. But today the new-look Andrea was hard to swallow. What on earth was the idea of trying it on with friends?

For her part, Andrea was also miffed. Lilah seemed quite unmoved by her meteoric rise in society.

By the time the coffee arrived, Dominique could see, both parties looked distinctly relieved.

'No, Lilah,' insisted Andrea, ostentatiously producing a gold American Express card, 'your birthday, my treat.'

'Thanks,' said Lilah, wishing she could feel more appreciative than she did.

Andrea looked at her watch. 'Now then,' she said briskly, 'about this meeting on the twentieth of August. I know you were hoping to get away, but couldn't you do it before you go?'

By this stage, Lilah was feeling in no mood to accommodate her friend.

'My client will make it worth your while,' continued Andrea crisply. For her, silence was never anything other than a negotiating tactic. 'With this particular person, money is a complete irrelevance.'

Lilah seemed unmoved.

'You do have all the requisite languages, don't you?'

Lilah could feel herself being bludgeoned. It put her on the defensive. 'The language spread is not the problem.'

Andrea saw her opening. 'Of course, this is an extremely confidential meeting. But I assume we can rely on your absolute discretion.'

Lilah felt a sudden rush of blood to her cheeks. 'For God's sake, what do you take me for? I've worked for heads of state and government.'

'Good,' said Andrea, smiling sweetly. 'So you'll do it.'

Lilah looked at her friend. It was true, after all. Intelligence and integrity were no match for guttersnipe cunning. 'All right,' she conceded, wearily. 'But my fee for the day will be two thousand pounds.' It was an outrageous request and she knew it. But at least it was some small compensation for having been manipulated.

Andrea never blinked an eyelid. Silly woman, she thought. She could have quadrupled her price and Roger wouldn't have cared. 'Of course,' she agreed immediately.

Lilah looked surprised. What, no quibble about the fee? 'Andrea,' she asked, 'precisely who is our client?'

'Roger Samson.'

'Roger Samson? Of Samson International?'

At last. Andrea was happy to have achieved some effect on her friend. 'Yes,' she said, trying to sound blasé. 'And it'll be an eight a.m. start at Samson Heights. Roger's a very early bird.' She signed the bill with a flourish. 'Tell me what you think when you've met him, but in my book, whatever *je ne sais quoi* is, Samson's got it in spades.'

Andrea's chauffeur was waiting as they emerged from the restaurant.

'Do you want a lift?' she asked, gesturing towards the Jaguar.

'No, thanks,' said Lilah. 'I'll walk home. It's only five minutes from here and I need the fresh air.' The two women embraced.

'We must do this again soon,' cooed Andrea, as the chauffeur helped her into the car. Humming merrily to herself, she sank back into the luxurious cream upholstery.

'The office, madam?' asked the chauffeur.

'No, Samson Heights, please, Norman.'

Andrea resumed her humming. Wonderful. After all her prevarication, she had finally nailed Lilah. Now that was another feather in her already well-plumed cap. Andrea smiled at her own reflection in the tinted car window. It would not be long before Roger realized that she could always deliver. One day she would be the woman Roger could never manage without.

*

'Lilah,' hailed Hugo from the other side of Kensington Park Road. 'I've been trying to phone you all day. You've forgotten to put your answering-machine on.' He wandered across the road, narrowly avoiding collision with a motor-cycle courier.

'You ought to be less of a dreamer.' Lilah kissed her friend enthusiastically. 'You nearly gave me a heart attack. Come on, let's go and have a stroll in the gardens. I need to walk my lunch off.'

The Ladbroke Square gardens were atypically quiet. Many of the small children and nannies who generally frequented them were already away on holiday. Instinctively, Hugo dead-headed a rose. Lilah smiled. He had an unwavering eye for detail.

'How about dinner tonight, then?' asked Hugo, as Lilah opened the gate.

'Love to,' replied Lilah. 'Although at this rate, I'm going to be the size of a house. Guess who I've just had lunch with?'

'Surprise me. Raisa Gorbachev?'

'That was over a fortnight ago.'

'Bloody show-off.' The two friends laughed.

'Actually,' continued Lilah, 'I've just been talking to Andrea Blackwell.'

'Ghastly, ghastly little woman,' sniffed Hugo, picking up an empty burger carton and depositing it in a litter bin. 'So much rubbish everywhere nowadays. Why are people so horribly uncivilized?'

'But she did write some wonderful pieces about you when she was still on the *Courier*,' protested Lilah loyally. God knows, it must have been a stock reaction. She always defended her friends. 'You can't say that didn't help in getting your business off the ground.'

Hugo grimaced comically. 'Ah, yes. That was when our Andrea was going through her "generous" phase. That was after her "outrageous", "obnoxious" and "facetious" phases, and slightly before her "sanctimonious" and finally "unctuous" phase.'

They continued laughing as they sauntered through the garden. Over by the tennis courts, a group of people were noisily mixing what looked like some highly exotic Pimm's. 'Let's sit down here on the grass,' suggested Hugo, as they reached the shade of an oak. 'I want to give you your birthday present. I just picked it up from a dealer friend of mine on the Portobello Road.' Carefully, Hugo extracted a small parcel from an old Sainsbury's plastic bag. 'Happy birthday, Lilah,' he said.

Excited, Lilah unfastened the red ribbon and unwrapped the glossy black paper. 'Oh, Hugo,' she exclaimed, extracting a beautiful porcelain figurine from a mass of tissue paper. 'It's beautiful!' She kissed him.

'I'm so happy you like it. Don't you think the woman looks like you? Tall, beautiful, elegant . . .'

'Stop it, Hugo.' Lilah threw the tissue paper at him. 'You're very naughty, you know. You're always spoiling me. What is this, Dresden? It must have set you back a packet.'

'Not réally, darling. You see, I'm afraid it's not Dresden. It's a Samson.'

'A Samson?' Lilah looked genuinely puzzled.

'After Edmé Samson,' explained Hugo. 'The nineteenth-century French porcelain maker. Good old Edmé used to turn out superb hand-painted and hand-made copies of anything you fancied. Chinese, Meissen, Chelsea, Derby – you name it, he did it.'

'Were they good?'

'Brilliant! In fact, they look so authentic, they still fool most of the people most of the time.'

'So that's a Samson, then?' A shaft of sunshine penetrated the oak tree's branches. Carefully, Lilah examined her figurine in the light. 'Charming and perfectly executed,' she mused. 'But nevertheless, a fake.' Suddenly she burst out laughing.

'What is it?' asked Hugo, intrigued.

'Just a funny coincidence. I'll tell you about it over dinner.'

Dinner at Leith's was wonderful although Hugo said he hated the décor. Too much black and white and tubular steel, it reminded him of a Brook Street Bureau. Both deliciously tipsy by this stage, Hugo insisted on walking Lilah back to her flat.

It was only a stone's throw away from the restaurant. But Hugo said he wanted to be sure.

Lilah could hear the phone ringing as she searched for her keys. Waiting patiently on the doorstep, Hugo suppressed a yawn. Handkerchiefs, lipsticks, biros, cheque books, throat pastilles – why on earth did women cart so much junk around in their handbags? Apart from the piercing wail of the telephone, the terraced Victorian house in which Lilah's ground-floor flat was situated was perfectly quiet – the silence of August.

'Are you sure you're OK here on your own?' asked Hugo solicitiously. 'It does seem very empty. You know you can always stay over at my place if ever you're feeling lonely.'

'Thanks,' said Lilah, finally extracting a small bunch of keys and kissing Hugo fondly on the cheek, 'but I'm perfectly all right. I'll be in touch very soon. And thanks for a lovely birthday. Where would I be without you?'

By the time she had negotiated three sets of Banham locks, the phone in her flat had stopped ringing. Damn it, she thought. Who could that possibly be? Dropping her coat on the bedroom floor and kicking off her shoes, Lilah went in search of her address book. No doubt it had been one of her brothers, calling to wish her a happy birthday. She would try ringing them all right now.

Disconsolately, Jonathan Morton returned to his Range Rover parked outside Johannesburg's Carlton Hotel. It had taken him over an hour to drive from Meroto to the city, and all to no purpose. All day long he had been looking forward to talking to Lilah and to wishing her a happy birthday. It seemed ages since he had heard her voice and he was badly in need of her laughter. The few phones that there were in Meroto had been out of order for weeks. What a pity! She must have gone out for the evening. Probably with some new boyfriend or other. She never mentioned them, but no doubt she had men queuing up in droves.

Jonathan turned the key in the ignition as a crowd of drunken revellers tumbled through the revolving door. Switching on his headlights, he moved into first and started on the lonely trip back to Meroto. For one sharp selfish moment, he wished he were back in England, preferably in Lilah's bed. He tried to conjure up her face, but tonight it eluded him completely. Oh, God, why was life so fucking complicated?

CHAPTER TWENTY

London, 20 August 1987

'GOOD MORNING,' said Lilah brightly, as she was ushered into the office by a handsome young security guard. 'I'm Delilah Dooley, the interpreter for Mr Samson's meeting.'

'Good morning, Miss Dooley,' replied Sally Kerwin, putting away a large bunch of keys in the top right-hand draw of her desk. 'I must say, you're very early. The meeting starts at eight.'

'I know. But I always prefer to be in plenty of time. Besides, I was hoping Mr Samson might be able to spare me a few minutes for a preliminary briefing.'

'I'll ask him.' Miss Kerwin admired professionalism in those she had to deal with. 'Would you like to wait in the meeting room?'

'Thanks,' said Lilah.

'I'd try to help you myself,' confided Miss Kerwin as she and Lilah walked briskly along the corridor, 'but I'm afraid I'm not entirely clear about the purpose of this meeting. I do know that Mr Samson has dealt with all these gentlemen before, but I rather think this is the first time they've all met face to face. Here we are.' Miss Kerwin opened the oak-panelled door leading into the room. 'If you'd just like to make yourself comfortable, I'll go and see if Mr Samson is available.'

Lilah parked her briefcase on a green leather chair and walked over to the window. It was a fine late summer's morning. Already the Thames below was full of commuter launches, cargo vessels and even pleasure cruisers. As usual, the river seemed to have a rhythm all of its own, relentless, unperturbable; it was perfectly hypnotic. The strong undercurrents made occasional eddies in the cold, grey water. Rivers were like people, thought Lilah. Who could ever tell from the surface what was bubbling away beneath?

Roger closed the door quietly behind him. Silhouetted against the window in the early morning light, Lilah stood there, tall, elegant and motionless. She was superb. The fitted red Ungaro suit showed every curve of her figure. Her thick auburn hair hung loose, just sweeping her shoulders. And those legs . . .

'Miss Dooley?'

'Oh, I'm sorry,' said Lilah turning, embarrassed to be caught off-guard. 'I'm afraid I didn't hear you come in.' She returned Roger's perfect smile. How long had he been standing there?

'How do you do?' said Roger. Where had he seen this woman before? 'I'm Roger Samson.'

Lilah felt the strength drain out of her body as her fingers touched his in a firm and formal handshake. It was perfectly ridiculous. She could not take her eyes off him. Like a rabbit caught in the headlights of an oncoming car, too mesmerised to bolt, she felt completely helpless. 'How do you do?'

He stared hard at her. What extraordinary eyes he had.

'Forgive me, Miss Dooley. From Mrs Watson-Smith's description, I'd expected you to be more – how shall I put it – more academic.' That was it! Roger suddenly remembered – Covent Garden. It must have been two or three years ago, but no one ever forgot a face like this.

'Perhaps I should have worn my blue stockings?' laughed Lilah, a trifle too loudly.

'I'm glad you didn't.' Blushing, Lilah felt like a schoolgirl again. She wished he'd stop looking at her. Eventually he broke the silence that hung between them. 'Do sit down.'

'Thank you.'

'About this meeting. Miss Kerwin tells me you'd like a briefing.'

'Yes, please, if you wouldn't mind.'

'Not at all. The fact is, for some years now I've been trying to put together several like-minded entrepreneurs.' He paused.

She waited. She felt slightly dizzy. What was it about this man?

'In this country, there's an old boy network, you know, people who've been to the same school, the same university. In France, they have their *grandes écoles*. In the States, it's helpful to be an Ivy League product. But I've been working on a different sort of network.'

'Based on business interests?' That was better. She'd managed an intelligent question. Now she felt she could cope.

'Mainly. But we also try to promote other – shall we say – worthwhile causes. Right now in South Africa, for instance, there's a group of people already benefiting from two million dollars' worth of our help.'

Lilah was impressed. 'So your group is heavily involved in charity?'

'We look very carefully into any worthwhile cause.'

Lilah felt as if a burden had been lifted from her shoulders. She'd been right, after all, to accept this assignment. At the same time, the mention of South Africa made her think of Jonathan and his hospital and that made her feel guilty. 'If it doesn't create too much hassle, could you possibly waive my fee and donate it instead to your South African project?'

Roger stared at her poker-faced. 'I don't think so,' he said. 'Believe me, it would create all sorts of problems. Besides, you mustn't get too carried away. We've all very hard-headed capitalists, you know. Our primary purpose here today is to help one another make money.'

'Of course.' Clearly, these were the sort of benefactors who preferred to remain anonymous.

'Now then,' continued Roger, 'about the participants. I'm sure there's no need to remind you that no mention of their names must ever go beyond this meeting room?'

'Of course not.' Lilah felt aggrieved. As a member of the International Association of Conference Interpreters, she was already committed to secrecy on such matters. It was part of the association's code. She need not have felt so cross. Roger's private detective had already run a thorough check on her. Lilah's discretion and credentials were above suspicion.

'Good,' replied Roger. 'Then let's begin with my American colleague, Jim di Pietro. He's a banker. In the past, he's been very helpful to me and Samson International. Without Jim, the Samson Tower development in New York would never have got off the ground.'

Lilah nodded. 'Would you mind if I made a few notes?'

'I'd rather you didn't,' said Roger smoothly. 'You never know where such things may end up.'

'No, of course not. I don't even know why I do it – taking notes, that is. It's just a habit. Once I've taken them, I never even need them. I tend to remember everything anyhow.' Lilah bit her lip. If only he would stop looking at her like that, perhaps she could stop this gabbling.

'Jim is also our Central and South American contacts man. Samson International has various schemes under way in that part of the world. Then there's our French connection, Pierre Lebrun, also a banker. He's been very useful to us in former French African colonies.'

'Does he speak any English?'

'He understands it but, if possible, he prefers to speak French.'

'No problem.'

'Then our Russian friend, Yuri Petroff, always works through an interpreter. It's a trick he learned from Krushchev. Whenever he changes his mind, he claims the interpreter made a mistake.'

'That's OK,' laughed Lilah. 'I'm used to working with the Russians.'

'The Japanese connection is Nobutaka Kurokawa, another industrialist. None of us would do any business in Japan if it weren't for him. He's of the old school – speaks nothing but Japanese.'

'That's fine. And the rest of the participants?'

'They'll all be speaking English.'

'Miss Kerwin told me this is supposed to be an informal meeting.'

'Yes, just a friendly get-together, really. I'm hoping it'll encourage greater co-operation in the future. Oh, and something else I ought to tell you. It's a bit of a joke, really – Jim di Pietro's idea. He's christened us "the Group".'

*

The meeting started on the dot of eight. 'Gentlemen,' began Roger, 'I know you're all very busy men and I hope we'll finish before lunch-time. I've called you all here today because I thought we should all make personal contact before the Group makes any further plans.' Roger watched Lilah as she translated for the benefit of the Group's non-English speakers. Her performance was mesmerizing. Even when she spoke Japanese, Jim di Pietro appeared to be hanging on to her every word. And Jim spoke nothing but Brooklyn.

'Before I report on the South African project,' continued Roger, 'I'd just like to repeat the advice I've been giving you all individually over the last six months. Jim and I are in total agreement over this one. We're both convinced the market is about to collapse.'

'Yes,' interrupted Fritz Reineke, a German banker, in heavily accented English, 'we have heard you say this many times, Roger. But the question is when?'

'No one can pinpoint precisely when,' continued Roger. 'But I reckon some time towards the end of 'eighty-seven – probably around autumn time.'

'So you would suggest selling as much stock as possible?' interrupted Pierre Lebrun. He was small and wiry. With his neat black moustache and somewhat fastidious mannerisms, Lilah thought he looked more like a *maître d'* than a major entrepreneur.

'Yes,' replied Roger emphatically, 'and as soon as possible. The name of the game is go liquid now.'

'I don't suppose George Hamish will need much convincing of that,' quipped Jim di Pietro. Lilah translated without really understanding. The rest of the Group just laughed.

'And now to South Africa,' resumed Roger.

Lilah started.

'As agreed, the first two million dollar tranche of the four million agreed has been deposited in Switzerland.' Members of the Group all nodded.

'And the project . . . ?' ventured Mr Kurokawa.

'I have good people on the ground overseeing the details,' said Roger. 'But as you know, gentlemen, these things all take time.'

Lilah translated away. Who knows, perhaps Jonathan's

hospital might even be benefiting from this aid.

By midday, Lilah was shattered, but not so shattered she did not notice Roger Samson's admiring gaze following her every movement. The Group had covered a multitude of topics – from disinvestment to reafforestation, from planning permissions to platinum.

'I think we've dealt with most points,' said Roger as the boardroom's clock struck twelve. 'Is there any other business anyone would like to raise?'

To Lilah's relief, nobody said anything. It had been a nebulous meeting, difficult to grasp. Although Lilah had interpreted everything perfectly, she felt she had understood nothing. It had been like trying to translate *The Waste Land*.

'In that case, I'd like to thank you all and call this meeting to a close.' Roger smiled at everybody. 'By the way, Miss Kerwin has arranged transport for those who have to leave immediately.' The Group started to gather their belongings.

'Do you have any private conversations you'd like me to stay on for?' asked Lilah.

Still staring Labrador-eyed at Lilah, Jim di Pietro waved farewell from the doorway.

'I'm afraid not,' said Roger, taking Lilah by the arm and guiding her to the far end of the meeting room. 'But I'd just like to thank you for doing a terrific job.'

Exhausted though she was, Lilah still had the energy to feel utterly flustered. 'It was nothing.'

Roger shook his head. 'Not at all. At one point, I thought old Petroff was going to blow his top. How did you manage to calm him down?'

Lilah managed a smile. 'I told him I'd misunderstood you.'

'Had you?'

'No, of course not, but it always works. I thought that'd give you the opportunity of suggesting what he wanted.'

'You mean a reduction on the second phase of the South African project.'

'Precisely.'

Roger laughed. 'Miss Dooley, you could sell poteen in Bordeaux. I've never met such a negotiator.'

He'd noticed she was Irish, then. He must have read her CV with care. 'I'm just a communicator, that's all.'

'I refuse to argue semantics with a professional linguist. But whatever you are, you're a genius. Thank God you were on my side. I've never known Kurokawa agree so easily to my proposals.'

Emboldened by this confidence, Lilah began to laugh. 'Well, shall we say it's all in the way you put things to people.' Oh, God, those eyes. If only he'd stop looking at her like that.

'All in the way *you* put things to people,' he insisted. Lilah affected to stare at the Kandinsky on the opposite wall. Roger was pleased to note her confusion. His, at least, was better hidden. 'Will you have dinner with me this evening?'

'I'm sorry,' said Lilah, unable to return that implacable gaze, 'I'm playing bridge tonight.'

'Then when are you free?'

'Well, I'm off on holiday in a few days' time.'

'Where are you going?'

Lilah knew it was none of his business, but somehow she found herself wanting to reply.

'Jamaica.'

'Not really the best time of year to be in the Caribbean. Too hot.'

'I know. But August and early September is my only free time. Apart from Christmas, I'm working the rest of the year.'

'I'm not surprised that you're in such heavy demand. How long will you be away?'

'About three weeks.'

'Would you mind if I called you when you get back? I really would like to have dinner with you.'

'Yes,' Lilah stammered. 'I mean no. No, I wouldn't mind at all.'

Arriving home, via an expensive saunter down New Bond Street, Lilah noticed a dark blue Corniche parked outside her flat. 'Miss Dooley?' enquired the chauffeur, stepping out onto the pavement as she rummaged around in her bag for keys.

'Yes?'

'I have a delivery for you.' The chauffeur gestured towards the Corniche.

'Oh, Jesus!' exclaimed Lilah. 'There must be dozens of them!'

'One hundred exactly,' replied the chauffeur, opening the back door and starting to unload an avalanche of lilies. 'And they come with the compliments of Mr Roger Samson.'

Roger smiled. It had worked. For the first time in his life he was positively desperate that it should.

'The name's Roger. We're not in a meeting now.' There was a slight pause at the other end of the line.

'Roger, what can I say? Thank you for the lilies.' Lilah laughed, her usual, good-natured, high-spirited laugh. 'Mind you, there are so many I'm afraid I've had to put them in the bath.'

'Don't mention it, Lilah. I'm going to do that every day until you have dinner with me.'

'Oh, please . . .' Lilah sounded horrified. 'Please, I don't like to sound ungrateful. But really, you mustn't. By the time I get back, no one in this building will be able to move.'

Roger smiled to himself. 'All right, then,' he conceded slowly. 'I'll have to think of something else.'

CHAPTER TWENTY-ONE

Ocho Rios, Jamaica, late August, 1987

'TIME to wake up!' Hugo rapped loudly on Lilah's bedroom door.

'What time is it?' Lilah's voice was thick with sleep. 'I'm still completely banjaxed.'

'Serves you right for climbing the Dunn's river falls twice in one afternoon,' replied Hugo, ignoring the question. No one in the West Indies kept track of trivia such as time. For Jamaicans, time was even more irrelevant than their impossible national debt. 'May I come in? I've brought you some breakfast.'

'Hang on a sec.' Lilah stumbled out of her monstrous emperor-sized bed and hurriedly pulled on a T-shirt. 'You can come in now. I'm decent.'

Hugo appeared, carrying a tray. On it were two plates of mango, papaya and grapefruit, a large pot of tea and croissants.

'Would Madam like breakfast outside?'

'Yes, please,' said Lilah, opening the peach and turquoise curtains and flinging wide the french windows which led onto the terrace. Immediately, sunshine spilled into the bedroom. By the side of the house, the river, one of the celebrated Ocho Rios, gushed noisily down to the sea. Already the heat was intense. Without the air-conditioning of the bedroom, Lilah could feel the cloying warmth clinging to her face. It was like being enveloped in a cloud of freshly made candy-floss.

'Another scorcher,' said Hugo, gazing out over the light, blue-green sea. A few waves broke white-crested over a nearby coral reef. A lone yacht, its pristine paintwork glistening in the sunshine, appeared on the distant horizon.

'Bliss!' said Lilah, licking mango juice off her fingers. Already the gaily coloured bullfinches, sugar-eaters and banana-quits were cheeping their interest in the leftovers. 'Another few hours on the beach this morning, I reckon, before it gets too unbearable.'

'If you think you still need it. You're already a wonderful colour.' Hugo gazed, disinterested but admiring, at her soft, golden skin.

'Thanks,' said Lilah, throwing a piece of croissant to a greedy little bird. 'By the way, have the others decided what they're doing today?'

'Alison and Des are going to Port Antonio. And Beth and Mat thought they might drive over to the Blue Mountains.'

'Are you going with them?

Hugo shrugged his shoulders, non-committal. 'I do have quite a bit of work to do on the Ciboney project up the road. I'm going to have to come up with some colour schemes before we leave. Peach and green, perhaps. So restful, don't you think, after the fierce, bright colours of the sun and the sea?'

'You don't have to hang around here on my account,' said Lilah, pouring out the tea. Hugo had been working so hard he needed a few days' respite and she knew he was staying behind only because he was concerned about her. He had always been deeply protective. 'I'm perfectly all right on my own,' she continued. 'After all, we do have half a dozen security guards included in the rent.' Below, in the garden, an armed guard sat down heavily on one of the seaward-pointing cannon and nonchalantly lit a cigarette.

'The privileges of staying in a government-owned house. You know, Lilah, heads of state and government have slept right there in that bed of yours. Not to mention HRH Princess Margaret herself.'

'So that explains the empties . . .'

'Lilah!'

'Sorry, Hugo,' she laughed. 'But I don't recall your being so mad about the monarchy.'

'Only queens,' agreed Hugo, pouring himself another cup

of tea. 'OK, then, if you're perfectly sure, perhaps I will tag along with Beth and Mat, after all. It gets so hot down here. I rather fancy the idea of some cool mountain air.'

'Good.' Lilah held out a few more croissant crumbs to the birds. Tamely, they fluttered down and ate them out of her hand. 'That means I can scoff all that leftover jerk chicken for my sad and solitary lunch.'

A thought crossed Hugo's mind. 'Be careful you don't go getting yourself burned, now. If you want, I'll leave my total sun block.'

'Thanks,' said Lilah smiling at him gratefully whilst gouging the last sliver of papaya from its greeny outer skin. 'You know, Hugo, I always said you were better than a wife. But the fact is, you're better than a wife and a mother all rolled into one.'

Paradise, thought Lilah, wandering down the bougainvillaea-shaded path which led to the private beach. The stone steps hugged the course of the fast-flowing river. Gingerly, Lilah put her toe in. God, it was cold. Agile as a cat, she hopped onto a rock jutting out of the water. Nimbly, rock after rock, she made her way down the river and into the sea. Unlike the river, the waters of the Caribbean were warm and velvety. Lilah floated on her back, staring mindlessly up at the blue infinity of sky.

Her skin tingled as she lay, wet and salty, in the fine white sand. She gazed across the endless expanse of sea. The yacht was now much closer. Almost – she laughed to herself at the memory of one particularly ghastly Law of the Sea conference – in her exclusion zone. Fumbling in her tote bag for the sunscreen, she smothered herself in cream. To hell with it, she decided, taking off her minuscule black bikini top. The security guards were nowhere near and there was no one else to see. Lilah stretched lazily as the sun beat down on her and, within minutes, she was dozing.

'Good morning.'

'Oh, my God!' Lilah sat up, opened her eyes and immediately grabbed a towel.

'Do you mind? This is a private beach.' The man's tall form was silhouetted against the sun.

'And I feel very privileged to have had a private view.'

Christ! Roger Samson! Here he was, standing there laughing at her, looking fit and relaxed in a pair of khaki shorts, sunglasses and an off-white seersucker shirt.

'How did you get here?' she spluttered, now securely draped in her towel. Roger pointed to the yacht, moored a few hundred yards from the beach, and to a motor boat bobbing right next to the shore.

'Easy,' replied Roger. 'I told the captain to drop anchor at Laughing Waters. And here I am. I hope I didn't frighten you.'

'But how did you know I was here?'

'A quick phone call to our mutual friend, Mrs Watson-Smith. I didn't even have to ask her. It just came out in the conversation.'

Still confounded, Lilah searched wildly for something, anything to say. 'About the flowers. I hope you got my thank-you note. I didn't think a phone call was sufficient.'

Roger sat down beside her. 'Yes, I did,' he said. 'And I keep it in my wallet to make sure I don't lose it.' Shooting a long, sideways look at Lilah's lithe, tanned body, Roger buried his hands deep in the warm sand. Lilah felt more confused than ever. She never really knew whether he was making fun of her or not. It was something about those eyes. Try as she might, she could not begin to read their message.

'Do you mind looking the other way while I put my top on?' she asked.

'If you insist.' Roger stared out to his yacht.

'There,' she said, feeling decidedly less vulnerable in its few square inches of fabric. 'That's better. So what's brought you out here to the Caribbean?'

'I've come for dinner.'

'All this way? It must be very important.'

'It is,' said Roger, removing his sunglasses to look at her. He stared deep into Lilah's eyes. 'I've come here to have dinner with you.'

None of the fifteen crew members aboard the *Samson I* had ever seen their boss so agitated.

'Christ Almighty,' said the captain, 'his lordship's like a cat on a hot tin roof. Frantic phone calls from London. "Leave

Newport immediately and head straight for Jamaica. Tell the chef I want to see him as soon as I arrive. Make sure the dining room and the lounge are full of lilies." I've never known his nibs so uptight.'

'Whoever she is, she must be pretty special,' replied the first mate, still irritated at having to leave that sweet little waitress in Newport at such short notice. 'It ain't like the boss to put himself out for a woman.'

'We don't know for sure it is a woman,' said the captain. 'You know Mr Samson. He never tells you anything you don't need to know.'

'Come off it, Cap'n. What about the flowers? Besides, I heard him talking to the chef before he went ashore. A candlelit dinner for two this evening. Don't sound like no big business meeting to me.'

'No, I suppose not. Anyway, whoever it is, you'd better put the men to work swabbing down the decks. His Majesty says he wants the place spotless by this evening.'

The cool sea breeze was welcome after the torrid heat of the day. Impatiently, Roger paced up and down the upper deck of the *Samson I*, waiting for his guest to arrive. He had spent the last two hours in his private gymnasium, trying to work off the tension. But for once that had failed. For the first time he could remember, Roger Samson was feeling nervous. The intercom rang loudly.

'Captain here, sir. Your guest will be arriving shortly. They've just picked the lady up in the motor boat. Would you like me to welcome her aboard?'

'No,' said Roger, 'I'll be down myself. Oh, and, Captain, I'd like you to keep the men off the sun deck, the upper deck and the main deck this evening. I don't want any intrusions.'

'Aye, sir.'

Roger ran down the illuminated stairwell and watched the motor boat pull alongside. Looking ravishing in a long cream silk shift, Lilah negotiated the steps with a little help from the first mate.

'Hello,' said Roger, kissing her on the cheek. 'I'm so glad you could make it.'

'How could I refuse? You sent your pirates to kidnap me.'

'Nonsense,' smiled Roger, 'you're free to leave whenever you wish. At least, after you've finished dinner. Come up to the main saloon and have a glass of champagne.'

Somewhere along the coast, a party was in full swing, the insistent, heady beat of reggae and soca music drifting out across the water. Lilah smiled. Hugo would be enjoying himself over there tonight. A few spliffs of ganja, a lot of rum punch and he would already be well away. Lilah gasped in admiration as Roger showed her into the luxurious dark grey and gold saloon. Tomorrow she and Hugo would have fun comparing notes.

'What an incredible boat,' said Lilah, as Roger handed her a glass of champagne. 'How big is it?'

'Sixty-five metres, if that means anything to you. I keep fifteen crew on board. And we can sleep ten guests.'

'You must have had some fabulous parties.'

'Well, on the upper deck I can entertain about a hundred people informally. I do that from time to time but only for business purposes. Sadly, I just don't have the time to use this thing for fun. Sometimes I come here to be on my own, but that's for some peace and quiet so that I can think more clearly.'

'And what do you do all day on your own?' asked Lilah. 'Sit and plot?'

Roger laughed. 'Some of the time. And when I'm tired of that, there's a sauna and steam-room – I bring my own masseur with me – and a gymnasium on board. It looks as though you work out regularly too.'

'Not since I lost my Reeboks.'

'And when was that?'

'About ten years ago!'

Roger threw his head back and let out a deep laugh, not something he did very often. What an extraordinary woman she was. Sophisticated yet ingenuous, she seemed to have no idea of the effect she had on people.

'When would you care to eat?' he asked, refilling Lilah's glass.

'Soon,' declared Lilah. By now, she was feeling far more relaxed in his company. A day in the sun, a few glasses of champagne, the proximity of this handsome, attentive, fascinating man – she was starting to feel quite giddy. 'I'm ravenous.'

Roger pushed a button. Immediately the large gilt screen separating the saloon from the dining room opened to disclose a black lacquered table. On either side of the screen, discreet lighting illuminated two skeletal Giacometti statues. 'Dinner is served,' he said theatrically.

Lilah's eyes sparkled in the candlelight as Roger helped her to her seat. 'Roger, this is so beautiful.'

'Nowhere near as beautiful as you.'

Lilah fiddled with her napkin. She was completely over-whelmed. She had never before felt so powerfully attracted to any man – not even Jonathan. She wasn't even sure if she liked the feeling, yet she found it impossible to resist.

'I hope you eat lobster,' said Roger, standing beside her as he filled her glass with wine. She could feel his body next to hers, strong and vital. She nodded, speechless for a second. Please, she prayed earnestly, as her hands began to shake, please let the chef have taken it off the shell.

As dinner continued, Lilah grew progressively more animated and amusing. Tales of pompous politicians, fatuous functionaries and crazy Irish relations, Roger felt he had never enjoyed himself so much. She almost succeeded in making him loquacious.

'No family?' exclaimed Lilah, as the Armagnac and coffee finally arrived. 'That's awful. I can't imagine life without siblings. It must make you feel quite lonely.'

It was too good an opportunity. Roger put his hand on hers. 'It does,' he said. 'Very.'

Lilah's head was swimming. 'Do you mind if we go out on deck for a breath of air?'

'Of course not. Here.' Roger placed his dinner jacket over Lilah's bare brown shoulders. Despite the heat, Lilah could feel the goose-pimples rising as the warmth of his coat met her flesh.

Pencil points of light pierced an ink-black Jamaican sky. Gripping the hand-rail, Lilah's knuckles seemed to glow luminescent in the dark.

Roger put his arm around her shoulders. 'Is that better?'

'Yes, much better, thanks.' Lilah could hear the waves,

gently lapping against the boat. 'I've had such a wonderful evening. Truly magical. It's like a fairy tale.'

'Lilah,' said Roger, a sudden sense of urgency in his voice, 'I have to leave for New York tomorrow morning.' She pulled his jacket around her more tightly. Suddenly she felt very cold. 'Believe me, it's the last place I want to be right now. But it can't be avoided. I want you to come with me.' Lilah's heart missed a beat.

'But, Roger,' she stammered. 'I'm here on holiday with friends. I can't just leave them in the lurch. Besides . . .'

'Besides what?'

'I'm sorry about the cliché, but the truth is, I hardly know you.'

Roger pulled her close to him so that their lips were almost touching. 'Perhaps not. But I know enough about you to know that I want you more than I've ever wanted anything or anybody.' He kissed her, gently at first. His lips were very warm. Then he opened her mouth with his and she felt his tongue caressing hers, confidently increasing the pressure. His hands were under the jacket and firm against her back. He pulled back and softly kissed the corners of her mouth.

'I want you,' he said at last.

'It's getting very late,' stammered Lilah, confused yet still desperately hoping he would kiss her again.

'I know,' said Roger, his hands still firmly on her back. 'So are you coming to New York with me or not?'

Lilah peered up at him. A vague memory of Jonathan flickered across her mind. 'I can't,' she whispered. 'I'm sorry, I can't explain, but it wouldn't feel right. Sorry, Roger. I've probably been wasting your time. I suppose I should go.'

Roger held her even closer. This was indeed a very special lady. How stupid of him to push things quite so fast. He might even have frightened her away. 'No, I'm sorry,' he said softly. 'I just didn't want to let you go, that's all.' He stood holding her for a minute in silence. 'You're right. It's getting late. I'll take you back to the house myself. But only on one condition.'

Relieved and yet somehow disappointed, Lilah forced a smile. 'Condition?' she queried. 'Does everything have to be a deal?'

Roger laughed again. 'I'm afraid so. I'm only taking you ashore if you'll see me back in London.'

'Then it's a deal!' said Lilah happily. Roger caressed her hair, took her face in his hands and kissed her eyelids and the tip of her nose.

'Good,' he said, slowly. 'I'm so glad you see it my way. But a good pirate king must always exact his ransom.'

Three days later, a parcel from New York arrived at Laughing Waters.

'What on earth . . . ?' exclaimed Lilah, tearing off the expensive gift wrapping and opening the box.

'Looks like a pair of Reeboks,' said Hugo, looking up from his week-old copy of the local paper, the *Gleaner*. 'Signed a sponsorship deal, have you, Lilah?'

'Don't be silly. I haven't worn a pair of trainers since I left school.' Intrigued, Lilah read the accompanying card out loud.

' "The Reeboks may not fit. But the rest will. All my love, Roger." Now, what on earth is that supposed to mean?'

'Beats me.' Hugo shrugged his shoulders and returned to his *Gleaner*.

'Oh my God!' Carefully wrapped in tissue paper and hidden in one of the shoes, Lilah discovered a glorious emerald pendant. 'Isn't it just fabulous?' she enthused, fastening the chain around her long, slender neck. Ecstatic, she started to twirl round and round the sitting room. 'Come on, Hugo, what do you think?'

But for once, Hugo could think of nothing to say. His mind was too preoccupied. For some reason, his thoughts had turned to nineteenth-century porcelain and to a man by the name of Samson.

CHAPTER TWENTY-TWO

Early September, 1987

'HELLO, Andrea. I'm happy to catch you in the office.'

'Roger. Where are you phoning from?'

'I'm here in New York at Samson Tower.'

'But I've been trying to get hold of you for days. What have you—?'

'I've been incommunicado,' interrupted Roger sharply.

It was all in the tone of voice. Andrea knew better than to pursue this line of questioning. 'Happy with everything at the hotel?'

'Yes, very. The place has ninety-five per cent occupancy. You're doing a great job here.'

Alone in her Bloomsbury office, Andrea smiled smugly.

'Andrea,' continued Roger, 'there's something of a far more personal nature I'd like you to deal with.'

'You know I'll do anything I can to help.'

'It's rather delicate. Simonetta is becoming something of a . . . liability. I want to tell her it's all over.' Andrea's smirk was growing wider by the minute. 'But I really don't want the hassle of a personal confrontation. I haven't the time for Italian histrionics.'

'So you're asking me to tell her?'

'Well, yes. But it's not quite as simple as that. She's been around with me for quite some time now, she's bound to have picked up a few names, ideas, information . . . you know the sort of thing.'

'Of course. The sort of things you wouldn't want finding their way into a national newspaper.'

'Precisely. That's where you come in. Andrea, I want you to make it clear to her that it would be in nobody's interest . . .'

Least of all yours, thought Andrea.

'. . . for such details to go any further. You can tell her that I'm willing to put a hundred thousand pounds in her account to ensure that she . . .'

'Keeps her pretty mouth shut?'

'Yes, that's about the top and bottom of it. I also want her to understand that I never want to hear from her again.'

'Christ, Roger, she must have really done something to annoy you,' said Andrea, intrigued.

'Not at all. As far as I'm concerned the relationship is over and that, quite simply, is that. When you've finished your meal in a restaurant, you don't expect to deal with the washing-up.'

'I see,' said Andrea, crisply. 'So I've been promoted to Samson International's head dish-washer.'

'I'm sorry. I didn't mean it to come across like that. But the point is, you're the only person I can trust to deal with these things for me.'

Andrea started to smile again. Yes, she *was* becoming indispensable to him. 'Don't worry,' she said, 'I'll fix Simonetta for you. But, Roger?'

'Yes?'

'What made you decide to dump her so suddenly?' Andrea was afraid she might have gone too far, but for once Roger seemed to open up.

'I've been thinking about it for quite some time. And recently I've understood that there's only one woman I really need in my life.'

She felt a tingling sensation down the length of her spine. 'Do I know her?' she asked coyly.

'Better than anybody,' replied Roger. 'Sure, I've been doing OK on my own. But together, she and I could move mountains.' Andrea clenched the receiver tighter.

'I understand,' she said, softly. 'And you needn't worry about Simonetta. By the time I've finished with her, you can be sure she'll never spill any beans.'

Simonetta was surprised to receive Andrea's phone call and even more surprised when she invited herself over to Flask

Walk for a chat. As soon as she put the phone down, Simonetta knew she should have said no. Tired and jetlagged, she was in no mood for unwelcome intrusions into her home. *Dio onnipotente*, did she need a day in bed! The deodorant commercial up the Amazon had overrun by a week and she was still exhausted from the shoot. Besides, it was weeks since she'd heard from Roger and, try as she might, she couldn't track him down. Trundling downstairs and into the kitchen, she switched on her espresso machine and listened while it bubbled. A couple of thick *ristretti* later, she was feeling human again.

Simonetta glanced at the clock on the double oven of her expensively fitted kitchen. What a joke! That was the only reason the oven was ever used – to tell the time. Yet like all Italian women, Simonetta loved to cook: pasta with home-made pesto sauce; veal in Marsala wine; fish with anise. How she wished Roger would let her cook for him once in a while. But he had never allowed that degree of domesticity to creep into their relationship. Simonetta sighed. The meretricious glamour of the modelling circuit was gradually beginning to pall. Home, food, a husband, children – deep down, what else did a good woman want?

She returned to her bedroom and climbed into her leotard. It was over an hour before that Watson-Smith woman was due so she might as well work-out. She started with her deep breathing exercises. Despite the caffeine, this basic yoga technique usually succeeded in calming her down. But not today. Today her mind would not stop racing. What on earth had happened to Roger? Of course, she ought to be used to these silences by now. Roger was always away on some business trip or other. But, somehow, this seemed odd. In – out. In – out. Simonetta tried hard to concentrate on her breathing.

For once Andrea was early. She had a good thirty minutes to spare. Feeling chirpy in the bright, autumnal sunshine, she parked her car in a side-street and sauntered through Hampstead village. Wandering down Perrin's Court, she stopped at La Villa Bianca to make a lunch appointment for herself. 'Just me,' she said, beaming at Giuliano, the indefatigable Italian owner. 'It's a very personal celebration.'

Crossing the road, she walked down Flask Walk to Simonetta's house and rang the bell.

'My word,' gushed Andrea, as Simonetta answered the door in her bright blue leotard, 'very hale and hearty, aren't we?'

Ignoring the remark Simonetta led Andrea into her pretty sitting room. Glancing around, Andrea noticed a photograph on the white wickerwork side table. It was of Roger and Simonetta being introduced to the Queen at a charity dinner. Andrea smiled. Soon, she would be the woman at Roger's side for such shots.

'Would you like coffee?' asked Simonetta, watching as Andrea made mental notes of everything in the room. She had never much cared for this woman, and felt no inclination to change her mind now.

'No thanks,' said Andrea breezily, making herself at home on the sofa. 'This won't take long and I don't want to interfere with your body-building exercises.'

Simonetta stared dismissively at her. Why would the English never learn? Women with fat legs should never wear short skirts. 'Perhaps you ought to try it yourself some time.'

Andrea was feeling too bouncy even to notice the remark. 'The thing is,' she continued, opening her briefcase, very matter-of-fact, 'Samson International is one of the world's most influential multinationals.'

Simonetta sat on the floor and crossed her legs. 'So what's new?' she asked.

'The chairman of the company, my employer—'

Simonetta exploded angrily. 'Get on with it, Andrea. You don't need to beat around the bush with me!'

Andrea was enjoying every minute. 'Please don't make my job any more difficult than it is. The point is, that in his position, Roger Samson cannot afford the possibility of even the slightest breath of scandal.'

Simonetta stood up and towered menacingly over Andrea. 'What the fuck are you talking about?'

'These,' said Andrea, handing Simonetta a large brown envelope. 'Take a look at the contents. Very interesting, I think you'll have to agree.' Andrea smiled sweetly up at her adversary. 'I must say, I love the one with those wonderful black men. I don't suppose you could have been more than fourteen at the time. However did you manage it?'

Simonetta turned pale. 'Where did you get these?'

The smile remained painted on Andrea's face. 'Oh, let's just say I still have my contacts in Fleet Street.'

Simonetta slumped back onto the floor. 'But it was all so long ago. I was broke. I needed the money.'

Andrea stood up and started walking around the room, casually studying Simonetta's *bibelots* as she went. 'Of course,' she said, preening herself in a mirror. 'But let's face it, it wouldn't do your career much good if it came out now, would it?'

Simonetta felt her blood grow cold. 'What do you want from me?'

'Me? From you?' Andrea laughed coarsely. 'Why, nothing at all. In fact, I've just dropped in to say hello and to give you a little present.' She handed Simonetta another envelope, a small white one.

'What's this for?' asked Simonetta, ripping it open and staring uncomprehendingly at a cheque made out for £100,000.

'Roger is a very busy man,' continued Andrea, sitting down on the sofa again. 'The cheque is just his way of saying goodbye and thanks for everything. Of course . . .' by now she was prodding like a picador, determined to elicit a reaction, 'I need hardly add that Roger does not expect to see any comments in the press about the ending of this little dalliance.'

'Dalliance?'

'Nothing that might embarrass either him or the company.' Andrea waited for the eruption. Nothing happened. For minutes, the two women sat facing one another in silence. Andrea felt badly cheated. 'If anything were to appear,' she added, desperate to draw blood, 'you do realize that I hold all the negatives to those interesting little snapshots.'

Simonetta stood up and walked across to where Andrea was sitting. For one frightening second, Andrea thought she was about to slap her. Then, slowly and deliberately, Simonetta started shredding the cheque into tiny pieces. Like outsize snowflakes they fluttered down onto Andrea's lap. Irritated, Andrea brushed them onto the carpet. 'Don't be ridiculous,' she shouted. 'That's a hundred thousand pounds you've just torn up. Now I'll have to go and get the bloody cheque reissued.'

Simonetta stared at Andrea with the deepest contempt. 'You really don't understand, do you?' she said, drawing herself up to her full impressive height. 'Please tell Roger from me that he should have known better. I don't want his money and I don't need to be blackmailed into silence. Tell him I would never do anything to harm him.'

On the way back to her car, Andrea cancelled her lunch-time celebration at La Villa Bianca. Vile-tempered and shouting at everybody in the building on her return, she slammed the door of her office and sat there fuming for the rest of the day. Simonetta, after all, was supposed to be have been the loser. Somehow, it seemed to Andrea, she had just come out on top.

Back in New York, Roger was in his penthouse suite preparing for a meeting.

'Good to see you, Jim,' he said, shaking di Pietro warmly by the hand as he was shown into the drawing room.

'And you,' replied the barrel-chested New Yorker.

'I thought the meeting of the Group went well.'

'You played them like a violin,' said Jim approvingly, 'you and that fabulous interpreter of yours. Jeez, what a body.'

Roger sat down and started to shuffle his papers loudly. Such comments were all right when applied to other women. But he did not want anyone, let alone Jim di Pietro, talking about Lilah in that way.

'Yes,' he replied, ignoring the remark, 'their confidence – and funding – certainly gives us a lot more leeway. How's your side of the organization shaping up?'

'Great, just great. I was in Bermuda the other day. Now I've left the details with my legal boys. By the time they're finished, we'll have more Mickey Mouse companies than Disney.'

'Good. I'll be going to Zug next week to do the same.'

Jim made himself comfortable on the sofa. 'How I love the Swiss. Such wonderful people to do business with. More tight-lipped than the Mafia.'

'And absolutely legit.' Roger and Jim both laughed.

'You want to start moving soon?'

'No,' said Roger emphatically. 'For the time being I just want to know the system's in place. I've been having a few problems with George Hamish recently. He's getting a bit jittery. I'm going to have to let things die down for a while.'

Jim nodded. 'Whatever you say's fine by me. You're the boss. But when you're good and ready, Roger, all you gotta do is say the word. The system'll be up and running and just waiting for you to go. The Group is right behind you now. And those boys have got the dough.'

'Yes,' agreed Roger, thoughtfully, 'that meeting was very useful – in more ways than one.'

'Good excuse to celebrate,' said Jim, smiling broadly. 'Hey, you up for a very special treat? I got the best bit of ass ever to come out of Vegas lined up for you tonight.'

'Thanks,' said Roger, staring out across the New York skyline. 'But for once I'll give your generosity a miss. Tonight I've got a very important phone call to make.'

Across the city, in the Pool Room of the Four Seasons restaurant in Park Avenue's Seagram building, Harold and Claudia Weiss were waiting for their daughter.

'I hope that boyfriend of hers remembers to wear a jacket,' sniffed Claudia, already scanning the menu. 'You never know with these Australians.'

'Be fair, honey,' said Harold. 'I know you'll never think anyone is good enough for Sophie, but Grant's a nice boy – interesting, bright, respectful.'

'Then why doesn't he make an honest woman of my baby? This living together business, it just isn't right.' Claudia stared gloomily into her mineral water. Since Sophie had hit twenty-three, her mother dreamed of nothing but glasses being broken under the *chuppah*. Every morning, when she awoke, the joyous cries of '*Mazeltov!*' were still ringing in her ears. Come on – no one was getting any younger! Claudia wanted to see some grandchildren before she went to meet her Maker. Harold patted his wife's hand.

'You know, these modern kids, they belong to a different generation.'

Claudia was not to be mollified. 'You can say that again. In my day, youngsters were on time. They didn't used to keep the older folks waiting.'

'If the two of them are late, you know it's got to be Sophie's fault. It's a miracle that guy ever manages to get her out of the office.'

Claudia shook her head disconsolately. 'Just like her father.'

'Yep,' said Harold proudly, 'just like her father. And that's the way I like it. Ah . . .' a huge smile illuminated Harold's wizened face, '. . . here they are.' He stood up to welcome them.

It was one of the reasons Sophie loved him. Grant Foster seemed totally unaware of the impression he always managed to create. Diners in the restaurant stared as the six-foot five-inch Australian shook hands with Mr and Mrs Weiss. Sophie looked on amused. God, he was handsome, with those shoulders as broad as a quarterback's from years of shearing sheep and baling hay in the state of Queensland.

'Hi, Mom,' said Sophie, embracing her mother. 'Sorry we're late. I had some business to tie up with Tokyo.'

'Told you so,' said Harold under his breath. 'Hi, baby. Don't I get a big kiss nowadays?'

'Sure, Dad.' Sophie kissed her father as he held her close in a bear hug.

'Good to see you again, Grant,' said Harold, pointing to a seat. 'Make yourself comfortable. I see your old mate Kerry Packer has been hitting the headlines again.'

'Good for him,' said Grant, laughing. 'TV stations, gambling, horses – you name it – it all seems to come up smelling of roses for Kerry. What a lucky bastard!'

Sophie saw her mother flinch. Claudia never swore.

'Grant used to play polo for Kerry Packer once upon a time,' explained Sophie, determined, in the teeth of obvious opposition, to gain her mother's approval. 'He has a seven handicap.'

'Used to,' said Grant, a broad, friendly grin illuminating his face. He had tried everything to ingratiate himself with Mrs Weiss, flowers, chocolates, deference, but none of it had worked. The last time he visited Sophie's parents in Palm Beach, she had virtually ignored him. Tonight he was determined to elicit some reaction. 'Not bad, hey, Mrs Weiss, for a larrikin who learned to ride as a jackaroo in New South Wales?'

Claudia stared at the water gently playing into the pool. Larrikins? Jackaroos? Do me a favour, why couldn't these Australians learn to speak proper English like Americans?

'You sure have produced some interesting entrepreneurs in your neck of the woods,' said Harold enthusiastically. 'Only the other day, I was reading a piece in the *New York Times* about Alan Bond.'

'The toast of Western Australia,' said Grant, nodding amiably to the waiter as he poured him a glass of wine. 'Or he was when he shafted your boys for the America's Cup back in 1983.'

Sophie glanced nervously at her mother. 'Grant learned all about mining in Western Australia,' she explained.

'Sure did,' continued Grant. 'And about the boys who used to sit around making fortunes ramping the shares.'

'Ramping?' asked Claudia. Always too busy spending it, Claudia had never taken much interest in how money was made.

'Yes, ma'am. Artificially pumping up the price of speculative shares – especially mining shares.'

'But isn't that illegal?'

'You're not wrong there. What's more, as me old mate Richie used to say when he was a few tinnies of Castlemaine XXXX over the top, "There's been many a good share fucked by actually drilling the mine." '

Harold started to guffaw loudly. He knew what the boy was up to and good for him. The son-in-law to suit his wife had yet to be born.

Sophie suppressed a giggle. 'That's where Grant developed his feel for the market,' she added quickly. 'Down at NYMEX, they reckon he's an absolute star.'

'Oh, do they?' said Claudia pointedly and then, turning to Grant, 'You must have found New York something of a culture shock.'

'You're not wrong about that either,' replied Grant, who had already downed his first glass of wine and was now looking for the waiter. 'Jeez, I used to think a crowd was a roo and a couple of joeys hopping across the Leeuwin coast road before I came to this place.'

Claudia stared at her daughter in puzzlement. Did she communicate with this man through an interpreter? Harold, on the other hand, was enjoying the performance enormously. He had taken to Grant the first time they had met. No wonder Sophie was so fond of him. With his roving past and his devil-may-care attitude, he reminded Harold of his long-lost brother Simon.

'Mind you,' continued Grant, 'you Americans make everybody welcome.' Harold nodded. As a German-Jewish refugee, he recognized the truth of that. 'You even make the bloody Pommies welcome,' continued Grant. 'Look at this bloke, Roger Samson. The way he's going, he'll soon be taking over Wall Street.

'It's interesting,' piped up Sophie. 'Off and on, I've been doing quite a bit of research into his company. You know, Dad, the last photo I could find of Uncle Simon was taken in Meroto. There's an outfit called Metallinc, a subsidiary of Samson International, who run a mining operation there.'

Harold looked intrigued. 'So you think Simon might have had something to do with it?'

Sophie shrugged. 'I don't know for sure. I'm working on it. But it looks that way. And there's something else turned up in his letters. Seems like Uncle Simon was a major beneficiary to the Convent of the Holy Rosary near Meroto.'

Horrified, Claudia stared at Harold. 'Your brother,' she exclaimed, 'funding a convent?'

By now even Harold was getting irritated with his wife. 'And why not?' he snapped angrily. 'When my brother and I left Germany, it was to escape religious persecution. In me that bred tolerance and understanding for all other religious persuasions. I reckon it did the same for Simon. Too bad none of that ever rubbed off on you.' Claudia started to study her perfectly manicured nails. Her nails were always perfectly manicured. The ladies of Palm Beach had nothing else to do.

'Anyway,' said Sophie, trying to avert a row, 'the point is, Dad – and Mom, I've been trying to get in touch with the nuns there, just to see what else I can find out about Uncle Simon.'

Harold was clearly excited. 'How about going to South Africa to have a look for yourself?'

'I intend to,' said Sophie simply. 'When I've done all the spadework here.'

'You could even get Metallinc to invite you,' added Grant.

'All these outfits are desperate to impress dealers like you. Say the word and they'd have you there quicker than Dennis Lillee through a Pommie middle order.'

Claudia sighed. It probably made sense to an Australian.

'No,' replied Sophie, laughing. 'When I do go, it'll be under my own steam. I reckon I'll discover more that way.'

'That's my baby,' said Harold. 'Always independent. Come on, let's order. Anything grab you, Grant?'

'Yes,' said Grant who was, as ever, starving. 'I reckon I'll have the shrimp in three-fruit-and-mustard sauce.'

Claudia raised her eyebrows. What do you want? she sighed to herself. The boy wasn't even *kosher* but he was more of a catch than Ernie.

CHAPTER TWENTY-THREE

Meroto, late September, 1987

IT HAD taken months of bureaucracy and paperwork, but eventually Jojo Matwetwe had been granted permission to stay permanently at the Christian Sight-Savers Mission Hospital. To Jojo, Jonathan Morton was nothing short of a saviour. The operation on her eye had been a complete success and when the bruising and the swelling had died down, her face had regained all its former sullen and unsmiling beauty.

As soon as she was fit and well, Jonathan had offered her a job at the hospital. After the incident in the shebeen, he knew she would be a marked woman back at the Meroto platinum mine. Despite her initial reservations, Jojo was grateful for the white doctor's concern and, gradually, she had begun to trust him. Working alongside him in the hospital, it was impossible not to marvel at his reserves of energy and compassion.

Jojo sighed with relief as the last patient on the operating list was wheeled back to the recovery ward. It was already nine o'clock at night and Jonathan had been on the go since six that morning. Jojo watched as, exhausted, he walked back to his consulting room to finish some reports. She had never met a man, either black or white, quite like him. In more ways than one, Jonathan had managed to open her eyes.

She popped her head around his door. 'You're looking tired. I'll make us both some cocoa.'

'Thanks, Jojo. I'm past feeling hungry but that would be great.' He returned to his heap of papers.

Five minutes later, Jojo appeared with two steaming mugs. They sat for a while in silence, sipping their drinks and listening to the wild Transvaal wind rattling the corrugated metal roof.

'Jonathan,' asked Jojo suddenly, 'what brought you to Meroto?'

By now Jonathan was used to her abruptness. At first, it had really bothered him. He had thought it a personal slight. As time went by he'd begun to realize that she knew no other way.

Apart from the ancient angle-poise lamp on his desk, there was no other light in the room, but Jonathan was aware of Jojo's eyes piercing the semi-darkness.

'D'you know, Jojo,' he answered, half weary, half amused, 'there are days when I ask myself the same question. In the end, I suppose it's all to do with upbringing.'

'So your father was a doctor?'

Jonathan shook his head and started to tell her about his family. Sipping his cocoa he described the strongest influences in his childhood – the redoubtable Morton women. He would never forget his mother campaigning to save the Elizabeth Garrett Anderson Hospital. By the time she had finished writing to national papers, lobbying politicians, addressing meetings, circulating newsletters, giving radio and television interviews, the authorities were so frightened they had to keep it open. And then, of course, there had been his grandmother, an even tougher case than his mother, by all accounts, totally unstoppable. In Victorian days, she had helped the so-called fallen women in the East End of London. Disinherited when she refused to give up her work, she had never returned home to her father's comfortable world of aspidistras and anti-macassars.

'Now I understand better,' said Jojo gravely. 'A family makes you who you are.' Jonathan watched as Jojo swirled her cocoa. It was now or never. He had not meant to open old wounds. Poor Jojo. She had been through enough already. All the same, ever since he had seen those eyes and that flawless light brown skin, he had been burning to ask the question.

'And what about you, Jojo,' he ventured at last. 'What about your family?'

Jojo shuffled uncomfortably in her chair. 'I never had a real family,' she said quietly. 'Only my mother.'

'Is your mother still alive?'

'Yes, she's still living at the Convent of the Holy Rosary not far from here. The nuns there took her in when she was pregnant with me. After that, they looked after both of us.'

Jonathan wondered how best to proceed. 'So there was no man to help your mother?'

'No. There was no man. When I was growing up, all the other children at the convent said my mother was a whore, that she slept around with white men.' Jojo's voice faltered. 'But when I told my mother, she started to cry and said it was not true, that she didn't sleep around and that, anyway, it was not her fault.'

Jonathan could feel her carapace of sullenness beginning to disintegrate. 'Did your mother ever tell you who your father was?'

'No, she always said she didn't want to talk about it. That it was never any of her fault, and that no one had the right to call her a whore.'

Jonathan could hear Jojo struggling to compose herself. For a while they sat in silence.

'I'm sorry,' she said at last. 'It hurts me to think of her.'

'That's OK,' replied Jonathan. 'So then you were educated by the nuns?'

'Yes. They told my mother that I was very clever,' Jojo laughed a strange hollow laugh, 'but that my attitude was all wrong.'

'Was it?'

'I suppose so. But I hated school. In my class all the children made fun of me and called me half-caste. They said I didn't belong anywhere – not with them and not with the white folk either. Then they said they would not play with me. I behaved badly to pretend I did not care.'

Jonathan felt an overwhelming surge of tenderness. 'Was there anything you ever learned to care for?'

'Yes,' said Jojo, more in control now. 'I loved my husband, Darius. He was a good man. Very kind to me. But he was killed in an accident in the platinum mine.' Her lip was quivering again.

'I'm sorry,' apologized Jonathan, 'I didn't mean—'

'No,' interrupted Jojo. 'I have been wanting to tell you. I want you to understand who I am and why.'

Jonathan got up and went to kneel beside her. 'You've had a very difficult life,' he said. 'But I'm very proud of you, Jojo. I've never known anyone who works half as hard as you do.' He put his hand on hers.

'You don't understand it all,' she cried, suddenly jumping up and making for the door. Jonathan stared after her in amazement.

'But—'

'No, Jonathan. The problem is being here with you at the hospital. I am learning to care again.' Confused, Jonathan tried to grab her by the arm.

'But, Jojo,' he said, 'look at me. Caring for people, isn't that a good thing?'

'No!' Jojo released herself from his grasp and turned once again to leave. 'At least, not always. Oh, I don't know. I hope one day you'll understand. But for what I must do, Jonathan, no, it isn't.'

Two miles down the road in a disused old shack, the central committee of the FAP was holding its monthly meeting.

'You're late, Jojo,' said Credo Sekese as Jojo took her seat at the rickety, melamine-topped table.

'Sorry,' said Jojo, breathless. 'We've been working very hard at the hospital. I had to run all the way here.'

Credo noticed Jojo's uneasy expression and immediately relented. 'Just to let you know what's been going on,' he repeated for her benefit. 'Our new comrades, the Group, have deposited two million dollars in the bank account they set up for us in Switzerland.'

'But, Credo,' objected Jojo, 'I told you at the last meeting that I was not happy about this. Who are they, this Group who are supposed to be helping us? How do we know we can trust them?'

'I know you're not happy,' said Credo soothingly. 'But, Jojo, if we're ever going to create any real trouble around here, we're going to need money for weapons and explosives.'

'If the Group pays up then the Group's OK,' said Kenny Maboi, slowly. 'Maybe we don't know who they are. But it doesn't matter any more. Already they've delivered what they promised. How can there be a problem?'

Tall and sturdy, Walter Ngobeni nodded his head. 'I agree with Credo,' he said. 'I'm tired of waiting for things to change. I left the ANC because our leaders said no to violence. At least, no to the kind of violence that's going to make things change. That is why I joined the FAP. Now the time has come for guns.' The only woman in the committee, Jojo often found herself in a minority of one. Far from bothering her, it made her all the more assertive.

'But why should this Group want to help us?' she argued heatedly.

Kenny shrugged his shoulders. 'Who knows?' he replied. 'And who cares? Maybe they're international terrorists – the Red Brigades, Colonel Gaddafi – I don't know. All I know is, whoever they are, they're trying to help us now.'

Credo had had enough. Democratic discussion was fine in theory but it took up so much time. 'Yes,' he said decisively. 'Besides, they are not ordering us to do anything yet. They are just helping us to get organized. When we have what we need to act, then we will work out our strategy.'

'But what kind of strategy? Are you going to let this Group we've never heard of decide what we are going to do?'

'It is not like that,' said Credo. 'We will plan our actions together. Our aims will be the same. We will do nothing that is not in the interests of our own FAP cause.'

Jojo frowned. 'I'm still not happy,' she said.

Suddenly, Walter Ngobeni banged his fist on the table, knocking over a half-empty beer can. It rolled onto the floor with a clatter. 'What happened to you, Jojo?' he shouted. 'You're not the same woman since you went to work in that white man's hospital. Seems like you don't believe in the black man's fight no more.'

'It's *not* a white man's hospital,' shouted Jojo angrily. 'That hospital's for you and me.'

'Shut up,' said Credo, glaring at Walter. 'Everyone here has the right to an opinion.' He sighed in frustration. It didn't really matter, of course. The majority of the committee were already decided. Yet, of all the comrades, Credo most wanted Jojo to be convinced. There was something about this woman. Her opinion mattered to him. But even as he sprang to his friend's defence, Credo knew Walter was right. Jojo Matwetwe was no longer the same comrade he had carried into the Christian Sight-Savers Mission Hospital. He had watched it happening. But Jojo had stopped hating and started caring. For the scale of subversion Credo had in mind, that could be very dangerous. He would have to keep an eye on her.

'Look,' said Credo, 'it's time we were all getting back to the hostel. I think we ought to take a vote. Those in favour of continuing to work with the Group.'

Kenny and Walter raised their hands immediately. Credo looked at Jojo. Slowly and half-heartedly, she followed suit. Credo looked relieved. The members of the committee got up to go.

'Jojo,' said Credo quickly, 'will you stay behind for a few minutes? I want to talk to you.'

Jojo sat down again and waited for the others to leave. Within minutes Kenny and Walter were gone, sidling silently into the cool Meroto night.

'Now then,' continued Credo, when they were alone together, 'I've known you long enough by now. Tell me what's the matter.'

'Nothing,' said Jojo, stone-faced.

'You can't fool me, Jojo. It seems like only yesterday you were giving me a hard time. "Credo, why don't we organize a strike at Meroto like they've done at Impala?" "Credo, why can't we have a sit in down the mine?" '

Despite her annoyance, Jojo laughed as Credo tried to mimic her voice. 'Yes,' she replied, 'and you used to tell me, "Wait, Jojo. We're not organizing anything for the sake of a few more rand in the pay packet." '

Credo peered into Jojo's tired but beautiful face. 'That's right, Jojo. And I still stand by it. When the FAP moves, I want it to be big. So big, the whole world will notice. Then everyone will look at the black people of South Africa and ask themselves what to do.'

Jojo looked contrite. Credo, after all, was so much wiser.

Perhaps she'd been wrong to have acted so awkwardly. 'Is that why we need the Group?' she asked.

Credo nodded. 'Yes, Jojo. We need their money. And their help. When the FAP moves, the entire capitalist economy must feel it. That is what I've always said. I want you to believe that, too.'

Jojo stared vacantly at the floor.

'What changed your mind?' insisted Credo.

'I don't know,' stammered Jojo. 'Since I've been at the hospital, I've watched Jonathan spending his whole life to make people well. He makes me want to do that, too. But then, I think of the cause and I know we must kill many people.'

'No, Jojo, you must not think of that. You must think that we are fighting for our freedom. And sometimes bloodshed is the price.'

Jojo started playing with a loose thread in the hem of her skirt. 'I suppose so.' She did not sound convinced.

'Believe me,' continued Credo. 'It is the only way. I have to be getting back. Should I walk with you to the hospital?'

'No, thanks, Credo. You get back before they catch you out of bounds. I'll be just fine.'

As the two comrades embraced, Credo noticed something strange – a new light in Jojo's eyes. Walking swiftly back to the hostel, he felt a sudden unexpected pang of jealousy. Of course! He had been so tied up with the Group and the FAP, he had failed to recognize it before. That was the explanation. Jojo Matwetwe was in love.

CHAPTER TWENTY-FOUR

London, late September, 1987

'DELILAH fucking Dooley!' Angrily Andrea threw her briefcase on the floor. It skidded across the hall.

'Andrea?' Charles appeared at the top of the staircase. 'Ah, there you are. I thought I heard the front door. I'm sorry, I wasn't expecting you home this early. Is everything all right? I must say, my dear, you're looking quite ill.'

'It's nothing,' replied Andrea, ashen-faced. 'I've had a terrible day at the office, that's all.'

'My poor darling,' said Charles, running down the stairs, 'you really oughtn't push yourself so hard. I keep telling you, it's time we had a holiday.' He put his arms around Andrea and kissed her fondly on the forehead.

'I don't want a bloody holiday!' snapped Andrea, pulling away impatiently.

'Come now, you're exhausted. Can I help? Why don't you come into my study and tell me about it?'

'Oh, for heaven's sake, Charles, leave me alone! There's nothing to talk about. I'm tired that's all.'

Charles looked sympathetic. 'Just as well Roger rang to cancel dinner this evening. He said he hoped we wouldn't mind – but he's decided to fly to Paris instead. He's taking your friend Lilah for dinner. And I must say, from the way he was talking, he sounds quite keen on her.'

Andrea felt like screaming. Thanks to a casual phone call from Lilah, she already knew of Roger Samson's plans. Quite keen on *her* then, was he? She wanted to lash out. So this was the new woman in Roger's life, the woman with whom he was going to make Samson International buzz. Storming up the stairs, she slammed her bedroom door and flung herself onto the bed. That bitch! That Miss Goody-Two Shoes fucking bitch! She wasn't even his type! And that bastard, Samson. How dare he treat her like this? How dare he lead her on and give her all the dirty work to do? That business with Simonetta! And all the time he'd been clearing the decks for Lilah, not for her. Andrea pummelled her pillow. It was too much. Roger was hers. She had created him in his own image and to her own liking. Now Lilah had stolen the only man she had ever really wanted.

'You'll pay for this,' cried Andrea out loud. 'Whatever I have to do, Lilah, I'll make sure you pay for this.'

Back in his study, Charles picked up the silver-framed photograph he always kept on his desk. How gay and beautiful Lydia had been in those days. So different from the ravaged creature he had nursed so tenderly to the end. The lump in her breast, so the surgeons had discovered, was a secondary cancer and the mastectomy had been futile. By the time Lydia came round from the anaesthetic, even she realized that she was irretrievably riddled with the disease.

'Promise me one thing,' she had whispered the night before she died. She was refusing to take her drugs by that stage, resolutely determined to stay awake and lucid. She wanted to remain capable of talking to her husband. Who else but her could help him to come to terms with his grief?

'Anything,' Charles had replied.

'Promise me you'll try to be happy again. I'd feel so much better if I thought you might find someone who would make your life less lonely.' Charles sighed at the recollection. He had hoped his second wife might fill the raw, emotional gap that Lydia had left. But nowadays he rarely saw Andrea. And even when he did, she was always so offhand. Gently, Charles kissed Lydia's photograph and replaced it on the desk.

'I'm sorry, darling,' he whispered at last. 'They were all right and I should have known it. I've been a silly old fool. Forgive me. I feel I've let you down.'

'Nothing like your own plane,' laughed Lilah, fastening her seat belt as the Samson International Lear jet taxied down the runway at Heathrow airport.

Roger leaned back in his grey leather seat and took her hand as at last the plane took off. 'It does save a lot of time.'

Lilah smiled at him and looked out of the window onto the lights below. She felt like pinching herself. Private planes, yachts, flowers, jewels – for the last month she felt as if she'd been living in a dream. Turning, she noticed Roger's face, for once in repose. He was so good-looking with his thick, dark hair, his high, sculpted cheekbones and strong even teeth. And yet there was something else, something oddly melancholic about that proud, handsome face, which she found even more attractive. How she wanted to believe she could make him truly happy.

'And what are you staring at, Miss Dooley?' he asked, suddenly aware of her attention.

'The one flaw in your Adonis profile.'

'You mean that bump on my nose?' Roger felt it with his forefinger.

'Got it in one,' laughed Lilah. 'How did you manage to acquire that?'

'A boxing incident at school.'

'Ugh, how barbaric! I can't abide boxing. No son of mine will ever be allowed to box. What sports do you play nowadays?'

'Golf, tennis. And I like to shoot and ride.'

'No team games, then?'

'No. Team games mean relying on other people.'

'And you don't like doing that?'

'Not unless I absolutely have to.' Roger's voice sounded hard and cold. Lilah shivered involuntarily as he looked at her. What was it about those eyes? They said nothing – or, perhaps, everything about the man. Like a dedicated poker player's eyes, they betrayed not one flicker of emotion.

'And what about you?' asked Roger. 'Now you've been equipped with the Reeboks you've no excuse.'

'Sorry, Roger. You've picked the wrong woman. Even at school, I was so hopeless at games I had to skive off to the library. At least, that was until Mother Mary Vianney caught me reading *Gone With The Wind* camouflaged as the *Collected Works of St Thomas Aquinas*. I was nearly expelled for that.'

'Sounds like you had a very strict upbringing!'

·'Yes and no. Of course, the nuns were disciplinarians. But my parents were extremely indulgent. Especially as I was the only girl among four brothers.' They sat for a while in silence as the stewardess poured them each a glass of champagne.

'I envy you,' said Roger, when she'd gone.

'Oh, don't be such a bullshitter,' teased Lilah. 'Roger Samson, one of the world's richest and most eligible bachelors, envious of me? What on earth have I got that a man like you can't have?'

'You'd be surprised.' He lifted her hands to his lips and gently kissed each of her fingers.

Situated two minutes away from the Champs-Elysées, the Samson International was easily the most luxurious hotel in Paris. The manager greeted Roger and Lilah effusively as they arrived in the foyer.

'I see what Hugo means,' said Lilah, studying the hotel's great round entrance hall with some amusement. The rotunda was full of antique statues on high pedestals and the walls were covered with dark red wallpaper with a greyish-blue shaded pattern.

'Ah, yes, your friend Mr Newsom,' said Roger, guiding Lilah towards the lifts. 'And what does he have to say about my foyer?'

'I'm sorry,' said Lilah. 'I shouldn't have mentioned it but it was something about the excess of Leona Helmsley meets the pretension of Susan Gutfreund.'

Roger laughed. 'I'd like to meet this Newsom fellow. I've heard he's very good. Besides, he sounds extremely amusing.'

'Oh, he is! The best. So you don't mind his criticism?'

'Not at all. I always said they'd overdone it with the gold leaf in here. The trouble was, I was far too busy with other projects when this was being done. Perhaps your Mr Newsom might find the time to come and sort it out?' The gilt-mirrored lift ascended to the top floor of the hotel.

'Dinner in an hour?' asked Roger, as the manager ushered Lilah into her suite.

'That'd be fine.'

'In my penthouse, then,' said Roger, kissing her lightly on the cheek, 'if that's all right with you.'

From the window of Roger's penthouse, Lilah could see the Arc de Triomphe illuminated in the distance. 'It's so beautiful up here,' she said, a macramé of confused emotions waging war in the pit of her stomach.

'Fantastic, isn't it?' Roger poured her a glass of pink champagne. 'Although before tonight I'd never quite realized how beautiful.'

Lilah gulped. 'How many Samson International hotels are there?' she asked, hoping the champagne might steady her nerves.

'Twenty worldwide, and all in prime sites.' Roger's arm was touching hers. 'I've just sold a large chunk of the stock to a Japanese conglomerate but Samson International still retains a controlling interest in the chain.'

'I see.' Lilah was fighting for small talk. 'Any reason for diluting your share-holding?'

'Just a feeling,' said Roger, vaguely. 'I've been selling quite a lot of stock recently.'

'Including your mining interests?'

'Oh, no,' said Roger, twiddling one of his Hans Muth platinum cufflinks. 'I'd never do that.'

'You know, I have a friend who's working near your mine in Meroto.' Thank God! At last, she had managed to say it.

'Oh yes?'

'An old university friend named Jonathan Morton. He's a surgeon out there in the black township.'

'Really? And is he still a friend?'

'Yes. I thought I ought to mention him.' Roger put his arms around Lilah's shoulders.

'So you were lovers?'

'Yes. But that's a long time ago now. We've both moved on.

We're still friends, of course.' Confused, Lilah took a large slug of champagne.

'And since Jonathan?'

'Nobody. I've never been a person for casual relationships. I could never really see the point. With me it's all or nothing. That's why I'm feeling so . . .'

'Nervous?'

'Yes, nervous. Especially with a man like you.' Lilah could feel the warmth of Roger's body close to hers. Her heart was thumping and the champagne didn't seem to be helping.

'You needn't be.' Roger turned to face her. 'I won't deny that there have been plenty of women in my life. But you're different, believe me. I've never *wanted* any woman before I met you.'

Lilah began to feel dizzy. 'I think I'd like to sit down,' she muttered, taking another gulp of champagne. Suddenly her face froze.

'Lilah, are you all right?'

'I'm sorry,' she was grateful for the diversion, 'but I think there's something in my drink.'

Roger looked on amused as Lilah fished a hard, sharp object out of her glass. 'Roger . . . oh, Lord . . . what on earth . . . ?' Lilah gasped as she produced an emerald-cut, pink diamond.

'Do you like it?'

'It's . . . why, it's . . .'

'It's approximately five carats,' ventured Roger. 'I only managed to get hold of it this morning. That's why I just had to have dinner with you tonight.'

'But, Roger . . .'

'If you like it, I'll get Buccellati in Milan to make it into a ring.'

'A ring?' Lilah blinked. In the distance, the lights of the Arc de Triomphe had become a blur.

'Yes, Lilah. It's the best way I could think of to ask you to marry me.'

Lilah was shaking. If only her heart would stop thudding so hard, she might decipher what it was trying to tell her. She thought of Jonathan. She knew, since meeting Roger, that she'd tried to push him to the back of her mind, and it had worked. He seemed so distant now. She must stop feeling guilty. She wanted *this* man, wanted him more than she'd ever wanted any person or thing in her life. Nothing else mattered any more.

'Yes,' she whispered at last. In an instant, Roger had swept her into his arms and carried her into the bedroom.

Slowly, he unbuttoned Lilah's ivory silk blouse. She noticed his hand was shaking too. He spread it wide and gazed at her breasts, something he'd been longing to do since that first illicit glimpse in Jamaica. How beautiful she was! Her breasts were still lightly tanned, though paler than her belly, which had the faintest tracing of pale down snaking towards her belly button, now revealed as he slid her blouse down over her brief white panties. He could see the triangle of darker hair beneath the lace. He mustn't go too fast. He cupped the lower part of her left breast with his hand and drew it up. The nipple was already hard. He began very tenderly to roll it between the thumb and forefinger of his other hand. It was unbearable. Lilah moaned. Her pants were soaking wet. He replaced his fingers with his mouth, warm and soft, and slid his hand down over her belly to cover the lace between her legs. Her still-brown legs were bare of tights. He felt the heat and dampness there.

'Oh, Lilah, Lilah . . .' It was the first time in his life he'd ever really wanted to please a woman. 'It's all right. There's no need to be nervous.'

He could feel her eyes, wide open, staring anxiously down at him. 'I'll try not to be,' she whispered, as he continued to undress her. She watched in silent admiration as, deftly, he undressed himself. His body was quite perfect: powerful arms and shoulders; small, flat stomach; neat, hard buttocks. Lilah stared at his magnificent erection, her need for him now urgent. She quivered with anticipation as she lay naked and prone on the bed. He returned to lie beside her and gently parted her legs. Lilah closed her eyes as she felt his tongue, hot and slippery, penetrating her mouth. Their tongues touched and caressed one another as, slowly, he slid a finger inside her. Her hips began to respond, slowly, rhythmically to the touch of his fingers as they sought for the swelling of her clitoris. It was too much. She came suddenly, clinging to him in pure, unalloyed ecstasy.

'Roger, Roger . . .'

But Roger did not stop. He continued to stroke her body for quite some time with the tips of his fingers – her breasts, her belly, her thighs – making sure she was perfectly at ease before he started again. Lilah cradled his erection in her hand and, desperate to please him now, guided him towards her pubic mound, urging him to enter her. He was impatient with desire, yet determined still to pleasure her. He slipped inside, deeper and deeper, moving together with her with blissful ease until she came again, her arms clasped tight around his neck, trembling with joy and relief. Roger climaxed almost immediately, overwhelmed by the aching need to be with her, to feel with her, to be part of her.

'I love you, Roger,' said Lilah, relaxing exhausted into his arms and softly kissing his face.

'And I love you.' Roger held her hard, almost too hard, to his chest. Already he was feeling frightened by the truth of his own admission.

CHAPTER TWENTY-FIVE

Early October, 1987

HUGO NEWSOM had never felt so miserable. In the last three weeks almost everything he really cared for seemed to have disappeared. First Marcus, his longstanding actor-lover, had left him for a film producer. It had been a devastating blow. He'd known Marcus even longer than he'd known Lilah. As undergraduates, they'd all trodden the Footlights boards together. In company, Hugo managed to laugh it off with a languorous shrug of the shoulders. The film producer, he joked, was the only way Marcus could reach those parts ordinary thespians could not reach. But underneath Hugo still felt deeply hurt and betrayed. The end of this relationship was as bad as any divorce.

And then his grandmother, the relative he loved best, had died. Divorce followed by bereavement, how much emotional turmoil could one man take in the space of a month? Day after day, Hugo paced around in the workroom of his Arundel Gardens duplex, too restless to concentrate on anything except his grief. Dear old Granny Sheridan. For years now, she had been both mother and father to him. Not that his own parents were dead. More's the pity, thought Hugo bitterly. For all the love and support he'd had from them, they might as well have been. Of course, he still saw his mother from time to time – surreptitious lunches at Le Caprice whenever his father was out of town. But she was such a timid doormat of a woman and so petrified of her husband finding out that such occasions were hardly red-letter days in Hugo's crowded diary.

Fun! No, there hadn't been much of that in Hugo's child-hood years. A slight, intelligent and sensitive boy, his father had insisted on packing him off to boarding school at the earliest opportunity. Bullied by physically stronger boys, Hugo had soon moved himself off the sports field and into areas where he could excel. Gradually, his sharp wit and ready tongue started deflecting the worst excesses of his tormentors. After that, it was an almost inexorable progression to the stage and to boys of a similar disposition.

It was then that the real trouble with his father had set in. For Mr Newsom senior, it was already a flogging matter when his son refused to play cricket at Eton. But the rumpus when he found his only son and heir was a practising homosexual! Hugo shuddered at the memory. After the most fearful row, his father had cut him off without a penny. To this day he still refused to speak to him, even at the funeral. Over on the mantelpiece, Grandmother's antique shagreen clock chimed three times. Good old Granny Sheridan. Thank God that woman at least had a mind of her own and was determined to right a few wrongs. Her will, read out to the huge conster-nation of the rest of the family, had left everything to her favourite grandson, Hugo. From now on, he need never worry about money again. Not that he ever had, of course. But all the same, it was nice to be genuinely loaded. It gave you so much freedom to behave precisely as you wished.

Hugo looked fondly at the priceless glazed Tang horse, recently arrived from Grandmother's estate. As a small boy, he had spent hours studying its every detail. Even now, with its hogged mane, flared nostrils and large eyes glaring from beneath heavy eyebrows, it looked as if it were just about to jump off the console table. Yes, dear old Granny Sheridan. Her actions had done little to improve relations between Hugo and his parents. But at least in the matter of inheritance she had managed to restore the balance. Hugo pulled out a handkerchief. He was missing her already.

And now, to cap it all, there was this lunatic business with Lilah. Hugo slumped down in his favourite leather armchair and mournfully shook his head. He had never met this chap, Roger Samson, but he had heard and read enough about him to know he was just not her type. Like Hugo, Lilah had always loved beautiful things, but money for its own sake had never impressed her. Until now, she had seemed to operate on the basis of more fundamental values. If Jonathan had been a bit too serious for Hugo's tastes, at least he was a decent sort of bloke. Hugo was sick with worry. Lilah was far too trusting to be caught up with a man like Samson. He had simply swept her off her feet. Nowadays she was turning down interpreting assignments so she could spend more time with him. It was all too quick, too sudden. She was already out of her depth.

Hugo sauntered into the kitchen to make himself a cup of mint tea. Swatches of carpets and fabrics, colour charts and plans lay strewn all over the work room. A fabulous mansion in Kensington Palace Gardens to be decorated from top to bottom and Hugo had hardly started. By this stage the owner, with a temper to match his short stature, was screaming for his plans. Let the bastard wait, thought Hugo, placing the mint tea sachet into his individual teapot. He was in no mood for work. Now that he, too, was rich and over-privileged, they could all go to hell. Uncompromising interior design – take it or leave it. From now on, that was to be the watchword for Hugo's operation.

He was taking his afternoon nap when he was awakened by the phone.

'Hugo Newsom?'

'Yes.'

'Roger Samsom here. I believe you're a friend of Lilah's.'

Hugo hated being woken up so brusquely. 'Yes,' he mumbled. 'And congratulations.' The word stuck in his throat, but, for Lilah's sake, he may as well mouth the platitudes.

'I'm a very lucky man. Look, Hugo, I know you're busy, but I have a proposal I'd like to put to you.'

'Mmmh?' No point pretending to be enthusiastic when he absolutely wasn't.

'We're planning a new Samson International hotel in Edinburgh. Things are still at the drawing-board stage. But I'd like you to take charge of the interior design. We've already had too many balls-ups in that department.'

For a moment, Hugo's wicked sense of mischief got the better of him. What an ideal opportunity for sabotage. Already Hugo could picture the honeymoon suite of the Edinburgh

Samson International: a large *lit à la polonaise* tricked out in Black Watch tartan, a few pairs of antlers on the bedroom wall and a set of bagpipes in the bathroom. Hugo scratched his head. That was always the problem with execrable taste. The Americans would probably love it.

'Was this Lilah's idea?' asked Hugo, suddenly suspicious.

'No,' replied Roger, 'it was mine, although I have to admit . . .'

'Yes?'

'I know it would make Lilah very happy if she thought you were working with us.'

Us! God, thought Hugo, almost amused, it hadn't taken Roger long to move into the first person plural. Already he was talking like a happily married couple. Hugo smiled wryly to himself. Perhaps, on the other hand, it was just a negotiating ploy. He must have known Hugo could never turn Lilah down.

'Well, I'd like to have a look at the project first.'

'Of course.' Roger was clearly delighted. 'Let's have dinner, the three of us, next week. I'll get Lilah to liaise with you. There are quite a few things we've got to discuss. I'm a great fan of your work. I've been wanting to meet you for quite some time.'

For half an hour after the phone call, Hugo sat thinking to himself. Yes, Lilah was right, Roger Samson was certainly charming. And very persuasive, and clearly determined to do everything to get Lilah's friends on his side. All the same . . . Hugo looked at his old mate, the Tang horse, and sighed. Perhaps, after all, it would work out. Perhaps they were both head over heels in love. But if so, wondered Hugo patting the horse's head, why was he feeling so bothered?

CHAPTER TWENTY-SIX

October, 1987

FEW OF the world's top businessmen felt like playing golf this morning, but Roger Samson was one of them. The previous day, 19 October, he had seen billions of pounds wiped off the world's leading share indices. Brokers were still reeling from the shock. Black Monday! In London, New York, Tokyo – everywhere – the mood was much the same. Confusion, gloom and spiralling depression.

The dark blue Corniche purred its way towards Virginia Water. Roger's chauffeur studied his boss's face in the rear-view mirror, searching for signs of stress. There were none. In fact, Roger was looking positively relaxed – happy, even. Mark knew better than to ask his boss any questions. But he had heard the radio and seen the papers and it was difficult not to feel alarmed. All the same, if the atmosphere in the car was anything to go by, his job, at least, was not yet on the line.

'The West at Wentworth, isn't it, sir?' asked Mark when Roger had finished his call to New York.

'Yes.' Roger was looking forward to his game. Only the other day he had flown over the course in the Samson International helicopter. Winding through Wentworth's large, heavily wooded estate, it looked like a vast, coiling snake. As the pilot had pointed out, it was no wonder locals referred to it as the Burma Road.

'What time are you teeing off, sir?'

'Eleven o'clock. But I'll be meeting Mr Watson-Smith in the club house at quarter to.'

'That's fine. We're in plenty of time. The roads seem almost empty this morning.'

'I'm not surprised,' said Roger, smiling broadly. 'I'll wager there's a lot of people who won't want to get out of bed this morning.'

It was a cold, grey day as Roger and Charles left the warmth of the club house for the challenge of the West at Wentworth.

'Congratulations on your engagement,' said Charles as, briskly, they made their way to the first hole. 'I saw the announcement in *The Times*.' It was a lie, but only a white one. Charles had indeed seen the announcement in *The Times* but for some weeks before he had already known that something was on the cards. Andrea's vile moods and temper tantrums had virtually spelt out the engagement.

'Thanks,' said Roger, smiling at his friend. 'Lilah's a wonderful girl.'

'She certainly is.' Charles fastened the Velcro of his golf glove. 'I've grown very fond of her myself. You've got someone very special there.' The two men walked in silence as the wind whistled around their ears. The caddies, discreet as ever, followed a few yards behind.

'And congratulations also on your hunch,' continued Charles, as soon as there was a lull in the wind. 'Your intuition about the market has proved remarkably correct. What can I say? You've made us all very rich men.' Charles spoke with no trace of either pleasure or excitement. It was a simple statement of fact. Nowadays money seemed to matter even less than ever before.

'Yes, Samson International went liquid just in time,' replied Roger. 'And right now, cash is king. Soon we'll be buying up stock all over the place at bargain-basement prices.'

'Yes, I suppose so.' Roger cast a sideways glance at his golfing partner. He looked tired and dejected, unusual for Charles.

'How's Andrea?' Roger could see he had struck a raw nerve.

'Very well,' said Charles loyally. 'Very well indeed. Busy, of course.' He made a stab at a smile. 'But then again, we're all busy, aren't we?' How could Charles confide his problem to anyone, let alone to a man like Roger? It seemed ages since Andrea had moved into her own separate bedroom. What, she had goaded, was the point of sharing a bed where nothing ever happened? Besides, she had continued, it was for his own convenience as well as hers. Increasingly, she had taken to coming home in the early hours of the morning. It was because she was working late in the office, or so she always said. But on the few occasions, late at night, when he had tried to phone her there, he had never found her in. There was no point in denying to himself what Andrea was really up to. Charles only prayed that she'd learned enough to keep things discreet.

Four hundred and seventy-one yards long, the first hole on the West at Wentworth was a par five. 'I'll have a driver, please,' said Roger to his caddy. Charles watched Roger's perfect, rhythmic swing as he hit the ball a searing shot, 280 yards straight down the middle of the fairway.

'Good shot,' said Charles, accepting a driver from his caddy. It was so unlike Charles not to concentrate, yet Roger could tell that his friend's mind was anywhere but on his golf. Those jerky head movements, that strained and awkward-looking posture. Bringing his driver down far too quickly, Charles sliced the ball.

'I'd say about two hundred and forty yards away,' said the caddy, replacing Charles's club in the bag. 'Can you see it there, to the right of the fairway?'

'Hard luck, old chap,' said Roger, jovially slapping Charles on the back. Both scratch golfers, Roger was used to playing a needle match with Charles. 'No doubt you'll make it up on the next shot.'

Roger was in terrific form. After a brilliant four iron, he was onto the green and two putted for a birdie. Poor Charles. Nothing seemed to go right for him. Playing over the gully with a five iron, he landed short of the green and caught the bunker on the right-hand side. After a difficult shot, he eventually chipped onto the green and two putted for six.

'One over,' muttered Charles, disconsolately.

'You're only warming up,' said Roger, trying to jolly his friend along. But it made no difference to Charles's game. For someone who stood to have millions of pounds added to his personal fortune, Charles was a very miserable man indeed.

Already the wintry Surrey evening was closing in and the beech, fir, and birch trees swayed like eerie sentinels in the growing gloom and dampness as the two men walked briskly back to the changing rooms.

'I'm thinking of bringing Lilah into the company.'

'She's very talented.' Charles tried hard not to shiver too visibly. It was odd. All those years in the Coldstream, Charles had never felt the cold. But now, for some reason, he felt frozen all the time.

'Yes, she's already showing quite an interest in the hotel chain. I thought she might do well in personnel and industrial relations. God knows, I hate that area of the business. I've had it up to here with men like Mike Patterson and his bloody Amalgamated Hotel Workers Confederation.'

'I'm sure Lilah will have them all eating out of her hand in no time,' said Charles.

Roger was pleased to see some glimmer of pleasure cross Charles's kind and careworn face. All the same, he was worried about him. Charles was still a very useful asset to Samson International. Perhaps he ought to have a word with Andrea. Or, better still, perhaps he ought to get Lilah to have a word with her. Silly little bitch. Already she had managed to forget which side her bread was buttered. 'We must all have dinner soon,' said Roger, as they neared the changing rooms. 'I'm sure the girls would like that. Especially now they'll be working together on the hotels.'

There was an angry ripping sound as Charles tore off his glove. 'Yes,' he said, as he kicked the turf off his shoes, 'I'm always happy to see you and Lilah.'

Soon after the engagement, Lilah moved in with Roger and put her own flat on the market. Refusing to take on any further interpreting assignments, she was now concentrating her mind on Samson International and its extensive hotel chain. Life with Roger was so full and exciting, she rarely had a minute to devote to organizing their wedding. Fortunately, there was always Hugo in the wings. He, too, was busy, especially with the new Edinburgh project, but wherever he was and whatever he was doing, Lilah knew he would always find time for her. Roger welcomed their friendship, fostered it, even. Hugo was no competition. And besides, there was no doubt about it, he was the best designer in the country. It was good to have him on board.

For the first time in their engagement, Roger was away on an extended business trip. Two weeks on her own to kill, Lilah had never felt so lonely.

'Lonely?' laughed Hugo, when Lilah called to invite him over for the week. 'But you've been rocking around the world for years on your own. Why lonely all of a sudden?'

'I don't know,' she replied, rather shamefaced. 'This house is so big. I feel weird just rattling around here without company.'

Hugo had heard it all before. 'Bullshit! You're missing him, aren't you?' Silence. 'Lilah, you're getting too dependent.'

He was right and Lilah knew it. Nevertheless, she felt aggrieved. 'Well, are you coming over or aren't you?'

Hugo could not bear to hear her cross. 'Of course, I'll come,' he said, relenting. 'You know I'd never let you down.'

Their second evening together, Hugo insisted on preparing dinner. After his whirlwind trip around the Samson International chain, he was tired of being waited on hand and foot. Besides, cooking had always been his favourite relaxation. A good dinner, he maintained, was like good theatre and he had always excelled in both.

After a delicious meal of exotic fruits in Pernod, fillet of beef and sorbet, the two friends retired to the drawing room sozzled with the remains of their second bottle of wine. Hugo was grateful for this period of peace and quiet together. After the hullabaloo of the engagement, it felt like old times again.

'Well, if you're happy, Lilah, so am I,' he said, trying not to sound too curmudgeonly. 'It was all a bit quick, that's all.'

Slowly, Lilah sipped her burgundy. 'I know. But Roger's so wonderful, I can hardly wait to get married. Please, Hugo, you'll have to help me plan the wedding.'

Hugo smiled wickedly. 'Of course. In fact, I insist. But you must draw up the guest list as soon as possible so I know what I'm letting myself in for.'

'Already? But the wedding's not till next July.'

'All these things take time. I suppose the dreaded Andrea will have to be invited.'

'Hugo, please . . .'

'Can't help it, Lilah. Never could stand her. All the same, I suppose one has to look on the bright side. At least nowadays she won't be pitching up in ski pants and stilettos.'

Lilah laughed as she refilled Hugo's glass. The more smashed he was the more vicious he became. After a few bottles, he was well away. 'I think we'll have the reception here at Regent's Park,' she said. 'Roger's given me *carte blanche* to revamp the house. Can you do the job?'

'An unlimited budget?'

'Yes.'

'Wonderful. Then I'll do my best to exceed it.'

Lilah giggled, a trifle embarrassed. 'You really don't like him, do you?'

'I have no feelings about Roger Samson one way or the other. But I do care for you.'

'I know,' said Lilah, kissing Hugo affectionately on the cheek. 'But, believe me, I know I'm doing the right thing.'

Hugo looked at her and wished he could believe her. 'Of course you do,' he said at last. 'I suppose I'm just jealous, that's all. A complete dog in the manger. Does Jonathan know yet?'

Lilah looked crestfallen. 'I've written to him. I couldn't quite muster the guts to tell him over the phone.'

'I see.' Hugo peered into her face.

'Look,' she said, almost angrily, 'I know he won't approve. And I know you don't approve. But Roger is the most thrilling man I've ever met. He's building Samson International into one of the world's most influential companies, and I'm going to help him go even further.' Suddenly Lilah burst into tears. 'Why is everybody being so awful? It's just the same with Andrea. I phoned her the other day to invite them to dinner and she could barely be bothered to speak.' The tears rolled down Lilah's cheeks. 'Why is nobody happy for me?'

Hugo put his arms around Lilah's shoulders. 'Don't be so naïve,' he said. 'I'm concerned because I'm fond of you. Andrea's upset because she's a jealous little madam.'

Lilah mopped her tears with Hugo's generous linen

handkerchief. 'I'm sure that's not true. She's just surprised, that's all. Everybody is. But she'll come round in the end.'

Hugo kissed her forehead. Who was he, after all, to tell her how to run her life? Besides, if he went on like this he was going to lose her as a friend. Standing up, he strode theatrically across the room and over to the window.

'Now then, Miss Dooley,' he said, pretending to measure for curtains, 'let's stop all this wailing and gnashing of teeth. If you're going to get married next summer there's work to be done, you know.'

'You're adorable.' Lilah smiled and sniffled simultaneously.

'Wait until you see my fees. Come on, grab a coat.'

'Where are we going?'

'Over to my place for Sotheby's latest sales catalogues. I'm going to turn this macho mausoleum into the most des. res. in Regent's Park.' Suddenly Hugo noticed a particularly gory hunting scene hanging in an alcove. Marching straight up to it, he removed it from the wall and, opening a window, pitched it into the garden.

'Hugo!'

'Uncompromising interior design,' said Hugo, without batting an eyelid. 'No whingeing, Lilah darling. You knew that when you hired me.'

It was quite unlike Jonathan Morton to snap at his patients but today the slightest irritation sent him into transports of invective. Of course, Jojo had seen him angry before. But that anger was always directed at the situation – poverty, ignorance – never at its victims. By the time he had finished his morning clinic he was in such a fiendish mood that Sister Ndaba retreated to the women's room in tears.

'Oh dear,' she wept as Jojo tried to comfort her. 'I've seen it all before. This place is getting too much for the doctor. It happened just the same with the last one. He ended up with a nervous breakdown.'

'Don't you worry, now,' said Jojo, still fuming at being called an incompetent in front of a waiting-room full of patients. 'Something must have happened to explain all this. Dr Morton is a good man. He isn't going to leave us. He loves this hospital too much.'

'No, I tell you, I've seen it before,' insisted Sister Ndaba. 'One day these doctors are just fine. The next day – snap. They can't cope no more.'

'Leave it with me,' said Jojo. 'I don't know what's the matter with that man. But I'm going to get to the bottom of it right now.'

'Jonathan, are you feeling OK?' Jojo was petrified to find Jonathan slumped motionless over the desk in his consulting room. Perhaps, after all, Sister Ndaba's diagnosis was correct.

Immediately Jonathan straightened up. 'Yes, I'm fine, thanks. I'm sorry for shouting at you this morning.'

'That's all right,' said Jojo, relieved now rather than angry. 'I'm used to it. All my life, people have been shouting at me.'

Jonathan felt even worse. 'No. It was completely out of order. And, besides,' he tried to raise a sheepish grin, 'you know it's not true. You're the most competent assistant I have in this hospital.' He stared listlessly at his desk. 'Now if you'll forgive me, Jojo, I've a lot of paperwork to get through.'

'No,' said Jojo, striding across to the desk and closing the file he was affecting to study. 'There's something worrying you, Jonathan, and I want to know what it is.'

'This is not a professional matter,' said Jonathan, refusing to meet her gaze and returning to his files. 'And it's not something I want to talk about.'

'Oh no?' said Jojo, planting her two elbows heavily on the pile of papers. 'If you don't tell me, then who are you going to tell? Or are you just going to go home on your own and let it fester and fester until you're feeling so sick and bad-tempered you're no use to anyone here?'

Jonathan shook his head. 'I'm sorry, Jojo. I told you I'm sorry.'

It wouldn't do. He was blocking her out. Suddenly Jojo was angry again. 'I keep telling you that you don't have to say sorry to me. All you have to do is treat me like a friend. Remember – there was a time when I told you everything about myself and it made me feel a whole lot better. So now you talk to me! You go on all the time about people being equal. Go ahead and treat me like one.'

Jonathan was surprised and shaken by Jojo's sudden outburst. 'You're right,' he said slowly. 'I know I'm behaving like a complete and utter prat. Of course you're my friend.' He studied Jojo's beautiful, angry, puzzled face and felt his stomach lurch.

'Come on, then,' said Jojo gently.

Jonathan stared at his desk again. 'There's a woman I was once in love with,' he started. 'She's just written to tell me she's getting married.'

Jojo's heart filled with a mixture of sympathy and envy. Quietly, she put her hand on Jonathan's sad, bowed head. 'Are you still in love with her?'

'Yes, I suppose I must be. And this is all my fault. I should have listened to her, tried to compromise a bit more. Now she's gone and got herself tied up with that bastard.' Jonathan felt embarrassed. Surely, after all this time, he ought to be above such visceral jealousy?

'Is he a bad man, the man your friend is marrying?'

Jonathan looked at her in despair. 'Jojo, she's marrying Roger Samson.'

'The man who runs Metallinc?'

Jonathan nodded.

'Now I understand,' she said softly, stretching out to touch his face. The contact was electric. Without thinking, Jonathan caught Jojo's hand and stood up. Pulling her towards him, he wrapped his arms tightly around her. Her warm, supple body felt so comforting against his. Her head tilted upwards, her eyes closed and her moist lips parted – Jonathan felt an overwhelming desire to make love to her. By now she was breathing fast and shallow, her mouth and tongue responding eagerly to his. Jojo moaned a deep, long moan, the voice of a thousand hurts erased in one embrace. Already she could feel his erection, rigid against her thigh. Jojo's heart was pounding. Quickly she began to unbutton her dress. Then suddenly Jonathan stopped her.

'No, Jojo. Oh, God, no. What on earth am I getting us into?'

Jojo looked devastated. 'You don't want to make love to me,

then?' she whispered, the pain of rejection branded lividly across her face.

'Of course I do. But you know it wouldn't be right. You've had enough pain and misery in your life without my adding to it out of selfishness.'

'But I want you to. You said I was your friend.'

'And so you are,' sighed Jonathan, peering down into her hurt, angry eyes. 'And my equal. That's why I can't make love to you, Jojo. You're far too precious just to use.'

CHAPTER TWENTY-SEVEN

Christmas, 1987

THE CHRISTMAS lights in Regent Street were more spectacular than ever: huge, white illuminated snowflakes, brilliantly suspended fir trees, garlanded with red ribbons and silver balls, myriad Santa Clauses complete with gift-laden sleighs, and hundreds of red-nosed reindeers named Rudolph galloping in brightly coloured bulbs across a dark December sky. Lilah loved it, the frantic bustle of last-minute Christmas shopping. At Hamley's, London's most famous toy shop, children stared wide-eyed and open-mouthed at the walking-talking robot. Hysterical mothers, the seasonal bonhomie of the lunch-time office party now wearing decidedly thin, were fighting one another for the few remaining Barbie dolls. Tired little boys, anxious now to get home, were hopelessly trying to prise their fathers away from the latest model train sets.

Lilah bought a fluffy pink elephant for her chauffeur's new granddaughter. Lord, she thought, glancing at her watch, there was still so much to do before the shops shut and everything was taking so long. She hurried into Liberty's before making her way to a teeming Piccadilly.

The food department at Fortnum & Mason's was so full it was almost impossible to move. A large American lady, bearing half a dozen boxes of crystallized ginger, almost flattened Lilah against the foie gras counter. There was no point in mentioning any of this to Roger. He would simply ask why she hadn't had everything delivered. Delivered! That was the whole point of Christmas shopping – the hassle of human contact. But Roger remained resolutely uninterested. How she wished he could show enthusiasm for anything other than business! The idea of Christmas spirit seemed quite alien to him. Tumbling onto the street with yet more carrier bags full of caviare and smoked salmon, Lilah hailed a cab. Gratefully ensconced in the back, she started to plan her Christmas Eve.

Lilah loved Midnight Mass, always had done, with the flickering candles, the carols ('Adeste Fideles' – that one always made her cry), the church decked out with holly and the Holy Family huddled happily around the crib. Tonight, the service at the Brompton Oratory seemed more beautiful than ever, the lights, the incense, the singing. Lilah only wished Roger had agreed to come. The bells rang and she knelt to pray. What a way to start the festive season, here in church all on her own. Her mind wandered to the happy, rowdy Christmases of her childhood. No, she'd never been on her own in those days. The house in Islington had always provided a focal point for such family occasions. Now her parents were gone, it all seemed so very far away. Lord, how she missed her mother and father – she still felt the loss like a physical pain. Nowadays, the five Dooley children, though emotionally very close, were scattered across the globe. Patrick, Lilah's eldest brother and a qualified barrister, had recently left Gray's Inn for a prestigious law firm in Boston. Sean, a foreign exchange dealer, was currently having a whale of a time in Sydney. Kevan, after a few failed wine bar enterprises in Chelsea, was now running the Shamrock, the most celebrated singing pub on the west coast of Ireland. And Declan (his mother's favourite) was in Rome, about to be ordained a priest. Lilah prayed for their health and happiness and hoped that someone was praying for hers.

By the time she'd driven up to Hertfordshire, it was three o'clock in the morning. Slowly, Lilah negotiated the long, tree-lined driveway which led to their country retreat. Standing in two hundred acres of prime farmland, the Oaks was an impressive Victorian building. Roger had found it soon after their engagement and Lilah had fallen in love with the place at first sight. Originally built as a large country house, it had subsequently been transformed into a young ladies' boarding school. Some time later, a soft porn king had bought it to entertain his friends. Lilah was now in the process of converting it back again to its former Victorian glory.

She could hear the horses whinnying softly in the stables as she opened the front door. Creeping upstairs, past the huge Christmas tree in the hall, she wandered along the endless corridor and into the bedroom. Exhausted by now, she undressed in the darkness and quietly slipped into bed beside Roger. 'Happy Christmas, darling,' she said, snuggling up close to him. But Roger did not stir. Tomorrow, an endless succession of people would be visiting, all of them Roger's guests. The very day she most wanted some time to share with him! Irritated at the prospect, Lilah rolled over and curled herself up into a tight, foetal ball. Within minutes she was asleep.

'No, no, no!' Roger's shouts pulled Lilah brutally from sleep.

'Roger, what is it?' Lilah switched on the bedside lamp to find him shaking by her side. The sight of her seemed immediately to calm him.

Moving across the bed, he grasped her tightly in his arms. 'You won't ever leave me, will you?' he said urgently.

Bemused, Lilah stroked his hair. It was she, after all, who was constantly being left. And it was he who had the track record. 'Don't be silly,' she soothed. 'I love you.' Releasing herself from his grip, she put her arms around his waist and kissed him lightly on the lips. Her hands came to rest on the strange band of whitish weals that scarred the bottom of his back. She had noticed them on their first night together, when Roger had fallen asleep exhausted after making love to her. Curious though she was, she had never thought to pry. No doubt he would explain things in his own time.

'Come on,' she said, holding him closer to her. She could feel his heart beating wildly in his chest. 'Let's try and get back to sleep.'

But Roger wanted to make love, and although she was tired, Lilah could not deny him. It was a short swift fuck, with none of the tenderness and care for her pleasure that he usually showed. Lilah was disturbed by his roughness but pushed her disquiet to the back of her mind. Perhaps he was simply getting something out of his system.

'I'm sorry, Lilah.' He flopped back onto the pillow afterwards, not looking at her.

'It's OK.' Despite the man in her bed, Lilah felt suddenly lonely. 'Goodnight, Roger.'

The next morning, Lilah was amazed to find him still sleeping when she awoke. He looked so peaceful that she was overwhelmed with tenderness. Lovingly, she kissed the handsome face on the pillow next to hers. He opened his eyes. For one brief moment it seemed as if they were struggling to convey some message to her.

'Happy Christmas,' said Roger, brightly. Leaning down to the side of the bed, he produced a small, perfectly wrapped parcel, an expensive gift from Asprey's. Already the moment had passed.

CHAPTER TWENTY-EIGHT

Spring, 1988

'Ir I didn't know you better, Sophie, I'd say you were a few bangers short of a barbie.' Sprawled out on the sitting-room floor, Grant and Ernie stared at the heap of letters and reports in which Sophie was immersed.

'I'm sorry, Grant,' said Sophie, looking up and trying not to squint. The bright spring sunshine poured in through the picture windows. Outside New York remained deceptively chilly. 'I hope you two boys aren't feeling neglected.'

'Oh, no, not at all,' said Grant laconically as he stroked the supine Blue Burmese. 'But just be grateful we're not in Queensland, Ernie, me old mate. And that you're not a bloody sheep.' Miaowing his alarm, Ernie hopped across the floor and onto his mistress's lap. He was soon engrossed in her untouched breakfast bagel. Smoked salmon and sour cream – Ernie's favourite.

Sophie removed her large, tortoiseshell reading glasses and made a funny face at Grant. 'How can you be so cruel to poor dumb animals?'

'You tell me, darling. You're the bloody banker.'

'What would I do without you, Grant?'

'I dunno. Probably become the world's leading expert on the life and times of Uncle Simon Weiss.'

'I really am sorry,' said Sophie, ostentatiously closing a folder full of correspondence and flashing Grant her most dazzling smile. 'I know it's become a bit of an obsession with me.

But I still can't help thinking there's something very odd about Uncle Simon's death.'

'But, Sophie, you got a copy of his death certificate. He died in a car accident after a massive coronary. Verdict – death from natural causes.'

'Sure, I know that,' said Sophie, gently putting Ernie on the floor and walking across the room to where Grant was still lying. 'But take a look at this.' Sophie handed him a letter handwritten in impeccable, black copperplate.

'From the Convent of the Holy Rosary, Meroto,' said Grant, lifting himself onto his elbows. 'Don't tell me, Sophie. You've succumbed to a sudden bout of poverty, chastity and obedience and you're taking Holy Orders.'

'Oh, do shut up and read it.'

Grant read for a few minutes in silence as Ernie peered over his shoulder.

'So?' said Sophie.

'So what? So this Reverend Mother Benigna confirms that Uncle Simon was a very generous benefactor.'

'Yes?'

'And that he promised to make a large bequest to the convent in his will.'

'Precisely.'

'Precisely what, Sophie?'

'That's precisely what's odd about his death. The convent never got that bequest. Why? Because, as far as we know, Uncle Simon died penniless and intestate.'

'What does that prove? Even your father says Uncle Simon was never too brill with the old paperwork. That's how the two of them lost contact.'

'Sure. But don't you see? If Uncle Simon had been feeling unfit or unwell, I'm convinced he'd have had a will drawn up.'

'Perhaps.'

'No perhapses, Grant, I'm sure of it. Besides, if he was so stony broke, how come he's promising the convent a major hand-out when he snuffs it?'

'Sophie,' said Grant, bemused and rubbing his head, 'where's all this leading?'

'Can't you see? Something must have happened. Perhaps

he lost all his money all of a sudden. Who knows? I just feel he must have had some terrible shock, something to precipitate the heart attack.'

'Look, you could be right. But all this happened over ten years ago. What can you prove now?'

'I don't know.' Sophie sounded deflated. 'In fact, I'm not even sure what I'm looking for.'

'Some connection between Uncle Simon and this bloke, Roger Samson?'

'I suppose so. Uncle Simon must have had something to do with opening up the Meroto mine. But I've read every Metallinc report I can lay my hands on and there's no mention of his name anywhere.'

'So you reckon Samson knew your uncle?'

'More than that. The way I figure it, they must have worked that mine together.'

'So what you're getting at,' Grant stroked Sophie's thick dark hair, 'is how come Roger Samson ends up a multi-fucking-millionaire while poor old Uncle Simon is six feet down pushing up the daisies?'

'Something like that,' said Sophie, laughing. 'You have such a way with words.'

'Have you anything else to go on?'

'Nothing except instinct.'

'The most important tool of your trade.'

'And the fact that this Roger Samson guy gives me the heebie-jeebies.'

'Ah, come off it, Sophie. Be fair. The bloke's a friggin' genius. His timing's even better than Don Bradman's in his hey-day.'

Sophie sighed. Grant was forever talking about Australian tycoons she had never even heard of. 'Maybe,' she conceded. 'But I've been doing my homework on Roger Samson. I guess by now I must have read every major interview he's ever given.'

'And?'

'Well, however far you dig with this guy, you never get to know anything about his early life.'

'I suppose that's because the punters are more interested in what he's gonna do next, not what he was up to twenty years ago.'

'Maybe. But don't you find it weird? When Roger Samson tips up in London in 1980, he's already thirty-two years old. Before that, forget it. The whole picture's a write-off.'

'Be reasonable, Samson wouldn't be the first bloke who didn't want to make a song and dance about his South African connections.'

'Perhaps not,' said Sophie, now lying flat on her back with Ernie strolling nonchalantly back and forth across her stomach. 'I know you think I'm wasting my time, but I'll keep on searching till I find it.'

'Sure,' said Grant, removing the cat to the sofa and rolling over to kiss Sophie. He started to paddle his fingers up and down her stomach, imitating Ernie. 'Find what was it again?' His hand continued its march, getting nearer to her crotch with each descent.

'I told you I don't know,' said Sophie, relaxing and beginning to enjoy this game. 'But whatever it is, I know there's got to be something.'

CHAPTER TWENTY-NINE

July, 1988

'JONATHAN?'

'Lilah, is that you?' Bleary-eyed, Jonathan looked at the alarm clock by the side of his bed. It was 3 a.m.

'Yes. I'm sorry to be ringing at this time of night – I just had to talk to you.'

'It's always good to hear your voice, Lilah. Very good.' Silence.

'You know I'm getting married tomorrow – well, it's today now I suppose.' There was a seemingly endless pause. 'But somehow tonight I just can't get to sleep.'

'I'm sorry I couldn't make it to the wedding,' said Jonathan, his voice still thick with drowsiness. 'I hope you understand.'

'I know you're very busy.'

'That's not the reason I can't come.'

'No, no – I suppose not.' Silence.

'Lilah, are you all right?'

'Oh, Jonathan.' By now Lilah's sobs were audible down the line. 'I'm feeling so confused.'

'What's the matter, Lilah? Do you want to call it off?'

'No, oh, no. I couldn't do that. Not at this stage. The arrangements have all been made. Everybody's here—'

'I don't call those good reasons,' said Jonathan sternly.

'No, I didn't mean that,' stammered Lilah, floundering. 'Of course I want to get married. It's just that it all seems so overwhelming at the moment. I'm sure it'll all seem much simpler in the morning.' Another long silence.

'Do you love him, Lilah?'

'Yes, of course I do,' retorted Lilah, rather too quickly. 'Why else do you think I'm marrying him?'

'*You* tell *me*, Lilah. You're the one who's lying awake confused, trying to figure it out.'

'Oh, Jonathan. You're no help at all. I thought I'd be able to talk to you of all people. I thought we'd always be friends.'

'No, Lilah. I don't know that we can be friends. If we can't be more than that, perhaps we can't be anything.'

'Oh, please!' Her voice was thin and weak, like that of a small, tired child.

'Does he love you?'

'Yes, I know he does. In his own way. He needs me.'

'*I* need you.'

'No, you don't,' she snapped. 'That was always half the trouble. You don't really need anything or anybody. That's why you're such a lucky man, Jonathan. The strength of your convictions has always been enough to keep you going.'

'Lilah, have you just rung up to argue with me? Because if so, I'm putting this receiver down immediately.'

'No.' Lilah's voice subsided. 'No, I'm sorry. It's just that I want to make sure that you understand. There's something about Roger – I can't put my finger on it – despite everything, all the money and the power, he seems, well, lost.'

'Come off it, Lilah. From what I've read, Roger Samson seems to know precisely where he is now and where he's going next. And he doesn't seem to allow many people to stand in his way.'

'Jonathan, you don't know him.'

'No, but I do know you.' By now Jonathan was out of bed and striding angrily around his bedroom. 'Wake up, Lilah,' he shouted. 'What the fuck do you think you're trying to do? Save this bastard's soul?'

'It's not like that,' cried Lilah. 'I do love him. He needs me.'

'So you said. Great! And now you're ringing me up in the middle of the night looking for my blessing. Well, forget it, Lilah. You know I don't go in for that kind of crap.'

'Why are you being so aggressive?'

'Can't you understand? If you told me you were marrying Samson for his money, I'd be a happier man. But I know you too well. I've been thinking about it ever since you got engaged and it's the only reason I can come up with. You're marrying Samson because you've convinced yourself there's some great big emotional void in his life that only you can fill. That's it, isn't it, Lilah? Tell me. I'm right, aren't I?'

'Yes.'

He could barely hear her whisper. 'Then don't go through with it,' thundered Jonathan. 'Please, Lilah. I'm begging you. Don't go through with it.'

'But, Jonathan . . .'

'Believe me, Lilah, one thing is for sure. Empty people are never satisfied.'

'Please, don't,' sobbed Lilah. 'I didn't ring you up to hear this kind of thing. I rang up because it's important you believe me, Jonathan. I'm marrying Roger because I love him.'

'That's the bloody tragedy,' said Jonathan, sitting down wearily on his bed, his heart palpitating with a combination of love and hurt and anger. 'And that's why I'm so bloody frightened for you, Lilah, my dear, darling Lilah, I believe you honestly think you do.'

The marriage of Miss Delilah Dooley and Mr Roger Samson was one of the society events of the year. Celebrated in St Patrick's Chapel at Westminster Cathedral, the ceremony itself was a deliberately low-key affair. Apart from Charles Watson-Smith (who acted as Roger's best man), Andrea and Hugo, the only guests at the chapel were Lilah's immediate family. Her youngest brother, Father Declan Dooley, recently ordained in Rome, officiated so beautifully that the ladies in the congregation were all moved to cry. All the ladies, observed Hugo, himself mopping up an impertinent little tear, with the single exception of Mrs Watson-Smith.

Despite her sleepless night, Lilah looked ravishing in an ivory corded lace and taffeta dress, its high neck and nipped waist showing every curve of her wonderful figure. Her auburn hair was simply dressed in a French pleat, neatly held in place at the back by a single diamond pin.

'A trifle pale,' whispered maiden aunt Bernie to Lilah's brother, Sean, seated next to her on the pew. 'But there again, whenever herself is after doing something important, she's always a trifle pale.'

Sean, back from Australia for the wedding, was studying his new brother-in-law with interest. Tall and dashing in his impeccably tailored morning suit, Roger Samson repeated his marriage vows in a clear and confident voice.

'In Sydney,' Sean whispered to his brother, Patrick, 'they say your man will be bigger than Kerry Packer.'

'Sure, an' which eejit is talkin' about spondoolicks on a day like today?' snapped Aunt Bernie. The old lady crossed herself immediately. 'Heaven forgive me for cursing in church. But in the end, your man's a poor orphan and he's nothin' else. He needs a good woman like Lilah to be lookin' after him, so he does.'

Patrick said nothing. It was neither the time nor the place. But in Boston he had heard a few things about the Dooleys' new brother-in-law. Nothing concrete – such gossip never was – just rumours about Samson's business associates. Of course, the partner in Patrick's law firm had not actually spelled it out. But the old money of Boston, he implied, would never do business with the likes of Jim di Pietro.

'I believe Lilah's taking an increasing interest in the hotel chain,' whispered Kevan, still hoarse from the previous night's hooley. 'Perhaps she could give me a few tips on increasing the profits at the Shamrock.'

Aunt Bernie's rosary beads rattled ominiously. A devout Pioneer, she had never touched a drop of alcohol in her entire seventy-year-old life. Nowadays Kevan's 'singing pub' featured increasingly in her novenas. Every night, Aunt Bernie prayed for the Holy Ghost to descend upon it and, in His infinite love and wisdom, blow the frigging thing to pieces.

The reception, by contrast, was a spectacular occasion. Hugo had spent months organizing everything right down to the tiniest detail. For the previous two days, the Samsons' Regent's Park mansion had been ringed with guards. Lilah had no intention of allowing the world's press to intrude on this, the most important day of her life. And with many of the world's wealthiest people on the guest list, not to mention the country's leading politicians and showbusiness personalities, Roger had demanded the highest level of security.

'How typical,' sniffed Andrea to Charles as they made their way through the mansion's magnificent entrance hall.

'I think it's very impressive,' replied Charles coldly. Andrea's snide remarks were getting increasingly on his nerves. Nowadays she never had a good word to say about either her best friend, Lilah, or her major employer, Roger. Ignoring his wife, Charles surveyed the room, with its black and white marble floor and white columns, with frank approval. On the left hung a fine Brussels biblical tapestry depicting Samson slaying the lion.

'How very beautiful,' said Charles to no one in particular.

'Just typical,' sighed Andrea once again. 'Typical Roger Samson megalomania.'

Charles stared at the young woman for whom he had once cared so much. It was strange how envy distorted even the prettiest of features.

A waiter appeared carrying glasses of vintage champagne. 'Thanks,' said Andrea, accepting a glass and immediately resting it on the priceless Spanish chest at the foot of the tapestry. The gesture was not lost on Charles. She knew, with a bit of luck, that it might leave some kind of mark. 'Oh dear,' continued Andrea loudly, 'how very *nouveau*. I'd have thought Roger would have known better. But I see the Samsons are into instant ancestors.' Andrea motioned towards a large portrait of a woman hanging on the adjacent wall.

'Eighteenth-century, French, a portrait of la Comtesse de Provence by Madame Vigier-Lebrun,' interrupted Hugo, sauntering through the hall. 'And I suppose, Andrea darling, that the Blackwells of Grimford are all hanging in the Tate.'

Furious, Andrea wished the cylinder candelabrum would come crashing down on Hugo's arrogant bloody head.

'You and Lilah have done a wonderful job,' said Charles, shaking Hugo warmly by the hand. 'Pay no attention to Andrea.'

'Have no fear of that,' said Hugo, who had always been fond of Charles. He hoped that one day the dear chap would finally see through his dreadful little wife. Judging by that comment, perhaps he already had.

'See you anon,' said Hugo, catching sight of William

Stanton, surreptitiously arranging his hair in the Italian gilt mirror at the opposite end of the hall.

'I say, Stanton,' said Hugo moving across to slap his old friend cheerfully on the back, 'you're looking very prosperous.'

'And so are you,' replied William, delighted to see Hugo again. He placed an expensively wrapped gift on the ebony and lacquer Weisweiler commode. 'And if I'm not mistaken, I think I can see your touch in this place, Newsom.'

'Absolutely. Lilah and I have had the most tremendous fun spending a few of the Samson millions on this pile.'

'How is she?'

'Well, she's looking wonderful, if that's what you mean,' replied Hugo vaguely. 'I suppose you saw the ghastly Andrea as you came in.'

'Did my best to avoid her. My word, though, didn't she do well for herself?' The two friends looked across the hall to where the Watson-Smiths were standing. Andrea, pert in a black and white Edina Ronay suit, seemed to be hanging onto every word the young duke and duchess were saying.

'Come on, before you throw up,' said Hugo, taking William by the arm. 'The bride and groom are receiving people in the garden. I know Lilah's looking forward to seeing you.'

'Hugo!' The two friends turned to notice a small frail figure slumped on the round ivory damask banquette in the middle of the hall.

'Aunt Bernie,' said Hugo, solicitously, 'may I fetch you a glass of water?'

'It's just the heat, darlin', that's all,' said Aunt Bernie, fanning herself with a Catholic Truth Society pamphlet she had retrieved from the bottom of her handbag. 'And the fact that I haven't worn these stays since Lilah's father's wake. Be a good boy, will you now, Hugo, an' give me a hand up.'

'Shall we escort you?' asked Hugo, helping the old lady to her feet. 'This is William Stanton, an old university friend of mine and Lilah's. And William, this is Lilah's Aunt Bernie.'

'Now that's a very handsome young man,' said Aunt Bernie to Hugo in a loud stage whisper. 'What does he do?'

'Nothing much,' said Hugo, affecting a grimace. 'He's a banker. Sad, really. He was a late developer.' William smothered a smile as the unlikely trio wandered past the sweeping stone staircase and towards the reception.

The french windows of the garden room were thrown open on to the formal Italianate garden with its clipped box hedges and charming stone statues. Outside, Hugo could hear the tinkle of high society laughter – as fake and evanescent as the fizz of a bottle of Asti Spumanti. Eschewing the sunshine, some of the guests had returned to the garden room which was cool and fresh with its bright green and yellow painted furniture. Filled to overflowing with caviare, an ice sculpture of a massive scallop dominated the centre table.

'Go and take William outside to meet the happy couple,' said Hugo to Aunt Bernie. 'I'll be along later.'

A raucous cluster of guests had congregated around Kevan who was enjoying himself enormously. 'And so I says to him, I says, then why do the Irish call a pound a punt? And he says to me, he says, Jaysus, Kevan, I don't know. Why do the Irish call a pound a punt? And I says to him, because it rhymes with bank manager.' The group howled with laughter, none more so that the young duchess herself.

'Kevan?'

'Yes, Hugo. An' what can I be doin' for you?'

'Could we have a word?'

'Of course.' The two men found a quiet corner.

'Heavens above!' exclaimed Kevan, tapping a gloriously gilded barometer for a reading. 'This looks like an interesting old yoke. What does this say? Made for the Dauphine of France and first hung in the Palais du Louveciennes.'

'Yes,' said Hugo, slightly impatient. He had not buttonholed Kevan to discuss important French furniture.

'I bet that must have set herself back at least a couple of hundred quid.'

Hugo was beginning to wonder whether he had chosen the wrong brother. 'Kevan,' he continued, regardless, 'have you spoken to Lilah recently?'

'Of course. I was talking to her about five minutes ago.'

'No. I mean *really* spoken to her. What I'm driving at is, do you get the impression she's happy?'

'Sure, she's as rich as Croesus an' this is one hell of a party,' replied Kevan. Hugo sighed. It was obvious where Lilah had acquired her sometimes impenetrable sense of logic. A waiter stopped to refill their glasses. Another arrived with a silver salver of exquisitely presented canapés.

'So the family thinks she's OK?' Discreetly, Hugo moved a fine early Ming blue porcelain vase away from Kevan's elbow.

'To be perfectly frank with you, Hugo,' said Kevan, his mouth full of champagne and smoked salmon, 'I haven't had the time to discuss it properly with the boys. But all I know is, once Lilah sets her mind on somethin', there's nothin' any of us can do to stop her. She's always been very headstrong.'

'I know,' said Hugo. 'Anyway, sorry for interrupting you. You must think I'm behaving like the spectre at the feast. Go on – back to your audience. I know they're missing you.'

'Hugo,' said Kevan, suddenly sombre. 'I do know what you're drivin' at. I've met your man, Samson, an' I can't help feelin' he's a very cold fish – not Lilah's sort at all.'

'And your brothers?'

'Well, Declan's never been known to say a bad word about anyone. But Sean and Paddy both seem a bit concerned.'

'Did any of you say anything?'

'It's a bit late now, isn't it? Besides, who are we to tell herself what to do and how to do it?'

'You're right,' agreed Hugo glumly. 'But why do you think she's marrying him?'

'Well, Declan says it's because she loves him. Aunt Bernie reckons she wants to look after him. An' Sean and Paddy say she's been dazzled by his money.'

'And which of them is right?'

'Oh, they're all right,' he said emphatically. 'But since you're askin' me, I think there's something else as well. If you want my candid opinion, Hugo, I'd say she was doin' it for the crack.'

'As I always said to Roger . . .' Hugo could hear Howard Anderson's voice booming from the garden as he moved back towards the hall. Draped around a particularly blonde and buxom starlet, Christopher Grafton was studying the centre-piece of the marble-topped Regency table near the foot of the staircase. 'Bloody fascinating,' he said, peering into the bowl, about to dip his finger in the water. 'I wonder what these little black buggers are?'

'I wouldn't do that,' said Hugo quickly. 'They're Japanese fighting fish.'

'Very pretty,' purred the starlet, disposing of her cigarette butt nonchalantly on the beautiful Aubusson carpet. 'Especially with those white orchids floating around on top.'

'Yes, they are attractive,' agreed Hugo. 'I've got them dotted all around the house. Rather more inspired than boring old floral arrangements, don't you think?'

'Oh, yes,' breathed the starlet, hugely impressed.

Hugo smiled at her pretty, vacuous little face. Women like that, they were no different from the Japanese fighting fish. Slightly less interesting on the conversational front, they were all mere decorative baubles for rich men's interior design. 'I'm going upstairs to check on a few things in the drawing room,' he said.

'Oh no,' breathed the starlet. 'Do stay and talk to us. I've read so much about you and I'm so fascinated by your work.'

'Sorry,' said Hugo, turning on his heel and swiftly ascending the staircase. 'Christopher should have warned you. I have a very low boredom threshold. And you, darling, have just reached it.'

Outside in the garden the champagne flowed freely as the bride and groom circulated among their guests.

'William, I'm so happy to see you,' said Lilah, kissing him on both cheeks. 'I hope Aunt Bernie has not been leading you astray.'

'On the contrary, she's just convinced me never to do business with anyone who drinks.'

'That rules me out, then,' said George Hamish, weaving his way across the garden to Lilah. 'Let me kiss the blushing bride.'

Two feet away, Madeleine Hamish looked on with ill-concealed opprobrium, her powder-blue petal hat wobbling precariously atop a stiffly lacquered perm. 'Congratulations,' she said primly. 'Ah, waiter, waiter, yoo-hoo. Do you think you could fetch me a glass of water? No, none of that fancy fizzy stuff. Tap water will do nicely. I do think drinking champagne in the sunshine is a bad idea, don't you, George?' She spoke slowly and deliberately, her words over-articulated, rather like Joyce Grenfell admonishing a five-year-old for accidentally wetting his pants.

Poor old George, thought Lilah, returning his embrace. No wonder he's always smashed.

'I agree,' piped up Aunt Bernie. 'Sure, drink is the devil's work.'

'Then let's all go to hell and merrily,' returned George, determined to enjoy the day despite the tap-water-drinking Madeleine. He offered his glass to a hovering waiter.

'I'm staggered nobody's managed to hook you yet, William,' said Lilah, trying to avert an argument.

'I don't think I'm quite ready for the ball and chain.'

Madeleine Hamish scowled through the veil of her hat. Lilah thought she looked like a flatulent toad peeping out from behind a hydrangea bush.

'Hugo always said that you were a late developer,' continued Lilah. Both she and William laughed. Private jokes – such bad form – another thing Madeleine Hamish really could not abide. 'D'you know, William,' continued Lilah, oblivious, 'I really do owe you an apology. I've been so bad at keeping in touch with people over the last few years. I'd love to see you and Hugo for lunch.'

'Just as soon as you get back from honeymoon,' agreed William. Out of the corner of his eye, he could see Sir Howard Anderson bearing down on Lilah. 'But right now, darling, I think I'll go and find old Newsom. Looks like you're about to be nailed.'

Hugo was surprised to find a slightly tipsy Miss Kerwin sitting upstairs in the drawing room.

'Oh, Mr Newsom,' she said, flustered, 'I hope nobody will mind. But it's too much for me downstairs. It's all so lovely . . . so very, very lovely.' Sniffing into her handkerchief, Miss Kerwin gestured vaguely around the room, her reflection shuddering silently in the carved giltwood mirror hanging over the fireplace.

'You are very fond of Mr Samson, aren't you?' said Hugo, sitting down next to her.

'He's been very good to me,' replied Miss Kerwin, tracing a

SAMSON AND DELILAH

pattern on the Savonnerie carpet with the toe of her sensible
court shoe. 'I've been with him since he arrived in this country
and I've watched Samson International grow. I suppose you
could say it's the most important thing in my life.'

'Are you happy for him?' probed Hugo, vaguely ashamed
to be taking advantage of Miss Kerwin's tipsy and emotional
condition.

'Oh, yes. Yes, of course,' said Miss Kerwin defensively.
'Miss Dooley's a lovely girl. I only hope Mr Samson isn't . . .'

'Yes?'

'Nothing. Oh dear. How dreadfully disloyal.' Miss Kerwin
rose to her feet. 'I'm afraid I'm not myself today. I hardly ever
touch a drink, you know. Perhaps I'd better leave before I do
something silly.'

Hugo watched as, slightly wobbly, Miss Kerwin made her
way out of the drawing room. Discreet people, thought Hugo,
peeved, they were so unutterably useless.

Two more guests filtered quietly into the drawing room.
Recognizing Jim di Pietro, Hugo sauntered across to the fireplace, affecting to admire the superb pair of BVRB commodes
and the Cézannes hung above them.

'Roger agrees with me,' Jim di Pietro was saying. 'We'd
better give it some time. Probably eighteen months or so. I
don't reckon the Group should move on this one before early
1990.'

'What about the South African connection?' The man spoke
impeccable English but with clipped Teutonic precision.

'No problem. We can keep them happy till then. Don't
forget, they also need time to get themselves into some kind
of shape.' The two men were speaking so quietly that Hugo
could hardly hear them. He moved across to study Jim's surprise wedding present to his friend – Roger's old Corniche
crushed and compressed by César. The two men were now
standing just a few feet away, next to the Riesner console.
Glancing up, Hugo could see their faces clearly in the Louis
XV mirror above.

'Is everything else in place?' asked the German.

'Sure,' replied Jim. 'The companies are all set up. When we
do move, we're going to have to buy thousands of relatively

260

small contracts. And we've got to keep the ownership of those contracts as untraceable as possible.'

'Otherwise the regulatory authorities will smell a rodent?' asked the German.

'Something like that,' said Jim. 'Did you get those figures I sent you?'

A waiter appeared at the large double doors and the two men turned to have their glasses replenished. Drat, thought Hugo. With their backs to him, he could no longer follow what they were saying. Swiftly, he sidled past them, pretending to study the stèle d'Arman.

'Oh, waiter,' said Hugo, slurring his words for the benefit of his audience, 'another tincture over here, please. I say, this thing is jolly colourful, isn't it? I wonder how whoever it was got all those tubes of paint to trickle down into the plastic. Bloody clever, I say.'

Neither the German nor di Pietro paid him the slightest attention.

'So you are saying that eighty per cent of the Western world's platinum is coming from South Africa?'

'Yeah,' agreed Jim di Pietro. 'And right now ninety per cent of that is being refined by South Africa's two major refineries.'

'Rustenburg and Impala?'

'You got it. All of which makes our job so much easier.'

'Hugo, Hugo, sure an' I've been lookin' for ye everywhere.' Hugo clenched his teeth as Aunt Bernie came bustling into the room. Hell, just as the conversation was getting interesting! Now, not even lawyer Patrick would be able to make sense out of what he could report. What a pity! Hugo knew Patrick was dying to know more about Roger's swarthy American friend.

'Yes, Aunt Bernie.' Already the two men had moved across to the far end of the room, well out of earshot. Hugo's mood was not improved by the sight of Jim di Pietro playing with the wedding present he had given Lilah – a beautiful Farhi backgammon set in yellow and red plexiglass.

'Come on, now, out into the garden,' insisted Aunt Bernie. 'Lilah's been askin' after ye.'

Shit! There was no way to refuse without making the two

men suspicious. Fuming, Hugo followed Aunt Bernie down-stairs and out into the garden.

Lilah smiled gratefully as soon as she saw him. For the last fifteen minutes she had been subjected to the most tedious ear-bashing from Sir Howard Anderson and was clearly in need of rescue.

'Lilah, darling, what a wonderful day,' said Hugo kissing her on both cheeks. 'I thought the ceremony went off very well.'

'Hugo, you know Sir Howard and Lady Anderson?' asked Lilah, comically crossing her eyes at Hugo.

'Yes, I do believe we've met before at some Samson Inter-national thrash or other,' said Hugo amiably. 'My word, though, Sir Howard, you're not looking terribly well today, are you?' He peered at Sir Howard's florid, dissolute face and smiled sympathetically.

'I keep telling him,' said Lady Anderson, concerned, 'but he won't have any of it. He works too hard, don't you, Howard, dear? Always at the House or in his office till the early hours of the morning. I've given up ringing him from the country. During the week, it's just impossible to get hold of him at the London flat.'

'I'm feeling just fine,' resisted Sir Howard, who had no intention of moving on. He was quite enjoying himself, regaling the new Mrs Samson with tales of how he had set her husband on the right track early in his career. 'And as I was saying to the Prime Minister only the other day . . .'

'Of course, that would be your flat in Holland Park,' said Hugo disingenuously.

'Why no,' said Lady Anderson, puzzled. 'Our flat's just three minutes away from the Houses of Parliament – on the bell.' Sir Howard glared at Hugo.

'How very odd,' insisted Hugo. 'D'you know, Sir Howard, I could have sworn I saw you early the other morning, coming out—'

'Ah,' said Sir Howard, interrupting him in mid-sentence, 'my dear Lilah, do forgive me. There's a cabinet colleague over there I must have a word with. Come on, Serena. Lovely party, Lilah. We must all have dinner soon.'

'Hugo, you are the limit,' laughed Lilah, taking Hugo by the arm as Sir Howard scampered off across the garden. 'Mind you, I don't think I could have stood another minute with that dreadful old buffoon. Tell me, have you seen Roger about?'

'No,' replied Hugo, casting around, 'he must be in the house.'

'I think I'll go and find him. I'm boiling in this dress. Ah, Charles.'

Hugo took his leave as Charles Watson-Smith arrived to greet the bride. With a bit of luck, Jim di Pietro and his German friend would still be in the drawing room.

Hugo peered into the room but already the two men had moved on. Instead, next to the games table, stood Roger and Andrea.

'You used me,' shouted Andrea raucously, the elocution lessons temporarily forgotten.

'I don't know what you're talking about,' replied Roger.

'Oh, yes, you do. You led me on. You made me think you wanted me and then you went and married Lilah.'

'It's all a figment of your own fevered imagination.' Roger's voice was icy. 'And I must say, apart from anything else, I think it's rather bad form to be behaving like this on my wedding day.'

'Don't you talk to me about bad form.'

'Now just you listen here. It's as simple as this, Andrea. Do you want the Samson International account or don't you?'

Andrea said nothing. Hugo could see her chest heaving with sheer frustration.

'Good,' said Roger breezily. 'Then I think that's all settled.'

'But you—'

'Andrea, I'm warning you. We'll have no more of this nonsense. Now, off you go and enjoy the party. Oh, and just one more thing before you join your husband.'

'Yes,' said Andrea, still clutching at straws of hope. Roger fixed her with his most terrifying blue stare.

'If you say so much as one word – one word I tell you – to upset Lilah, believe me, Andrea, I'll ruin you completely.'

The singing had already started by the time Lilah and Charles reached the garden room.

'Oh, Mary, this London's a wonderful sight,
With the people here workin' by day an' by night.
No, they don't sow potatoes, nor barley nor wheat,
But there's crowds of 'em diggin' for gold in the street.'

Lilah smiled indulgently. Despite the previous night's excesses, Kevan was clearly back in fine voice.

Still badly shaken, Andrea wandered into the room, depositing the classic PR kiss on everyone of importance. 'Washington kisses', Hugo called them. Brief lip/cheek interface, gaze firmly focused beyond the ear, eyes scanning the room for further potential recipients. 'Lilah, darling,' she gushed, 'how wonderful you look. I'm so happy for you both.' Lilah looked relieved, pleased that the tensions of the previous months seemed to have evaporated.

'Thanks,' she said, radiant. 'I know you've been a bit worried about me – probably thought I was rushing into things. But I'm so happy, Andrea. And you've always been such a good friend. I knew you'd come round in the end.' Andrea smiled her most saccharine, snuggle-bunny smile. Charles gazed out into the garden.

Excavating large mounds of beluga from the carved ice scallop, Hugo and William could not help overhearing the conversation. 'Don't listen,' warned William, catching a dangerous glint in Hugo's eye. 'It'll only annoy you.'

'I like to practise being annoyed,' replied Hugo, tapping a silver spoonful of caviare rather too vehemently on his plate. 'Otherwise I might lose my edge. Come on, let's find a quiet corner somewhere else before I deck that little bitch.'

Upstairs in the drawing room Father Declan Dooley found Roger studying the two Giacometti sculptures Lilah had transferred from the yacht. 'Tortured souls,' declared Father Declan, looking at the elongated and skeletal human figures and back again at Roger.

'Yes,' said Roger, flashing the priest his most dazzling smile. 'Sad, lonely, miserable beings. Terrible, really. I suppose that's why the Church is so hot on marriage and the family.'

'A person can be isolated – I mean, spiritually isolated –

even within such institutions,' replied Father Declan pointedly.

'You're right, Father,' said Roger casually. 'That's why it's so important for a man to find the right wife.'

Declan did not know whether Roger was taking the rise or not. 'So you're convinced Lilah is the right wife for you?'

'Absolutely. We make a great team.'

'Marriage is not a ball game, you know.'

Roger laughed. 'I'm sorry, Father. I didn't mean to sound so crass. What I meant was, Lilah and I – well, we complement each another. She has qualities – I don't know – people just do things for her – for no reason – just because they like her. Me – it seems I always have to pay or threaten to get things done.'

The two men stared silently at the figures for a minute. Father Declan turned to Roger. 'You don't want to talk to me, do you,' he asked quietly, 'about anything – anything at all?' Roger bit his lip. For a split second Father Declan thought he might open up, get whatever it was that was bothering him off his chest. But the moment was soon lost.

'Roger.' Jim di Pietro appeared at the doorway. 'About that TV deal. Spare me a minute on your wedding day?'

'Sure,' replied Roger. 'Just go upstairs to my study, will you, and make yourself at home. I'll be with you in a minute.' He turned his attention back to the priest. 'Thanks for the offer,' he said jauntily, 'but there's nothing I need to talk to you about, Father. At least, nothing I can't handle.'

By now, guests were swarming all over the house. In the dining room, where an exquisite seafood buffet of lobster, dressed crab, king prawns and smoked salmon had been laid out on the long, eighteenth-century English dining table, a group of showbusiness personalities had congregated and were already picking anorexically at the fare.

'These folk don't even talk to one other,' noted Patrick *sotto voce* to Sean. Unlike the *glitterati*, the two brothers had healthy appetites and were busily helping themselves to generous servings from the buffet.

'No,' agreed Sean, highly amused, 'they don't converse, they just *network*.'

'I've always been so interested in your career.' Somehow Christopher Grafton's starlet had appended herself to a celebrated northern footballer and was now giving him the full benefit of her fatuous infatuation. Barely twenty years old and already a millionaire, 'Bonker' Billings was drinking champagne straight out of the bottle.

'One of Andrea's less felicitous PR coups,' whispered a peeved Christopher Grafton to the Dooley brothers. 'She put this yobbo on an annual fifty-thousand-pound retainer to promote Samson International hotels. So far all he's done is smash up a few suites and pee all over the potted plants in the foyer at the Samson International, Park Lane.'

Both Sean and Patrick laughed. Here was one guest, at least, who did not give a toss about the nuances of networking.

'Mind you,' continued Christopher, 'he's cleaned up his act a lot since your sister came onto the scene. Apparently she sat him down one night and told him he was upsetting his old mum back in Liverpool. Since then, he's stopped smashing up suites and is simply sticking to the plants.' Patrick glanced down at the glorious Heriz carpet and prayed that today 'Bonker' was on his best behaviour.

Sir Howard Anderson was sitting in a corner, his head slumped against the yellow silk stripe wallpaper while Lady Anderson scuttled around, busily filling the great man's plate. 'Mr Newsom,' he called, as Hugo made his way through the dining room and into the conservatory. 'Young man, I want a word with you.'

'I can see that,' replied Hugo, barely bothering to look back over his shoulder. 'I can see your mind, cranking up to conjugate.'

The conservatory had filled up with what Hugo called the 'money mob'. 'Interesting, William, don't you find?' he said, decidedly sloshed by this stage and glancing around the room. 'All Lilah's guests are personal friends. And Roger's are all business associates.'

'Does he have any friends?' asked William.

'Nope,' said Hugo, clinging unsteadily onto a wall bracket bearing a priceless figurine. 'Except Lilah.' He hiccupped loudly. 'Christ, I hope Bonker doesn't catch sight of all these potted plants.' William stared at the impressive array of palms and hanging ferns.

'Oh, my God.' William caught sight of an extremely affluent-looking Arab gentleman half-hidden in the foliage. 'Is that who I think it is?'

'Dunno,' replied Hugo, swaying dangerously close to a palm tree.

'You know – what's-his-name – the arms dealer. I thought he was wanted by the police for questioning in this country.'

'Nothing would surprise me about Roger's guests,' said Hugo, eyeing the assembled company with obvious disdain. 'Come on, Stanton, I suppose we'd better have something to eat before I keel over.'

Upstairs, on the second floor, Jim di Pietro stared across the desk at Roger. Christ, this guy was a difficult one to read. Never, in all his sixty years, had Jim found it so difficult to relate to a man. Roger Samson – he was not like any other business associate he had ever dealt with. It was not so much that Samson was hard and ruthless. Heck, Jim had seen plenty of hard and ruthless guys in his time. He was hard and ruthless himself, for Chrissake, though deep down everyone knew he had a soft and generous streak.

But Roger – no, there was something about Roger. Or rather something missing. Jim had met it once before with a guy they called the Viper. Never had di Pietro come across a hit-man so lacking in human feelings, so totally incapable of guilt, fear or shame. Jim caught Roger's eye. Despite his wealth and prestige, he was just the same. Roger Samson was a man completely devoid of affect.

'As someone I once knew used to say,' smiled Roger, perusing the papers on his desk, ' "turnover is vanity, profit is sanity".'

'Yeah, very neat,' replied Jim, testily. 'But I've bust my ass over this deal, Roger. And what I want to know is, is it yes or no?'

'They're conning you on the advertising revenue.'

'Nobody cons Jim di Pietro,' he retorted, his fingers clenched hard on the gilt-bronze border of Roger's desk.

'Hell,' said Roger, standing up and walking round the desk. 'I'm not expressing myself very well today, am I?' He put his hand on Jim's shoulder. 'Look, Jim, get them to lop twenty million dollars off the price, and tell them we have a deal. The lawyers can sort out all the crap about citizenship of the owner.'

'OK,' said Jim, his face now wreathed in smiles. 'I'm sure they'll bite.'

Roger nodded.

'Thank God we went liquid when we did,' continued Jim. 'Right now, you can call any shots you want. You're still saying early nineteen ninety for our South African venture?'

'Yes. I've told you, I'd rather we sat tight for a while. You have everything you need to keep the FAP contacts happy?'

'Sure. Mind you, it's not easy to keep the young bloods completely quiet. Thank God that guy Credo Sekese wants to hang out for the big one. All the same, I hear some security guard bought it at the Meroto plant the other day. They found the poor bastard pulverized in one of those big ore-crushing machines.'

'In a ball-mill?'

'Yeah, that's the one. Seems this guy was an ex-cop. A few years back he beat up real bad on some FAP girl. Anyways, by the time they opened this thing up, all that was left of him was a small pool of blood, dripping out of the door.'

'Christ Almighty! Still, when it comes to blowing up the refineries, it looks like there'll be no qualms on the FAP side.'

'No,' said Jim. 'No, I reckon not.'

Sitting together in the relative calm of the print room, Father Declan had just been buttonholed by a decidedly maudlin Hugo.

'Declan, Hugo, have you seen Roger anywhere?' asked Lilah. Declan looked up at his sister. She seemed somewhat fraught.

'Last I saw,' he replied, 'Roger was going up to his office to talk to some American gentleman.'

'I'm just sick of it,' exploded Lilah suddenly. 'It's supposed to be *our* wedding not *my* wedding. And I've spent the last few hours on my own entertaining all *his* bloody guests.'

'Ghastly people,' said Hugo, his head lolling slightly to one side.

Lilah nodded her agreement. Politicians who had outgrown their wives and the wives who so despised them. Millionaires who had purchased the latest trophy wife. Girls who had traded love and youth for an old man's bed and cheque book. Lilah sighed, exhausted. Where did she fit into all of this? 'Thanks,' she said. 'I'll go and drag him down.'

'So you see, Father,' continued Hugo, unabashed, 'AIDS has changed everything for a person like me. Why, since coming down from university, I've had only three real lovers.'

'Three?' repeated Father Declan quietly. His years of training in the seminary had taught him never to sound shocked or offended, no matter what the confession. Hugo nodded his head. First there had been Marcus, the actor and the best-looking. Then Daryl, the sculptor – the best in bed. And then there had been Garry, the cricketer. Hugo could no longer remember what had been so appealing about Garry. Perhaps he'd been the best at short forward square-leg. Declan took a deep breath as he pondered his response. Not all the cardinals in Rome could have prepared him for a case like Hugo Newsom.

'Roger!' Lilah found her husband making his way down to the dining room.

'Lilah, darling . . .'

'Don't you Lilah darling me. Where have you been all afternoon? I've been here—' Lilah caught sight of Jim di Pietro following close behind Roger.

'You're right, honey,' said Jim emolliently. 'But it's all my fault. Now don't you two lovebirds go fighting on your wedding day. Like I said to Mrs di Pietro on our happy day, there's the rest of your life together for that.'

Lilah forced a smile as Jim continued on down the stairs.

'I'm sorry, darling,' said Roger, catching Lilah by the hand. 'But there was something Jim and I had to talk about. Besides,' he drew Lilah closer to him, 'today I just can't deal with a crowd of people. All I want to do now is escape somewhere quiet with you.'

'Oh, Roger,' said Lilah, her annoyance evaporating, 'you know we can't do that. Come on, you'll have to see a few more guests. I know Sir Howard Anderson is dying to talk to you.'

'All the more reason to escape,' sighed Roger, with a rare flash of humour. He kissed Lilah hard on the lips. 'I love you, Lilah. I want to make love to you.'

'And I love you, too,' said Lilah, surprised by the force of his embrace.

'Good. So, you're not going to divorce me just yet?' He held her closer.

'No, of course not.' She looked up at him, her eyes now twinkling mischievously. 'Not unless you keep party-pooping at your own bloody parties.'

Aunt Bernie's screams were clearly audible even at the top of the house. Hand in hand, Roger and Lilah raced down the staircase to see what had happened to her. By the time they reached the hall, Hugo and Declan were already there, trying to calm the old lady.

'Whatever is the matter?' shouted Lilah, alarmed.

'My fault entirely,' said Hugo, shamefacedly. 'I knew there was something I'd forgotten. The bloody oxygenating plants.'

The small group stared at the bowl on the table near the foot of the stairs. Starved of oxygen, the black Japanese fighting fish had started fighting one another and were now all floating belly up among the orchids.

'Jesus, Mary and Joseph,' muttered Aunt Bernie, deathly pale and clasping her rosary beads tightly to her generous bosom. 'Sure, death at a wedding, 'tis a terrible omen.' And with that, she passed out on the floor.

CHAPTER THIRTY

Spring, 1989

IF OVER the next few months anyone had asked her, Lilah would have said that she was ecstatically happy. Rich and glamorous, with houses in London, Hertfordshire and Cap Ferrat, not to mention their international hotel chain, the Samsons cut a brilliant swathe through high society everywhere. Of course, Roger often travelled alone on business but that, as he reminded Lilah whenever she tried to complain, was the price of running one of the world's leading industrial conglomerates. To begin with, his frequent and often unexplained absences bothered her. But soon Lilah was so busy with her own career in Samson International that she managed to blot out qualms from her conscious mind. Moreover, any misgivings about the quality of their relationship were quickly submerged under the plethora of social functions which the new Mrs Samson was called upon to organize.

Lilah continued to correspond with Jonathan, though her letters became gradually more restrained. Nowadays, after all, there were far too many no-go areas between the former lovers, a range of subjects that could never be discussed. How, for instance, could Jonathan be expected to sympathize with her over her too-often lonely bed? She missed their earlier intimacy and tried to compensate with generous donations to the Christian Sight-Savers Mission Hospital. But Jonathan was far too prickly to accept such largesse without certain reservations. As usual, he struggled with his conscience. In his view, Samson money was tainted and he wanted none of it. In the end, however, after Lilah's protestations, he relented. Even so, he could never be cajoled into accepting anything more than essential medical supplies.

Yes, Lilah missed the warmth and openness she used to share with Jonathan. There were so many new fears and feelings she longed to talk about but somehow, married to Roger, she seemed more isolated than ever. Andrea, though ostensibly charming in company, seemed frosty and withdrawn in their personal dealings. And as for Hugo – well, there was no point asking him for advice about Roger. He had disliked him from the outset. Sometimes Lilah would catch herself sighing in the mirror. It seemed there was really no one left to talk to.

And yet Roger's nightmares were a cause of much anxiety. It was not so much the nightmares themselves which hurt her so deeply, more Roger's stubborn refusal to discuss them. Such reticence was alien to Lilah's nature. She tried to persuade him into therapy but he just laughed at the suggestion. Therapy was like sleep, he maintained, a refuge reserved for the wimpish and inadequate.

But perhaps what bothered her most was Roger's reluctance to talk about his parents or his early life. Even now the scars on his back remained resolutely unexplained. Sometimes Lilah felt as if her husband had only come into being on his arrival in London. His time before that was very vague and, for large tracts, a positive mystery. But if Roger's past was an enigma, so increasingly was his present. Even on evenings when they were both at home at Regent's Park, he sometimes elected to sleep alone in his interconnecting bedroom. There were always valid reasons – a deal somewhere to be finalized and international phone calls to be fielded throughout the night. All the same, although sex was still frequent, sometimes very tender and sometimes almost painfully passionate, it was always on Roger's terms, precisely when, where and how he wanted it. Sex, like everything else in his life, was a matter of control.

At first Lilah tried to reach out to her husband but soon discovered that his charming carapace of reserve was impenetrable. With all the business and social commitments there were few opportunities for quiet dinners together. But even when such occasions arose, Roger often seemed preoccupied and distant. During their love-making, for the few moments that his guard was down, Lilah believed he loved and needed her. But whereas Lilah's love for Roger was absolute, his seemed more conditional. She suspected that he loved her for himself not for herself, that was the difference between them. Certainly he was enormously proud of his wife and her instant success within the company, but already Lilah was beginning to feel like the prize asset in Roger's empire – beautiful and expensive, but once acquired, no longer to be fought for. Something kept surfacing in her thoughts, a line vaguely recalled from the letters of Madame de Sévigné: 'You intrude on my solitude without affording me company.' How many women, she wondered, felt the same way about their husband?

Such reflections, though disturbing, were swiftly brushed aside. The intelligent mind has an almost infinite capacity for successful self-deception. If there were large areas of Roger's past and present life from which Lilah felt excluded, she refused to let it get her down. There was no point wasting sleep over seemingly intractable problems. Unconsciously Lilah had done a deal. Within six months of marrying Roger, she had managed to convince herself that there was no problem whatsoever. In the end, it was easy. She simply did what she had always done – kept herself on the move. More dangerous still, she hoped that the arrival of a baby might solve this undefined problem.

The 1989 'Save the Baby Fund' spring dinner was to be held at Samson Tower, New York, and both Lilah and Andrea had worked hard to make this fund-raiser one of the city's most glittering occasions. Jim di Pietro, who was very fond of the new Mrs Samson, had called in all his markers and done everything to ensure that her efforts were crowned with the utmost success. Lilah was pleased with the way the guest list was shaping up. The old recipe, a judicious amalgam of the rich and famous – wealthy businessmen rubbing shoulders with their favourite film stars, pop idols and sporting heroes – seemed guaranteed to do the trick.

'I can't thank you enough,' said Lilah, when Jim called her in London to confirm another tableful of guests at $1,000 a head. 'You know I wouldn't have known where to start in New York without your help.'

'Don't mention it,' said Jim, from the depths of his tinted-window stretch limo. 'I wouldn't be doing it if I didn't like you.'

'That's kind. Would you mind if I gave you a special mention in the programme?'

'Jesus Christ, don't. Thanks all the same, but that's the last thing I need. Like my father used to tell me when him and me were both still in the plumbing business, "Jimmy, boy, rich guys who go looking for publicity, they end up broke or in the slammer."'

Lilah laughed.

'You better believe it,' continued Jim seriously. 'Anyways, bye for now, Lilah, I'm looking forward to seeing you over here.'

It was eight o'clock on the evening of the dinner. Already the majority of guests had arrived and were drinking cocktails in the recently refurbished foyer of Samson Tower.

'You've done a wonderful job here, Mr Newsom,' said Jim di Pietro, casting an appreciative eye over the new marble floor and mahogany inlaid walls. Little gasps of delight were audible all over the room as the assembled guests surveyed Hugo's wonderfully eclectic choice of *objets*. His own special trade-mark, a few pieces of underglazed blue Ming, plus works by Poliakoff, Klein, Matta, Rothko, Schiele, Klimt and Hockney, and a beautiful Brancusi head. New York's agonizingly thin ladies and their portly tuxedoed husbands were in agreement: this was more like a private collector's gallery than the foyer of an international hotel.

'Thanks,' said Hugo, graciously.

'You know, you've done yourself no harm tonight, young fella. Tomorrow half of Hollywood'll be on the phone to you, trying to buy themselves your style.'

'Style,' replied Hugo, arching his eyebrows ever so slightly. 'My dear Mr di Pietro, if you haven't got it, you just can't buy it.'

Upstairs in the Samsons' private suite, Lilah was beginning to fret. Already they were running thirty minutes late.

'Roger, I really do think it's time we went downstairs.'

'Just another few calls to London and I'll be right with you,' Roger shouted from the sitting room.

Wrestling with her temper, Lilah tried breathing deeply. She did not want to start the evening with an argument. On the other hand, it was high time she told Roger what she thought about this ridiculous affectation. She knew who was behind it. Once from Grimford, always from Grimford. Andrea thought it chic and sophisticated to arrive late. Somehow she had convinced Roger to cultivate the habit. It drove Lilah wild. 'I'm afraid I can't hang around here waiting for you any longer,' snapped Lilah. 'This is your hotel and this is my function. To turn up any later would be the most appalling manners.'

'Cool down, darling,' called Roger, dialling yet another number. 'Andrea reckons a late entrance creates more of an impression.'

'Of course it does,' replied Lilah, angrily. 'An execrable impression.'

'Look, I know you're probably feeling a bit nervous – what, sorry George, yes, I'll be with you in a minute – I'm just talking to Lilah . . . Sure – Lilah, George sends you his regards – says he hopes the fund-raiser—'

'I'll see you downstairs,' shouted Lilah. Taking one last look at herself in the mirror, she slammed the door behind her.

'Lilah, honey, where've you been?'

'Sorry, Jim,' answered Lilah evasively. 'Roger's still tied up on the telephone.'

'I understand,' said Jim sympathetically. No, you don't, thought Lilah. 'Anyways, as usual, you're looking just great, honey,' continued Jim, admiringly. Tall and elegant in a simple, strapless, red silk evening gown, Lilah stood out in a crowd even as dazzling as this. 'Come on,' he said, taking her proprietorially by the arm, 'let me introduce you to a few people. Oh, and, honey, if any of those low-life press bums starts giving you a hard time, just give my boys a shout.' Jim gestured to two Neanderthals hovering silently in the background. The last time a photographer from New York's *Daily News* had importuned Jim, he had ended up with the initials JDP carved neatly in his buttocks.

'Thanks, Jim,' said Lilah, eyeing the pair of heavies with some degree of alarm, 'but I'm sure that won't be necessary.'

Across the room, Andrea was chatting up a large man from Pittsburgh with a dangerously florid complexion. 'Armoured cars – how very interesting. So that was how you made your first billion?'

'Yes, ma'am. And now I reckon it's time to put something back into this great nation of ours.'

'Of course,' smiled Andrea amiably, wondering just how large Mr Apelbaum's armoured car PR budget might be. 'And so that's how you became interested in ante-natal screening and post-natal care?'

Mr Apelbaum stared at Andrea as if she had arrived from another planet. 'Oh, sure.' He suddenly twigged. 'Yeah, that's right.'

Oh, sure, thought Andrea, giving him the full advantage of her navel-plunging neckline. Why bother pretending? He was here, like everyone else, to make some useful contacts. 'Mr Apelbaum,' said Andrea, placing her small, plump arm on his, 'there are quite a few people here I'm sure you'd like to meet.'

'Why, Mrs Watson-Smith,' beamed Mr Apelbaum, 'I'd be very grateful, very grateful indeed, if you'd introduce me to a few folk.'

Andrea smiled again. Trying hard to focus his attention on the Brancusi, Charles could not help noticing his wife's all too obvious overtures. 'If you'd be so kind,' he called to a passing waiter, 'I'd like another Scotch.'

'Of course, sir,' said the waiter, instantly obliging. It was not for him to comment, of course, but that was already Charles's seventh.

On Sophie's suggestion, Horneffer & Salzmann had taken a table at the dinner. 'Sophie, do I understand it right?' asked Earl Shallit, the chairman's bespectacled son-in-law. 'I've just been looking at the seating plan. Seems we're in a no-smoking area.' Earl fiddled nervously with his glass. He was a fifty-smokes-a-day man.

'All the best tables are no-smoking,' explained Sophie. 'That's to say, the ones closest to the cabaret and to where the

Princess of Wales will be sitting. But if you want, Earl, I'll see if I can change it.'

Earl thought for a minute as his ego waged war with his addiction. 'No, no, that's fine. Let's just leave things as they are.'

'Is that who I think it is?' asked Grant, pointing across the room.

'Don't point, it's rude, even for an Australian.' She dug him in the ribs.

'You're not wrong,' replied Grant, totally unabashed. 'But is it?'

'Yes,' said Sophie, admiring the fifty-five-year-old film star who still looked not a day over thirty. 'Heck, and to think she was in the first movie I ever saw when I was seven years old.'

'Yeah. Looks like she's being escorted by that up and coming tennis star everybody's talking about.'

'Good for her,' laughed Sophie, who was looking stunning in a classic black number. 'I hope I'm still pulling the boys when I'm her age.'

'They'll have me to deal with first,' said Grant, putting his arm around Sophie's shoulders and kissing the top of her head. Bud Hollingway stifled a miserable sigh. If only he had shown Grant's nerve, maybe he would be kissing that girl.

'This Mrs Samson, she's some looker,' said Sophie, watching Lilah as she worked the room, smiling graciously to everyone she met.

'They say that industrial relations in Samson International hotels have improved exponentially since she moved in,' interjected Bud. 'A twenty per cent rise in productivity. A thirty per cent drop in absenteeism. A fifty per cent reduction in petty larceny . . .' Bud bit his lip. Why did he always have to sound like a computer print-out? It was all to do with his job, of course. But no wonder he had never managed to win Sophie Weiss's heart.

Arthur, Drew and Martin, Sophie's colleagues on the platinum desk, were enjoying themselves enormously. Despite the recession, they were having a good year, thanks mainly to Sophie. 'Come on, Sophie, have some more champagne,' urged Arthur.

'No, thanks,' said Sophie, covering her glass with her hand.

'I reckon at least one of us has got to be on the ball tomorrow morning.'

Grant recognized Roger Samson from his photographs in the press. Confidently, the chairman of Samson International strode into the foyer, stopping to shake hands with sportsmen and business associates, and to kiss any number of drooling society ladies. 'Over there,' said Grant, gently nudging Sophie. 'It looks like yer mate, Roger Samson, has finally tipped up.' Sophie stared at Roger: handsome, rich, urbane, he seemed without a care in the world.

'What is it, Sophie?' teased Drew. 'Boys, it looks like Sophie's having another of her intuitions.'

'You're right,' replied Sophie, seriously. 'That man really bothers me. I don't know what it is about him, but I swear I'm going to find out.'

'Well, better late than never,' said Lilah, glancing pointedly at her watch as Roger finally reached her. 'Are you sure you wouldn't like me to find you a mobile telephone? You never know. You might feel the urge to speak to the talking clock over dinner.'

'I do love you,' said Roger, laughing and kissing her on the lips. For once, Lilah remained cool. Tonight she was not to be so easily mollified.

'Mr Samson?'

'Yes,' said Roger, turning round to face a tall, white-haired man who looked as if he was in his late sixties. 'How do you do?'

'How do you do?' replied the stranger, shaking Roger by the hand. 'The name's McCloughlin, Sam McCloughlin. Not that you'd remember me, I don't suppose. But your father and I, we knew one another way way back in the fifties.'

The colour seemed to drain out of Roger's face. 'Really?' he said.

'Yes,' continued Sam, 'we were both in the mining business in those days. Of course, I left South Africa over twenty years ago, once I'd made my pile. But I heard your father came a cropper down a mineshaft sometime in the seventies.'

A vein in Roger's neck started to pulse. 'Yes,' he said, clipped. 'It was a terrible blow.' He tried to steer Lilah away towards Jim di Pietro, but Sam McCloughlin followed them, relentless.

'My sources told me it was probably murder,' he continued. Lilah took a sharp intake of breath. This was the first time she had heard the story of Roger's father's death. Surreptitiously she searched her husband's face for signs of surprise or shock.

'Nothing quite so dramatic,' smiled Roger, smoothly. 'The police said it was an unfortunate accident, that's all.'

'Baloney,' replied the man. 'There's no way someone like your father could have just have fallen down that shaft. Someone must have pushed him.'

Lilah noticed the vein in Roger's neck, pulsing now quite violently. She began to feel afraid.

'I think you'll find the police were right,' said Roger, abruptly taking his leave. 'It's been nice meeting you, Sam. But now we really must go into dinner.'

A thousand people sat down to dinner in the Samson Tower's glorious mirrored ballroom. Seated at the top table, Roger immediately called the waiter and ordered a double Scotch. About to remonstrate, Lilah caught the look on his face and changed her mind. 'Is everything all right?' she asked, sorry now for her previous fit of pique. Poor Roger, there was so much she had yet to learn about him. This story about his father, it sounded desperately traumatic. No wonder he had nightmares. Whatever had happened, she wanted him to know that he had her total love and support. She put a reassuring hand on his knee. Roger remained impassive.

'It's nothing,' he snapped. 'Just forget about it.'

The diners progressed smoothly through a superb menu. Some of the ladies actually ate, but mostly they just pushed the food around their plates, oohing and aahing about how delicious everything was. Roger seemed even more preoccupied than usual, barely speaking throughout the meal. Witty, voluble and amusing, Lilah tried to compensate, earning herself instant entry into the hearts and homes of New York's *nouvelle* society.

Glancing briefly to the next table, Lilah could see Andrea,

draped across some clearly besotted man. Charles, sitting perfectly straight and still, was affecting not to notice.

'Poor Charles,' whispered Lilah to Roger, trying to engage him in some conspiratorial confidence. Roger watched as Charles accepted yet another glass of Château Ausone '64.

'I do believe she's driving him to drink,' mused Roger. 'I hope the poor bastard doesn't make a fool of himself in front of all these people.'

Angry, Lilah sniffed at her friend's behaviour. 'If he does,' she said, 'that would be the first time Charles ever embarrassed Andrea.'

The cheese came and went followed by a magnificent pudding of spun sugar fruits piled high into multicoloured pagodas.

'Some dessert!' exclaimed Sophie, who tonight had eaten her first square meal in God knows how many weeks. 'Sure, I'm going to have some,' she said to the waiter in attendance. 'Someone's got to make up for the Jane Fonda brigade here tonight.'

After coffee, the Princess and her party left, leaving the assembled guests to enjoy an hour's cabaret from their all-time favourite crooner.

'Look!' Sophie's eyes had hardly left the top table all evening. 'Seems like Roger Samson's leaving too.'

Lilah had rarely felt so angry or humiliated. With a perfunctory apology and some vague excuse about 'urgent business', Roger had taken his leave and left her to entertain their guests for the rest of the evening. 'Of course, he's in the middle of some terribly important deal,' she explained, forcing a smile. 'Phone calls day and night, it's just dreadful.' Everyone nodded sympathetically. After all, Mrs Samson was such a lovely lady.

'Lilah, would you mind if I came and joined you?'

Lilah looked up. Thank God for dear old Hugo. 'Of course. Please, take Roger's place. He won't be coming back.'

'What a relief!' exclaimed Hugo, pouring himself a glass of port from the heavy, crystal decanter on the table. 'I've just escaped from appalling Mrs Gluzgold.'

'Mrs Gluzgold?'

'Yes, you remember. All those years ago, when I was still at

Sotheby's, I went to value old Gluzgold's porcelain collection.'

'Yes, I remember now.' Lilah's spirits were raised immediately by Hugo's presence. 'Wasn't he the pharmaceuticals billionaire?'

'*Was* is the operative word, darling. Apparently he popped his clogs six months ago. Now Mrs G wants me to go and revamp the house on Long Island – *carte blanche* and tra-la-la.'

'You must accept. You can't spend all your time working on Samson International hotels.'

Hugo looked at Lilah, a long, penetrating look that forced her eventually to avert her eyes. 'That's precisely what I intend to do.' Hugo put his hand over Lilah's. The warmth and kindness, the unspoken understanding, it was all Lilah could do not to burst into tears. 'At least,' continued Hugo, 'until I'm sure you don't need me to be around.'

It was well past 2 a.m. by the time Lilah returned to the Samsons' private suite.

'Is that you, darling?' called Roger from the bedroom.

'Who else do you suppose it might be?'

'How did the cabaret go?'

'Fine, just fine,' Angry though she was, Lilah was far too tired to have it out with him tonight.

'Are you coming to bed, darling?'

Lilah almost laughed out loud. Men – they were so unbelievably stupid! They ignored you all day, did their best to wreck your fund-raiser, succeeded in making you totally miserable and then seriously believed you might want to top off your evening with a quick roll in the sack with them. 'Yes,' she said, kicking her shoes into one corner and throwing her evening bag on to the sofa. 'I'm going to sleep in the spare bedroom.'

It was not in Lilah's nature to keep resentment burning. But over breakfast in their suite the next morning, Roger offered no hint of remorse, no word of explanation for his behaviour the previous evening. It drove Lilah to distraction.

'By the way, Roger,' he looked up from his *New York Times*, clearly oblivious of any tension, 'I'll be leaving for London this afternoon.'

'Oh,' said Roger. 'I was hoping we could have dinner with Jim at 21 this evening.'

'Sorry, but I did tell you yesterday, if only you'd been listening. Tomorrow I have a very important meeting with Mike Patterson of the Amalgamated Hotel Workers Confederation. If someone doesn't talk to him soon, and in a half-way civil fashion, there's going to be major trouble in the Park Lane hotel.'

'Lilah.' Roger stood up and made his way around the circular glass table to where she was sitting. 'Lilah, I bought this for you the other day.' Roger placed a small leather box on the table. She stared at it then picked up the box and opened it.

'It's lovely,' said Lilah, staring at a diamond-encrusted brooch, the tears welling in her eyes.

'It's a bee,' said Roger, gently, 'because you're such a busy bee.'

'Oh, Roger,' sniffed Lilah, 'can't you see? It's very beautiful. But I don't want your presents. All I want is a bit more of your time – and your confidence. I can't bear it any longer, Roger. You have to trust me.' Even through her tears, Lilah could see that she had touched a raw nerve. She could have kicked herself. Already he had clammed up again.

'I am what I am,' he said tersely.

'But all I want to do is share—'

'I am what I am,' he repeated, his voice cold. Suddenly, Lilah felt a wild, thunderous noise vibrating in her head.

'In that case,' she screamed, standing up and hurling the brooch the entire length of the room, 'you can keep your bloody trinkets. You don't have to buy me, Roger. Perhaps you can't get a handle on that. But my love for you is freely given. All I'm asking you for is a little fucking trust.' And with that, she stormed out of the room.

Dinner with Jim and his wife was a very low-key affair. The di Pietros missed Lilah's ebullient company almost as much as Roger did. Through by ten o'clock, Roger decided to go straight back to the hotel. Quietly, the limousine purred its way down 52nd Street and across to Samson Tower. Subdued, he pulled his dark blue cashmere coat about him and stared out through the window. What on earth could he do about Lilah? How could he tell her all she wanted to know about himself without the certainty of losing her? He felt totally drained. Commitments, relationships, they were such an enormous waste of energy. And yet, he wanted Lilah. More than anything else in the world, he wanted her. But how could he square the circle? She would not be the woman he wanted if she were not horrified by his past. It was an impossible situation. How could she, kind, loving, loyal, compassionate Lilah, ever be expected to understand? Sometimes even Roger himself could barely comprehend what still drove him on and on. But then, the same old fear would return to haunt him, the dream of a small, defenceless, terrified boy, and Roger knew that he had to keep on hustling and winning and amassing and acquiring. Now, even now, that same small boy was there inside him, desperate to be secure, petrified of being left alone with no one there to love him.

Roger ran his fingers through his still-thick hair. Nowadays, there was a frosting of grey at the temples – nothing too ageing, Lilah had decided, really rather attractive. Roger smiled. The sooner she had a baby the better. A baby would divert her attention and, so he hoped, bond her to him more effectively. Suddenly, Roger caught sight of his own reflection in the tinted glass window and shuddered. That look – Roger knew what it was. He had seen it often enough on other men's faces. It was the look of fear. Goddammit! This woman was really getting through to him. He dug his nails hard into the palm of his hand, leaving livid little crescent shapes in the soft flesh. He was becoming *dependent* on her. He *cared* for her. Caring was not like needing or wanting. Caring was a weakness. For a man like Roger Samson, there were no weaknesses. This could not be allowed to happen.

As soon as he opened the door, Roger was aware of another person in the suite. 'Lilah, is that you?' For one split second he thought – hoped, even – that his wife had missed her flight.

'No, Roger. It's me.' Sprawled across the sofa and covered only with his own burgundy silk dressing gown, Andrea helped herself to another glass of champagne from the bottle in the ice bucket. God, what a brazen little bitch.

'What the hell are you doing here?'

Andrea smiled the same winsome, slightly myopic smile that had once captivated Charles. 'Well, Charles and Lilah have taken the same flight back to London. So here we are, Roger, you and I, two lonely people left to their own devices in the big bad apple of New York.'

Roger threw his coat over a chair and poured himself a glass of champagne. 'How's Charles?'

'Oh, in his usual state – a state of moderate paranoia. We had a big bust-up before he left. He claims I flirt with other men right under his nose. He says I do it just to annoy him.'

'And he's right, isn't he?'

'No, he's not.' Andrea moved across to the window where Roger was standing. He could see her nipples, hard and insolent, straining against the silk. 'If you really want to know, I do it to attract *your* attention.'

Roger stared hard at her greedy little mouth. 'Charles is a good man,' he said at last.

'Sure,' sneered Andrea. 'And Lilah's a good woman. Straight as a die. Never disloyal. Couldn't tell a lie. So unbelievably bloody good. Perhaps too good for you, eh, Roger?' Andrea allowed the dressing gown to slip from her shoulders. Roger resumed his gazing out of the window.

'I'm right, aren't I?' she continued. 'In fact, from what I've seen, I'd be inclined to say that you were frightened of her.'

'Don't be so bloody stupid.' Roger gave one of his clipped, humourless laughs. 'Come on, Andrea, get your clothes on. It's time you were back at your apartment.'

'Admit it,' she insisted. By now the dressing gown had fallen to the floor and Andrea was standing in front of him, naked, blatant, demanding a response. 'You need a woman who's as hungry as you are, don't you? A woman who won't judge or condemn you.'

Roger refused to look at her, but she could see the vein pulsing in his neck. 'Fuck off, Andrea. I want you out of here.'

'What a joke! Superstud Roger Samson! Next thing you know, it'll be two point four kids and church on Sundays.'

'Shut up!'

'Oh, yes, Roger. I can just see you by the time she's finished with you. She'll have you running around after her like her prize bloody poodle.'

'You bitch!'

'So very good and sweet, our dear Lilah. Does she make you pray for forgiveness every time you fuck her?'

He brought his hand down hard across her face. She reeled backwards and fell to the floor. Her cheek burned angrily as she stared up at him, unblinking. Reaching over towards the ice bucket, Andrea grabbed the bottle. For a split second, he thought she was going to throw it at him. She smiled at his obvious confusion. Then parting her lips, she took a long slow slug of champagne.

Roger looked at her with a mixture of lust and loathing. Then suddenly, as if in a dream, he was on top of her, his prick hot and hard, jabbing her like punches. He came almost at once, shuddering with relief and contempt. He had not made love to this woman. This was barely even sex. No, this coupling with Andrea had been something else: an act of defiance and of liberation, a desperate effort to escape from the tendrils of commitment to his wife.

Andrea smirked. Even sex with Mr Apelbaum that afternoon had been more satisfying. But that was fine by her. Sex was only the means. Now she had precisely what she wanted: something over Roger. Without saying a word, she went off to take a shower. Twenty minutes later, dressed and ready to leave, she found Roger still sitting motionless on the sofa. 'I'll be off, then,' she said, brushing his cheek with a kiss. She opened the door. 'Oh, and, Roger, I'll need to see you for dinner next week. There are so many things we've got to talk about.'

Three hours later, Roger was still staring out of the window and across the illuminated New York skyline. His father – well, his father had had it coming. And Simon Weiss – that had been a purely business matter. But Lilah – there had been no reason to betray Lilah, no reason on earth except his own terrible fear of betrayal. Roger rubbed his eyes. Some evening's work! Now he had this frigging bitch, Andrea, to contend with.

The next thing Roger knew, the phone in the sitting room was ringing loudly. He picked up the receiver.

'Roger, I hope I didn't wake you up.'

'No, no, of course not.' Roger paused for a second. 'Lilah,

I'm so glad you rang. I can't tell you how much I wish you were here right now.'

'Roger, I don't suppose you even gave it a second thought but I picked up the busy bee from the floor the other day. And I just wanted you to know that I'm wearing it for my meeting with Patterson this afternoon. For luck. And to remind me of you.'

Roger felt a strange sensation, something vaguely recalled from childhood, the sharp, unaccustomed pain of tears, pricking behind his eyelids.

'I also want you to know that I'm sorry for walking out like that. I was tired and angry. But it was unforgivable – you must have such a lot on your mind.' A slight pause. 'Believe me, I love you, Roger.'

Roger bit the knuckle of his forefinger hard. 'And I love you too,' he said. 'Whatever happens, Lilah, remember I really do.'

CHAPTER THIRTY-ONE

London, January, 1990

'GOOD MORNING, the chairman's office.'

'Hello. Andrea Watson-Smith here. I'd like to speak to Roger.'

Miss Kerwin pursed her lips. She had never liked Andrea – such a common little madam for all her airs and graces.

'*Sir* Roger,' said Miss Kerwin pointedly. It had been the high point of her career, Roger's knighthood in the Queen's Birthday Honours List the previous year.

'*Sir* Roger,' repeated Andrea, aggravated. 'And I'd still like to speak to him.'

'Sir Roger is preparing for a board meeting later this morning. He's left instructions to be disturbed by no one.'

'He'll take my call,' snapped Andrea and then, elaborately polite, 'so if you'd be good enough, Miss Kerwin, I'd be very grateful if you'd just put me through immediately.'

'I'm sorry.' Over the months, she had become increasingly disturbed by Andrea's constant calls. 'But my instructions are *no one*.'

'In that case,' said Andrea tersely, 'get *Sir* Roger to ring me back as soon as the meeting's over.' She slammed down the phone.

Sally Kerwin frowned as she studied her buffed and manicured nails. Sometimes it seemed as if she had spent all her life with Samson International. But the fact was, before joining the company, she had spent quite some time as a secretary in

the Foreign Office. It was there that she had first become
acquainted with the concept of 'Need To Know'. In the Foreign
Office as, indeed, in all governmental departments, nobody
was ever apprized of anything they did not absolutely need to
know. It was good for security, so the powers-that-be maintained. And also, as Miss Kerwin had soon discovered, good
for the most grotesque inefficiency.

All the same, mused Miss Kerwin disconsolately, the system
occasionally worked. Sometimes there genuinely were things
it was better not to know. If Sir Roger and Mrs Watson-Smith
were – well, it didn't really bear thinking about, did it?
Especially not now Lady Samson was expecting. Such a nice
woman, always so cheerful and polite. And so kind – why,
there had been absolutely no reason for her to come to Miss
Kerwin's mother's funeral. Reluctantly she wrote a memo for
Sir Roger. '9.30. Mrs Watson-Smith phoned. Please return her
call.' Yes, Sir Roger was her employer and, as such, deserved
her total loyalty. Nevertheless, although she knew nothing for
certain, Miss Kerwin strongly disapproved. She noticed one of
the red lights on her phone winking at her insistently.

'Miss Kerwin?'

'Yes, Sir Roger.'

'Could you please bring me the files I told you to put in the
boardroom – the one on pensions and the other on cut-rate
insurance. Oh, and while you're at it, you may as well bring
me the one on company cars, planes and helicopters and the
other on company houses.'

'Of course. I'll go and fetch them immediately.'

Sir Roger Samson leaned back in his chair and smiled a low,
self-satisfied smile. Yes, everything was turning out very much
according to plan. Now it was up to the rest of the Group to
play their part as well. Roger dialled a number.

'Hello, Samson International, Park Lane. Mary speaking.
How may I help you?'

'Roger Samson here. Could you please put me through to
Mr di Pietro's suite.'

'Of course, Sir Roger.' A quiet click, a few bars of Beethov-
en's Fifth and Jim was on the line.

'Hi, Roger. What lousy London weather! How's your meeting shaping up?'

'Fine, thanks Jim. I've come up with a package of perks that'll have the directors doing cartwheels across the boardroom floor.'

'You don't say. That's great, Roger. But unless they're a bunch of bums, that ain't gonna be enough. How's your market capitalization looking?'

'Three point one five billion at the end of last year,' said Roger, idly tapping a few figures into his personal computer. With a current stake of 22 per cent in Samson International, that made his own personal holding worth over £600 million. Roger made a note on his memo pad. He'd better have his shares transferred into Lilah's name – at least for the time being. The platinum scam looked an absolute cert but, still, it was an open-ended liability. Best to be on the safe side.

'Now that does sound healthy,' said Jim, coughing up his early morning catarrh, 'very healthy. OK, Roger, that's more like it. Your boys are going to think you're God Almighty – no interference from that side for the next twelve months at least.'

'And I should bloody well hope not,' laughed Roger. 'OK, Jim, the real reason for my call. As I said the other evening, the time is right to move. I'm going to start buying platinum figures between now and February for delivery early October. I want you to get onto the rest of the Group and tell them to do the same. They should be buying at between four hundred and fifty, five hundred dollars, no more. The experts are all predicting a glut of the stuff. Five hundred is top whack.'

'Got it.'

'And tell them to buy from anywhere and everywhere – London, NYMEX, TOCOM, private investors, I don't care. But remember, no massive, individual contracts. We don't want the authorities getting suspicious.'

'I know the drill. A whole bunch of smaller contracts . . .'

'Yes, widely held, at least, ostensibly, and ownership untraceable.'

'I'm ready to move right now,' said Jim. 'How much are you going in for?'

'One million ounces. No point in being greedy.' The two men laughed.

'Not that it's any of my business, but how are you going to fund your end of the operation?' Jim's voice was smooth.

'Shall we just say,' said Roger, closing the top of his personal computer, 'that there's no point speculating with your own money when you happen to be running one of the world's most successful conglomerates.' The two men laughed again. 'So when are you off to South Africa to see our FAP friends?'

'The day after tomorrow,' replied Jim. 'They'll be so gung-ho now that things are finally on the move. D'you know, Roger, I'm actually starting to like that guy Credo Sekese. He's done a good job for us, just keeping those boys of his in check.'

'Now don't go getting too sentimental about your terrorist friends,' said Roger, amused. Credo and his mates could have all the fun they wanted blowing up Rustenburg and Impala. But when it came to Meroto, the security forces would be there, primed and waiting for them.

'No problem.' Jim laughed hoarsely. 'I've been known to lose a few good buddies in my time.'

'Have you decided on a date?'

'Yes, September thirtieth. It's a Sunday. Credo wants to keep bloodshed down to a minimum. There's not so many workers around on a Sunday.'

'The thirtieth of September it is, then,' said Roger, ringing the date in his diary. 'Have a good trip, Jim. I'll see you in New York next week.'

'Sure. Oh, and, Roger, remember to send my regards to Lilah. How's she doing?'

A sudden shadow crossed Roger's face. 'Fine, just fine. This baby business seems to be agreeing with her. She says she's never been so happy.'

'Well, that's just great,' enthused Jim, who himself had five strapping sons. 'You just look after that little lady, will you, Roger?'

As soon as Roger replaced the receiver, there was a knock on the door.

'Come in.'

'The files, Sir Roger,' said Miss Kerwin, placing a multi-coloured stack on his desk. 'Oh, and a message from Mrs Watson-Smith.'

The shadow across Roger's face grew darker.

'She'd like you to return her call as soon as the board meeting's over.'

Roger did not care to catch his personal assistant's eye. 'Thank you, Miss Kerwin,' he said, immediately opening a file. 'Perhaps now you could go and look after any early arrivals in the boardroom. I'll be along in fifteen minutes.'

'Congratulations, Lady Samson,' said Mike Patterson, shaking Lilah warmly by the hand. 'What are you hoping for?'

'I really don't mind,' smiled Lilah, radiant and still enviably slim. 'But what I do mind is being called Lady Samson by people who are supposed to be my friends.'

'Sorry, Lilah,' said Mike, 'This is my first board meeting in this place. I'm feeling a bit overwhelmed.'

'Don't give me that! Mike Patterson – overwhelmed? If I weren't such a lady I might just say something like "Bullshit!" '

'Lilah, Mr Patterson, I hope I'm not interrupting anything?'

'Of course not!' Lilah kissed Charles Watson-Smith on the cheek.

'I just want to say how very happy I am for you, my dear.'

Lilah looked up at Charles's kind, noble face and wished she could say something to erase the all too obvious pain. 'Thank you, Charles,' she said. 'I can't tell you, I'm so over the moon about it. I think the only thing that could make me happier is if you'd agree to be godfather.'

'I'd be delighted,' said Charles. 'I feel very honoured. Let's just hope that we have a little girl.'

We? It was a strange word to use, but before Lilah could turn it over in her mind, Miss Kerwin arrived dispensing coffee.

Charles moved across to the window. He stared out at old Father Thames, dull and dirty beneath the gloomy January sky. Never in his life had he felt quite so hopelessly miserable. No, not even when Lydia died. That, at least, had been out of his hands. But this – Charles shook his proud and handsome head – what on earth could he do about this?

'Everything all right?' asked George Hamish, still rheumy-eyed from Yuletide excess.

'The company's been doing very well,' replied Charles, elusively.

'Sir Roger Samson, Superstar,' sneered George, looking out with Charles across the river.

'Any surprises on today's agenda?'

'Not really. I suppose you already know that your wife has talked Roger into a twenty per cent increase in her already enormous fees.'

Charles said nothing. No, he did not know. But then again, nothing Andrea managed to talk people into surprised him any more.

'Oh, and I suppose you're aware of Roger's package of perks for directors of the company.'

'It's a bloody disgrace,' interrupted Mike Patterson, who had come over to see George on quite a different matter. 'I don't see the point of company cars. Waste of company money if you ask me. I go everywhere by tube.'

'How very intriguing,' piped up Christopher Grafton, who had also joined the group by the window. Anything to escape Sir Howard Anderson pontificating about the European Exchange Rate Mechanism. 'It must be twenty years since I took a ride on the underground.'

'But then, of course, as I said to the Prime Minister at Chequers only the other day, I said, "Prime Minister, once you've decided to shadow the D-Mark . . ." ' Sir Howard was surprised to find himself trying to convince the wall. It was an unnerving experience, not unlike being interviewed by Mr Jeremy Paxman.

Seated at the head of the huge, horseshoe-shaped table, Roger smiled beatifically. As anticipated, the board meeting had gone off almost without incident. Thank God for Lilah! At one point it looked as if that bolshie bastard Patterson was going to make waves over the proposed directors' perks. But, fortunately, Lilah's suggestion of a private health care plan for all Samson International staff had soon put paid to his objections.

Roger was about to close the meeting when he saw Patterson, trying to catch his eye from the far end of the table.

'Chairman?'

'Yes, Mr Patterson.'

'I don't know if it's in order, but on behalf of the union, I'd just like to say how much better things have been since we've had Lilah – I mean Lady Samson – to deal with. No insult to yourself intended, Sir Roger.'

The other directors laughed politely.

'None taken,' said Roger.

'And now,' continued Mike, 'I've been instructed by the membership not to leave this meeting without wishing Lady Samson all the best from everyone.' Mike turned to where Lilah was sitting. It was an awkward little speech but its sincerity was beyond doubt.

'Hear, hear,' chorused the rest of the board.

'Thank you,' said Lilah, moved. 'That's very kind. But I want you all to know, I wouldn't have been able to do any of this without the support and backing of my husband.'

The shadow returned to haunt Roger's face. Andrea – the one blot on his otherwise perfect landscape. Roger closed the meeting and slowly collected his files. He had to get rid of this woman. She was like a cancer, increasingly difficult to manage and capable at any minute of destroying his life completely.

The following week, the evening before his departure to New York, Roger and Lilah shared one of their rare dinners à deux.

'You ought to eat more,' said Roger, watching Lilah tenderly as she struggled with a small piece of poached salmon.

'I can't help it. Sometimes I feel quite queasy. Other times I have extraordinary cravings – sometimes for the most ridiculous junk.' She poured herself another glass of carrot and celery juice.

'Look,' said Roger suddenly, 'why don't you come with me to New York tomorrow? I'd really like to have you there.'

'I'm sorry,' said Lilah, her eyes shining in the candlelight, 'I'd love to but I've got meetings organized for the rest of the week. And besides, the doctors have advised me to cut down on long-haul flights.' Roger continued to sip his wine. Damn it! If only Lilah could accompany him that would keep the predatory Andrea at bay – at least for this trip. Roger tapped the side of his glass, irritated. Damn it and damn her, the conniving little bitch. Nowadays, she made it her business to know every detail of both his and Lilah's schedules. It was impossible to shake her off.

'You should slow down, you know, darling,' said Roger. 'Give yourself some more free time. You'll be busy enough once the baby arrives.'

'I know, I know,' said Lilah. 'I suppose this is what they'd call advice from the pot to the kettle.'

'I suppose so,' laughed Roger, getting up from the table. 'But you know, I have to look after my two most important assets.'

'OK, OK, you've convinced me,' replied Lilah, snuffing out the candles. 'Anyway, this evening I am feeling tired. I think I'll have an early night.' Lilah peered lovingly up at Roger's face. 'I suppose you'll be in your study for another few hours at least?'

'I'm afraid so,' he said, encircling her waist with his arms. 'There are quite a few things I must sort out before I leave.'

'So I shouldn't stay awake, waiting for you?'

'No. I think it's going to be one of those nights,' said Roger, kissing her gently. 'Now you go and get some rest. And don't worry, I won't disturb you at some ungodly hour.'

'I wouldn't mind, Roger, really I —'

'No,' said Roger, kissing her again. 'you need your sleep. I'll see you in the morning.'

Lilah closed the bedroom door behind her. Quickly, she took off her jewellery – tonight just a simple strand of pearls, a pair of pearl and diamond earrings and, of course, her magnificent engagement ring. On the small Carlin writing desk, just beneath the window, stood a red leather jewel box. Lilah traced its embossed crest with her forefinger: three fleurs-de-lis, the royal crest of France. Carefully, she opened the lid. The jewel box of the ill-fated Marie-Antoinette, it was her most coveted possession. Poor silly wretch, mused Lilah. Was there ever a woman so out of touch with the reality of her situation?

Lilah placed her own pieces in the box, everything except

the small antique emerald ring which never left her right hand, and closed the lid. Ten minutes later, curled up in her large four-poster bed, Lilah was fast asleep.

It was well past midnight when the phone in Roger's study rang. He picked up the receiver.

'Roger?'

He clenched his teeth. 'Look, Andrea, I've told you before. I don't want you ringing me at home.'

'Temper, temper.' Her voice was soft and wheedling. It made him want to hit her. 'Hope we're in a better mood by the time we reach New York.'

Roger grasped the receiver hard. This business had to stop. It was getting out of hand. 'Look, Andrea, I'm going to be very tied up this trip. I just won't have time to see you. There's really no point in your coming.'

Andrea's voice was calm and cold. 'You don't say. So Roger's very tied up, is he? Well maybe you're right. Maybe I'll just stay in London and have a nice little lunch with Lilah. Such a long time since we had a good heart to heart. And there's so much I've got to tell her.'

Roger's blood ran cold. This woman was capable of anything. He'd been right about her the first time they'd met. Yes, they were kindred spirits, all right. Nothing and nobody was allowed to get in the way of whatever it was they wanted. Friendship, honesty, trust and decency, these were merely obstacles on the road to their brand of success. His voice was more placatory now. Until he could figure a way out of this, he had to keep her sweet. 'Andrea, you have to understand . . .'

Lilah woke up. The insistent pangs of hunger were rumbling beneath the sheets. A bacon sandwich, she thought, with a few gherkins, perhaps, and a generous dollop of Marmite. Switching on the light, she pulled on her dressing gown and quietly slipped out of the bedroom. The door to Roger's study was ajar and a narrow shaft of light streamed out onto the landing. Poor darling, thought Lilah. He must still be working.

Perhaps he, too, would like a sandwich? She padded over to the study where Roger, quiet but insistent, was trying to reason with someone on the phone.

'Listen, you can't seriously expect me to be at your beck and call every day of the week.'

Intrigued, Lilah stopped to listen.

'Besides, I'm sure Charles is beginning to suspect something – he was very offhand with me at last week's board meeting.'

Lilah froze, her legs suddenly numb and leaden. Heavily, she leaned against the wall for support. It was all she could do to stay standing.

'Yes, I know all that. But it's getting very difficult for me. Lilah's at home much more.' There was a pause. Roger's voice sounded tense. 'Of course, Andrea, you know I wouldn't want anything to upset the applecart. I'm just asking you to be more discreet, that's all.'

Lilah's cheeks began to burn. Her head felt as if it had been kicked and thrashed by a thousand manic hurling players.

'And if we keep meeting in New York someone at the hotel is bound to say something.'

By now Lilah's heart was palpitating so wildly it seemed it might shatter her rib-cage.

'No, Andrea, you know I'm not trying to get rid of you.' A pause. 'All I'm saying is, we've got to be careful.'

Lilah covered her mouth with her hand, willing herself not to vomit. She dragged herself back to her bathroom and was immediately and violently sick. The room, her head, everything seemed to be spinning on a new and terrifying axis. She crawled back into her bedroom and, hauling herself up, collapsed heaving onto her bed. A single tear rolled down her cheek, spilling onto her soft silk pillow. What on earth was happening to her? In one short minute she had lost her hero, her best friend had died and her whole world had collapsed.

Roger put the phone down feeling drained and exasperated. The frustration of being controlled! That fucking woman, she was never going to let go gracefully. No, Andrea had neither the decency nor class of a woman like Simonetta. How could he get rid of her without the most almighty ructions?

Exhausted, Roger closed his eyes. By the time he opened them again, it was time to leave for the airport.

Lilah rolled over on her side, pretending to be asleep as Roger came in to say goodbye. Not wishing to disturb her, he kissed her gently on the forehead and quietly left the bedroom. For hours, it seemed, she lay there motionless, staring at the wall. Eventually the phone rang. A strange, muffled, distant sound, it seemed cocooned in cotton wool, a thousand miles away from the monstrous cacophony of noise pounding in her head. Instinctively, she reached for the receiver.

'Lady Samson?' It was Babs, her tirelessly efficient secretary, ringing from her office in the Samson International, Park Lane. 'Is everything all right?'

'I'm sorry,' said Lilah, still completely dazed, 'what time is it?'

'Ten thirty-five,' replied Babs. 'I've already had to cancel your nine thirty and ten o'clock meetings. What would you like me to do about the rest of the morning?'

'I don't think I'll be coming in today . . .' Lilah's voice trailed off into a whisper.

'Lady Samson,' said Babs, concerned, 'what's the matter?'

'Nothing, nothing. I don't know. Perhaps a touch of flu. I'll be all right. I . . .'

'I'll cancel all your engagements until further notice,' said Babs, by now positively alarmed. Why, she had seen Lilah only the previous afternoon, fit, blooming and bursting with energy. What had this vague, disembodied voice to do with yesterday's Lady Samson?

'Yes, yes . . . if you would . . . I'll call you later on today . . . when I'm feeling a bit better . . . I . . . I . . . I . . . Goodbye for now.' Lilah dropped the receiver back onto its cradle. Frantic, Babs rang Mrs Owen. Within minutes, she was knocking on Lilah's door.

'Lady Lilah. Lady Lilah. Please may I come in?'

Lilah gasped, as the first searing wave of pain ripped across her body.

'Please,' she cried, breathless and frightened as Mrs Owen opened the door. 'Please call me an ambulance at once.'

CHAPTER THIRTY-TWO

ON A plane, somewhere between Johannesburg and London, Jonathan Morton was writing notes. It was important, of course, this presentation he was due to make to the College of Ophthalmologists. But if he was feeling nervous, it was more the prospect of seeing Lilah again that filled him with trepidation. The last time they had met, Roger Samson was not yet on the scene. Until then, Jonathan still believed he and Lilah might somehow work things out. Now all that seemed like ancient history. Lilah – Lady Samson – was now another man's wife, carrying that other man's child. Slowly, Jonathan sipped his glass of mineral water. His work in Meroto might make for riveting presentations but, in Jonathan's mind at least, it had cost him the woman he loved.

In the Lindo Wing of St Mary's Hospital, Paddington, Hugo Newsom paced up and down the waiting room, desperate for news. He glanced at his watch – 4 p.m. It was over five hours now since Lilah had been admitted and Hugo was sick with worry.

'Cup of tea, Mr Newsom?' asked the pretty blonde receptionist, popping her head around the door.

'No, thanks,' said Hugo. 'You haven't by any chance . . .'

'No, nothing yet,' replied the receptionist, kindly. 'But please try not to worry. Lady Samson is in excellent hands. Professor Cranmer hasn't left her side all day.'

Hugo was still pacing the room some two hours later when Professor Cranmer appeared. A tall, ascetic-looking man, with thick grey hair and a grave, intelligent face, his presence engendered confidence.

'Professor . . . ?'

'Sit down, Mr Newsom,' said Professor Cranmer, gently. 'Mr Newsom, I have to tell you we tried everything we could. But I'm afraid Lady Samson has lost the baby.'

Slumped motionless in his armchair, Hugo tried to choke back the tears. The professor put a comforting hand on his arm. 'You seem very close to her,' he continued, shaking his head. 'In fact, you were the one person she asked to be informed of her admission in here.' Professor Cranmer coughed discreetly. It was on his own instructions that Miss Kerwin had been asked to track down Lady Samson's husband.

'Yes, we've been friends a long time,' murmured Hugo, hardly knowing what he was saying.

'Then perhaps you can help me understand. Last week I examined Lady Samson. She was fit, strong and healthy, the last sort of person I'd have expected to have a miscarriage.'

'And she so desperately wanted this baby.'

'That's precisely what I'm driving at. I'm still aware how much she wanted this child. And yet today – how can I explain – it seemed as if she'd lost the will to fight for it.'

Hugo groaned. 'How is she?'

'To be honest, I'm very worried about her. Before this, she was as strong as a horse. But now, I don't know, she seems so very distant.'

'Please, will you let me see her?'

The professor thought for a while. 'Well, she's heavily sedated now, of course. But she knows you're here and I don't think a few minutes with you can do her any harm.'

'Thanks, Professor. I'll leave whenever you tell me to.' Picking up his coat, Hugo followed Cranmer into the corridor.

'When she's less tired,' continued the professor, as they both waited for the lift, 'I hope I'll be able to get her to discuss the matter with me. In the meantime, Mr Newsom, I feel I ought to warn you. In my opinion, Lady Samson was already in trauma when she arrived at this hospital. She isn't talking much at the moment. But it's clear she's been subjected to some extremely violent shock.'

The bedroom, soothing in shades of pale grey and pink, was lit by muted wall-lights. A surprisingly small, strange figure lay curled up in the bed.

'Lilah, old girl,' said Hugo, struggling to hide his emotions. 'I'm . . . I just wanted to say I'm . . .' It was no use.

'Hugo, is that you?' Staring at the ceiling, Lilah did not even turn her head to look at him. Quietly, Hugo went over to the bed to kiss her and was shocked by what he saw. Pale and drawn, Lilah seemed to have aged twenty years overnight. But that was not what frightened him. There was something far more terrifying about her aspect. The fun and laughter in Lilah's eyes had disappeared.

'Yes,' said Hugo, groping for something to say, 'it's me. At least, for as long as they'll let me stay. Don't worry, old thing. You're going to be all right. And Miss Kerwin is trying to locate Roger. I'm sure he'll be back just as soon as he knows what's happening.'

A peculiar look crossed Lilah's face. She continued to stare at the ceiling.

'Is there anything I can do?' asked Hugo, increasingly alarmed.

'Just hold my hand, will you?' whispered Lilah, her voice a dull monotone.

'Of course.' Hugo reached for Lilah's hand. It felt insubstantial and rigid with cold. He pressed it against his cheek for warmth. Then suddenly, the tears started to cascade down Lilah's face, silent tears of sorrow and sadness but, above all, of self-reproach. 'I couldn't see,' she murmured, too exhausted to sob. 'I thought I was so happy, Hugo. But the truth was, I couldn't see.'

Roger Samson had barely arrived in his suite at Samson Tower before the telephone rang.

'Hello?'

'Sir Roger?' said the telephonist, 'I have a call for you from London. Your personal assistant. She says it's urgent.'

'Put her through.' Roger felt vaguely alarmed. It was the

first time he had heard the unflappable Kerwin talk in terms of urgent. Important yes. Most important, occasionally. But urgent?

'Sir Roger.' By the sound of her voice, oddly thin and broken over the phone, Roger could tell something was horribly wrong. 'I'm afraid something dreadful has happened.'

Roger waited impatiently as Miss Kerwin blew her nose. A strike, a fire, an accident – why on earth could she not get on with it?

'Yes?'

'I'm afraid Lady Samson has been rushed into hospital.' Miss Kerwin sobbed out loud. 'Oh, Sir Roger, she's lost the baby.'

Roger's head began to swim. His son, he was sure it was going to be a son. His heir. Someone he could give everything to. A piece of himself to be proud of. And now . . .

'How's Lilah?'

'I don't know, sir. I just heard about the miscarriage from the professor. As for Lady Samson,' Miss Kerwin dissolved again into tears, 'I felt it wasn't my place to probe.'

By now, the pounding in Roger's eardrums had grown intolerable. 'I'll be back just as soon as I can. Oh, and, Miss Kerwin, do you have the hospital number? I'll try and get through right now.'

Despite Roger's protestations, Andrea had insisted on coming with him to New York. That morning, he had dropped her off at her (or rather Charles's) apartment before continuing on to the hotel. Already she was making him pay for trying to give her the brush-off. Despite his hectic schedule, she had made him promise to take her to lunch.

Impatiently she paced around the apartment, waiting for his call. She had spent the previous day at the beautician's and was quite pleased with the results. She stared at herself in the mirror. Cut on the bias, the new blue Lacroix suit made her look inches slimmer. Her blonde hair, just made even blonder, courtesy of Ricardo at Samson International, Park Lane, was curled and teased and looked twice its volume. She smiled at her own reflection. It was just as well she had not heard Ricardo himself sniggering behind her back.

'Looks like Madam's just emerged from a de Havilland wind tunnel,' he said as soon as she left the salon.

Andrea poured herself a glass of wine. What on earth could have happened? He'd better not try breaking their arrangement. She went into the kitchen and rummaged in the cupboard for a packet of pretzels. God, she was starving. How dare he keep her hanging around like this? Angry, Andrea dialled Samson Tower and asked for Roger's suite. The phone was engaged so she left a message. In fifteen minutes, when Roger had failed to return her call, she phoned again and this time managed to get through.

'Roger, what the hell is holding you? We're supposed to be having lunch, remember, and I'm ravenous. Don't think you can start taking me for granted just because—'

Roger held his head in his hands. Who needed this fucking harridan?

'Lilah's had a miscarriage. I'm flying home immediately.'

'But I've come all this way to be with you.'

Suddenly Roger snapped. 'Didn't you hear what I said? Lilah's had a miscarriage. Doesn't that mean anything to you? You're supposed to be her fucking friend.'

Peeved, Andrea checked her stockings. Sheer, black, the way Roger liked them. Or, at least, the way Lilah's were.

'Oh, come off it, Roger. A miscarriage, so what? It happens all the time. If you want to fill your house with little Samson juniors, I'm sure Lilah's young enough to have plenty.'

Roger shook his head. This had been the worst mistake he had ever made in his life. 'You bitch! You stupid little bitch! How dare you speak like that? You'll never be half the woman Lilah is. Now fuck off back to your husband.' Roger slammed the phone down. Seething, Andrea sat with the phone, now dead, still grasped tightly in her hand. No, she refused to let him go like that. He was frightened – and guilty – that was all. Slowly she replaced the receiver. After all this fuss and nonsense was over, she would soon lure him back again.

The next day, Jonathan phoned the Samsons' residence to confirm his lunch appointment with Lilah. Poor Mrs Owen, she was so beside herself, it took her all of fifteen minutes to tell him what had happened. Immediately Jonathan caught a cab to the hospital and asked to speak to Professor Cranmer.

'I'm afraid she's in a very precarious mental state,' explained the professor. 'It's very odd. She's been refusing to take her husband's calls. He was in New York when it happened. We expect him back some time this morning.'

'May I see her, please?' asked Jonathan earnestly. 'I know she's not well. But I am a doctor. And besides, Lady Samson and I, we were once very close.'

'Yes, I do know,' replied the professor. 'Your name has come up in her sleep. Yes, of course, you may see her, if she's not too tired. She needs good friends around her at the moment.'

Lilah's hospital room was full of lilies, a delivery from Roger. As Jonathan entered the room, a red-eyed Hugo gestured silently towards Lilah, sleeping fitfully in her bed. The two men went into the corridor.

'How's she taking it?' asked Jonathan, disturbed.

'Very bad,' replied Hugo, who looked dreadful. 'I've been here all night. She didn't want to let go of my hand, so they decided to let me stay. All I can say is, she's in a terrible state. Most of the time she just stares at the ceiling – doesn't really talk much. Then occasionally she mutters something about not being able to see. And now, just before she nodded off, she was rambling on about the wind of the wing of madness. It's a line from Baudelaire, I think.'

'Poor Lilah.'

'Yes,' said Hugo, rubbing his eyes, 'poor Lilah. Honestly, Jonathan, I really have been frightened for her. I can't tell you how pleased I am to see you.'

'And Roger?'

'Don't talk to me about Roger bloody Samson. I don't know for sure, but something's going on. Lilah won't even talk to him.'

Jonathan's jaw set hard. 'Look, Hugo, you're exhausted. Why don't you go back home and get some sleep? I'll stay here with Lilah.'

'OK – just so long as she's not on her own when Roger tips up. I tell you, I don't know what it is, but whenever his name is mentioned, she seems to seize up.'

'Don't worry,' said Jonathan slowly. 'If that's what Lilah wants, I won't leave her alone for a minute.'

It was worse, far worse, than Jonathan had expected. Of course he had seen depression before, acute depression, even, but never had he witnessed such a radical change in a person as now he saw in Lilah. She had cried when first she saw him, but then resumed her gazing into thin air for hours and hours on end. Morning tea came and went, but she made no attempt to touch it. For once in his life, Jonathan felt utterly helpless. It was as if the life was draining out of her drop by drop and there was nothing he could do to stop it. Already she seemed gaunt and frail, a ghost of the glorious green-eyed girl he had once known and loved.

As the morning wore on, Jonathan tried to read the paper as Lilah continued to sleep sporadically. There was a gentle tap on the door and a tall elderly gentleman appeared carrying a large bouquet of flowers.

'How do you do?' said the gentleman. 'I hope I'm not intruding. How is Lady Samson?'

'Sleeping at the moment,' said Jonathan quietly.

'In that case I'll come back later,' said the gentleman, depositing the flowers on the bedside table. 'Please, when she wakes up, could you tell her that Charles Watson-Smith came to see her and sends all his love?'

'Charles . . .' Lilah's eyes flew open, yet their expression was dull. She turned her head towards him. 'Charles,' she whispered urgently. 'Roger . . . Andrea . . .' She closed her eyes again. She hadn't meant to say it. Why drag Charles into this?

Charles strode across to the bed and took her hand. 'I know, my dear. Perhaps I should have told you. But I'm afraid I've known for months.'

Jonathan closed the door behind him and went in search of a telephone.

'Are you sure?' asked Hugo, who was feeling much better after a few hours' sleep and a prolonged stint under the shower. 'Roger and Andrea? The fool. The complete and utter fucking fool. That little bitch!'

'I suppose Lilah must have found out,' surmised Jonathan. 'And that's what caused the miscarriage.'

'Has Roger been in yet?'

'No, not yet. I left Lilah with Charles. I thought it best to give them a few minutes on their own. I'm going back straight away.'

'Fine. I'll be round in about half an hour. Whatever happens, Lilah mustn't be on her own when that bastard arrives. God knows how she's going to react.'

Charles was on the point of leaving as Jonathan entered the room.

'I'll come and visit you tomorrow, my dear, if I may,' he said, kissing Lilah gently on the forehead. Lilah nodded vaguely. Already she was dozing again. 'Goodbye, Jonathan,' he said with a grateful smile as he passed him in the doorway. 'I've heard such a lot about you from Lilah. Thank God you're in London. We're going to have our work cut out, helping her through this.'

'Yes,' stammered Jonathan, his attention focused elsewhere. 'Yes, I'll see you here again tomorrow.'

Charles nodded to the man who had just entered the room, and left Jonathan facing Sir Roger Samson.

'Thank you for all your help,' said Roger, staring distractedly across the room. 'I came back as soon as possible. But how could anyone have imagined?'

Jonathan stared at the man he hated most. Of course, he had seen photographs of him. But no photograph could do justice to those piercing ice-blue eyes. Suddenly Jonathan shuddered. It seemed hardly credible, but he knew he had seen those eyes before! Jojo!

'. . . and so, in your opinion . . .'

Jonathan shook himself. He had not been listening to a word the man was saying.

'Gentlemen.'

He felt a wave of relief as Professor Cranmer came in to check on his patient.

'Professor, what can I say?' Suave and charming, Roger thanked him effusively. It was the only way Roger knew how to play it in front of people: miscarriages happened, just bad luck, soon everything back to normal. How else could he manage to control the misery that was already crowding in? 'Will it be long before she can try again?'

Professor Cranmer caught Jonathan's gaze, full of silent loathing. He paused for a second. It was not in his nature or in the nature of his profession to be judgemental, but he found Sir Roger Samson's reaction extraordinarily insensitive. 'Sir Roger,' said the professor calmly. 'I don't think you've really understood. Your wife is in shock. These things take time. There's a whole cycle of grief, sorrow and depression that has to be worked through gradually.'

'Lilah needs care and understanding,' snapped Jonathan suddenly, 'not a bloody timetable.'

'Jonathan . . .' The voices had woken Lilah. 'Jonathan, is that you?'

'I'm here now, darling,' said Roger, racing to her side. Desperately, he peered into Lilah's face, searching for some glimmer of recognition. Jonathan watched for her reaction, she appeared not to see her husband, staring straight through him and onto the wall beyond.

'Lilah, Lilah. It's me – Roger.' Frantic, Roger turned to Professor Cranmer, looking for reassurance. Jonathan stared at Roger. Foolish, arrogant man, even now he failed to grasp what had happened. Of course Lilah did not know him. For the first time in their relationship, she was seeing him for what he really was.

After ten days, Professor Cranmer allowed Lilah to return home. She agreed to see a counsellor twice a week but was showing few signs of improvement. Already she had lost over twenty pounds in weight and was still unable to regain her appetite. Roger was at his wit's end. As far as he was concerned, the affair with Andrea was over. He had not seen or even spoken to her since New York and even she knew better than to pester him right now. Three weeks went by, and still Lilah was making no progress. She refused to go out, rarely bothering to wash her hair. Worse still, she never opened a book or a paper and could not even bear the noise of the radio or television. Jonathan visited her every day, his concern being gradually augmented by both fear and frustration. By the time he had to return to Meroto, Lilah was barely functioning.

For hours, Jonathan weighed the risks involved and decided to go ahead. Whatever Lilah's reaction, it could be no worse than her current state of suspended animation. Besides, he had to try something, however desperate, before he left. He did not dare entrust her recovery to mere pious hopes and Roger.

She was in the drawing room when Jonathan called to visit.

'Lilah,' he said, after Mrs Owen had brought tea, 'you know I'm leaving tomorrow.'

Lilah said nothing, just continued to pour.

'Lilah, it can't go on like this,' he shouted, suddenly. Lilah looked up at him – a flicker of response.

'You're killing yourself. Yes, that's what you're doing. You're bloody killing yourself. And all for what – for that bastard husband of yours and some little tramp you called a friend.'

Lilah's hand began to shake violently. She put the teapot down.

'I'm not going to let it happen, you understand?' said Jonathan, standing up and striding around the room. 'I'm not going to sit back and watch you waste away over two examples of human trash.' He took her by the shoulders. 'Stop it, Lilah!' he shouted, shaking her hunched, emaciated body. 'They're not worth it. There's no point grieving over something that never was. What you're going in for now is nothing but self-pity.'

'How dare you?' exploded Lilah, her arms flailing, her fists raining blows on Jonathan's chest. He did not try to stop her as this carbuncle of poisonous fury suddenly erupted. At last, a reaction, some sign of fight, some ray of hope, some trace of the old Delilah. 'For God's sake,' she cried, 'let me grieve for my child. Let me at least do that!'

'Come to Meroto with me,' said Jonathan, holding her tightly as her rage subsided. 'You know you're never going to get better here. It's too close to the source of pain.'

'But, Jonathan, I'm not ready . . .'

'No, Lilah, don't get me wrong. I'm not asking you to make any major decisions – it's too early for that. I'm just suggesting you take a break. Who knows, perhaps you can work with me in the hospital?' Jonathan smiled wryly. 'The change would do you good.'

'But I can't help . . .'

'Nonsense, Lilah. Believe me, you can do plenty. What's more, you'll see plenty.'

In vain, Lilah tried to protest.

'No,' continued Jonathan, deaf to her objections, 'I don't expect you'll ever forget the baby you lost. But at least in Meroto you'll have a genuine yardstick to measure your suffering by.'

For the first time since her miscarriage, Lilah managed a smile. She should have known better than to argue with Jonathan. 'You're always right, aren't you, Mr Morton?' she whispered mischievously. Jonathan could have leapt for joy. The first real hint of the girl he'd known. This really was a breakthrough.

'Of course.' He laughed out loud. 'I'll vouch for it myself.'

'OK,' she said, peering up into his dark brown eyes. 'I'll come with you to Meroto. But only on one condition.'

'Anything.' Jonathan felt like hugging himself.

'This time, dinner will be at *eight*.'

When Roger arrived home that evening he was pleasantly surprised: for the first time since her return from hospital, Lilah had actually dressed for dinner. Tonight, though pale and pitifully thin, she was at least looking alive again.

'Roger,' she began, as they waited in the drawing room for Mrs Owen to call them through. 'I've decided to take a holiday.'

Roger looked alarmed. 'But, darling, you're still not fit to travel. And Professor Cranmer and your counsellor are both here in London. Why don't you leave it for a few weeks? If you give me a few weeks I'll work it so we can take a break together.'

Lilah shook her head. 'No, Roger. I want some time on my own. I need some space to think.'

Roger was feeling more disturbed by the minute. On the one hand, he was pleased to witness a few flashes of the good old Lilah. On the other, he was not at all convinced that she should be spending long periods away from him right now.

'Where are you thinking of going? The house in Cap Ferrat would be very peaceful but the weather's not too brilliant. If you want, you could go to the Caribbean – it's ideal.'

Lilah smiled. No, she had never even noticed it before: how gradually and insidiously Roger had managed to organize her life. She had been a willing victim, of course. It had all seemed so natural at the time. The job, the lifestyle, this whole bloody charade of a marriage. Lilah's cheeks began to burn. 'I'm going to Meroto,' she said.

Roger looked aghast. 'That dump! But, Lilah, if you want to go to South Africa for some sunshine, I've got contacts down in the Cape.'

'I'm not going for the sunshine,' she snapped. 'I'm going to help Jonathan in his hospital.'

'But, Lilah . . .'

'It'll do me good. It'll take my mind off . . .' Lilah's voice faltered.

Roger shook his head. The idea was a dreadful one. But she did need a complete break, a total change of environment. Besides, he was in no position to argue with her. But, of all places, Meroto!

'Are you sure?'

'I'm leaving on tomorrow's flight with Jonathan.'

'Tomorrow. But, Lilah, this is all a bit sudden. Have you asked the professor's advice?'

Lilah nodded. 'He thinks it's a good idea. I'll be in excellent hands. Jonathan is a doctor. And, besides, in the hospital I'll have something to keep me occupied. Here, all I do is sit around and mope.'

Roger moved closer to her on the sofa. Her mind was clearly made up. 'You won't be gone long, will you?' he asked.

Lilah shot him a strange, sideways glance. 'I'm sure you'll hardly notice. Let's face it, you're always so busy, what with one thing and another.'

He made to hold her hand, desperate to say something. But the words just would not come.

'I'll make it up to you,' he said, at last. Lilah said nothing, just returned his gaze.

Yes, she thought, standing up and moving towards the dining room, and I'll make it up to you.

Surprised though he was by her sudden decision, Roger saw Lilah's new-found determination as a welcome sign of recovery. She still looked worn and haggard, but at least, as they drove to the airport, she was communicating and even smiling from time to time. True, most of her conversation seemed to be with this interfering Morton chap. All the same, Roger tried desperately to feel optimistic. It was difficult to tell, of course, especially with Morton always coming between them. But as Roger left her at Heathrow airport, he felt Lilah was responding to his kiss.

'Goodbye, darling,' he said, as she made to follow Jonathan through Passport Control. 'I'll phone you every day.'

Lilah picked up her matching leather hand baggage. 'Sure,' she said, turning on her heel and moving off.

'Look after yourself, darling. I want you to come back fit and well. I love you.'

But already Lilah was out of earshot.

Roger stood and waved until she had disappeared. Only then did it really strike him. For the first time in his adult life, Roger felt alone and frightened. Quickly, he turned and left the departure hall.

Lilah's spirits improved with every mile away from London. As the plane flew on into the night, Jonathan watched her as she slept, a new look of serenity now spread across her face. It would not happen overnight, of course, but gradually she would come to terms with her loss and her grief.

CHAPTER THIRTY-THREE

February, 1990

SOPHIE WEISS was clearing her desk at Horneffer & Salzmann.
As usual it had been a busy week and innumerable ends
needed tying up before she left for a fortnight's trip to Meroto.
Sophie's letters to Reverend Mother Benigna at the Convent
of the Holy Rosary had yielded some useful information, but
there were still far too many question marks over the death of
Uncle Simon. In the end, Sophie had decided, there was
nothing else for it. She would have to visit the place and trace
the truth for herself.

'Looking forward to your holiday, Sophie?' asked Drew on
his way out of the office.

'Like I told you a hundred times, wise guy,' remonstrated
Sophie, 'this is not what you'd call a holiday.'

'Whatever you say, Sophie. Research trip, fact-finding mission – anything you wanna call it. Now let's take it from the
top, are you looking forward to it?'

'Sure,' replied Sophie who, as far as her colleagues were
concerned, was off to observe a few platinum mines. 'I'll bring
you back your very own chunk of Merensky reef, if you like.
Just to remind you what it is you're buying and selling here
all day long.' Immediately, Drew became more serious.

'Talking of buying and selling,' he said, 'have you picked
up on anything strange over the last month or so?' Sophie
looked at Drew and and felt like kissing him there and then.
At last – someone else on the desk had felt the vibes. So far,

there had been nothing she could put her finger on. Nothing she could prove. But Sophie could have sworn that something odd was happening in the market.

'Strange? How d'you mean, strange?'

'I don't know for sure,' said Drew. 'Perhaps I'm way off line. But I can't help feeling there's been more than usual interest in October platinum.'

He watched as Sophie scribbled Stars of David all over the cover of her memo pad. 'I knew it,' she said, emphatically. 'It's been bothering me since about – what? – about mid-January I thought I was picking something up. But then, when I worked it over, I couldn't find a reason or a pattern, nothing I could put it down to.'

'It could be just a blip.'

'Sure it could. In fact, the chances are it is. All the same, Drew, I'd like you to keep an eye on October trading till I get back late February.'

'Happy to be of service,' said Drew, continuing on his way. 'Oh, and by the way, Sophie, you won't forget to come back to us, will you now, honey? You know I'm relying on you to pay for my new apartment in Key West.'

Sophie was still busy tidying away her notes when the phone on her desk rang.

'G'day, Sophie. Am I still taking you to the airport?'

'Grant – what a star you are. I'm afraid I'm running a little late.'

'No worries, we're still in plenty of time. Anything you want a hand with?'

'Well, now you come to mention it, Grant, there is just one thing.'

'Just say the word, Sophie, darling. You know I'd do anything for you.'

'Anything?'

'Anything. I'd even go to Detroit.'

Sophie laughed. 'I've been talking to Drew here in the office. It's just a hunch, but we both reckon there's something going on with October platinum. Could you sniff around, find out who's been picking up a lot of offers?'

'I'll see what I can do. But, of course, strictly speaking—'

'Who the hell speaks strictly down at NYMEX?'

312

'You're not wrong. All the same, it'll take all my Aussie guile and charm to winkle out which clients the boys down here are buying for. You know, the traders' code of confidentiality and all that baloney.'

'I know everything there is to know about confidentiality at NYMEX,' said Sophie, 'and I promise I'll pay the bar bill.'

'Then it's a deal. It may be dark and dirty work, but someone's got to do it. Now then, when do you want me to come and pick you up?'

'Could you pass by the apartment in about an hour? I've still got some packing to do.'

There was a pause at the other end of the line. 'I'm going to miss you, Sophie.'

'Me, too,' said Sophie and smiled.

Jojo Matwetwe was not a happy woman. Right from the beginning she had been suspicious of the Group and now, it seemed, these faceless men were running the FAP's entire operation.

'But they are not faceless,' argued Credo, as Jojo voiced her objections perhaps for the hundredth time. 'I've met Jim di Pietro many times.'

'Yes,' interrupted Jojo. 'You've met Jim di Pietro, Credo. How come the rest of us never got to see him?'

'Security,' answered Credo. 'It's the same reason we don't know who the other members of the Group are. These people, they believe in us and our struggle. That is all we need to know.' The other members of the FAP central committee nodded in agreement. If Credo trusted Jim di Pietro and his anonymous friends, that was good enough for them.

'Anyway,' said Walter Ngobeni, who was getting increasingly tired of Jojo's protestations, 'whoever they are, it is clear that we are all now working to the same objective – the thirtieth of September.'

Jojo looked surprised. That was the first time she had ever heard anyone mention a date. She looked accusingly at Credo.

'I am coming to that,' he continued, smoothly. 'It has been decided, we decided, Jim and I that is, that the best day to act is the thirtieth of September. I insisted on a Sunday, because

Sunday is the only day there are no workers down the mines or in the crusher plants—'

'No,' interrupted Jojo, 'but there are still men in the mills and refineries.'

'I tell you, we are doing everything we can to keep casualties down to a minimum.' Credo sounded weary.

'But if we are blowing up the smelters and refineries, there are bound to be—'

'Listen,' shouted Kenny Maboi, angrily, 'no one is happy about the chance of our own people dying. But this is the risk we have to take. In a war, innocent people get killed. And this is war.'

'Jojo, you know, I am not a man of violence.' Credo spoke quietly. 'It's true, with this plan, we will blow up the smelters and refineries at Rustenburg, Impala and Meroto. But don't you see? In one operation, we will bring major chaos to the whole of Western capitalism. In one operation, we will achieve more than five, ten, fifteen thousand deaths in South Africa. That is what we must remember.'

Jojo sat deflated in her corner. Credo was right, of course. All the same, a definite date had now been set and the prospect of bloodshed and violence was a reality. That was what Jojo was finding hard to stomach.

'Already FAP members have infiltrated the security services,' continued Credo. 'And we have men in key positions throughout the mines. But we must keep our plans as secret as possible. Only those directly involved in the operation will be told.'

'But what about the . . . ?'

'No, Jojo,' said Credo, sternly. 'My word is final. If every member of FAP knows what is going on, the authorities are bound to find out. I cannot take that risk. Until the thirtieth of September, work in the mines must continue as normal. The security services must have no reason to suspect trouble. Is that agreed?'

Everyone, except Jojo, nodded his silent approval.

'And what about you, Jojo,' said Credo, gently, 'don't you trust me?'

'I trust *you*, Credo,' said Jojo, getting up to leave the meeting. 'It's not you I'm worried about.'

*

Both Lilah and Jonathan blinked as they emerged from the plane into the fierce early morning sunshine. At that time of the day, Jan Smuts Airport was pleasantly empty and, for once, their baggage came through almost at once. They swept through customs and were soon outside the airport building, waiting for the car Jonathan had organized to take them to Meroto. Suddenly, a few yards away, a white Mercedes pulled up and a man with a briefcase jumped out.

'Good Lord,' said Lilah, tapping Jonathan on the arm. 'Do you see that man over there – the one just disappearing into Departures? That's Jim di Pietro, a major American banker. He's one of Roger's closest business associates. I wonder what he's doing here?' A sudden pained expression crossed her face and she caught her breath.

'Are you all right?' asked Jonathan, concerned.

'Fine, fine,' said Lilah, relieved that their car had now arrived. 'It's almost three years ago now. But, you see, the day I met Jim di Pietro was the day I first met Roger.'

'It's OK,' said Jonathan, helping Lilah into the car. 'I know these things still hurt.' Jonathan made himself comfortable on the seat beside her.

'Jim and Roger were both in a meeting I was interpreting,' she went on. 'God knows – they talked about everything under the sun, platinum among other things. And then, let me think, there was something about a four-million-dollar project in South Africa – some sort of charitable donation.'

'Can you remember what the money was for?'

'No, it was never mentioned. But I assumed it had to be for charity. I know it struck me at the time because I felt bad that I'd so misjudged Roger.'

'And who are "they", this bunch of benefactors with four million dollars in small change for any worthwhile cause?'

'Curiously enough,' said Lilah, as the car slid away from the airport building, 'it was Jim di Pietro who gave them their name. It was supposed to be a bit of a joke, I think. They call themselves the Group.'

Jonathan insisted that Lilah rest as soon as they reached Meroto. She objected, of course, arguing that she had slept perfectly well on the plane and now wanted to see the hospital.

'My word, Miss Dooley,' laughed Jonathan, 'oh, excuse me, m'lady, I mean Lady Samson. We are getting better, aren't we?' He studied his patient intently. She needed to gain at least twenty pounds and her face was still sunken and pale. But at least now she was standing up straight again, no longer hunched and defensive.

'Now the old pig-headed Irish stubbornness is back, you reckon I'm on the mend, right?'

'Spot on.' Jonathan carried her suitcases into the spare bedroom.

'All this is new.' Lilah sat herself down on the bed and kicked off her shoes.

'Yes, m'lady, and you've even got your own *en suite* bathroom.'

'Get lost, Morton,' said Lilah, aiming a shoe at him. 'Call me m'lady once more and . . .'

'And what?' asked Jonathan, turning around to face her. She stared back at him so tenderly he thought his heart would break. How he longed to take her in his arms, caress her, make love to her, wipe away all the pain and suffering. But that, he realized with a pang of sorrow and desire, was the last thing Lilah needed. Right now, she needed nothing but time – time to heal herself.

'I'm not sure yet,' she smiled, lying back on the bed. 'But I'll think of something. Run along now, I know you're desperate to see your patients.'

'Promise me you'll rest. I'll come back for you later this afternoon and then I can show you around the hospital. Nothing too strenuous today, mind. I don't want you doing too much too soon.'

Jonathan frowned as he left the house. Back in London, it had all seemed so simple. Here in Meroto there were still a few awkward details that had to be ironed out. For a start, how was Jojo going to react to Lilah's presence in his house? And, more important still, how would Lilah react to Jojo, to the extraordinary and bizarre fact of those eyes?

*

The hospital had been ticking over nicely during Jonathan's absence. Without him there had been no operating list but the staff were trained to deal with minor ailments and they had all been kept very busy.

'So, you're back, then?' said Jojo, bumping into Jonathan within minutes of his return.

'Yes,' he replied, trying to ignore her sullen expression. 'I suppose you've been rushed off your feet?'

'The work was no problem. We managed OK.'

'I'm sure you've all done a wonderful job. Anyway, now I'm back. And I've brought a friend from England with me. I'd like you two to meet.'

'I know,' said Jojo, sharply.

Jonathan forced a smile. So that was it. Clearly, he had underestimated the speed of the bush telephone in Meroto. He decided it was better not to react.

'Do you remember I told you about that friend of mine – the one who married Roger Samson?'

Jojo's look remained thunderous.

'She's in a very bad way. She's had a miscarriage and – let's just say she's been going through a lot.'

'You're looking after her?' asked Jojo, whose sympathy for anyone tied up with Samson was strictly limited.

'Yes,' replied Jonathan. 'And I'd like you to be involved too. I think it would be good for her to come and help out in the hospital.'

Jojo said nothing.

'Believe me, Jojo, Lilah is not at all like her husband. In fact – well, never mind. I'm just asking you to make her feel welcome, that's all.'

Jojo nodded sourly and continued on her way down the corridor. The FAP was plotting death and devastation for God knows how many of their own people, and here she was, being asked to feel sorry for Roger Samson's wife!

Her figure like that of a gawky teenager, in a white T-shirt and faded blue jeans, Lilah waited for Jonathan to return to his consulting room. During their visit around the hospital, she had been impressed by the improvements and by the new professionalism of the staff. But why had Jonathan insisted she hang around simply to meet Jojo? She was here for two or three weeks at least and surely tomorrow would do? Idly, Lilah studied the old framed photograph of Trinity behind Jonathan's desk. Hospital politics, she decided. Clearly, if she was going to work here, it was better not to stand on Jojo's toes.

'Lilah,' said Jonathan, coming into the room, 'I'd like you to meet Jojo Matwetwe.'

Lilah gripped the end of the desk as Jojo entered behind him. 'I'm sorry,' stammered Lilah, sinking heavily into the chair. It was just not possible. Desperately, she glanced at Jonathan for support.

'Is she OK?' asked Jojo, concerned despite herself.

'Yes, I'm sorry . . .' said Lilah, staring at the woman. 'It's just – I'm sorry – how terribly rude – it's just that you remind me of someone.' Lilah turned in appeal to Jonathan. 'Jonathan . . . ?'

'What is going on in here?' asked Jojo, alarmed. By now she was convinced that Lilah was having a nervous breakdown. Anxiously, Jonathan studied Lilah's face. He had taken another risk, of course, by introducing her so soon to Jojo. But in his view, it was a risk worth taking. Somehow, in Jojo's strange eyes lay the clue to Roger Samson.

'It's all right, Jojo,' continued Jonathan calmly. 'Look, I can't explain now, but Lilah and I need to talk to your mother. Do you think that would be possible?'

'I can phone her at the convent,' said Jojo, perplexed but intrigued. 'I've not seen her for many months. If she agrees, perhaps we can visit her on Sunday?'

'That would be great,' said Jonathan. Jojo's expression was anxious. 'Please, Jojo. You've got to trust me. Until we meet her, I don't want you to mention the name of Samson to your mother.'

'No, please don't,' pleaded Lilah. 'You mustn't tell her who I am. At least, not until we meet face to face.'

'But why not?' Jojo looked at Jonathan in confusion.

'Please, Jojo, believe me, it's best we do this as I say.'

Jojo shrugged her shoulders. 'OK,' she agreed at last. 'I'll ring her tomorrow morning and I'll let you know.' Moving to leave the consulting room, she turned to look at Lilah.

'And if you need anything doing while you're here,' she said, 'you just let me know.'

Jonathan smiled as Jojo closed the door behind her. 'Now that,' he smiled, playfully ruffling Lilah's hair, 'is what I call progress.'

The nuns of the Convent of the Holy Rosary filed silently out of chapel and into the blistering Transvaal heat. How peaceful they all looked, thought Lilah enviously. The serenity of celibacy – it had much to recommend it.

'That is Reverend Mother Benigna,' said Jojo, gesturing towards the tall impressive woman walking briskly towards them. The wind caught the folds of the nun's long white robe, inflating it immediately. Veil and robe both flapping, Reverend Mother continued to march across the garden. Lilah smiled. She looked like a magnificent tall ship just rolling along on the breeze.

'Good morning to you all,' she said, her kind, unlined face breaking into an easy smile. 'My dear Jojo, how nice to see you again, my child. Naomi has been looking forward to your visit. Go and wait for her in the house.'

'Thank you, Reverend Mother,' replied Jojo, for once extremely subdued. 'I've brought two friends who wish to meet my mother.'

'Jonathan Morton and Lilah Dooley,' said Jonathan, with a slight inclination of the head in deference to the old lady.

'Ah, Dr Morton. Of course, I've heard of you and your work at the hospital. You are constantly in our prayers.'

'Thank you,' replied Jonathan solemnly. Lilah suppressed a smile. So even the atheists got a mention in the prayer department. How very comforting for Jonathan.

'Come,' said Reverend Mother, gesturing towards the house. 'You mustn't stand outside here in the sun. I'll ask Mother Vianney to bring you some refreshment in the drawing room. Now, if you'll please excuse me. I'm also expecting a visitor.'

It was like being transported back in time. Lilah inhaled deeply the atmosphere of the convent and was once again at school. The smell of beeswax polish permeated the parquet floor, the glistening mahogany banister and the well-nourished oak panelling of the hall. Somewhere down the corridor, a waft of boiled cabbage had escaped from the kitchen and was now wending its way through the whole house and up into the rafters. Lilah smiled. If experience was anything to go by, thin gravy and mashed potato would also be on the menu.

In the drawing room, where Jojo sat waiting, the brass candlesticks had been rubbed and rubbed to a burnished red glow. A simple crucifix hung above them, its twisted, tortured body buffed to shiny, bright perfection, its stigmati, Lilah noticed, recently repainted red.

Mother Vianney placed some glasses and a large jug of home-made lemonade on a table before going off in search of Naomi. Silently, Jojo stared out of the window and onto the garden she had spent so many hours weeding as a child. If only Reverend Mother had known. Designed as a punishment for her insolence, Jojo had always preferred the solitude of the garden to the torments of her classmates. At the far end of the room, Jonathan studied a picture of Christ, his heart exposed and riven by an ugly-looking knife. They were strange, macabre folk, these Catholics. What a miserable religion!

It was Lilah who first noticed Naomi as she entered the room. Now in her early fifties, she was still a handsome woman, tall and erect with the simple elegance of her people.

'Jojo,' she whispered softly, walking across to embrace her daughter near the window. For a few minutes the two women clung to one another.

'Mother,' said Jojo, at last, 'this is Jonathan Morton, the doctor who runs the hospital.'

'How can I thank you?' asked Naomi, lowering her eyes.

'Please,' said Jonathan, slightly embarrassed, 'whatever I did for Jojo, she's already paid me back a thousand times.' There was an awkward pause. 'Naomi,' continued Jonathan, watching her intently, 'I'd like to introduce you to a friend of mine from England. This is Lilah – Lilah Samson, the wife of Roger Samson.' Lilah watched as Naomi's body froze, her face a silent testament to a mass of conflicting emotions.

'Samson – Roger Samson . . .' she stammered. She lurched towards the sofa.

'Mother,' cried Jojo, alarmed. 'What is it?'

'Here,' said Jonathan calmly, pouring Naomi a glass of lemonade. 'Sit down and drink this.'

'Tell me . . .' faltered Naomi, gazing up at Lilah. 'Did Roger ever mention me?'

'What?' exclaimed Jojo. 'Mother, you know Roger Samson?'

Lilah ignored the interruption. 'No, Naomi,' Lilah said softly. 'He's never really told me anything about his time in South Africa. Perhaps you could tell me.'

Naomi took a long, slow sip of her drink. 'Jojo,' she began, looking imploringly at her daughter, 'I always hoped I would never have to tell you this. I was always too ashamed.'

'Please,' urged Lilah, 'I'm sure, whatever happened, there's nothing for you to feel ashamed about.' Holding her mother's hand, Jojo nodded.

'It was all a long, long time ago,' continued Naomi reluctantly. 'About thirty-five years now. But still I think of it and I feel bad inside. In those days, I worked for Mrs Samson. I was nanny to the *kleinbaas* Roger.'

Jojo's jaw dropped.

'The madam was very kind. But she was never very well. The *kleinbaas* was a strong little boy. We spent plenty of time together.' Naomi paused. 'I loved him very much.'

Lilah coughed awkwardly.

'But the *baas* was a very wicked man. He used to beat all the servants. He even beat the *kleinbaas*.'

Lilah shuddered as she recalled the nightmares and the unexplained weals on Roger's back.

'Then one day, he broke into my hut . . .' Naomi's voice was barely audible. 'I begged him no, no, no. I tried to stop him. I said, what if the madam found out? But he was too strong for me. He . . .'

Jojo held her mother's hand tightly in her own.

'After that, I could never stop him. Every night, he came to my hut. I did not know what to do. I felt bad for the madam. And I felt frightened for myself . . . And then, one day, I . . .' Naomi peered beseechingly at Jojo, 'I found I was having a child. The *baas* said I was a trouble-maker and he kicked me out of the house. I had nowhere else to go. So I came here to the convent. The nuns here looked after me and Jojo.'

The group fell silent as the full impact of Naomi's story began to sink in.

At last, Jojo managed to speak. 'My half-brother?' she gasped, incredulous. 'Roger Samson is my half-brother?'

Naomi nodded sadly.

'I'm sorry for making you relive all this,' urged Lilah, 'but, please, can you tell me what happened to the family after that?'

'A girl who came to work here in the convent told me the madam died in childbirth. She said the madam had no will to live. She said all the servants cried the way the *baas* keep beating that small boy. He just kept beating and beating him. Even worse when the madam died. But no one could do anything about it.'

Jonathan looked at Lilah. Her confusion was evident. At last she felt she was beginning to understand the enigma of her husband. She was even feeling sorry for him. But would sorrow and understanding ever lead to real forgiveness?

'What happened to Roger's father?' she asked.

'The police said he died in an accident,' replied Naomi, still clinging tightly to Jojo. 'But no one really believed it. The people say he was murdered. The truth is, no one really cared.'

Jonathan shook his head. 'Sounds like a nasty piece of work. No wonder Roger's such a—' Catching the look on Lilah's face, he stopped himself in time. No point rubbing salt in the wound. She knew these things already.

'Thank you, Naomi,' said Lilah, going over to the sofa to kneel beside the woman. 'I know what this must have cost you.'

Jojo looked at her mother with new admiration and affection. 'I love you,' she said softly.

Jonathan could see the tears welling up in Naomi's eyes. Taking Lilah by the arm, he moved quietly towards the door. 'We'll just leave you two together for a while,' he said.

Across the hall in Reverend Mother's study, Sophie Weiss was scanning a file of yellowing correspondence.

'Of course, your uncle Simon never spoke to me of his business affairs,' explained Reverend Mother. 'And, I must admit, I was never moved to ask.'

'You mean, he never mentioned the Meroto platinum mine?' prodded Sophie. 'Not even in passing?'

'Miss Weiss,' said Reverend Mother kindly, 'your uncle was a wonderful man and, for many years, a generous benefactor to this convent. That was all I ever needed to know.'

'Did he ever mention his family?'

'No,' replied Reverend Mother, shaking her head, 'never. And I never pursued that matter either. As you know, with Jewish people of a certain age, family is often a deeply traumatic subject.'

'So, what did you talk about when he came to visit?'

'The things that seemed to concern him most,' replied Reverend Mother, smiling wistfully. 'Injustice. Inequality. Man's inhumanity to man. I suppose he'd had his fill of that in Germany.'

'And here,' added Sophie, wryly.

'Yes, and here. But your uncle was also an optimist. He believed in our mission to educate poor black children in this country. I think he hoped, as we all hope, that their future would be that much brighter.'

Sophie continued to flick through the correspondence. 'When was the last time you saw my uncle?'

'About three weeks before he died,' replied the old lady, suddenly more animated. 'In fact, that's something I've never been able to fathom.'

'What, his death?'

'Why, yes, that, of course. So sudden, so unexpected. But there was something else as well. The last time I saw him he was very excited. He told me that the convent need never worry about money again, that he was about to see to that.'

'And then he went and died intestate.'

'Yes, but of course we never knew that until some time after his death.'

'And that's what surprised you?'

'My dear Miss Weiss,' explained the nun, somewhat embarrassed, 'as you can see, I'm no business woman. I've always believed that God will provide.'

Sure, thought Sophie, so do I. God and Dow Jones between them.

'All the same,' continued Reverend Mother, 'six months after

Simon's death, we'd still heard nothing about the legacy. So I decided to phone his bank in Johannesburg.'

'Which bank would that be?' asked Sophie, busily scribbling notes.

'Gregory's Bank,' replied Reverend Mother. 'All Simon's donations to the convent were channelled through them. You'll find copies of their letters in that pile.'

'And what did they say?'

'Well, that's the thing that's always bothered me. The gentleman at the bank told me that Simon had nothing to leave when he died. He said that his home and his land were all mortgaged up to the hilt. There were also certain land rights, I believe, but they were all swallowed up by debt.'

'And yet three weeks before his death Uncle Simon was talking about leaving you a substantial sum?'

'Precisely.'

'I've got to say,' said Sophie, puzzled, 'it does seem kind of weird. Was there anything else?'

'Just one more thing,' replied Reverend Mother slowly. 'I don't know if it's of any significance but the gentleman also mentioned that the day he died, Simon had been involved in an argument.'

'Did he say with whom?' Sophie could barely conceal her excitement.

'No. And I never asked. I just prayed that whoever that person was, he would somehow find the grace of God's forgiveness.'

Walking out into the garden, Sophie was amazed to see Lilah as she wandered arm in arm with Jonathan through the grounds of the convent. God, what a change in a woman! Pale and gaunt, Lady Samson looked a shadow of the beautiful socialite she had been less than twelve months ago. Sophie was shocked. Of course, she had read of Lilah's miscarriage in some gossip column or other. But what on earth was such a woman doing here at the Convent of the Holy Rosary?

'Good afternoon,' ventured Jonathan, as Sophie passed them on the way to her car.

Sophie smiled. An English accent. Whatever Grant might say about bloody Pommies, this sort was invariably polite. 'Hi there,' she replied. 'Lovely weather here. Sure does make a change from New York.'

'New York?' Jonathan looked mildly surprised. 'You're a long way from home.' The statement seemed to invite an explanation.

'Sure am. An uncle of mine died out here some time ago. He'd lost touch with the rest of the family. I'm just tying up a few loose ends.' Sophie laughed. 'What else would a good Jewish-American girl be doing in a South African convent?'

'Did you discover anything useful?' asked Lilah, instantly taken by this breezy American woman.

'I guess so. I've just been talking to the Reverend Mother of this place. Seems the day he died, my uncle was at his bank, arguing with someone. Luckily, the guy who overheard the argument still works there. I've just fixed to meet with him first thing tomorrow morning.'

'You think that may be important?' chipped in Jonathan.

Sophie shrugged her shoulders. 'Who knows? I'll just check the story out and take it from there.'

Lilah looked at the woman in frank amusement. 'You make yourself sound like some kind of private detective.'

'Strictly white-collar crime. I'm in the platinum business.'

'You're a geologist, then?' guessed Jonathan.

'No,' replied Sophie, handing them both a business card. 'My Uncle Simon was the guy who pulled the stuff out of the ground. I just buy and sell it.'

'Sophie Weiss,' repeated Lilah, slowly. 'Hornetfer and Salzmann.' Lilah thought hard for a minute. 'I know I've come across that name somewhere before. Didn't your bank take a table at the Save the Baby spring fund-raiser?'

Sophie was hugely impressed. 'You got it. And I have to admit, Lady Samson, I recognized you from that.'

Lilah looked embarrassed.

'And I'm Jonathan Morton,' interrupted Jonathan, sensing Lilah's unease. 'Lady Samson is staying with me for a few weeks' rest and recuperation.'

Now it was Sophie's turn to feel embarrassed. 'I'm sorry,' she stammered. 'I read about it . . .'

'It's all right,' said Lilah, quickly. 'I'm feeling a lot better

325

already. So much better, in fact, that Jonathan here has decided to put me to work in his hospital.'

'You're some tough guy!' The tension swiftly subsided. 'Which hospital is that?'

'The Christian Sight-Savers Mission Hospital in Meroto,' replied Jonathan. 'Perhaps, if you've got a free evening, you'd like to come for dinner?'

'That'd be great,' said Sophie. 'First a Catholic convent. Next a Christian hospital. Just wait till I tell the rabbi what I do for vacations.'

Jonathan laughed. This woman was just the sort of tonic Lilah needed at the moment. 'How about tomorrow, then?'

'Just fine,' replied Sophie. 'I'm due at the bank in the morning, and then I've gotten myself invited to lunch at the Meroto platinum mine.'

'The infinite munificence of Metallinc,' sniffed Lilah, her smile suddenly extinguished. 'Another of my dear husband's fascinating little affairs.'

Sophie blinked with surprise at the sarcasm in her voice.

'Here's how to find us,' interrupted Jonathan. He was sketching a map for Sophie. 'Come straight over from the mine if you've got nothing better to do.'

Sophie put the map in her bag, at the same time retrieving her car keys. 'Thanks,' she said. 'I guess by then I'll be able to fill you in on my long-lost uncle Simon.'

CHAPTER THIRTY-FOUR

OILED and polished to perfection, the brass lift in Gregory's Bank whirred slowly up to the directors' floor.

'Miss Weiss?' enquired the well-coiffed secretary. Sophie nodded. 'Mr Russell's expecting you.' The woman stood up and led Sophie along the corridor. Its walls were lined with ageing photographs of mine shafts and smiling miners. Sophie would have liked to stop and study them, but the woman just marched on ahead. She was ushered into Mr Russell's office.

'Good morning, Miss Weiss.' Mr Russell stood to welcome her. In his sixties, Ben Russell was a tall man with a slight stoop and around forty pounds of excess weight. He had small, nervous eyes and a weak mouth. Sophie took an instant dislike to him.

'It's very good of you to see me at such short notice,' she said, taking a seat. 'But, like I told you, I don't have much time in Johannesburg.'

Mr Russell smiled, a stick-on, ineffectual smile. 'That's why I've already had your uncle's file brought up from the archives,' he said, his eyes darting around the room.

'Thanks.'

'If only I'd known,' he continued awkwardly, 'I'd have had all this sent on to you. But until your phone call yesterday, I'd no idea that Simon Weiss had any living relatives.'

Sophie shrugged. 'It's not your fault my father and Uncle

Simon lost touch,' she said. 'I guess they were both too busy trying to make a buck.'

'I suppose so,' nodded Mr Russell. 'It happens to us all. Now, Miss Weiss, as you know, Simon Weiss left no will when he died. And, as the documentation will show, he was on the verge of bankruptcy.' He coughed. 'So what can I do for you?'

'Mr Russell,' began Sophie, earnestly, 'did you know my uncle well?'

The man's eyes refused to meet Sophie's. It was deeply annoying.

'Simon Weiss was a very private person,' he muttered. 'But for ten years or more I did advise him on financial matters – goodness, how Simon hated paperwork! Even so, I don't think I could honestly say I knew him well.'

'I believe from Reverend Mother Benigna that he was here the day he died.'

'Yes, that's true. I told Reverend Mother myself. He was here that day for a meeting. You see, Simon had invested everything he owned in what is now the Meroto platinum mine.'

'I knew it! I knew somehow Uncle Simon must have been tied up in that operation.'

'Tied up?' repeated Russell, bemused. 'My dear Miss Weiss, your uncle was more than tied up in Meroto. He was the guiding force behind the entire operation. He did the prospecting. He located the platinum. As I told you, he sank every cent he had into that mine. That's why the whole thing seemed so extraordinary.'

'What, the investment?'

'No, the investment was as safe as houses. That wasn't the problem. The point was . . . now when was it . . . ?' He flicked through the file. 'Ah, yes, here they are, my own notes from that meeting.' He handed Sophie several pieces of foolscap and continued. 'By nineteen seventy-five, your uncle had decided to float Meroto on the Johannesburg Stock Exchange. The results of the feasibility study he'd commissioned were outstanding. Simon was cock-a-hoop.' He drummed his fingers nervously on the desk. 'The day he came, there were about half a dozen of us here, stockbrokers and merchant bankers, all extremely optimistic. Then someone asked to see the documentation on the mineral rights.' Mr Russell paused.

'And being so bad a paperwork, I guess Uncle Simon had lost them?'

'Oh no. Not at all. The point is, he had never owned them.'

'What? Then why did he plough all his money into the mine in the first place?'

'With mining,' Russell shook his head, 'things are often far from clear. Simon owned the land rights – as I recall they'd been purchased from a farmer named de Jongh in nineteen seventy-one.'

'So when had the mineral rights been sold?'

'At precisely the same time. But not to Simon.' Sophie stared hard at him. 'To a friend and business associate of his.'

'And who was that?'

Russell seemed to be studying the top of his desk. 'A man named Roger Samson,' he said at last.

Sophie had never felt such torrents of anger. Round and round they raged in her head until she thought she was going to scream. 'You're telling me that bastard stitched my uncle up?'

Russell looked distinctly anxious. 'Come, come, now, Miss Weiss. You can't go around making allegations like that. You have no proof. After all, even I assumed that this was the arrangement your uncle wanted. It seemed reasonable enough. He'd always treated Samson like a son.'

'Sonofafuckinbitch!' shouted Sophie. 'Didn't you realize what was going on?'

'Well, no.' His tone was sheepish. 'At least, not at first. You see, at that meeting, when this was all pointed out to Simon, he didn't say a word, just sat there thinking. Then he asked me if he could make a private telephone call. So I took him down the corridor to my office.'

'And that's when you overheard the argument?'

'It was almost impossible not to. There was so much shouting going on.'

'And who was Uncle Simon shouting at?'

'Why, I can't be sure – I couldn't swear to it, you understand – but it seemed to be Roger Samson.'

Sophie hit the roof. 'And when my uncle died, you said absolutely nothing. You just sat there and let Samson get away with it?'

Russell bowed his head. 'What else could I have done? Legally, Samson's case was watertight. He owned the mineral rights. As you know, soon after Simon's death he went ahead with the flotation.'

'Yeah,' said Sophie bitterly, gathering up the file. 'And the rest is history.'

Russell got up quickly, trying to catch her arm. 'I'm sorry Miss Weiss, I—'

'Forget it,' snapped Sophie, brushing him aside. 'Business is business. And, please, let me guess, Samson International is now one of your biggest clients, yes?' Sophie stood up and turned on her heel to leave. 'That's OK, then,' she said, shooting him a look of deepest contempt. 'I won't be knocking on your door looking for more help. From now on, I'll deal with this myself. But I'm telling you one thing, Mr Russell. That bastard Roger Samson is going to pay for this.'

For over an hour, Sophie paced Johannesburg's Main Street, trying to cool down. So Roger Samson had stolen her birthright and betrayed her uncle – that wasn't bad for starters. Finally, she returned to her car and headed back to the Santon Sun hotel. It was not so much the money – hell, the Weiss family was rich enough already. No, this was something else entirely. Sophie racked her brains for the expression. *Zelbst gloibn*, that was it, self-esteem. Sophie was Jewish and proud of it. Why the hell were her people – *her uncle, for God's sake* – always being turned into victims? She had to find some way of turning the tables, of making that bastard Samson suffer. Sophie pressed hard on the accelerator. Now she knew everything she needed to know, Metallinc could stuff their lunch. The last thing any relative of Simon Weiss should want was Samson International hospitality.

Back in her hotel room, Sophie dialled Grant's number in New York. The phone rang for minutes before he eventually picked it up.

'G'day, sport,' mimicked Sophie, 'is Ernie pining for me?'

'Jesus, Sophie, do you know what time of morning it is?'

'I thought only Poms were allowed to whinge.'

'You got me there.' Grant came to immediately. 'Let me try again. Sophie dearest, how wonderful to hear from you. Both the cat and I are missing you to the point of desperation.'

'That's more like it.'

'How are your investigations going?'

'Interesting. Looks like that shit Roger Samson double-crossed Uncle Simon over the Meroto mine. The day Uncle Simon found out was the day he had his heart attack and died.'

'Roger Samson, Roger bloody Samson – that bloke's name keeps popping up everywhere.'

'What do you mean?'

'Well, I bumped into Larry O'Connor, an old mucker of mine, in a bar the other evening.'

'Grant, you're supposed to be spending your leisure time investigating October platinum trading.'

'Put a sock in it, will you, Sophie, and let a bloke have his say.'

'*So* sorry.'

'Apology accepted. Well, the thing is, Larry's now working for Kroll Associates.'

'The Wall Street investigators?'

'The smartest financial detective agency in the world. Now, since you left, I've been doing a bit of asking around at NYMEX, trying to find out who's heavily into October futures.'

'And who did you come up with?'

'That's the problem, Sophie. No one in particular. It seems like hundreds of companies are in the frame.'

'So there's no evidence of punters operating in conceit, then?'

'Not on the face of it. But anyway, I'm there having a few beers and talking to Larry and I ask him what he's doing—'

'Getting smashed with you.'

'Sophie!'

'Sorry.'

'And he says it's all hush-hush and all the rest of it, but he's involved in tracking down where Saddam Hussein has stashed the goodies.'

'Big potatoes.'

'Right. Larry reckons the old crook must have skimmed off

anything up to thirty-three billion dollars from government deals.'

'Those Middle Eastern guys sure don't mess around in nickels and dimes.'

'Anyway, looks like Larry is quite an ace at tracing funds back to holding companies . . .'

'And then finding out who ultimately runs the holding companies?'

'You got it.'

'Great. Three cheers for good old Larry. So how does that help us?'

'Sophie darling, are you losing your grip? Anyone'd think it was you and not me who'd just been woken up at some ungodly hour . . . get lost, Ernie, I'll feed you in a minute.' A loud miaowing blotted out Grant's voice.

'It's OK, Ernie. I'll be home real soon to feed you myself.'

'Bloody cat,' growled Grant. 'A cat like that in Australia, we'd feed it to the dingoes.'

'Grant!'

'Like I was saying, so Larry's a bit of a star when it comes to tracking down the dough. So I say to him, "Look mate, I'm having a bit of a problem here. There's a whole heap of companies buying October platinum. As far as I know, it could be completely legit. All the same, a friend of mine thinks there's a bit of a whiff about it. Could you help me out?" Larry says no worries and runs a few things through the computer for me.'

'And did he find anything interesting?'

'Well, it's early days yet. These things take time. But so far, he's looked into a few Bermuda-registered companies and guess what he's come up with?'

'Come on, Grant. Stop spinning it out.'

'A guy called Jim di Pietro . . .'

'The banker?'

'Yes,' replied Grant. 'Seems like he's been buying heavily through a complicated network of companies. And then there's somebody else as well.' Grant paused. 'Guess who's really up to his bloody eyeballs in October platinum? Your mate, Roger Samson.'

Sophie whistled. 'You don't say.'

'Are you still going to the Meroto mine today?'

'No, I decided to call that off.'

Grant could almost hear Sophie's mind ticking at the other end of the phone.

'You know, Grant, I'm sure Samson and di Pietro are up to something. But I'm damned if I know what.'

'Well, I'll just keep hacking away my end.' By now Grant had given up and allowed Ernie into bed with him.

'You're A-one, Grant.'

'Don't mention it. Keeps me out of trouble while you're gone. What are you up to for the rest of the day?'

'I guess I'll go visit with my new best friend,' Sophie teased.

'Not a bloke, I hope?'

Sophie was pleased to hear the edge in his voice. 'No, just someone I ran into yesterday. You're never going to believe me, Grant. But it's Roger Samson's wife.'

As usual, with Sophie, it was nothing but a hunch. A glance, a sentence, an expression, nothing she could ever put her finger on. But unless her celebrated intuition had taken a hike, there was something seriously wrong between Roger Samson and his wife. If so, mused Sophie, following Jonathan's map to the township, Lilah might turn out to be her most formidable ally.

'Hi, there!' shouted Sophie, jumping out of the car and waving to Lilah who was sunbathing in Jonathan's tiny overgrown garden.

'Sophie,' said Lilah, putting down her book, delighted. 'How nice to see you. We were only expecting you later on this afternoon.'

'I cancelled my lunch.' Sophie sat down beside Lilah. 'I thought it might be more fun here for the day.'

'How did you get on at the bank?' Lilah quickly pulled on a T-shirt over her bikini. She was still so thin, her skin seemed stretched translucent over her too-obvious bones.

'Oh, fine,' said Sophie evasively. 'I found out what I needed to know. Or, at least, I figured out what must have happened to my uncle.'

'I'm sorry,' said Lilah, more sensitive now than ever to other people's losses.

'It's OK,' said Sophie, a sudden steely gleam transforming

her dark brown eyes. 'Some guy double-crossed my uncle and now I'm going to fix him.'

Lilah nodded sympathetically. Vengeance. It was probably the only way. She stared vaguely up at the sky. Sophie looked concerned. It was as if this woman, Lady Samson, was floating in and out of consciousness. Hell, she must have something on her mind.

'How long do you reckon on staying here?' asked Sophie.

Lilah shrugged her shoulders. 'I'm in no hurry to get home. Right now, there's nothing for me there.'

'Oh, please,' teased Sophie. 'Married to one of the richest guys in the world and you're telling me there's nothing to go home to. Come on, lighten up.'

Lilah turned to look at her. Why not? What did it matter? What the hell did anything matter now? 'My husband and my best friend are having an affair,' she said simply.

'Oh, my God, I'm so sorry. I always seem to be putting my foot in it. Really, I didn't mean—'

'Don't apologize. I feel better for telling you.'

Sophie looked at Lilah's face and knew she was on her side. 'How do you feel about him now?'

Lilah leaned across to put a marker in her book. 'I don't know. Everything seems to be up in the air. That's why I'm here – trying to work it out. The trouble is, whatever happens, I know I'll always blame him for the loss of my baby.' The wound was still a gaping hole, as raw and as deep as ever.

'It's OK,' said Sophie, putting her arm round Lilah's thin and shaking shoulders. 'You just cry out loud if you want to. It's best to let it out. Here, thump this cushion. It's great therapy.' Lilah gave the cushion such a vicious punch that the seams burst and a cloud of duck-down stuffing exploded into the air.

'You like that?' asked Sophie, handing a handkerchief to Lilah. 'Feels great, doesn't it? I'm telling you, honey, sounds like the time has come to fight.'

Lilah blew her nose, peered hopelessly at Sophie. 'But how?'

'Look, Lilah, you've been straight with me. Now I'm going to square with you. Way back in nineteen seventy-five, someone double-crossed my uncle. As sure as planting a bullet in his head, that guy did him in.'

'And now you intend to find the man who did it?'

'I don't have to look for him,' said Sophie, her voice disturbingly quiet. 'That's where you and me have got something in common. That guy was Roger Samson.'

For a while they sat together in silence, two women united in their anger and hatred. Eventually, Sophie explained to Lilah the details of Roger's treachery. 'And so Meroto became the basis of Roger Samson's wealth,' she concluded. 'If you want to look at it another way, the whole of Samson International has been built on Simon Weiss's back.'

Lilah said nothing, her head still spinning from the enormity of it all. 'What can I say,' she spoke at last, 'except that I believe you?' She looked up as Jonathan's Ranger Rover came roaring to a halt outside the house. The doors opened and, to Lilah's surprise, Jojo also emerged from the car. Lilah frowned. It was unlike Jonathan to spring an unexpected guest on her.

'Quite a party,' he called, opening the gate for Jojo. Despite the warmth and confidence generated by their trip to the convent, Jojo seemed to have resumed her sullen expression.

'Hi there, Jonathan,' replied Sophie, vaguely annoyed at the intrusion. Just as she and Lilah were really getting places!

'Hello, Sophie,' said Jonathan, stopping to drop a kiss on Lilah's cheek. 'This is Jojo. She works with me at the hospital.'

Sophie smiled at Jojo who looked distinctly ill at ease.

'It's all right, Jojo,' said Jonathan, guiding her to an old striped deck-chair. 'There's no need to be alarmed. I simply want you to repeat to Lilah the story you've just told me.'

Jojo looked at him. 'Please,' she murmured. 'I only told you so we can avoid my people dying.'

'That's why I'm asking you to tell Lilah,' insisted Jonathan. Sophie watched as this extraordinary blue-eyed half-caste squirmed miserably in her seat. For days Jojo had agonized, trying to summon up the courage to confide her fears to Jonathan. But now things were moving far too fast. Jojo began to sweat. Now she had started this ball of betrayal rolling, there seemed no way to stop it.

'I belong to a movement . . .' she began at last, 'the Freedom for the African People movement. For many years, I have worked with them and believed in them. Our leader, Credo Sekese, is my friend and a good man.' Jojo shot a glance at Jonathan. 'You must not think I want to betray my friends.'

'You know nothing would make me believe that,' Jonathan protested. 'Let's face it, during all the years I've known you, you never even mentioned the FAP until today.'

'It was not that I did not trust you,' Jojo said, staring at her feet, 'but we are all pledged to secrecy.'

Jonathan put a hand on her shoulder. 'The important thing is that you trusted me enough to tell me this.'

By now, Sophie and Lilah were growing impatient.

'For years, the FAP had no funds,' said Jojo. 'And for years Credo argued against strikes and sit-ins. He said we must wait. He said one day we would strike a major blow against Western capitalism.' She paused. 'Then, a few years ago, a man approached Credo. He said he represented people who were behind us in our struggle. He promised us money to buy guns and explosives. He—'

'Tell Lilah the man's name,' interrupted Jonathan.

'I never met him,' said Jojo, quietly. 'Only Credo did. But his name is Jim di Pietro.'

'Jim di Pietro?' echoed Lilah and Sophie both at once. They stared at one another in amazement.

'Yes,' replied Jojo. 'And the people who wished to help us, we knew them only as the Group.'

'Jesus!' exclaimed Lilah. She was trembling despite the heat.

'You know these people?' asked Sophie.

Lilah nodded. 'They're a group of businessmen,' she replied. 'Roger and di Pietro are both members. But why on earth would they be funding a terrorist organization?'

'I'm sorry, Jojo,' said Jonathan, acutely aware of her apprehension. 'I'm sure Lilah understands that you're freedom fighters not terrorists.'

Jojo looked unperturbed. 'It's all right. When I see what has happened to us, even I can no longer be sure.'

'So your organization and this Group,' interrupted Sophie, 'you had some kind of strategy going?'

Immediately Jojo's face turned stony. '*They* had the strategy. It was all *their* idea. I was against it from the beginning. But *they* decided that the FAP must blow up the refineries . . .'

'Refineries!' Sophie was unable to contain her growing excitement. 'Which refineries?'

'Rustenburg, Impala and Meroto. The plan was for us to blow them all up on the thirtieth of September.'

Lilah could feel a headache coming on. 'But that doesn't make any sense at all,' she argued. 'Why would Roger be involved in a plot to blow up his own refinery?'

Sophie shook her head. 'Poor *schmucks*. You can bet your bottom dollar the security forces at Meroto would be sitting there waiting for them. No. Impala and Rustenburg, that's all the bastards are really after.'

'But why?' insisted Lilah. 'I still don't understand. Will someone please explain to me what the hell is going on?'

To Sophie it all made perfect sense. 'What a scam! And you have to hand it to these guys, they almost brought it off.'

Lilah stared at her, still bewildered.

'Look,' explained Sophie, her mind still fitting together the jigsaw, 'South Africa produces about eighty per cent of the world's platinum, and between them Rustenburg and Impala refine about ninety per cent of that.'

'So with those two out of action,' ventured Jonathan, 'Roger's Meroto stock becomes even more valuable.'

'That's only the cherry on top of the cake. Just lately there's been some heavy buying in October platinum futures. If there was a sudden shortage late September the prices of the stuff would rocket sky-high.'

Jonathan looked nervously at Lilah. Just how much more could the poor darling take?

'It's OK,' she smiled, acknowledging his concern. 'Nothing about Roger surprises me any more. It is Roger, isn't it, Sophie? Roger and di Pietro are behind all this.'

'I'm sorry.'

'Don't be. If it's any use, I can even give you the names of the other members of the Group.'

Sophie smiled at her gratefully.

Jonathan turned to Jojo. 'We must talk to Credo as soon as possible.'

'Yes. He must tell this di Pietro man that we will not carry out their plan.'

Sophie held up her hands. 'For God's sake, no! Don't you see? He mustn't tell di Pietro anything of the sort. The Group must never suspect that anyone knows their game.'

'No?' queried Jojo and Jonathan in chorus.

'No,' insisted Sophie. 'If you play it my way, all the FAP has to do is to sit tight and do absolutely nothing. The thirtieth of September will come and go and the Group will be down by billions.'

Lilah stared at Sophie with admiration. 'I suppose Roger stands to lose a fortune?'

'I guess so,' said Sophie. 'Right now, I can't tell just how much. But I reckon it must be plenty.'

'Good,' said Lilah, softly.

Sophie smiled. The plan in her agile mind was already shaping up beautifully. 'You're right.' She looked over at Samson's wife. 'It's time that shit got shafted.'

It was late Sunday evening before a meeting could be organized with Credo. Silently he listened to Sophie's explanations, looking up only once or twice to focus his gaze on Jojo. For her part, Jojo sat motionless in Jonathan's sitting room, a thousand conflicting emotions still raging around in her head. Jonathan's heart went out to her. Never had he seen her looking quite so worn and miserable. Divided loyalties – always the legacy of the half-caste. But Jojo had been neither a traitor nor disloyal to any race or colour. If only Credo would believe that, thought Jonathan earnestly. It happened to be the truth.

It seemed ages before Credo spoke. His hair was greying at the temples now, but he was still as fit and wiry as a much younger man, although his years as a rock-drill operator had taken their toll and left him slightly deaf. He compensated by concentrating twice as hard on everything said to him.

'Now I know I have made a mistake,' he finally conceded.

Jojo heaved a huge sigh of relief. She knew how stubborn he could be. 'Do you forgive me?' she asked nervously.

'You did what you thought was right.' Credo, his face still severe, looked at Jojo. 'And it is good that you did.'

Jojo's tense face relaxed. Thank God! That was all that really mattered. Credo had understood.

'So you agree to do nothing?' Sophie wanted to know. She was impressed by Credo's quiet dignity. Hell, terrorists, freedom fighters, whatever they wanted to call themselves, at least this guy knew how to behave.

'Of course,' said Credo, with the vaguest hint of a smile. 'This way, the FAP will still strike its blow against capitalism.'

Sophie started to laugh. 'We're not all such lousy scum-bags, you know.'

'No,' said Credo, looking around the room, 'you're not. That is why this new way is even better. This way only the evil ones get hurt.'

Sophie turned to Lilah. 'You know, I'd give anything to know more about this operation. Roger must be keeping the information somewhere. Any ideas?'

'His most sensitive files are kept in his office at Samson Heights.'

'Any way we could get hold of them?'

'Difficult, security's very tight,' replied Lilah, racking her brains.

'We don't want a break-in,' said Sophie. 'That would put Roger on his guard. There must be some way—'

'I've got it!' said Lilah. 'A birthday present, of course. The most natural thing in the world. Jonathan, push the phone over here, will you, please? I must get hold of Hugo.'

CHAPTER THIRTY-FIVE

YES, thought Sally Kerwin, that was so like Lady Samson. Despite her own grief, she had nevertheless found time to plan a surprise birthday gift for her husband. It had been quite a feat of organization, especially with Lady Samson herself still recuperating in South Africa. But Miss Kerwin was thrilled to be included in the plan and had played her part sublimely.

Poor Sir Roger, she mused, meticulously clearing her desk for the evening. The poor man really was in need of something to cheer him up. How she hoped Lady Samson would come back soon. Sir Roger had looked so worried and dejected since the miscarriage. Even after he had spoken to Lady Samson on the phone, something he did every day, his mood did not improve. If anything, he seemed even more restless and depressed. Miss Kerwin sighed. Perhaps after this evening's gesture things would begin to get better.

She sat and waited for Mr Newsom and his assistant to arrive. No, it had not been easy to arrange. For a start, there were so few evenings when Sir Roger could be guaranteed to be out of his office. But tonight, thank goodness, was one of those charity boxing events. Sir Roger was hosting a table and would be stuck there until midnight at least. Miss Kerwin glanced at the clock on her wall. This evening, a rare treat, she was going to the theatre. Excellent seats, too – tickets Sir Roger had asked her to book and subsequently failed to cancel. Miss Kerwin opened her handbag and took out a pressed powder compact. She was about to open it when Hugo Newsom and his handsome assistant arrived.

'Good work, Miss Kerwin,' whispered Hugo, conspiratorially.

'I'm sure there's no need to whisper,' said William Stanton, sternly. 'You failed actors, you're all the same. Any excuse for a bit of cloak and dagger.'

Miss Kerwin smiled at the pair of them. 'You won't be disturbed,' she said, eyeing the large painting Hugo was carrying under his arm. 'I've told the security guards what's happening. They all know how to keep mum.'

'Thanks,' said Hugo. 'And what do we do when we've hung it?'

'Just ring extension three nine seven.' Miss Kerwin collected her belongings. 'Someone will come and lock up.'

William helped Miss Kerwin with her coat.

'May I have a look at the surprise?'

'Of course,' said Hugo, holding up the picture on the desk. 'It's a Klein.'

Miss Kerwin pursed her lips as she studied the apparently random blue arrangements. 'Oh dear,' she said, shaking her head. 'Not my sort of thing at all, I'm afraid.'

Hugo looked on with frank approval. 'A bit of a gamble with Roger, I suppose,' he said cheerily. 'Never mind. If he doesn't like it, Lilah says he can always stick it in the boardroom.'

'I'll be off, then.' Miss Kerwin picked up her umbrella. 'No need to hurry. Sir Roger won't be back here tonight. And I know you interior designers don't like being rushed. At home, I'm constantly moving my bits and pieces around. It takes time to decide where things should go.'

'Interior designer, indeed,' snorted William, as Miss Kerwin disappeared down the corridor. 'Do I look like an interior designer?'

Hugo shot him a comical look. 'No, more's the pity,' he sniffed. 'You look like a bloody banker. Now put down that tool bag for a minute and make sure she's really gone.'

William peered down the corridor while Hugo started rummaging in Miss Kerwin's neatly ordered desk. Miss Kerwin got into the lift.

'Top right-hand drawer, wasn't it?' asked William, closing the office door.

'Yes.' Triumphantly Hugo held up a large bunch of keys.

'Lilah was right. Here we are. A spare set of keys to Roger's office.'

The blood drained from William's face. So far it had seemed like one hell of a lark. Now it was beginning to feel serious. 'You know we could go to prison for this,' he said.

Hugo laughed. 'Oh, do shut up, Stanton. If I'd known you were going to be such a ninny I'd never have invited you along.'

'I'm beginning to wish you hadn't.'

'Come on. You know I need you to decide what's relevant. I'm hopeless with figures. Now let's get weaving. Whatever we're looking for, we've got to find the little beauties.'

The Cure Cancer Campaign's annual boxing evening was being held in the Samson International, Park Lane. A men-only event, the heady amalgam of drink, dinner, gambling and a succession of bar-room brawlers beating each other up always proved a popular occasion with the dinner-suited businessmen of the City of London. For once, however, Charles Watson-Smith was feeling uneasy about the evening. After the recent tragic coma victim, he was beginning to have qualms about the morality of such an event. He had even gone so far as to voice his objections to the fund-raising committee. But Lady Swinden, the co-chairwoman, and her allies had voted him down conclusively. After all, they countered, the boxing evening had always proved a major money-spinner for the charity. And besides, as Lady Swinden had argued at her juggernaut-ish best, who on earth could tell whether any man was clinically brain-dead or not?

'Useful to have friends in high places,' said Sir Howard Anderson as Roger welcomed him to his table. Charles started to study the advertisements at the back of the sponsors' brochure. Too bad Anderson's recent knighthood had done nothing to alleviate his unutterable boorishness. Sir Howard took his seat with a nod to the assembled company.

'A ringside position, no less,' he guffawed loudly. 'Like I always told you, Roger, no point investing in anything but prime sites.'

'I think you know everybody here,' said Roger, ignoring Sir Howard's pointed references. The other dinner guests nodded vaguely in the direction of the former cabinet minister.

'Welcome aboard the Samson International board,' shouted young Christopher Grafton, inordinately pleased with his pun. As usual, Christopher had primed himself with a few hefty toots before leaving home. Now he smiled at the former Secretary of State with an amiable vacancy. What was it he had read about Anderson in *Private Eye*? Christopher wished he were not becoming quite so forgetful. Something about a knighthood for services to Uganda. If the opportunity arose during the course of the evening, he must ask the old buffer what he thought of the place.

'Thanks,' said Sir Howard, smiling broadly, his spider-veined jowls wobbling alarmingly. 'Hello there, Charles. Haven't seen you for ages. That busy little dolly-bird wife of yours keeping you all tied up, is she?'

Roger smirked as he recalled the lurid details of the private detective's report on Sir Howard. The chunk about bondage had been particularly interesting. Charles acknowledged Anderson's remark with the barest of nods and continued to flick through his brochure.

'My dear George.' Sir Howard shook hands warmly with George Hamish, seated on his right.

'I see you're retiring from politics at the next election,' said George, who had been drinking since lunch.

'Yes. Pressures of business, more quality time with the family – you know the sort of thing.'

'Bollocks,' said George, unsteadily lighting up another nine-inch Davidoff cigar. 'More a question of getting out before you're found out, eh, Sir Howard?'

'Are you interested in boxing, Sir Howard?' said Roger, staring daggers at George.

'Not really.' Sir Howard proffered his glass for champagne. 'I think most people would agree that my *forte* has always been more in the line of jousting – verbal jousting, don't you know.' Delighted with his own *bon mot*, he scanned the table for approval.

'Give me strength,' George groaned, taking a long draw on

his cigar and staring up at the ceiling. Roger shot a meaningful look at Piet van der Hoorn who immediately tried to divert George into less hazardous waters.

'Congratulations on your recent takeover of Fortune TV,' ventured Piet affably.

George stared unblinking at the large Afrikaner. ' "The slings and arrows of outrageous fortune",' he muttered, taking a fortifying slug of champagne. 'Mind you, I don't suppose Roger ever bothered with anything quite so primitive. Nothing but state of the art for the good of the nation, eh, Roger?'

'Shut up, George,' rasped Roger. 'You're drunk.'

George stared at him oyster-eyed. 'Sticks and stones . . .' he hiccupped. 'Oh no, we had to be more sophisticated than that, didn't we, Roger? Far more sophisticated.'

Roger was relieved when the soup arrived. If that did not sober George up, it might at least shut him up for the next ten minutes or so.

'All well at Meroto?' asked Charles, politely turning his attention to Piet.

'Just fine,' replied Piet. 'Profit margins have been on the up and up since we opened our own refinery.'

'Yes,' said Charles, 'I'm sure I must have read something along those lines in the annual report.'

Piet studied Charles's face. Could this be the same bright and jaunty gentleman who had once insisted on a trip down the platinum mine? He was so thin, his skin so sallow. Piet hoped it was not cancer.

'What's the form?' shouted George across the table to Christopher.

'There's no form,' replied Christopher. 'Tonight's boxers are all unknown amateurs, most of them just out and out bruisers.'

'How many bouts are there?' However sozzled he managed to get, George always remained completely numerate.

'Ten bouts, three rounds each.'

'You want a bet?'

'Is the Pope Catholic? I'll have a grand on the red corner for every bout.'

George's head nodded, a waving sort of nod, the kind evinced by velveteen dogs in the back of Cortinas. 'Fair enough,' he warbled. 'And I'll meet you with a grand on the blue corner.'

'George, is that entirely wise?' Charles was very fond of George, despite his increasing unpredictability. Even if he was a lush, the man was basically straight and honest. Besides, who could ever tell what drove another man to drink?

'Don't be so fucking patronizing,' said George. 'You think I can't afford to lose ten grand?'

Roger glared at his finance director.

'Oh, no, we're all rich men, now,' continued George, turning suddenly maudlin. 'We're all on the gravy train now. Just don't anyone try and stop the train or ask the driver where it's come from.'

The assembled guests made an embarrassed attempt at laughter. George withdrew into an increasingly sullen silence. To Roger's relief, the rest of dinner passed to the anodyne drone of banalities and banter.

'Of course, Roger was quite a boxer in his youth,' ventured Piet good-naturedly as eventually the spectacle began.

'Too bad he's not boxing this evening,' piped up Christopher. 'I'd put my shirt on Roger any day of the week.'

Roger responded with a self-deprecating smile. Men like Grafton were so easy to deal with. They were too idle or stupid to ask any awkward questions. All you had to do was make a profit and you were immediately a hero. Why couldn't men like George just try to see things that way?

The first nine bouts passed in a post-prandial haze of cognac and cigar smoke. As the evening wore on, Charles seemed to relax. So far, at least, there had been no major injuries and George, thank God, was £3,000 up on Grafton.

'Now this pair look like real fighters,' said Piet admiringly as the final two contestants stepped into the ring.

Roger, who had remained ominously quiet throughout the evening, was studying the two boxers with interest. The older man, Bethells, was powerfully built, three inches taller and fourteen pounds heavier than his young opponent, Thomas.

'I'll tell you what,' shouted Christopher to George. 'Double or quits.'

'OK,' said George, by now perfectly amiable again, and

taking a large slurp of cognac. 'And just to show I'm a sports-man, I'll let you choose which one you're backing.'

'Bethells,' said Christopher decisively.

'Good choice,' said Sir Howard. He turned to George. 'Your man's at a disadvantage in height, weight and reach.'

'Stick with Thomas,' said Roger quietly, almost to himself. Roger continued to stare at the young boxer's body, his muscular midriff honed to a state of impressive hardness.

The bell for the first round rang to a pandemonium of loud and bibulous exhortations. Bethells danced out of his corner with a sprightliness which belied his 250 pounds. Immediately he started to drive his young opponent across the ring with a flurry of straight and murderous punches. Within minutes, Thomas was bruised and cut around both eyes. Soon the blood was dripping from his cheeks and mixing with the sweat of his body to form pink smears across his white, satin trunks.

'Come on, youngster,' shouted George, nervously lighting another cigar. 'Come on, show him what you're worth.'

It was as if the young boxer had heard. Springing off the ropes to escape the vicious barrage, he responded with two thudding right hooks followed by a succession of terrible, swiping blows.

'Good man,' murmured Roger, as Bethells weaved drunkenly around the ring, sucking deeply for air. 'Come on, now, look for his chin.'

But the youngster was too impetuous, charging across the canvas with a predator's relish, his eyes glazed and desperate. Bethells was waiting for him with a malevolent combination of punches – jabs to the body, upper-cuts to the face, and then, a few short wicked shots to the bridge of his nose. Roger could hear the crowd groaning as Thomas fell to his knees, the blood pouring down his face and onto the canvas.

Suddenly Roger began to feel quite dizzy. The searing arclights on the roof of the hall, the smoke, the shrieks of the crowd, the smell of the cognac – the whole oppressive atmosphere began to assail his senses. Then suddenly, like a thousand red-hot needles, the excruciating pain of splintered bone shot across Roger's face. Unconsciously he lifted his hand to rub the tiny bump on his nose. Immediately, Roger Samson was ten years old again, helpless and petrified, crying out to an empty house as his father's brutal blows rained down on his boyish, tearstained face. As the bell for the second round went, Roger could feel the adrenaline coursing through his veins, the dry, bitter taste of hatred in his mouth.

His bleeding nose now staunched, Thomas charged out of his corner like an angry young bull, goaded beyond endurance. Within seconds he was attacking Bethells with murderous precision, every blow intensifying the ferocity of the next.

'Come on, Thomas,' yelled George, punching the air with his fist. This time the boxer needed no encouragement. He tore into his opponent, catching him with a right hook, then a left, then another right. Bethells staggered under the onslaught, his bruised right eye now closing over, blood oozing from somewhere behind his dislodged gum shield.

'Get on with it, Bethells,' screamed Christopher. By now the older man was down to the dregs of his stamina, desperately trying to husband his dwindling resources and attempting to box behind a jab.

'Oh, my God,' moaned Charles, as the youngster resumed the ugly protracted attack. Lefts to the head, more blows and upper-cuts to the body, then a scuffing right, high on the head, which sent the older man reeling.

Roger could not hear the crowd for the sound of blood thundering around his eardrums. Now he was twenty-two years old, desperate and angry like the youngster in the ring. He could feel the vein in his neck, twitching violently.

Bethells was up on the count of seven, but Thomas, rapacious as a starving coyote, was there waiting for him. It was all over within seconds, the older man hammered to the canvas by a remorseless succession of punches and the evil concussive left hook which finally did for him.

Roger stared at the lifeless figure and started to feel sick. God knows, he had never meant to kill his father. He had not even wanted to fight him. But Martin Samson was an impossible man to reason with. Roger closed his eyes. He could still recall the sickeningly dull thud as his father's head hit the rock. Oh God, there had been no alternative! He had to make it look like an accident, or suicide, or even a terrorist attack. Roger felt suddenly drained. The cheers of the crowd grew louder and more hysterical. Roger could hear nothing but the sound of his father's heavy body, plummeting to the bottom of the mine shaft.

Roger's office was like Roger, Hugo always thought. With its deep green leather upholstery and dark panelled walls it made one simple statement. Wealth. Lots of it. And very little else.

Hugo gave a whoop of joy as the drawer of the large mahogany cabinet slid open.

Looking at the accumulated mass of papers, William felt distinctly ill at ease. 'Haven't you even the vaguest clue as to what we're searching for?' he asked. 'By the look of this lot, we could be here all night.'

Hugo shrugged his shoulders. 'There are smoked salmon sandwiches in the tool bag.'

'Thanks,' said William, shaking his head. 'I'm beginning to get the picture.'

'Just anything and everything that could incriminate Roger,' said Hugo good-naturedly. 'Remember, we're doing this for Lilah.'

Success came sooner than expected. 'Christ Almighty!' exclaimed William, scanning the reams of figures and accounts. 'Wait till Lilah gets hold of this little lot. It's dynamite.'

Working his way through Roger's desk diary, Hugo nodded vaguely. 'Sure, I'll photocopy them all in a minute. Just hang on . . .' Suddenly Hugo felt a strange sinking feeling. He had not wanted to believe it – not even of Roger. But Lilah was right. There it was – the date of 30 September, heavily ringed in red.

It was well into the early hours of the morning before the two men were finally through.

'Isn't security going to think it a bit odd?' asked William, wearily packing the mass of photocopies into the tool bag.

'How do you mean, odd?' said Hugo, replacing the files in immaculate order and locking the cabinet door.

'Well, we came at seven o'clock to hang a picture and we're both still here at two the next morning.'

Hugo smiled beatifically. 'I already thought of that,' he said.

'That's why I had to tell Miss Kerwin and the security boys that you were my latest lover.'

William looked aghast. 'You what?' he yelled.

'Sssh,' said Hugo, handing him a hammer. 'Too much macho aggression – very bad for the heart. Now be a sweetheart, will you, dearie? Hammer in this nail for me.'

PART III

1990–91

CHAPTER THIRTY-SIX

·

LILAH leaned back in her seat and closed her eyes. Cocooned in the affluence of British Airways first class, the privations of Meroto already seemed light years away. Meroto. In the end it had taken every ounce of self-discipline she possessed to tear herself away. But right now she had a job to do – even Jonathan understood that. Not that his sympathy and understanding had made their parting any easier. On the contrary, the more Lilah realized what a true friend he was, the more she blamed herself for her own blind stupidity. She felt for the antique emerald ring he had given her all those years ago. Like a talisman, it seemed to give her courage and strength. Of course, such thoughts were nothing but silly superstition. But so what? Right now she needed all the help she could get.

Tanned to a light golden brown, Lilah looked serene and relaxed after her break in the South African sunshine. She had also put on weight, still not as much as she needed, but anything was progress. Her face had lost that sunken, haunted aspect and at least she was laughing again.

'A blanket, Lady Samson?'

'Yes, please.'

Lilah wound the blanket around her legs and closed her eyes again. Jonathan – she was missing him already. Not once during her four-week stay had they chosen to make love – not because they didn't care but because they cared so much. Better than anyone, Jonathan understood what type of woman

Lilah was. Despite everything, he knew she was still too deeply
involved with Roger. She needed time. Only time would stop
her caring for the hero she had created. Poor Lilah. It was
always so much easier to bury a reality than a phantom.

Lilah stretched her long legs and touched her cabin baggage
with her toe. Stowed away under the seat in front, her briefcase
bulged with copies of Hugo's findings. A shadow crossed
Lilah's face. 'Enough shit to sink a ship,' Sophie had declared
after studying the documents in detail. Yes, William Stanton
had certainly done a good job in ferreting out Roger's most
sensitive information. Lilah felt suddenly chilly and pulled the
blanket up around her shoulders. 'You'll have to learn to fight
dirty,' Sophie had warned her. 'If not, you'd better just walk
away now.'

Unconsciously, Lilah shook her head. She had come too far
already to think about backing out.

Lilah's heart lurched as she saw Roger waiting for her at Heathrow airport. How was it possible? How could she love and
hate this man at the same time? She held tightly onto her
briefcase as the porter wheeled her baggage across the arrival
hall.

'Roger!' she called. With every step towards him, she could
feel her resolve draining away. He turned to greet her and
smiled that perfect, easy smile. Oh, God! Then, even then, if
only he had asked for her forgiveness, told her how much he
loved her, even then she would have faltered.

'Hello, darling,' he said, kissing her briefly on the lips. 'We'd
better get back on the motorway as soon as possible before the
London-bound traffic builds up.' It was too late – he had blown
it. Lilah threw back her shoulders and marched briskly to the
car.

There was no opportunity for conversation. The car phone
saw to that. 'Yes, sure, I'll be over in New York the day
after tomorrow . . . Lilah? I've just picked her up from the
airport . . . Fine, just fine. She's in great shape . . . Of course
I will. And mine to Annie. See you Thursday, Jim.'

Lilah stared out of the window, disturbed. She was still far
more vulnerable than she had imagined. Disentangling from

Roger – it was like trying to kick a drug addiction. Toxic and pernicious, he was the last thing she needed. And yet, despite everything, he was still the thing she wanted most in life. Lilah held on, white-knuckled, to the handle of her briefcase. One day at a time. Wasn't that how addicts talked about beating their dependency? She must not expect too much of herself. Just one day at a time.

'You're right, George . . .' As usual Roger seemed immersed in a world of his own, oblivious to what was going on beside him. 'I agree. I don't think property prices here can sink much further. Just keep on looking. If you of all people can't sniff out the bargains, I don't know anyone who can.'

The car turned into Regent's Park and from there into the Samsons' driveway. 'I'll be home for dinner tonight,' said Roger, helping Lilah out of the car. He paused for a moment. If only he could tell her how much he'd missed her, how frightened he'd been and how lonely he'd felt without her. If only . . . But such words belonged to a long-forgotten world and to a language of which Roger knew nothing.

'Fine.' Lilah gave him a remote, unreadable smile. It bothered Roger for several seconds until the car phone rang again.

Within days, Lilah had thrown herself back into a frenetic range of activities. Having always eschewed fitness freakery, she now took to swimming fifty lengths every morning in the Samsons' indoor pool. After that, she would spend at least an hour working out with Alice, her personal fitness trainer. Alice was amazed by the power and energy her client poured into their daily workouts. Lilah trained so aggressively, it was as if she were trying to exorcize some demon from her body. At first Alice was worried but Lilah soon allayed her fears. It was, she argued as she gained in strength and endurance, the best therapy she could think of to expel her pain and grief. It was also, although she never admitted it to Alice, a form of preparation.

Lilah resumed her social round and was soon back at work within Samson International. She resigned her directorship of the company, claiming that she wanted less responsibility and more free time to pursue her own ideas. Nevertheless, she agreed to stay on as personnel consultant for the hotel chain and, perversely, seemed to put in even longer hours at the office. Mrs Owen despaired of her. It was rare that her cherished Lady Lilah was home before ten o'clock at night. But if Roger noticed any change in his wife, he never mentioned it. He put her remoteness down to trauma and assumed it would fade with time.

Sophie was back in New York and, with Grant, was poring over Larry O'Connor's latest batch of information.

'D'you see this?' Grant stretched out in his favourite position on the carpet and handed Sophie a printout. 'It's unbelievable. Looks like Roger's put no stops in.'

'What!' Sophie grabbed the sheet and started to read the figures avidly. 'No stop-losses. You mean, if the price of platinum goes through the floor, he's left no way of bailing out?'

'That's about the size of it. Tightrope act without the safety net. No insurance policy whatsoever.'

'Hell's bloody *Lutine* bells!' Sophie's eyes raced up and down the columns. 'That guy's a bigger lunatic than I thought.'

'Or just plain cocksure of himself. Look,' Grant handed Sophie another sheet of paper, 'according to Larry, Samson's in for at least a million ounces of October platinum.'

Sophie scanned the page with an expert eye. 'All purchased at between four hundred and fifty and five hundred dollars.'

Grant nodded. 'Right. Now let's just suppose Credo and the boys came good with the fireworks at the end of September. How would you be calling it in October?'

Sophie thought for a minute. 'Difficult to say for sure. On top of the immediate shortage there'd be a lot of panic buying. The price could go anywhere – who knows? – a thousand to fifteen hundred dollars an ounce – maybe even more.'

'Leaving our good mate, Sir Roger Samson, with a neat, little profit of anything up to a billion dollars.'

Suddenly there was a loud clatter. Gingerly, Ernie emerged from the kitchen with a pot of double cream on his head. 'I bet Lucrezia Borgia never had this kind of stuff to deal with,' said Sophie, rubbing Ernie down with her handkerchief. Ernie licked his mistress's face and settled down beside her on the documents.

'Even the cat wants to be part of this plot,' said Grant, stroking him fondly. 'Just you and me together again soon, hey, Ern old mate?'

'I'm sorry,' said Sophie, twiddling a stray strand of Grant's hair around her finger. 'Seems like I'm away a lot right now. You don't mind looking after Ernie, do you, Grant? I won't be gone long this time.'

'Course not,' said Grant, removing Ernie to the sofa and rolling over next to Sophie. 'You got everything all fixed up?'

'Well, Dad's done most of the fixing. He's set up the meeting for me in Amsterdam. When I spoke to him on the phone this morning, he seemed real excited about it all.'

'What about your new best friend? You sure she's not going to jack out on you at the last minute? It's going to take real guts to pull this whole thing off.'

'You needn't worry about Lilah. She hates Samson as much as I do. Besides, if it all works out, she stands to gain everything.'

'Everything?' asked Grant, pulling Sophie closer to him and starting to stroke her neck. 'You call control of Samson International everything?'

Slowly, Grant started to undo the buttons of Sophie's black silk blouse. Soon they were down among the printouts, with Ernie miaowing his approval.

'No,' said Sophie at last, her eyes shining, the flow of satisfaction warm and pink on her cheeks. 'But for a girl married to a shyster like that, it can't be bad to start with.'

It was such a wonderfully bright spring morning in Amsterdam that Sophie decided to walk to the meeting. After an early breakfast of bread, cheese and delicious Dutch coffee, she left her hotel, stopping momentarily on the steps to check the details in her diary. Herengracht 600 at 10 o'clock. Sophie glanced at her watch. Excellent. That gave her a good two hours to stroll along the celebrated Gentleman's Canal before the meeting was due to start.

She turned up the collar of her beige cashmere coat. Despite the clear blue sky the wind was keen and after the heat of South Africa, Sophie was still feeling the cold. As she walked along the canal, the gables of the tall, steep-roofed merchants' houses glistened in the sunshine. Stopping for a few minutes to admire the redbrick and stone of the Bartolotti House, she walked briskly past the white sandstone façade of the Bible Museum and on towards the Golden Bend. Sophie smiled. Bankers, burgomasters, captains of industry, they were all the same if you let them loose on a city's architecture. Even here in this elbow of Herengracht, elegance and charm had been pushed aside in the quest for corporate and civic grandeur. She quickened her pace, marching past the Mayor of Amsterdam's official residence and as far as number 600. Among the dozen or so plates by the side of the door, Sophie searched for the name her father had given her. Stam N.V. Just the sort of company, he'd assured her, to front her operation. There it was. Pressing the well-polished bell, she felt a tingling of anticipation and excitement. If it worked out, this would be the biggest deal she had ever done.

'What a beautiful room!' exclaimed Sophie, charmed, as a fresh-faced young secretary led her into the meeting room.

Rijnhard van Polen smiled, delighted. A round, friendly man, with golden half-moon spectacles, he had the sort of ruddily healthy complexion which belied his age. 'Most people seem to think so,' he said, walking across the room to welcome his old friend's daughter. Glancing briefly out of the window, Sophie could see the *achtertuin*, the back garden of the building. It was, she thought, as charming a view as the Gentleman's Canal itself. But it was not the view outside which most attracted her attention. Inside, the walls and ceiling of the room were covered in exquisitely painted panels, each one depicting a different allegorical scene. Classical temples, gods, goddesses, nymphs, satyrs – the whole place seemed light years away from the brutal functionalism of Horneffer & Salzmann.

'Must be a wonderful place to work,' murmured Sophie, silently wondering about its efficiency. Rijnhard's bright brown eyes twinkled with intelligence. It was as if he could read her mind. Gently, he tapped one of the panels which, to Sophie's surprise, creaked open.

'I'd never have believed it,' she gasped, as shelves upon shelves of ancient books and records were suddenly disclosed.

Amused, Rijnhard gestured to the long, oak table in the middle of the room. 'Please, Miss Weiss, take a seat while I order some coffee. We may be from the old world, but we have our ways of getting things done.'

Intrigued, Sophie studied Rijnhard as he phoned down for refreshments. He was, her father had told her, a leading Dutch banker and a brilliant financial mind, highly respected in international circles and well known as a 'results man'. It was almost half a century ago that Rijnhard had started his long and outstanding professional career in the trustee department of Bank Mees and Hope. It was during this time, dealing with trustee relationships with Mees in the Dutch Antilles, that he had come across Harold Weiss. After his experiences in Germany, Harold always felt it wise to keep part of his considerable wealth offshore. And where better, he had always maintained, than with Mees in the Dutch Antilles? The two men maintained contact even when Rijnhard left Mees to set up as an independent trustee and Rijnhard had even been a guest at Harold and Claudia's wedding. Harold had never been a person to give his confidence lightly, but if anyone had ever asked him, he'd have said that Rijnhard was the one man he'd trust with his life.

'So, Miss Weiss,' began Rijnhard, once the coffee had been dispensed, 'I believe from your father that you have a problem for me to solve.'

Sophie smiled at the Dutchman's tangential approach. If she didn't know better, or if they'd been in New York, she might have thought him either slow or dumb or soft. Fortunately, Harold had already forewarned her. In his youth, Rijnhard had played hockey for Bloemendal. No one who had ever witnessed that would doubt this man's agility and naked aggression. 'Yes,' said Sophie, sipping her coffee. 'I know you and Dad didn't go into details over the phone. I wanted to explain the situation to you myself. You see, there's a friend of mine who controls twenty-two per cent of a certain company.'

Nodding, Rijnhard helped himself to a chocolate biscuit. Dutch coffee and chocolate – they were both so very good. 'And your friend has acquired this stake recently?'

'Fairly recently. Her husband is into a certain . . . open-ended liability. He transferred the shares into her name just to be on the safe side.'

'Very wise,' said Rijnhard, offering the biscuits to Sophie. She declined.

'The point is,' she continued, 'my friend would like to find a way of acquiring a further twenty-nine per cent of this company.'

A broad smile flashed across Rijnhard's face. 'You mean she wants to gain control of the company?'

Sophie nodded. 'That's why I'm here. I need you to figure out a way of buying those shares that would be self-financing.'

Behind his half-moon spectacles, Rijnhard van Polen blinked just once. 'A tall order, Miss Weiss,' he said, his voice betraying not the slightest hint of surprise.

Sophie finished the remains of her coffee and put her cup down on the table. 'I happen to know that this company is headed for some real bad press.'

'How very unfortunate.' Rijnhard shook his head. 'And we all know what bad publicity can do to a share price.' He stared at Sophie in frank amusement. Oh, yes, she was her father's daughter.

'So you see, Mr van Polen, that must give us an opportunity somewhere.'

'I would think so,' agreed Rijnhard. 'Is there anything else I should know?'

'Yes,' said Sophie, beginning to gather her belongings. 'Like I said, my friend needs to acquire the shares. But she also needs a discreet and respectable corporate home to put them in.'

Rijnhard nodded. Discretion and respectability were what he was all about. He stood up to shake Sophie's hand. 'Leave your problem with me. I'm sure we'll be able to come up with something.'

Sophie was surprised by the strength of his grip. 'Thanks. I'm flying back to New York this evening. Could you please phone me when you've figured things out?'

'Of course. Oh, and, Miss Weiss,' he said it almost as an afterthought, 'the name of this company your friend wishes to take over?'

The smile vanished from Sophie's face. 'Samson International.'

Polite as ever, Rijnhard opened the door for her. Samson International! Even Rijnhard was moved to blink twice.

A week later, Rijnhard was still wrestling with the problem as he sat transfixed at the opera. The home of the Dutch national opera and ballet companies, Amsterdam's *Muziektheater* was a hideous modern monstrosity a stone's throw away from the beautiful Amstel river. Built of bright orange-red brick and glaringly brash white marble, the complex also housed the city's new town hall. Rijnhard hated the building with a passion, as did most of his fellow citizens. Throughout the 1980s he had been a leading light in the campaign to prevent this blot from appearing on the Amsterdam cityscape. But for once his efforts had failed and the project had gone ahead. Rijnhard had been bitterly angry. All the same, if he loathed the building he still loved what happened inside it. Tonight, Verdi's *Don Carlos* was being performed. A trifle long for some people, it was, nevertheless, one of Rijnhard's favourites.

It was extraordinary, he thought, how the powerful amalgam of music, drama and emotion could free the mind for creative thinking. Within minutes of the curtain, Rijnhard was miles away, far enough away at least not to mind his wife, Anneke, fidgeting in her handbag. Anneke was not an opera buff, although she tagged along to humour her husband. Thank God, Rijnhard had invited the van Lindens along. At least she could gossip to Magda during the interval.

By the fifth act, as the protagonists Elisabeth and Carlos met for their last farewell, Rijnhard thought he'd figured out a plan.

'You seem preoccupied,' said Willem van Linden, as they left the theatre together. The two women were lagging behind, discussing children. The two men had been friends for years. At Stam, where Rijnhard served as chairman of the management board, Willem was now finance director. He was the only man in Amsterdam who could read Rijnhard like a book.

'A slight problem, yes,' mused Rijnhard. 'I'm wondering if the market will let me write a large volume of puts at two hundred pence. They have to be valid for six months at least.'

Willem shrugged his shoulders. 'Long-dated puts. I don't see why not. What's the price right now?'

'Two hundred and forty pence. But, according to my sources, this particular company is in for a bit of trouble.'

'Rijnhard, unless I'm very much mistaken, I'd say you were hatching a plot.'

'Perhaps.'

'Come on, tell me, who are you after?'

Rijnhard looked at his friend. 'Samson International.'

Willem whistled. It was a loud piercing whistle, the one he had used to encourage his friend in his hockey-playing days. 'Heavens above,' he laughed as the two men reached the car, 'seems like Roger Samson would be well advised to watch his ankles from now on.'

CHAPTER THIRTY-SEVEN

'LILAH? Sophie here. How are you doing?'

'Fine, fine, just waiting for the word.'

Back home again in New York, Sophie laughed out loud. 'Well, now you got it, honey. I've just been speaking to van Polen. Boy, has he figured out some scheme! We'll explain the details when we see you. But believe me, Dad was right. The man's an out and out genius.'

Sitting alone in her office at the Samson International, Park Lane, Lilah could feel Sophie's enthusiasm being transmitted down the line. 'When do you want me to start?' she asked.

'As soon as possible. But remember, just bits of information at a time. We want this show to run and run. That is, until we decide to close it.'

It was lunch-time in Harry's Bar and already the dining room was filled with the nation's great and good. At one table Tim Bell, Mrs Thatcher's favour PR man, was holding court with a group of expensive-looking clients. Over by the window, Lord Hanson and Sir Gordon White were gripped in earnest conversation.

'Good afternoon, Lady Samson,' smiled Mario, the gracious manager. 'Your guest is already waiting for you.' Mario guided Lilah to her favourite table and helped her to her seat.

'Good to see you looking so well, old girl,' beamed Hugo, casting an appreciative eye over her light grey Kenzo suit.

'I feel well,' replied Lilah and ordered a Bellini. Hugo was already on his third. 'In fact, I've never felt better in years.'

'I take it your friend Sophie's trip to Amsterdam worked out all right?'

'Like falling off a log – or so she keeps assuring me. Seems like this chap van Polen's got the whole thing set up. Now it's up to you and me to make it happen.'

Hugo took a large gulp of his cocktail. 'Ready when you are, Lilah, but not before we've had our lunch.'

Lilah scanned the menu and ordered the most calorific dishes she could find. Pasta followed by even more pasta. Hugo stayed with the smoked salmon and beef.

'So you still think the *Courier* is the best paper to get things humming?' she asked, when the waiter had moved away.

'Of course. Roger's got his spies at all the heavies. If we went to any one of them, they'd be bound to warn him in advance. All we need now is an injunction and everything we've done is down the Swanee. Besides,' Hugo peered mournfully at the bottom of his empty glass, 'I don't think it matters who runs the story. Once it's in print, the damage is done. Oh, waiter, if you don't mind, same again, please.'

'Have you been in touch with the editor recently?'

'Yes,' said Hugo, smiling. 'Freddie Higgins and I have downed quite a few beakers discussing our shock-horror revelations. Now everything's been OK'd by the lawyers, old Freddie can't wait to get going.'

The waiter arrived with Lilah's lasagne and a plateful of smoked salmon for Hugo. Another waiter swiftly followed, carrying a basket of lemon halves covered in fine, white muslin.

'You know you're in a rough joint,' whispered Hugo, helping himself, 'when the lemon comes wrapped in a jock-strap.'

Lilah laughed. 'You never change.' The waiter poured the wine.

'And neither do you.' Hugo raised his glass. 'A toast to the woman who never changes.'

'You'd be surprised,' said Lilah, leaning across the table, her green eyes flinty-hard. 'I want Higgins to run that story in the *Courier* before the week is out.'

*

It was only seven o'clock in the morning but already Samson Heights was under siege. Press, photographers, television crews – Roger felt his temper rising as he ran the implacable media gauntlet.

'BBC World at One. Sir Roger, will you be resigning?'

'No comment.'

'Jack Lane, *The Times*. Sir Roger . . .'

'Simon Webster, *Financial Times*. Please, Sir Roger . . .'

'Come on, Roger. Look over 'ere, mate. That's it. This way.' Somewhere a flashbulb popped.

'Gentlemen, gentlemen,' said Roger, pushing his way up the steps, 'I do assure you, you are wasting your time. There will be no comment from me, or anyone else within Samson International, until I've had time to consult my lawyers. Thank you. Now, if you don't mind . . .'

Eventually Roger made it into the calm of his security-guarded citadel. Press, they were all the same, a pack of bloody gannets just waiting for a kill. Furious, Roger took the lift to his office. The plexiglass module moved silently up to the top floor of the building. Press. Wasn't Andrea being paid a fortune to keep these bastards off his back? Suddenly the warning bells started ringing in Roger's head. The *Courier*? Of course. Why hadn't he made the connection before?

Miss Kerwin was already in her office, numb with shock. Hearing the story on her wireless, she had rushed straight over to Samson Heights to see what she could do. Swiftly, she hid her copy of the *Courier* as Sir Roger appeared at her door. Never had she seen him looking so angry. His face was actually white with rage.

'I'll be taking no calls this morning, Miss Kerwin.'

'Yes, sir. I've already had—'

'I said none, do you hear?' The door shook as Sir Roger slammed it shut behind him.

Alone in his office Roger brought his fist down hard on the leather-topped desk. Just when everything was going so well! Everything – the company, the Group – why, even Lilah was on the mend. Roger grabbed the phone and dialled his wife at home. God knows how this sort of scandal was going to affect her. Nowadays with Lilah it was difficult to tell but her silence this morning was a very bad sign. The last thing he needed now was for her to slip back into that dreadful depression. Impatiently, Roger punched the automatic redial button. Bloody press! The line was constantly engaged. Poor Lilah! Already the bastards must be on to her at home. Roger clenched his fist in frustration, desperate to get through. It was only minutes but it seemed like hours before the line became free.

'Lilah – are you all right? What's been happening since I left?'

'Well, the phone's not stopped ringing. I was about to put the answer machine on.'

Roger felt relieved. From the tone of her voice she seemed completely in control. 'Good idea,' he agreed. 'Look, Lilah, I know I don't have to warn you, but say nothing to any of these bastards. Nothing.'

'No, of course not. Why should I? I haven't got anything to say.'

'Right. Now, I'm taking no calls at the moment but I'll ring you later in your office. Just to let you know what's going on.'

Lilah paused. 'Roger?'

'Yes?'

'Would you let me know something else as well?'

'Sure.'

'Is there any truth in these allegations?'

There was a momentary silence. 'I'm going to fight it,' he replied.

'That's fine, then,' said Lilah, putting down the phone. It was the clearest possible answer.

At home in Montpelier Square, Andrea Watson-Smith lay back on her pillow and groaned. What the hell did Freddie Higgins think he was playing at? This was nothing short of complete annihilation. Andrea could already feel the migraine starting as she reread the *Courier*'s headline: SAMSON INTERNATIONAL IN BRIBES SCANDAL! She reached for her Migril tablets and quickly washed one down. Rarely had she read such a comprehensive hatchet job. The *Courier* was not exactly renowned for its intrepid, investigative journalism but, by anybody's standards, this was an extraordinary scoop. Andrea could barely bring herself to return to the inside pages. Despite everything she had to give Freddie credit. This was sensational journalism at its very best. Allegations of bribes in return for planning permissions. Veiled and not so veiled references to politicians and prominent figures. Andrea took a deep breath and heaved herself out of bed. What a morning to have a hangover – just the day she needed to be at her very best. She staggered into the bathroom. The whole thing was quite extraordinary.

The phone rang just as she emerged, refreshed and tingling from an ice-cold shower.

'Andrea, what the fuck is going on?'

'Roger . . .' stammered Andrea, shocked by the tone of his voice. 'I've only just seen it. What can I say? I'm sorry. I had no idea.'

'You're not paid to have no idea,' he shouted. 'You're paid a fortune to make sure these things don't happen.'

For a second, Andrea was completely stunned. Now Lilah was getting better, she had hoped she and Roger might resume their affair. With a bit of organizing, this crisis might even have brought them together again. But now . . . Suddenly Andrea felt used and angry.

'There's no point swearing at me,' she yelled. 'I'd check your security, if I were you, Roger. Whoever it was, it wasn't me who sold this story to Freddie Higgins.' Andrea bit her tongue. She should never have mentioned his name. Now it was already too late.

'Oh, no?' shouted Roger, incensed. 'You had the motive, didn't you, you bitch? I dumped you and you went straight to your old boyfriend at the *Courier*. That's how it happened, isn't it?'

'No!' cried Andrea, distraught. The very thought was so ridiculously unfair. 'You've got to believe me, Roger. I'd never do that to you.'

'Come off it, Andrea. You'll always belong in the gutter. I don't know where you got your information—'

'But, Roger,' Andrea was crying now, 'I give you my word. There was no information. I didn't *have* any information. Please, you must believe me.'

There was a terrible silence.

'You're fired,' said Roger, suddenly very calm. 'And what's more, Andrea, when I've finished with you, you'll never work again in this city.'

Freddie Higgins had been in his office since six o'clock that morning. No, there was nothing like an exclusive to make a newspaper man feel on top of the world. Humming happily to himself, a rhythmic yet tone-deaf rendition of Sinatra's 'The Best Is Yet To Come', he put his feet up on the desk and, closing his eyes, he waited.

The call came sooner than expected.

'Mr Higgins?' said the switchboard operator. Freddie's secretary had not yet arrived. 'There's a Mrs Andrea Watson-Smith on the line for you.'

'Fine,' said Freddie, a huge grin spreading across his face. 'Put her through, will you? I've waited a long time for this.' There was a click as Andrea's call was connected. 'Andrea, love, great to hear from you again. How are you doing?'

'Freddie, where the *hell* did you get that story?'

Freddie's grin spread even further. 'Story?' he mused, leaning back in his chair. 'Sweetheart, the *Courier* is fifty fun-packed pages of news, views and sport. Which particular story did you have in mind?'

'Don't mess me around!' shrieked Andrea. 'You know bloody well which story I'm talking about. The Samson International story.'

'Lovely stuff,' cooed Freddie. 'You know, darling, for today's edition, I've had an extra million copies printed. Corruption in high places – our readers just can't get enough of it.' Andrea realized the aggressive approach was getting her nowhere in a hurry.

'Freddie, you've got to help me,' she begged, swiftly changing tack. 'My entire business is on the line. Samson International are my biggest clients. And Roger Samson is convinced I sold you the story.'

'Now that is a bugger, love, isn't it?' soothed Freddie. This was even better than he'd anticipated. 'I mean, it's bad enough him thinking his PR lady can't keep tabs on Fleet Street. But to think you'd actually set him up . . . I can see you must be gutted.'

'Please, Freddie, I'll be ruined. Can't you make it clear I had nothing to do with it?' Andrea dissolved into tears. It was monstrous, grovelling to this odious little toad. But what else could she do? That long journey out of Grimford – everything she had striven to achieve – it was all disintegrating before her eyes. 'Please . . .'

There was a long pause as Freddie poured himself a celebratory Scotch. 'I'd love to help you out, sweetheart,' he replied, savouring the moment. 'But I'm afraid no can do. The *Courier* can't go getting itself involved in a process of elimination now, can it?'

'But, Freddie—'

'Sorry, love. But you know as well as I do. A good journalist must never reveal his sources.'

'Freddie, please . . .' But already the line was dead.

Still clutching the receiver, Andrea lay sobbing on her bed. Eventually she dialled the number. It was a long shot but, under the circumstances, anything was worth a try. Of course, the frostiness that had entered their relationship had been entirely her own fault. But after all, Lilah was such a kind-hearted fool, she was bound to help her out.

Andrea grimaced as she heard the recorded message playing at the Samsons' home. Reaching for her Filofax, she looked up the number of Lilah's car phone and tried that one instead. 'Lilah,' she gushed, as soon as the call was connected, 'it's Andrea here. Long time no see. How have you been keeping?'

Lilah smiled. It was the first time she had heard from Andrea since the miscarriage. 'Well, thanks,' she replied, casually. 'And you? You must be awfully busy.'

'And how!' said Andrea, grateful for the ready-made excuse. 'But we must make time to do lunch soon – my treat.'

God, thought Lilah half amused, why had she never seen through Andrea before? She was so blatantly transparent. 'Sure,' she said vaguely. 'That'd be lovely.'

'Great. I'll give you a call.' So far so good. Andrea was

gaining in confidence. 'That story this morning,' she continued, 'it's dreadful, isn't it? That bastard at the *Courier* has certainly pulled a fast one.'

'Roger said he's going to fight it,' said Lilah, staring out of the window. The traffic around Marble Arch had brought the car to a standstill. Eamonn, her chauffeur, tapped the steering wheel impatiently.

'Of course. He must. It's nothing but libellous gossip. The *Courier*'s always been like that.'

'You should know,' said Lilah.

Andrea paused for a second, then chose to ignore the barb. 'Lilah, I wonder, could you do me a favour?'

'Anything to help a friend.' By now the traffic was moving again, and Lilah's black BMW filtered into Park Lane.

'Well, it's all too silly really,' said Andrea, affecting a giggle. 'But I suppose Roger was so angry this morning he had to lash out at someone.'

Lilah said nothing.

'You see, Lilah, the thing is, Roger seems to think that I gave Freddie Higgins the story.' Lilah almost pinched herself. Roger blaming Andrea – this was indeed an added bonus.

'Really?'

'Yes, as I say, it's all too stupid for words.' Andrea coughed nervously. 'But the point is, well, in the heat of the moment, he went and fired me.'

'You mean he's taken W&S Communications off the Samson International account?' Lilah wanted to laugh out loud.

'Yes,' continued Andrea, her voice momentarily faltering. 'You can imagine how that will be seen in the City.'

'Disastrous,' agreed Lilah. 'Absolutely disastrous.'

'So you'll help me out, then, won't you, Lilah? You'll tell Roger that he's got it all wrong and that it was nothing to do with me?' There was a seemingly endless silence. 'Lilah, are you still there?'

'I'm sorry, Andrea. But you know Roger as well as I do . . .' the pause was almost imperceptible, '. . . so you know he never changes his mind.' The car pulled up outside the Samson International hotel. The place was swarming with journalists.

'But, Lilah . . .'

'Sorry, Andrea. Got to dash. The press are snapping at my heels.'

'But, Lilah. You've got to—'

Lilah put down the receiver and caught Eamonn's eye in the mirror. 'Do you want me to drive on, Lady Samson?' he enquired. 'I don't want this pack of bloody whores pestering you today.'

'Don't worry, Eamonn,' said Lilah, beaming her most perfect smile. 'If you wouldn't mind opening the door for me, I'll be happy to see them all.'

By the time Andrea arrived in the breakfast room, she was in an evil temper. Charles had just finished his breakfast – a single round of wholemeal toast and a pot of Earl Grey tea – and was now immersed in his copy of *The Times*.

'Good morning, my dear,' he said, glancing up. 'Did you sleep well?'

'Have you heard the latest on Samson International?' snapped Andrea. She was in no mood for small talk.

'Yes, I'm afraid I heard it on the *Today* programme. It doesn't look at all good, does it?'

'Oh, Charles, for God's sake, why do you always have to be so bloody stiff-upper-lip? "Doesn't look at all good." Don't you understand anything? For me, this is a complete disaster.' Andrea sat down heavily and poured herself a cup of tea.

'I do control one of Samson International's major shareholdings,' said Charles quietly.

'Oh yes, just typical! My entire business is falling to pieces and all you can think about is one of your hundreds of investments.'

Charles returned to his paper and Andrea slammed a slice of bread in the toaster.

'And do you know what that bastard Roger has done? He's gone and sacked me. Lilah won't even intervene. Some friend she turns out to be.' Charles sipped his tea in silence.

'And you – just look at you. You're just as bloody bad. I don't see you jumping to my defence. You could have a word with Roger if you wanted to. But nothing – not a dicky-bird.

You're all so superior and smug and selfish – you make me sick the lot of you.' Charles folded his papers neatly and stood up from the table.

Andrea looked at him in surprise. She had not yet finished her tirade. 'Where do you think you're going?' she snapped.

'I have an appointment with my lawyers,' he said calmly.

'On a day like today,' sniffed Andrea, 'you ought to be seeing your bloody stockbrokers. You don't know him like I do. But once Freddie's got his teeth into Roger, you won't be able to give Samson International shares away.'

'Yes, I realize I don't know Freddie like you do. I'm seeing my lawyers.' He picked up his mail from the table. 'I've decided to file for divorce. This marriage has been a sham for as long as I can remember. I've had enough of it. And, my dear, of you.'

'You wouldn't dare!' Andrea was terrified. 'I'll ruin you if you do. You'll see. I'll get the best divorce lawyers in the country. We'll take you to the cleaners.'

'Do as you wish,' said Charles, opening the breakfast-room door. 'But you know, Andrea, you were never such a thorough journalist as you imagined. Nowadays, I'm really a man of very modest means. As your lawyers will soon discover, almost everything I have is tied up in discretionary trusts. You have what you always wanted – W&S Communications. I strongly advise you to take that and to leave me in peace.' Quietly, Charles closed the door behind him.

'Charles!' cried Andrea at the top of her voice. 'Please, please come back. I didn't know what I was saying. I've been under a lot of pressure recently. Please . . .' But Charles was already half-way up the staircase.

Andrea flung her half-full cup across the room. It shattered against the wall, tea trickling down in light brown rivulets onto the carpet below. But even she knew it was pointless. Her passport to the good life had suddenly expired.

George Hamish could feel his pulse racing and he was painfully short of breath. Thank God, for once the Esher train had been more or less on time. At Waterloo station he hailed a cab.

'Samson Heights,' he wheezed.

'Cor, guv,' said the cabbie, as George almost fell into the back, ''ave you seen today's paper? There ain't 'alf been some argy-bargy going on down there by the looks of it. Back 'anders all over the show, accordin' to the *Courier*.'

George tried to control his breathing. The cabbie looked vaguely concerned.

'Asthma attack,' lied George. That generally shut them up.

'Friend of mine 'ad asthma,' continued the cabbie, relentless, 'before he died, that was . . .'

George closed his eyes in silent prayer and tried to stifle a groan.

By the time he reached his office, he was feeling dreadful. Dropping his overcoat on the floor, he lurched across to his desk and slumped leaden into his chair. For all of fifteen minutes he just sat there, staring up at the ceiling and hoping for inspiration. Switching on his computer, he called up Samson International's latest share price. Already it had dropped 100p from 240p to 140p and was still falling. Suddenly, George felt a sharp, insistent pain, like a jackboot stamping on his chest. That story in the *Courier* – how the hell was Roger going to wriggle his way out of that?

'Ah, George.' He looked up to find Roger, standing in the doorway. 'I'm glad to find you in.'

'What did you expect?' George's voice was dull, toneless. 'Today the shit has really hit the fan.'

Already Roger had regained his composure. 'Not necessarily.' Roger strode across the room and sat on the edge of George's desk. Towering there above him, Roger looked strong and menacing.

'Not necessarily?' gasped George. 'Roger, who are you trying to kid? The shares are already in free fall.'

'Not if we keep cool. We'll get the legal boys to issue a couple of writs and in a few months the whole thing will be forgotten.'

'But what if it ends up in court?'

'We'll be OK,' smiled Roger. George shuffled uncomfortably in his chair. It seemed as if Roger's eyes were boring into him. 'So long as you and I just stick together.'

By now, an entire army of jackboots was goose-stepping across George's chest. 'Roger, I can't. I can't just go on lying and covering up—'

'George, whatever you say, you're in this right up to your neck.' Roger's voice remained threateningly quiet.

'But I never knew about these bribes. Or—'

'Or the half a billion dollars I've just borrowed from the company for – what shall we say? – special projects?' Roger put on his most charming, mirthless smile.

'Oh, Jesus, Roger,' groaned George, 'will it never stop?' The jackboots were stamping harder and harder. George's face was white with pain.

'Look,' said Roger, patting George on the shoulder, 'there's really nothing for you to get so worked up about. Believe me, just do as I say and everything will be fine.'

'Do as you say!' protested George angrily. 'That's why we're in this fucking mess. I should have put my foot down years ago.'

'Oh, yes. I'm sure you'd make a very touching spectacle in the witness box. But you're in this with me, George. And I for one have no intention of spending the next few years at Her Majesty's pleasure.'

George put his head in his hands. Prison. He would never survive a stint in prison. The experience would probably kill him. 'OK, Roger. What do you want me to do?'

'That's more like it,' said Roger, hopping off the desk and walking over to the window. 'I knew I could rely on your loyalty.'

George ground the nib of his fountain pen into his blotting paper.

'We'd better get moving right away. We're going to have to buy to protect our position.'

George nodded wearily. That was all he needed now – a hard day's hustling.

'And then, of course,' continued Roger, moving across to the desk again, 'we're going to have to stop people selling.'

'But we can't . . .' George's pulse was racing again, in strange little blasts.

'Oh, yes we can. Everybody does it. George, I want you to do some ringing around. Promise the banks we'll pay them advisory fees if they agree to retain our shares.'

'But, Roger,' protested George feebly, 'that's illegal.'

'And do whatever's necessary to encourage them to buy some more.' Roger stared down at George, hard and implacable. Unable to return his gaze, George focused his attention on the wreckage of his fountain-pen nib.

'So it's all fixed, then,' said Roger, slapping George jovially on the back. 'Believe me, in three months' time we'll be wondering what all the fuss was about.'

It was some time after Roger left before George finally reached for his telephone. He was no criminal – he knew that. But would anyone else believe it? Bracing himself, he started to dial around. Men like him were just weak and cowardly. Perhaps that was just as bad.

It had been unusually warm weather for late April in New York and Sophie was feeling drained. After a hard day in the office, she wanted nothing more strenuous than a quiet night in with 'the boys'. Sophie gazed fondly at her lunatic Aussie, slim and muscular in his denims and open-necked check shirt. Thank God for Grant. Without him her vendetta would have become a total obsession.

'Take-home pizza and vintage champagne!' he laughed, as Sophie carried the supper tray into the living room. 'Is this some kind of celebration?'

'You got complaints – go take a hike.' Sophie put the tray on the floor and started feeding anchovies to Ernie.

'No complaints,' said Grant, holding up his hands in mock horror. 'I just don't want any whingeing that I never take you out.'

'I want to go out, I'll let you know,' replied Sophie, beaming up at him. 'But right now I guess I'm happy just here at home with you.'

Grant smiled and kissed the top of her head.

Copies of *Newsweek*, *The Economist*, *Time* magazine and a slew of other publications lay scattered across the carpet. Even now, two weeks after the original revelations in the *Courier*, the name of Samson International remained firmly in the headlines.

'I've got to take my hat off to you,' said Grant, reaching for *The Economist*. On the cover, a cartoon of Samson in full admiral's regalia showed him clinging onto the helm of his ship. 'SIR ROGER SAMSON' ran the caption. 'TIME TO SINK OR SWIM?' He showed the cartoon to Sophie who laughed.

'If Samson thinks he's struggling now, he ain't seen nothing yet. We're going to keep this pressure up at least until the fall.'

'Pressure up – share-price down.' Grant opened the champagne with a flourish and poured each of them a glass. 'So what's the next nail in the coffin, Sophie?'

'We'll let the dust on this one settle. Then we'll start putting it around that the Securities and Exchange Commission on insider dealing is looking into Samson International's operation over here in the States.'

Grant whistled. 'Christ, Sophie. Are they?'

'No, of course not – leastways, not that I know of. But you got to admit, with that kind of rumour, the smell always lingers.'

Grant raised his glass to Sophie. 'I tell you what, I'm one bloody happy bloke that I'm on your side. By the time you're through with him, he won't own the shirt on his back.' Ernie miaowed his agreement.

'Just the way we want it, eh, Ernie?' said Sophie, stroking the Blue Burmese's immaculate coat. 'What's more, if the price of platinum starts dropping, he'll have to come up with the margin.'

Grant did a few quick mental calculations. 'You're right, Sophie. He can't afford to let the boys sell his position before October. And on the basis of a million ounces, that's what I'd call serious grief.' He took a slug of champagne.

'Poor old Samson,' laughed Sophie. 'He just won't know what's hit him.'

A sudden doubt crossed Grant's mind. 'Is his wife still bearing up?'

Sophie nodded. 'She's doing just great. Much better than I'd figured. And, boy, does she cotton on quick. All the same, honey – ' there was never a good time to say these things, ' – come the fall, I'm going to have to be hanging around here.'

'But our trip to Oz?' He sounded so hurt.

'I'm sorry,' said Sophie, gently. 'That's going to have to wait. I'll make it up to you, Grant, honest I will, just as soon as this thing is over.'

They sat for some time in silence. 'But I wanted you to meet me ma,' said Grant, at last.

'I said I was sorry. Anyway, we'll meet up next spring. We can make a real holiday of it then.'

Grant reached out for Sophie's hand and pulled her towards him. For once, it occurred to Sophie, he looked almost embarrassed. 'I don't think you understand what I'm trying to say,' he murmured into her ear. 'What I mean is – when you've got a minute – I'd like you to be my wife.'

CHAPTER THIRTY-EIGHT

'I'LL BE going over to Amsterdam for a few days,' announced Lilah one morning after breakfast. It was a glorious day in early May and, as usual, Mrs Owen had laid the table in the conservatory. Outside in the garden, the buds on the beech, oak and cedar trees were already bursting into leaf.

Roger looked up from his *FT* and smiled. 'Trouble at the hotel?'

'No, not really. But there are wage negotiations coming up next month and I don't want to be faced with any unpleasant surprises. Forewarned is forearmed.'

Roger nodded, pleased that Lilah was making such remarkable progress. 'When are you off? I might be able to join you over there for an evening.'

'I don't think so,' said Lilah hurriedly. She had checked Roger's diary and scheduled her trip accordingly. 'I'll be leaving tomorrow afternoon. I thought you said Jim would be over from New York.'

'Yes, but he'll be here for over a week. I don't really need to see him for dinner tomorrow evening.'

'You mustn't cancel,' said Lilah, alarmed. 'I'll only be gone forty-eight hours.' She prayed for inspiration. 'Why don't we meet in Paris for the weekend instead?'

Roger seized the opening. 'I'd like that,' he smiled, folding his paper deliberately. 'It's time you and I had a few days alone together.'

Lilah froze. Every effort he made to get close to her, the more distant she felt. 'That would be wonderful,' she found herself mouthing. Anything, just anything to stop him joining her in Amsterdam.

Roger stretched his hand across the table. 'I hope you haven't forgotten,' he said, noticing the absence of her engagement ring, 'but Paris is the place where I proposed to you.'

'Hugo? It's me, Lilah. I'm calling from the airport.'

'You seem to have taken up residence there. How long will you be away this time?'

'Only a few days. I'm going to meet this van Polen chap to see where we go from here. And then . . . well, never mind. It doesn't matter. I have to go to Paris. Look, Hugo, would you mind? I think it's time to call our friend Mr Higgins again.'

'What do you want me to give him this time? The stuff about arms sales to South Africa?'

'Yes, that would be good.' Detailed accounts of how Samson International and its subsidiary Metallinc had managed to violate UK embargoes. The story would be nothing short of dynamite.

'I'll ring him straight away,' said Hugo. 'It'll all have to be vetted and whatnot. I can't promise anything, but I suppose it will appear some time early next week. Will that do?'

'Fine. Thanks, Hugo.'

'Look after yourself, Lilah. You've been pushing yourself very hard just recently.'

'Don't worry about me.' Lilah wished she felt as confident as she sounded. In the British Airways executive lounge, the Amsterdam flight was being called. 'I'll be OK. I'm just starting to sort things out.'

The next day, Sophie and Lilah were to meet for lunch in the celebrated Dikker-en-Thijs in Prinsengracht. Downstairs, on the ground floor, the delicatessen was, as usual, doing wonderful business. Lilah made a mental note to drop in later for some delicious *extra-oud* Gouda. She made her way up to the first-floor restaurant where she was surprised to find Sophie already waiting for her.

'My goodness,' laughed Lilah as the two friends embraced, 'you're even earlier than I am.'

'I didn't feel like breakfast,' replied Sophie. 'I was still too jetlagged so right now I could eat a horse.'

Lilah studied her friend with renewed interest. Sophie looked absolutely radiant despite the claims of jetlag. 'Are congratulations in order?' She looked pointedly at the large ruby and diamond ring Sophie was now sporting on her left hand.

Sophie coloured a fraction. 'Yes. Grant decided to make an honest woman of me. Mind you, it's a bit hush-hush at the moment. We haven't had time to go see my folks.'

'I'm sure you'll be very happy,' said Lilah. The slightest hint of a shadow swept across her face.

'And you're going to be happy too,' said Sophie, putting a reassuring hand on Lilah's. 'Just as soon as we've gotten a few of these details out of the way.'

Sophie spent the next half-hour describing the technicalities of Rijnhard's plan to Lilah. It was complicated, and she was amazed at Lilah's ability to assimilate even the tiniest nuance. Already, she explained, while Samson International's price was still standing at 240p, Stam N.V. had taken out a whole series of put options, which, she continued, would enable Stam to sell the shares six months from the date of purchase to the counter party of the put at a small discount to Samson International's price of 240p. At the same time, Stam had acquired a number of call options at a quarter of Samson International's 240p share price. These call options of 60p, she added, covered almost one third of Samson International's share capital. Sophie stopped briefly to sip her mineral water.

'You've all been very busy on my behalf,' said Lilah, gratefully.

'Come on, honey,' said Sophie, 'you've played your part as well.'

Their attention was diverted by the noise of a hundred car horns, all hooting loudly in unison. Outside on the bridge, Lilah could see a huge traffic jam building up. A single delivery van, parked in a road behind the tram stop, was creating absolute havoc. 'Look,' she said, pointing out of the window and smiling in wry amusement. 'Seems like it's easy to organize chaos even in the best orchestrated systems.'

Sophie drained her glass. 'You better believe it,' she said, returning the smile. 'Now if you want some real disruption, let's go see what Rijnhard's got planned for Roger next.'

Twenty minutes later, after a brisk walk along the canal to Herengracht 600, Sophie and Lilah were being shown into the gracious, panelled room. Seated at the long, highly polished table, Rijnhard stood up to greet them. 'Today,' said Sophie smiling as Rijnhard shook her hand, 'I've brought my friend along.'

If the Dutchman was in any way surprised by the identity of Sophie's friend, his face gave nothing away. So this was the mysterious person who wanted control of Samson International. He would never have guessed.

'Lady Samson,' he said, his eyes twinkling. 'I've seen your photograph so often in the papers. I'm very honoured to meet you at last.' Lilah smiled and shook his hand.

Sophie felt cheated. These Europeans – they were impossible to read. It was as if they were at a garden party. Sophie had expected Lilah's arrival to create quite a stir here at Stam.

Rijnhard smiled across at Sophie, aware of her confusion. American women! However switched on they were, they understood precious little about Europeans and their behaviour. Despite the façade, Rijnhard was inordinately pleased at the latest development in the plot. So far he'd wondered whether this entire affair wasn't a wilder Weiss idea. But now with Lady Samson's involvement, he knew they really meant business.

Having introduced his friend and finance director, Willem van Linden, Rijnhard organized the inevitable coffee and the small group sat down at the table. 'Shall we make a start?'

Willem van Linden nodded politely. He was a small man with a kindly face and a slow, punctilious manner. In the fifty years Rijnhard had known him, he never once heard Willem raise his voice in either anger or frustration. Lilah heaved a pile of documents out of her briefcase and placed them on the table before her.

'Good,' smiled Rijnhard. 'Willem, have you checked Samson International's price today?'

'I've been onto the floor brokers at van Meer James Capel.'

Willem handed him a printout. 'Today they're down to eighty pence.'

Rijnhard shook his head in disbelief. 'Such bad press of late, I'm afraid. From two hundred and forty to eighty pence – who would wish to be running such a company? And how very wise of us at Stam to have spotted such an interesting opportunity when we did.'

Rijnhard was enjoying this little charade. Dutchmen, he had always heard say, were either bureaucrats or pirates. While Rijnhard enjoyed all the respectability of a bureaucrat, deep down he was a pirate. That, after all, was why he had left Mees and Hope all those years ago. After their acquisition by the Algemeine Bank Nederland, he felt stifled by red tape. Nowadays he had the freedom to do precisely as he wished. For what he needed to do right now, that was just as well.

'I think,' chipped in Lilah, 'that we can rely on further revelations in the weeks and months to come.'

'Excellent. In that case, Lady Samson, if the transaction Miss Weiss has explained to you can be executed, then I believe Stam can make a massive profit on your behalf. That profit will enable you to take control of Stam. You're going to need that as a vehicle for the second phase of our little . . . operation.'

'You mean acquiring twenty-nine per cent of Samson International. But how are we going to manage it?' Lilah looked nervously at Sophie.

Rijnhard sipped his coffee, non-committal. 'Don't worry about that,' he said. 'There are techniques available which will enable me to acquire control of blocks of shares through the European Options Exchange. To guarantee your anonymity, I shall take the protagonist's role. All I ask of you is that you continue to play your own less obvious yet very important role.'

Sophie glanced across at her friend with concern. She knew of the up-coming trip to Paris with Roger. How could anyone keep up that act?

For the first time in ages, Roger Samson was feeling good. Really good! Yes, Paris certainly did do things for people. The day before, he and Lilah had raced around town like a couple of sightseeing adolescents: the Eiffel Tower, the Arc de Triomphe, Sacre Coeur, the booksellers by the Seine – Roger vowed in future to spend more time enjoying married life together. Of course, with the share price languishing in the dumps, things were too hectic at the moment, but he'd sort that out soon enough. At some stage, in some vague, undefined future, he promised he would find the time.

Sprawled out next to him in bed, Lilah stirred in her sleep. Gently he reached out to her, his hand just touching her smooth cheek. How peaceful she looked, her face at rest and framed by that mass of auburn hair. Roger felt his erection grow beneath the sheet. Lightly he kissed her forehead moving down to her lips and throat, willing her to react. Lilah slowly opened her eyes.

'Good morning, darling,' he said. He began to tease her nipples with his soft slippery tongue. Still half asleep, she realized to her horror that she was responding. The tips of his fingers made circles in the springy hair of her pubis. He found her clitoris and worried it gently back and forth until she grew wet and ached with anticipation. Lilah said nothing as he slid inside her. She cried out as she felt him come with strong, hot spurts inside her, and she clung to him as he collapsed, exhausted, by her side.

'I love you,' he said, his eyes flickering open at last. Still Lilah said nothing. Her body had betrayed her but her resolve was intact. Men were such foolish creatures. Just one simple act and they thought to re-establish your dependence and their dominion. Lilah bit her knuckle. It was difficult not to grin.

CHAPTER THIRTY-NINE

Two weeks after his meeting with Lady Samson, Rijnhard van Polen was sitting in his office reading the latest copy of the *Courier*. 'SAMSON INTERNATIONAL – ILLEGAL ARMS TO SOUTH AFRICA SCANDAL', ran the front-page headline. There was no doubt that the editor, Freddie Higgins, had gone to town on this one. Diagrams of evil-looking guns and maps of possible delivery routes via Zambia and Zimbabwe – the whole story had been given what Freddie called 'the treatment'.

Rijnhard reached for his phone and dialled his friend, van Linden. 'Some more unfortunate publicity for Samson International. What's their price today?'

'Down to sixty pence.'

He felt the old thrill. It was like lining up for a goal. 'Time to move,' he said. 'Could you get hold of our people at van Meer James Capel? I want them to start exercising the calls and buy blocks of shares at sixty pence.'

'Of course,' replied Willem, waiting for the sting. 'I'll get onto it right away. Anything else?'

'Yes,' he said, slowly. 'Within the week I want to put them out at two hundred pence.'

'A profit of a hundred and fifty a share.' Willem tapped a few figures into his personal computer. 'By my reckoning that will mean an overall profit of over one point eight billion. Lady Samson should be a very happy woman.'

Rijnhard opened the box of Hajenius cigars and helped himself to one. 'Time for a small celebration,' he said. 'But remember, Willem, this is only the end of Act One.'

Sometimes it seemed as if it was becoming an almost daily occurrence – a posse of pressmen waiting to pounce on him at Samson Heights. Stony-faced, Sir Roger Samson walked up to the entrance, the spring in his step decidedly less pronounced. The *Courier* had been first to jump on Stam's recent coup and the rest of the media had swiftly followed suit. What a nightmare! Whispers of insider dealing were rife in the City. Already the London Stock Exchange was in uproar and the Serious Fraud Office had been called in to investigate the affair. Angrily, Roger pushed his way through the assembled crowd of hacks. Today it was all he could do not to deck one of them.

'No comment,' he replied to the familiar barrage of questions. Resignation, fraud, the future of Samson International – how on earth could anyone be expected to think rationally under such enormous pressure?

'Sorry, gentlemen,' he repeated, as Clive, the doorman, struggled to bar their entrance to the building. Roger nodded his gratitude and turned to face his tormentors. 'An official statement will be made as soon as possible,' he shouted above the general hubbub. 'But I'm a very busy man. I'd just like to get on with the business of looking after my shareholders' interests.'

The mood in the boardroom was less vindictive than Roger had anticipated. Although none of them would openly admit it, many of the board members had remained unmoved by the so-called scandals in the press. 'So Roger's been handing out a few sweeteners,' Sir Howard Anderson had confided to an old political ally in Annie's Bar. 'How else do the buggers expect a major multinational to do business nowadays?'

This latest development, however, was far more worrying. For once, Roger took the time to chat to each of his fellow directors in turn. Whatever his own problems, the effect he had on most of them was still quite uncanny. By the time he opened the emergency board meeting, he was feeling decidedly less defensive. Whatever was happening to the company – and that was still far from clear – they were all in this together. No team player himself, this was, nevertheless, the strategy he was trying to promote. In Roger's view, there was nothing wrong with team games – as long as he still called all the shots.

'Gentlemen,' began Sir Howard, as soon as the meeting had been called to order, 'I have never seen such a sustained and malicious smear campaign orchestrated by the press. I have contacts in the British security services who are convinced that there is a left-wing conspiracy to discredit the good name of Samson International and its chairman. You may rest assured, I shall leave no stone unturned . . .'

Charles Watson-Smith did not react as Sir Howard blundered on. Since initiating divorce proceedings, he seemed so much more rested and at peace. Poised and erect, his back ramrod straight once again, it seemed as if a weight had been lifted from his shoulders. Others around him had started to fidget while Mike Patterson, the man Roger knew he could least rely on, was looking like a pressure cooker about to explode. Roger looked at Charles. Thank God Andrea was completely off the scene. Charles never even mentioned her name now. After putting her ailing public relations business on the market she had moved to somewhere in Tenerife. Roger winced as he thought of their brief and potentially disastrous affair. What an aberration! If either Lilah or Charles had ever found out.

'As I was saying in the House only the other day,' Sir Howard was still going strong, 'it is companies like Samson International who have turned this country—'

'If you'd forgive the interruption.' The whole board looked at Charles as Sir Howard was stopped in his tracks, 'I'm sure Sir Howard's insights are of immense value to all of us.' Charles fixed the politician with a gracious, patrician smile. 'Now it may well be that Samson International is being targeted by subversive left-wing elements in the press.'

Sir Howard nodded knowledgeably.

'But does Sir Howard honestly believe that these *reds* and *commies* are now operating through channels such as James Capel and the Hong Kong Bank?'

There was a collegial guffaw around the table. Sir Howard seemed visibly to shrink.

'Quite right,' added Mike Patterson angrily. 'I've heard enough of this codswallop. Since when, I'd like to know, have smear campaigns been the monopoly of the left?'

'Gentlemen,' said Roger, 'I don't want this meeting to degenerate—'

'It already degenerated the minute old fatso there opened his gob,' interrupted Mike. With difficulty, Roger suppressed a smile.

'—into a political slanging match,' continued Roger. 'The allegations in the press are being dealt with by our lawyers. Charles is quite right. Today, what should concern Samson International most, is who is behind this massive option and share trade.'

'Who the hell is this Stam crowd, anyway?' piped up Christopher Grafton.

Roger turned to George, hunched up in his chair, looking as if Mike Tyson had been using him for target practice. 'They're an investment and holding company,' replied George, who up till now had spent the meeting wondering how Lord Lucan had managed to swing it.

'Listed on the Amsterdam Stock Exchange?' asked Charles.

'Yes,' said George, pouring himself a glass of Malvern water and dreaming of the Scotch he would have later. 'You know the sort. One of those Gentleman's Canal jobs.'

Charles nodded. 'And have the Amsterdam Stock Exchange been called in to look at Stam's latest operation?'

'I believe so,' said Roger, pleased to see his old friend on the ball again.

'Have they offered any explanations?'

'Not really,' answered George. 'Stam say they saw an interesting opportunity for their shareholders and they went ahead and took it.'

'So who are these shareholders, then?' asked Mike. It was important for him to know. If those bloody Japanese were planning to move in on him and his Amalgamated Hotel Workers Confederation with high-productivity no-strike deals, the sooner he knew the better.

'That's just the problem,' explained George, as patiently as he could on Malvern water. 'We've been trying to find out who's behind all this. But, unfortunately, Stam are not obliged to disclose the ultimate identity of their shareholders.'

Mike Patterson looked horrified. What was his hero Jacques Delors doing about this kind of nonsense?

'That's right,' corroborated Charles, turning to Mike. 'If the shares are all in bearer form, there's no need for Stam to divulge who the new beneficial owners are.'

'Talk about keeping the masses in the dark,' said Mike, bitterly. 'Sounds like the sort of situation Sir Howard and his Tory mates would love.'

'Chairman,' exploded Sir Howard, 'I will not have—'

'Gentlemen, please,' said Roger, trying to sound annoyed. In truth, he was far from angry. The more his directors bickered with one another, the less attention they would focus on his own recent string of failures.

'Do I take it, then,' asked Charles, 'that neither the Stock Exchange nor the Serious Fraud Office is likely to find any real grounds for investigation?'

'That's the way I read it,' replied George, lugubriously. 'Not that I can see how it helps us. Let's face it, Samson International is already teetering on the brink of collapse.'

The whole room fell silent. Mike Patterson stopped taking notes. Sir Howard Anderson stopped writing memos. Christopher Grafton stopped smoking in mid-drag.

'That's not the way I see it,' said Roger, quietly. From his calm, immobile expression, it was impossible to tell that inside Roger was boiling. Just to think! The only display of disloyalty so far had come from his own finance director!

'Who's the top man at this Stam outfit?' said Sir Howard, intervening quickly. He had not survived so long in politics without an ability to sense an impending storm. 'Whoever he is, I think Sir Roger should go and parley with him.'

Roger smiled amiably at the former cabinet minister. He might be a contemptible old hypocrite but at least once paid, he had the courtesy to play your tune. Not like that snivelling bastard George.

'I agree,' said Charles smoothly. There were murmurs of 'Me, too' and 'So do I' around the table.

'If nothing else,' continued Sir Howard, pleased at last to have come up with a suggestion which found favour with his colleagues, 'it might give Sir Roger a chance to assess Stam's intentions.'

More murmurs of overall consensus.

'If there are no objections,' said Roger, 'I'd be happy to set up a meeting with the chairman of their management board . . .' he looked down at his notes, '. . . Rijnhard van Polen.'

'And as soon as possible,' urged Sir Howard, loath to stop riding his new-found wave of support. What a wonderful feeling. It was like arguing for hanging and flogging at a Conservative Party Conference.

As the meeting continued, George found it increasingly difficult to concentrate on the agenda. What was the point of carrying on like this? For him, all the fun and zip had long since gone from Samson International. Nowadays, George spent many an inebriated hour trying to plot his escape. Even with his shares at their current level, he could still bail out with a tidy sum. George sighed as he poured himself yet another glass of Malvern water. He sipped it and tried to ignore the dreadful tremor in his hand. He would have to talk it over with Madeleine some time – some time when they could snatch a few minutes to communicate with one another.

'George?'

He looked up to find Roger's icy blue glare fixed mercilessly on him. It sent a shiver down his spine. What was the point of dreaming? His thoughts of freedom were an illusion. He was manacled to Roger for life.

'Yes.'

'Perhaps, as finance director, you could enlighten us.' The sarcasm dripped from his voice.

'I'm sorry. I wasn't really listening. What's the problem again?'

Charles intervened smoothly. 'I was just wondering,' he said, 'why it is that Stam are buying and selling large blocks of our shares and yet they appear on our shareholder register as beneficial owners of only ten per cent?'

George shrugged his shoulders wearily. 'Beats me,' he said,

ostentatiously rubbing his eyes. 'Perhaps when our illustrious chairman meets their illustrious chairman he could put the question to him.'

'Lady Samson?'

'Mr van Polen, how nice to hear from you. I've been following your movements very closely. Seems like your name is cropping up everywhere nowadays.'

'Then perhaps you have also heard of our very useful little profit of around one point eight billion?'

Alone in her bedroom, Lilah sat down heavily on the day bed. 'Good Lord!'

'Enough,' continued Rijnhard, 'for Stam to acquire twenty-nine per cent of Samson International and also . . .' Rijnhard coughed discreetly, 'a little profit besides.'

'Mr van Polen, I . . .'

'No thanks, Lady Samson. It is not all over yet. Now, however, you will be able to take control of Stam. I'm in the midst of organizing the paperwork. You are to become a shareholder via a Swiss nominee company. I thought it might just interest you. They're called Gaza nominees.' Rijnhard was delighted to hear Lady Samson laughing.

'Gaza – of course. The place where Samson bit the dust. How very, very funny.'

'They're managed by the Union Bank of Switzerland. So rest assured, Lady Samson, no one – but no one – will know of your involvement.' He paused before continuing. 'I thought I ought to tell you that your husband, Sir Roger, seems very keen to see me.'

Lilah thought for a second. 'Put him off for a while. At least until Stam has control of the shares. I think it's time for a little more bad press. After all, now I'm in charge, I reckon Stam should be buying as cheap as possible.'

At the *Courier*, Freddie Higgins was having the time of his life. Within months of the initial Samson International scandal, he had added over 500,000 to the paper's circulation. Now there was even gossip that the *Courier* might be voted Newspaper of the Year. (And all, thought Roger Samson angrily whenever he thought of it, at his expense.) Freddie had never felt so elated. Overnight he seemed to have been transformed into the people's champion, the guardian of public morality and the terror of the multinationals all rolled into one. The more Roger tried to muzzle him with injunctions, the more he enjoyed it. Pictures of the *Courier*'s fearless editor emerging triumphant from the court room only served to increase his personal charisma. Nowadays, of course, it seemed like everyone was jumping on the Samson International bandwagon. But for Freddie it was still *his* story. When it came to Samson International, he was like a dog with a bone.

'Lovely stuff,' he said as Hugo showed him the latest batch of information. 'Organized prostitution in those nice posh Samson International hotels. Brilliant. I'll push it past the lawyers and we'll probably run with it next week.'

Hugo nodded. 'It's quite a crusade you've got going here at the *Courier*,' he said.

Freddie eyed him slyly. 'It sells papers, sunshine, that's my angle. I've often wondered what yours was.'

Hugo smiled amiably at the editor. He'd always assumed Freddie had him down as some miffed gay with a personal vendetta against Roger. 'Oh, just a general desire to clean up the City,' he replied airily.

Freddie reached for the Scotch. 'Bollocks,' he said, pouring himself and Hugo a glass. 'That's the last thing any of us wants. No sex, no fraud, no corruption in high places – Christ, we'd never sell a bleeding copy.'

CHAPTER FORTY

WITHIN hours of the *Courier*'s latest damning revelations, Samson International was down to 50p. Over in Amsterdam, Rijnhard continued buying heavily, and within weeks Stam N.V. had acquired its twenty-nine per cent stake in Samson International. Once again, the London Stock Exchange was in uproar, demanding to know what was going on. But Rijnhard remained unmoved.

'Have you seen this?' yelled Roger, flinging a sheet of paper on George's desk. 'It's a press release. That character van Polen has just sent it out on the wire.'

Wearily, George picked it up. 'Samson International is a fundamentally good company,' it ran. 'Its current share price does not reflect its true underlying value. We therefore think it makes an excellent investment for Stam N.V.'

'Seems nice and vague,' he said, handing the piece of paper back to Roger. 'Have they been pressed for information on their future plans?'

Roger's face was etched with anger. 'Of course they have. The answer was "No comment".'

Standing up slowly, George sauntered over to his drinks cabinet and poured himself a Scotch. At half past eleven in the morning he did not bother offering one to Roger.

'You're going to have to insist on a meeting with this van Polen bloke,' he said.

'You're right,' said Roger, turning to leave. 'And the sooner the bloody better.'

It was two weeks before the meeting could be arranged but Roger made use of every minute of it. For once, however, his tactics yielded no results. The private detective hired in Amsterdam could find absolutely nothing on Rijnhard. Well respected as a leading banker throughout the community, he seemed to spend the little spare time he had either in church, at the opera, or on bicycling outings with his family. Roger's face darkened as he read the reports. There was nothing, not one shady deal, not one illicit liaison, just nothing he could pin on van Polen. Roger read on with a mixture of exasperation and boredom. There were just no chinks in his adversary's armour. Van Polen's two children, both girls, had been model students at the University of Leiden and his wife, Anneke, had a prize collection of Delft china. Roger snapped the file shut in utter frustration. It was like trying to dig the dirt on Mother Teresa – absolutely hopeless.

He was surprised when van Polen himself suggested meeting in London. Inured to all the usual games of psychological warfare, Roger had assumed that he would go for the advantage of home territory for their discussions. But either the Dutchman was too naïve or too intelligent for this kind of manoeuvring. Roger bit his lip in annoyance. Just when it mattered most in his life, he was dealing with an unknown quantity.

It was a grey, wet August day in London. Roger stared out of his office window and onto the gloomy Thames below. The English summer at least was predictably unpredictable. Roger glanced at his watch. Five to ten. How much had van Polen managed to find out about him? Nothing beyond the allegations already printed in the papers, decided Roger. The platinum scheme was a closely guarded secret among the members of the Group. And as for anything else . . . If only George could be guaranteed to keep his mouth shut, such skeletons as still existed could remain firmly in the cupboard.

Roger was surprised by the small, suave gentleman Miss Kerwin introduced into his office at the stroke of 10 o'clock. From the information in his possession he had been expecting someone far more dour and ascetic but, as the two men shook hands, Roger felt something akin to relief. It was all right, his intuition told him. They were going to reach an understanding.

Before long, Roger was feeling completely relaxed. It was easy to take to Rijnhard van Polen with his old-world charm and his no-nonsense observations.

'You're quite right,' said Roger, as Rijnhard stared disapprovingly at the Klein hanging just above the sofa. 'I've never been able to understand it either. Now you come to mention it, I think I'll have it moved to the boardroom.'

'A good Vermeer – cool, controlled, precise, classical, that is what is needed.'

'You seem to place a lot of store by precision and control,' Roger probed.

'In my view,' replied Rijnhard, 'these things are fundamental to any work of lasting value.'

'And Samson International? Do you see that as a work of lasting value?'

'Sir Roger,' Rijnhard began, 'you've built a wonderful company, no one would deny it. Of course, you've had some unfortunate publicity of late. But I can assure you that we at Stam would like to see this sorted out.' He smiled. 'Stam are long-term investors in international industrial groups.'

By now Roger was feeling he had the measure of the man. There was nothing here he could not cope with. 'I'm very pleased to hear it,' he said. 'It sounds as if we can work very well together.'

Behind his half-moon spectacles, Rijnhard van Polen blinked. 'I have one suggestion.'

No such thing as a free lunch or a free major shareholder either, thought Roger.

'Now that Stam owns twenty-nine per cent of your company, it might help restore confidence if I were elected to your board as a non-executive director.' He paused. 'In the Netherlands we call such people *commissaris*.'

Roger was silent for a minute. 'Mr van Polen,' he said at last, 'what are you after?'

Rijnhard peered straight into his eyes. 'A profit on my shares.'

A profit on his shares – a most reasonable answer. Roger, of all people, could understand the profit motive. 'Then I don't see any problems,' he replied.

'I hope not,' said Rijnhard, shaking Roger firmly by the hand. The two men left the office and walked down the corridor to the lift.

'I'll be in touch very soon,' said Roger as the lift doors slid open. 'I know we're going to work things out together. We seem to have quite a lot in common.'

Rijnhard smiled as the lift doors slid closed again. Far more than you could ever imagine, he thought, as the plexiglass module descended gracefully to the ground. Far more than you'd ever imagine.

At 4 o'clock the same afternoon George tumbled back into his office. It had been a mistake to have lunch with Reggie Hawkins and all his old mates from the National Westminster Bank. Conservative and careful almost to the point of stasis, Reggie had never seemed to have the makings of a high-flyer in the City. But to look at him now, happy and successful, thought George miserably as he lit up another Davidoff cigar, Reggie epitomized everything George wished he had going for himself. George thought of his tedious, frigid wife and their two ungrateful teenagers. To think he was doing it all for them! All this lying, cheating and juggling – it was no life for a man. Increasingly maudlin, George staggered across the office to his drinks cabinet and poured himself a gargantuan Scotch. He downed it in one. Christ, he wished Reggie hadn't told him. At least, not today. However well he had meant it, that had really wrecked his lunch.

Suddenly the battalion of jackboots resumed their offensive, smashing their heels down hard as they marched relentlessly across George's chest. Gasping for breath, he lurched across the room to the telephone on his desk. 'Miss McEvoy,' he wheezed, barely able to speak, 'Miss McEvoy, I think I'm having a heart attack. Could you please call an ambulance immediately.'

Miss McEvoy was the first to arrive in George's office, swiftly followed by Roger and Miss Kerwin. They found him collapsed on the floor, the receiver of the phone still dangling by its wire down the side of his desk, his cigar smouldering next to him on the carpet.

'Don't worry, Mr Hamish,' said Miss Kerwin, stamping out the cigar immediately and taking charge. After her evening course in first aid, she, at least, knew not to panic. 'Miss McEvoy, fetch me Mr Hamish's coat, will you? Then please go and get your own. We must keep Mr Hamish warm.'

Miss McEvoy was back in an instant and Miss Kerwin did her best to make George comfortable.

'It's OK, George,' said Roger, alarmed yet hardly surprised by the attack. He had known for months that George was a walking time-bomb. 'The ambulance will be here any minute.' God, he looked dreadful. The florid drinker's glow had left his face to be replaced by a dark grey patina. Around his eyes, black rings of fatigue conveyed an almost spectral impression. The top button of his shirt was already undone and his blue silk tie was splattered with the detritus of today's lunch-time session.

'Thanks,' he whispered.

'It's all right, Miss McEvoy. You can wait outside. I think Miss Kerwin and I can cope on our own.'

'Thanks, Sir Roger,' said Miss McEvoy, trying hard to hold back the tears. She was very fond of Mr Hamish. For all his faults and foibles, he was a kind and generous boss. 'I'll try to ring Mrs Hamish.' She held George's hand for a minute before quietly leaving the room.

'It can't go on . . .' rasped George, his voice barely recognizable. 'The boys won't buy it any more.'

'Don't talk,' said Roger firmly. God knows, he didn't want George making any eleventh-hour confessions in front of Miss Kerwin. 'You must conserve your strength.'

'Everybody's had enough,' continued George, breathlessly. He tried to gesture with his hand. 'Goodnight, Vienna. *Arrivederci*, Roma. *Hasta la vista* and . . . well, you get the picture.'

Roger shook his head in irritation.

'Please try to drink this,' urged Miss Kerwin, putting a glass of water to George's lips.

'Water?' asked George.

'With soluble aspirin,' replied Miss Kerwin, trying to sound professional. Perhaps she was being silly. But she thought she remembered reading it somewhere – maybe in one of her women's magazines – something about aspirin being used in the treatment of coronaries. In any event, at this stage, anything was worth a try.

'Forget it,' said George, his voice suddenly much stronger. 'Get me a large Scotch.'

Miss Kerwin frowned and looked at Roger.

'Do it,' insisted George. 'Another one won't matter now.'

Roger nodded at her and gestured towards the drinks cabinet. 'You're going to be fine,' he said. No, George mustn't go. Not now. Not when Roger most needed him. Just another six months – that's all that would be necessary. The presence of Rijnhard van Polen was bound to restore confidence in Samson International. Soon it would be plain sailing again. Miss Kerwin returned with the Scotch. 'Here,' continued Roger, taking the glass from her and holding it to George's mouth.

'Just a wee dram afore ye go,' muttered George, his eyes closed, the lines on his face disappearing as he sipped.

'George,' protested Roger, frightened, 'listen to me. You're only going down the road to St Bart's. Please, George, just hang on in there. You're going to be as right as rain.'

With difficulty, George opened his eyes to look at Roger. 'They're calling in your lines of credit,' he whispered.

'George, you're ramb–'

'Believe me, Roger, Nat West – they've had enough. They're calling in your lines of credit.' George smiled, a peaceful, beatific smile, before closing his eyes again. 'I'm off now, Roger,' he murmured. 'You can sort that one out by yourself.'

Roger looked frantically at Miss Kerwin. 'George,' he said, shaking him by the arm, 'George . . .'

But George was no longer listening. Right now he was dipping his toes into the same clear loch where he used to play as a child. It was cold, icy cold, and his feet felt numb and heavy. But the place was so quiet and beautiful it hardly mattered. Not a single sound – nothing, nothing except the sound of his own heart beating ever more faintly within his chest. And by now his legs were also feeling cold and heavy, too heavy – he may as well leave them behind . . . they only dragged him down as he tried to soar upwards into the sky to join the eagle who seemed to be calling him. And at last he was up there, flying alongside this great, majestic bird, and the peace was absolute, not even the slightest murmur, nothing except the sky and the wind . . . the unfettered freedom of infinity.

By the time the ambulance arrived at Samson Heights, George Hamish was already dead.

The funeral was a quiet, sober affair – precisely the sort of send-off George would not have wanted. After the burial service, Madeleine Hamish had organized tea and sandwiches back at the house – not a drop of alcohol to send him on his way.

'Can't see old George enjoying this,' whispered Charles, wandering into a corner of the drawing room with Lilah.

'Don't,' said Lilah. It was extraordinary. In a matter of weeks, Charles had regained all his old confidence and sense of humour. He was more active than ever in his charity work and was again enjoying life to the full. 'Though I must say,' she added conspiratorially, 'I do agree.'

'Perhaps you and I can escape to the pub for a quiet drink later on,' he suggested.

'Charles,' Lilah tried to look horrified, 'I don't think I recognize this behaviour. You're a changed man.'

'I feel years younger since . . .' Charles could not bring himself to mention Andrea's name, 'since she went.'

'Do you hear from her?'

'Nothing. I made it a stipulation. It's a chapter in my life that's ended. I only wish it had never begun.'

Lilah said nothing, just continued to sip her tea.

'You've been racing around quite a lot recently,' continued Charles. 'Never any time for lunch with an old friend.'

Lilah looked slightly embarrassed. 'That's why I can't have lunch with you,' she said quietly. 'Because you *are* an old friend.'

'Curiouser and curiouser. Am I to take it that there are certain things you wouldn't want to tell an old friend?'

'Not *wouldn't want*,' said Lilah. '*Can't*. Or, at least, can't just yet. I'm sorry, Charles. I know it all sounds a bit cloak and dagger. But you are a director of Samson International. And right now, there are things it's better you just don't know.'

Charles looked into Lilah's face with a mixture of admiration and affection. 'It's you, isn't it?' he said at last. 'The revelations, the scandal – I knew you'd never forgive him.'

Lilah bowed her head in silence.

'And Roger has no idea?'

'Why should he? I'm the last person he'd suspect. As far as he knows, I've no reason to try to hurt him.'

Charles patted her arm fondly. 'I know you'll tell me everything in due course,' he said, 'but in the meantime, you know I'll do anything I can to help.'

'In that case,' she said, smiling at him, 'please support Rijnhard van Polen's election to the board.'

Charles nearly dropped his plate in surprise. 'You don't mean to say . . . ?'

'I didn't say anything,' she said. 'But now you know why I've had to avoid you.'

'Charles!' Roger hailed him from the other side of the room. Leaving Sir Howard Anderson, he moved across to where Charles and Lilah were standing. 'Charles, I wanted to have a quick word with you about this Stam proposal.'

'Of course,' said Charles. 'I read your memo. Wonderful idea, in my opinion. This van Polen chap's a good man by all accounts.'

'So I believe. Excellent. I'm glad you agree. The rest of the board seem happy about him, too.'

Lilah turned to Charles. 'I'll leave you two to talk business,' she said. 'I can see Mike Patterson over there on his own. I'll just go and say hello.'

'About this Rijnhard van Polen chap,' said Charles, as soon as Lilah had left them. 'Now George has gone, it might be worth inviting him to take over as finance director – at least for the time being. A man of his reputation would do us no end of good right now.'

Roger thought for a minute. A finance director, living in

Amsterdam and already extremely busy, it sounded just the ticket.

'Do you know, Charles,' he said, 'that's a bloody brilliant idea. I'll ask him if he'd be prepared to take it on.'

CHAPTER FORTY-ONE

September, 1990

THE NEXT week Roger strolled along to his office, feeling more confident than he'd felt for months. It was still a struggle. There were new stories in the press to be refuted and denied. In-depth interviews with call girls, complete with scabrous details of their trade in Samson International hotels. More revelations of gun-running to South Africa. And further terrified squawks from government and council officials, distancing themselves from allegations of corruption. Roger had never had to fight so hard to maintain the company he'd built from nothing. But at least there were compensations. As expected, after the announcement of Rijnhard's appointment as finance director, the bank agreed to extend its lines of credit for another six months. Moreover, now George was gone Roger did not have to waste hour after hour placating the spineless old soak.

All the same, this was not business the way Roger understood it. This was not building, planning and creating, it was merely a matter of stopping the rot. How Roger yearned to have the company back on an even keel again. It was beginning to get to him. Every day, he worked his frustrations out in the gym. Sometimes it seemed the only area of his life where he still maintained control.

On the plus side of the balance sheet, there was always Lilah. Roger was amazed at her fortitude in the face of such adversity. Many wives would have cracked up and gone screaming to the health farm. But the tougher the going got, the more Lilah seemed to gain in strength. Often, in the mornings, she and Roger would swim together. Nowadays, she was fitter than she had ever been. As the crisis escalated, so his admiration grew. Her dealings with the media were always hallmarked by dignity and restraint. Even that rat Higgins at the *Courier* described her as 'The Jewel in Samson's Crown'. Despite himself, Roger had begun to accept his increasing dependence on his wife. When the odds were stacked against you, what a woman to have on your side!

As Roger walked down the directors' corridor, his thoughts turned once more to George. In the end, it was a blessing that he'd gone. Despite his life-long love affair with the bottle, deep down he'd always been a Scottish Presbyterian prude. The dissection of Samson International under the media microscope had frightened him to death. Roger despised that kind of weakness in his associates. Thank God this chap van Polen had taken over now. He was tough and teetotal and, better still, in Amsterdam.

'Sir Roger,' Miss Kerwin was hurrying along the corridor after him, 'I have a message from Mr van Polen. He says he'd like to speak to you as soon as possible.'

'Fine. I'll call Amsterdam immediately.'

'No, you don't have to do that. Mr van Polen's not there, he's here, in Samson Heights. In fact, he's in Mr Hamish's old office.'

Roger's heart sank as soon as he opened the door and smelled the office.

Rijnhard looked up from George's desk and smiled. 'Ah, Sir Roger. Do come in. I've already got some coffee on the go.' Roger came in and closed the door. On George's drinks cabinet was a brand-new coffee machine. Rijnhard crossed the room, poured two cups and handed one to Roger.

'Thanks.' Roger surveyed the scene with increasing apprehension. Occupying prime position on the desk was a framed photograph of Rijnhard's family. Complete with dogs and bicycles, they looked fine and upstanding, the image of Calvinistic bliss. Next to that was a box of Hajenius cigars and a tin of *hopjes* sweets. Dotted around the room were various bulbs being carefully nurtured in Delft china pots. Beside the coffee machine stood a photograph of a hockey team, taken, if the length of the shorts was anything to go by, quite some years ago. Next to that was an old silver trophy, polished so it gleamed.

Roger sipped his coffee. 'When did you arrive?' he ventured, trying desperately to camouflage his alarm.

'Early this morning,' said Rijnhard brightly. 'The early bird catches the worm, isn't that one of your English sayings?'

Roger tried to smile. 'You seem to have made yourself very much at home,' he said.

Rijnhard returned the smile. 'I think it's important to be happy in your environment,' he said, offering Roger the tin of *hopjes*. He declined. 'And since I'll be spending three or four days a week here – at least to begin with – I thought I may as well be comfortable.'

It was all Roger could do not to splutter into his coffee. 'As much as that? My word, I hope our little problems here won't cause your Amsterdam business to suffer.'

'If a job's worth doing, it's worth doing well,' said Rijnhard, gesturing towards the hefty wodge of files already on his desk. 'As you know, Samson International has a thirtieth September year end. That only gives me four weeks to put the year-end results together.'

Roger was beginning to feel as if he'd just been slugged in the stomach with a very large bag of cement. 'I wouldn't be too concerned,' he said hurriedly. 'We have plenty of good accountants to lend a hand.'

'It's no problem,' replied Rijnhard, draining his cup. 'We Dutch are used to hard work. Besides, since Stam own such a sizeable chunk of this company, it's useful to know what's going on. Now if you'll forgive me, Sir Roger, there's so much to be done.'

As the days went by, Roger became more and more nervous about his industrious new finance director beavering away down the corridor. This was all he needed! God knows what Rijnhard might find out in the space of a month – anything was possible. There were times Roger wished George was back. At least he could push him around. But Rijnhard was a completely different kettle of *matjes*. At the outset, Roger had assumed that he would be ignorant of the ins and outs of the British Regulatory system. The little Dutchman, he thought, would be all at sea. Rijnhard might have been a big commercial banker, but when it came to the intricacies of the London market, Roger had expected to have a beginner on his hands. For once, however, it was Roger who was all at sea. Rijnhard van Polen never ceased to surprise and annoy him with probing questions on the accounts. Roger gritted his teeth. He could not keep covering up for ever. Now it was all a question of hanging on until the platinum scheme came good.

It was late September and London was enjoying a balmy Indian summer. At Samson Heights Roger was working through lunchtime when the phone in his office rang. He was pleased to hear Jim di Pietro, on the line from New York.

'So the FAP are fine and raring to go?' asked Roger, after a brief initial exchange.

'I saw our friend, Credo Sekese . . . when was it now? – day before yesterday. I'm telling you, Roger, there's no holding that boy. Looks like you'll soon have the answer to all your prayers.'

'I'm counting on it,' replied Roger. 'I've got this new finance director ferreting around here at Samson International. God knows what he's going to turn up. And apart from that, I'm hoping for increased profits at Metallinc to help Samson International stock.'

'You sure have been having a rough time of it,' said Jim sympathetically, 'but, trust me, it'll all be coming good real soon.'

Roger's carefully constructed façade slipped, ever so slightly. 'It has to.'

'You're going to be OK,' said Jim, encouragingly. He had been in many a tight corner himself in the past and now he genuinely felt for his friend. 'Just one more week now, Roger, and you'll be laughing all the way to the bank.'

As the month drew to a close, Lilah noticed Roger becoming more and more withdrawn. By the time the thirtieth came round, he could barely converse at all, communicating only in short, clipped and often dislocated sentences. Definitely on edge, thought Lilah. Only she would have noticed the small tell-tale signs which spelt stress in her husband. The Scotch, for instance. Roger rarely drank spirits during the day and here he was, already on his second. Lilah returned to the Sunday newspapers. No respite for Roger there. The city pages were stiff with speculation over Samson International's future. Lilah turned to the *Sunday Times*: 'SAMSON INTERNATIONAL – INVESTIGATIONS CONTINUE INTO PROPERTY BRIBES SCANDAL.' In the *Observer* a highly critical piece concentrated on the company's asset stripping activities – 'SIR ROGER SAMSON – UNBUNDLER EXTRAORDINARY', while the *Sunday Telegraph* focused on further allegations of massive transfer pricing.

'No good news, I'm afraid,' said Lilah, looking up. Staring out of the window, Roger seemed miles away. In the garden, the trees were tinged with the russets, browns and golds of early autumn. The evenings were closing in and chill morning mists were not uncommon. The best, it seemed, was already over. There was only worse to come.

'I said, no good news, I'm afraid.' Roger turned to face her. He looked lean and fit in slacks, an open-necked shirt and a navy blue cashmere sweater. But for once his eyes were dull and tired. It was the only physical sign of strain.

'I'm sorry. No – no, it's not brilliant, is it?' The muscles in Roger's jaw tightened as the drawing-room clock chimed one. For God's sake, what was going on? Hadn't the explosions been set for eleven o'clock English time? Surely, he should have heard something by now. Roger started as the phone rang.

'It's all right, darling, I'll get it.'

Lilah moved on to the colour supplements, smiling as she read the latest limited edition offer. This week, a personalized mock-Fabergé egg could be yours to treasure on a five-point instalment plan. Who could ever live without one?

'That was Hugo.' Roger's voice sounded terse and irritated. 'He wants to know if you're up for a game of tennis. I told him you'd ring him back.'

'Why didn't you let me speak to him?' asked Lilah, all innocence. 'Are you expecting a call?'

'No, nothing in particular,' said Roger, hastily. 'But it's almost lunch-time. And you know when you two get going, you're likely to be there for hours.'

There was a tap on the door.

'Lunch is ready,' announced Mrs Owen, popping her head into the drawing room.

'Thanks, Mrs Owen,' said Lilah, as she got up from the sofa. 'I hope the cook isn't feeling put upon, having to work today.'

'Now don't you be talking silly.' Since the miscarriage, Mrs Owen had taken to speaking to her adored Lady Lilah like some fragile and occasionally wilful child. 'I can't remember the last time you were both here over the weekend. Believe me, she's just thrilled to pieces to be doing a proper Sunday lunch.'

Impatient, Roger walked through to the dining room. How it aggravated him, the way Lilah concerned herself about the staff and their wishes. They were paid – and handsomely – to do a job. The relationship ended there.

'Mmm – roast beef and Yorkshire pudding,' said Lilah as she followed Roger in to lunch. 'It smells wonderful. Please tell the cook I'm feeling ravenous today.'

Roger hardly said a word throughout the meal. Lilah watched as he picked sporadically at his food. It was ridiculous. She was almost beginning to feel pity for him. Quickly, she steered her thoughts away to Sophie's uncle Simon, to Jojo's mother, Naomi, to Andrea and to the child she herself should even now be playing with. The rare beef on her plate seemed suddenly less appetizing.

'Something wrong?' asked Lilah, sipping her glass of red burgundy. 'You seem very preoccupied.'

Roger poured himself another glass of wine. 'Seems like I wasn't that hungry, after all,' he replied, glancing briefly at his watch. Two o'clock. What the hell were those FAP bastards playing at? They were already three hours late.

'Oh dear,' said Lilah. Her appetite returned and she helped herself to more roast potatoes. 'Cook will be disappointed.'

Roger brought his glass down hard on the polished table. 'For Christ's sake, Lilah, don't you think I've got enough on my mind without worrying about the servants?'

'There's no point attacking the furniture,' said Lilah sweetly.

Exasperated, Roger stood up and strode across to the door. 'I'll be in my study for the rest of the afternoon,' he snapped. 'If I want anything, I'll ask for it. So you can tell that house-keeper of yours not to keep pestering me with cups of tea.'

'Will do.'

He slammed the door behind him. Lilah poured herself another glass of wine and savoured it slowly. It was only five past two.

After lunch, she wandered back into the drawing room and returned Hugo's call.

'How's Roger?' he asked.

'Beside himself.'

'Ugh – they must make a dreadful pair.'

Lilah made an attempt to laugh. 'Don't, Hugo. I've almost started feeling sorry for him.'

'Get a grip, darling. We're talking about your husband.'

'I know but—'

'Too late for all that now, old girl. Fancy a game of tennis?'

'No, thanks. I think I'll hang around here. Just to see how he's taking things.'

Hugo paused for a second. 'I'm worried about you, Lilah.'

'Don't be so ridiculous,' she laughed. 'I'm having the time of my life.'

'Perhaps,' said Hugo, slowly. 'Perhaps you think you are. But I'm afraid you can't fool me.'

'Hugo, what are you talking about?'

'Come off it, Lilah. Why should you give a damn about how Roger's taking things? That's what concerns me, darling. I'm afraid you're still in love with him.'

Alone in his study, Roger could barely sit still for a minute. During the course of the afternoon, he phoned Jim di Pietro at least half a dozen times but Jim had heard nothing either. As the evening wore on, Roger tried New York again.

'Look, Jim,' he said, his voice still level despite the tension. 'It's midnight here in the UK – one in the morning in South Africa – and there's still no sign of activity.'

'What can I say?' replied Jim, also extremely anxious. 'I'm just praying that Credo and the boys haven't screwed up.'

'Look, Jim, I'm taking delivery of a million ounces of platinum tomorrow. Do you hear me? A million ounces.'

'I know, Roger, I know. I've got almost as much riding on this as you have.'

'And right now, platinum is standing at around four hundred and fifty dollars an ounce. That means, on average, I'm down about sixty dollars an ounce.'

'You don't have to tell me, Roger. It's bad, real bad. But we're all in this mess together.'

'That's sixty million dollars,' continued Roger, ignoring the interruption. 'Sixty fucking million dollars I'm going to have to find from somewhere.'

There was a long pause.

'There's still time,' soothed Jim, trying to convince himself. 'There's no way a man like Credo is going to let us down.'

Roger smashed the receiver down. Sixty million dollars. There was a time, not so long ago, when he would have shrugged off such a sum. Now those days seemed light years away. Exhausted, Roger laid his head on his desk, willing the phone to ring. All night long he kept his vigil but the message never came.

For the men of Rustenburg, Impala and Meroto, the next day was work as usual.

CHAPTER FORTY-TWO

October–December 1990

IT HAD been a blisteringly hot day in Meroto and Jonathan was relieved to be home. Both the clinic and the operating list had been longer than usual and he was totally drained. Despite everything, however, he could still bring himself to sing under his tepid and erratic shower. It was a fairly eclectic selection of music, ranging from Dire Straits to Gilbert and Sullivan with a little Elton John thrown in for good measure. His voice was loud, occasionally in tune, and unrestricted by any formal training. It was hardly surprising that it took some time before he heard the knocking on his front door.

'Shit!' he said, tying a white bath sheet firmly around his middle and slithering across the water-splattered floor. At this time of the evening it could only be an emergency and he was in no mood to return to theatre. Opening the door, Jonathan was surprised to find Credo and Jojo standing on the step. 'Come in,' he said, happy to see them. 'There's some whisky on the sideboard. And, Jojo, there's Coke in the fridge. Why don't you pour yourselves a drink while I go and get changed?'

By the time Jonathan returned, casual in jeans and a T-shirt, Jojo and Credo were ensconced side by side on the worn leather sofa. 'So what's new, Credo?' asked Jonathan, pouring himself a Scotch. He saw Jojo every day. There seemed no point in asking for her news.

'I saw Jim di Pietro again last week,' replied Credo, extremely matter-of-fact. 'He was very, very angry.'

Jonathan laughed. 'I'm not at all surprised,' he said. 'How did you go about explaining things?'

Credo shrugged his shoulders. 'I said the security forces at Meroto were acting very strange. I said my men got very worried so we decided to call off the plan for all three refineries.'

'And what did he say?'

'He says he is stopping our funds.' Credo paused for a second. 'Jojo and I, we have just come from a committee meeting. Tonight we decided to disband the FAP.'

'Not because of that bastard di Pietro?'

'No,' replied Credo, slowly. 'Such men do not matter. But he – and you and Jojo – you have all taught me an important lesson.'

Jojo looked at Credo with a new light in her eyes. Never before had Jonathan seen her looking quite so relaxed and pretty. At the hospital, he was always so busy, there was never any time to notice. But now . . . Jonathan brushed the thought aside.

'Now I know that violence is not the answer,' continued Credo simply. 'Peace and co-operation, that is what we need. That is how we must work towards a united and democratic country.'

Jonathan nodded. 'I've always liked to hope so.'

Credo sipped his Scotch. 'That is why I have come to see you. Very soon I am leaving Meroto to join Mandela in his work.' The move came as no surprise to Jonathan. Ever since Nelson Mandela's release in February of that year, the pressure for an interim multiracial government had been building in South Africa. Already the momentum for change seemed virtually unstoppable. It was in that melting pot of ideas and ideologies that a man like Credo now belonged.

'I'm happy to hear it,' said Jonathan at last. 'The future of this country depends on men like you.'

'And you,' replied Credo earnestly. 'Before you came to Meroto, I never knew a white man I could honestly call my friend.'

Embarrassed, Jonathan stared at Jojo who was sipping her Coke in silence. It seemed so unlike her to remain so quiet for so long.

'Don't worry,' he said, for want of something to say. 'Even without the FAP, I'm sure you'll find other ways of keeping yourself in trouble.'

For some reason, Jojo could not return his gaze. 'Credo has asked me to go with him,' she blurted out.

'I see,' said Jonathan slowly. 'Now that's really a bolt out of the blue.' For some time the three of them sat nursing their drinks in silence.

'I'll miss you at the hospital.' Jonathan spoke at last. 'We all will.'

'You mean you don't mind if I go?' For the first time that evening, Jojo dared to meet his eyes.

'Of course I mind. You're a bloody good nurse and I'll never find anyone to match you.'

In the lamplight he could see Jojo's bright blue eyes brimming with tears. He had been a hard taskmaster over the years and it was lucky that his staff had always been so understanding. But perhaps, after all, a little more overt gratitude might not have gone amiss.

'I'm proud of you, Jojo,' he said, gently laying his hand on her shoulder. 'But Credo's right. There's another job to be done now. And I'm relying on you to fight your corner.'

'Don't worry about her,' laughed Credo, who had moved closer to Jojo on the sofa. 'I never met a woman with more fire in her belly.'

Or more genuine goodness in her heart, thought Jonathan, kissing Jojo on the forehead. Sitting back in his own winged armchair, he felt overcome by a sudden wave of loneliness. For all her sullen behaviour, he would miss Jojo rather more than he cared to admit. Now almost forty, Jonathan had devoted the last ten years of his life to the people of Meroto. Not that he resented it, not one single minute of it. But perhaps, after all, it was also time for him to think of moving on. The Christian Sight-Savers Mission Hospital was up and running. Now there were other challenges to be met, other problems to be overcome. Jonathan thought of Lilah and wondered what was happening. Although she phoned him often, it was becoming increasingly difficult to tell what was going on in her mind. Jonathan poured himself and Credo another glass of Scotch.

'To freedom,' said Credo, raising his glass in a salute. Jojo and Jonathan followed suit.

'To freedom,' replied Jojo, finishing the dregs of her Coke.

And to happiness, thought Jonathan, downing a sizeable shot of whisky. Whatever that word might mean.

By Christmas of 1990, Sir Roger Samson was beginning to feel that he'd successfully weathered the storm. The final year accounts, to be announced in January 1991, were poor but not terrible. Despite his worst fears, Rijnhard had failed to come up with anything untoward. Yes, there was plenty to be grateful for. Samson International's price was still in the doldrums, but at least van Polen's appointment had restored some semblance of stability and credibility to the company. Of late, certain sections of the media had been in congratulatory mood and some City pages were even predicting an upswing in the company's general fortunes. By the end of the year, Roger was feeling sufficiently at ease to suggest a holiday to Lilah.

'But I'd rather spend New Year in London,' said Lilah, looking up from her copy of *Cambio 17*. Exhausted and running a temperature, she had spent the last few days in bed. At this stage, the idea of a holiday alone with Roger filled her with apprehension.

'It's time we got away together for a while,' argued Roger, sitting down beside her on her four-poster bed. 'We've both been under a lot of pressure recently but I think we're through the worst of it now and the break would do us good.'

Lilah plucked a tissue from the box next to her pile of papers. Fortunately this was nothing but a slight head cold. Now she would have to play it for all it was worth. 'That's really sweet of you,' she said, sniffling loudly. 'But you've been taking the brunt of things. Why don't you accept Jim di Pietro's invitation? You know you love Aspen and the skiing's fabulous this year.'

'But, Lilah,' protested Roger, 'what about you? I don't want to leave you here on your own.'

'It wouldn't be the first time.'

'Lilah . . .'

'No, honestly, I'm quite happy here in London. Besides,'

Lilah sneezed several times into her tissue, 'I don't want this flu to develop into anything worse.'

Gently Roger encircled her with his arms as Lilah tried hard to shiver.

'You've been so wonderful,' he said, burying his face in her hair. 'Do you know, there were times this year I couldn't have gone on without you.'

Lilah closed her eyes tightly and fought hard to remember her part. God knows, she couldn't keep this performance up for very much longer. The stress of all this deception was taking its toll.

'I only did what most wives would have done in the circumstances,' she replied pointedly. By now she was genuinely trembling.

Roger tucked the bedclothes around her more securely and took her hand. 'Next year, I want you to start taking things more easily,' he said, kissing her fingers one by one. 'It's time we started trying for another baby.'

Lilah's hand stopped shaking as her whole body suddenly froze. 'A week in bed will do me a power of good,' she said. Her voice was dull and toneless.

'If you really think that's best,' said Roger, disappointed. 'Perhaps early in the spring . . .'

But already Lilah's thoughts were miles away. And for the very first time since she had known him, not one of them included Roger.

One evening, a couple of weeks after Jojo and Credo had left, Jonathan sat alone at home. For some reason he could not bring himself to go to bed. For hours he sat in his stifling sitting room, staring at the small, square table that had become such an integral part of his life. How many pints of midnight oil had he burned on its cheap red melamine top, poring over papers for international organizations and journals, and all, in the end, for whom and for what? Jonathan emptied the remains of the whisky bottle into his glass. Unusual, for him, tonight he was tired of caring for faceless humanity. The memory of Credo and Jojo, so happy, had left him feeling unashamedly selfish. Tonight all he wanted was a home and some children and Lilah beside him in bed.

He knew instinctively who it was as soon as he heard the phone.

'Made your New Year's resolutions yet?' asked Lilah, trying hard to sound jovial.

'Nope. Only thing to report is a letter from Jojo and Credo. They seem to be settling in.' Jonathan's speech was slightly slurred, but so what if he was drunk?

'I'm sorry,' said Lilah, sensing the despondency in his voice. 'I'd like to have seen Jojo before she left.'

There was a seemingly endless pause.

'Lilah, I'm thinking of leaving, too.'

Lilah could barely contain her delight. 'You're coming back to England?'

'I don't know. There's a post going in Jamaica. Sounds interesting. Quite a bit of research into sickle-cell anaemia.'

Lilah sank back into her pillows. It was the same old story all over again. Only this time there was so much more to lose. 'Please, she begged, 'please don't go making any decisions yet. I don't know how much longer it's going to take. But Rijnhard's very thorough. This bloody business is bound to be stitched up soon.'

'Roger, Rijnhard, Sophie, Stam – I can't tell you how sick I am of the lot of them.'

'Jonathan, you've been drinking—'

'Yes, I have,' he shouted angrily. 'But not half enough to help. What's happening to you, Lilah? All this lying and double-crossing – why don't you just walk away from the whole sordid mess?'

'I can't believe I'm hearing this,' cried Lilah. 'I didn't hear any objections when I was in Meroto.'

'No,' said Jonathan bitterly. 'But who was to know that this game was going to go on for so long? You're fighting as dirty as Roger, Lilah. And what's worse, you're beginning to be like him.' There – he had said it, his love, frustration and jealousy all tumbling bitterly out.

'I thought you understood.' Lilah sounded very shaken. The words had wounded her deeply, as deeply as only the truth can wound. 'Roger's got to be punished.'

'Aren't you the one who's supposed to believe in divine retribution?'

414

'Don't be such a smart-ass. That's your trouble, Jonathan. You're so tied up in your own little world, you've never really understood anything except medicine. It's just like Roger. All he cares about is power and money.'

'That's it, isn't it, Lilah?' yelled Jonathan. By now he was up and pacing around the floor, kicking any piece of furniture that happened to stand in his way. 'Ask yourself if that isn't the truth of it. That bastard Samson has poisoned you. It might have started off as vengeance but now you're in it for precisely that. The power and the money.'

There was a terrible silence.

'I thought you were my friend,' said Lilah, her voice thin and broken. 'I was even hoping, after all this was over, we could still make a life together.'

'Lilah, that's why I can't bear to sit back and watch—'

'You've already said enough,' said Lilah. 'I won't be phoning again.' She put the receiver down, her hand trembling, numb with shock. How could it have come to this?

By the time Hugo came to visit her two days later, Lilah seemed genuinely ill.

'I don't know what's got into her,' clucked Mrs Owen as she took Hugo's hat and coat in the hall. 'Sir Roger didn't want to leave her here alone. Not with the state she's in at the moment. But she insisted he should go. Then this morning, when I suggested calling the doctor, she just wouldn't hear of it. I wouldn't mind so much, but she's completely off her food.'

'Don't worry, Mrs Owen,' said Hugo, fond of her despite her relentless prattle. He knew it was only her affection for Lilah that made her so over-protective. 'I'll knock some sense into her. She can't fob me off with any of her usual nonsense.' Hugo started up the stairs and found Lilah, still in her dressing gown, sitting in the drawing room.

'Mrs Owen's worried about you,' he said, kissing her on the cheek. Pale and listless, Lilah's recent sparkle seemed to have disappeared overnight.

'I'll be OK,' said Lilah, absent-mindedly pushing a counter around the Farhi backgammon board.

'But will you?' Hugo put his finger on the piece to stop her moving it any further. Lilah looked up at him, surprised. 'Life is not a game,' he continued quietly. 'At least, not for a woman like you. You're tearing yourself to shreds, Lilah.'

'It's just a bout of flu, that's all. And I'm telling you, I'll be OK.' Lilah stood up and walked across to the fireplace where a fire was blazing. Still she was feeling cold.

'You can stop it all right now,' said Hugo, ignoring her excuses. 'You can do the honest thing and divorce Roger. Or you can tell Rijnhard to lay off. But, Lilah darling, I know you too well, you can't go on like this.'

'I can't stop it now.' She stared vaguely into the flames. 'It's already gone too far.'

'Then for Christ's sake,' snapped Hugo, 'let's get the whole thing over with and quickly. You've got to stop play-acting and start living life again.'

'Living for what?'

Hugo was alarmed to hear her talk like this again. For the last twelve months vengeance had been the organizing principle of her life. It had been the basis of her energy and motivation. Now it had become a familiar but vicious old friend whose company she had kept too long. 'Stop it!' he shouted, getting up and angrily striding across the room towards her. 'You can't talk like that. You've got everything going for you . . .' Hugo saw Lilah's face, reflected in the Italian giltwood mirror and immediately understood. 'Oh God,' he groaned, 'you do still love him, don't you?'

'I love them both,' sighed Lilah, a single tear trickling slowly down her cheek. 'But Jonathan is such a bloody hero and Roger is such a shit. Somehow I could never make it with either of them.'

'Lady Lilah.' Hugo swung round to find Mrs Owen standing in the doorway. God knows how much of the conversation she had heard but it hardly seemed to matter.

'Yes, Mrs Owen?' Lilah kept her face firmly pointed towards the wall. Right now, she did not need the additional fuss of Mrs Owen's smothering sympathy.

'I know you don't want to be disturbed,' continued the housekeeper, 'but there's a gentleman on the line from Amsterdam. A Mr von Poland, I think he said his name was. He says it's very urgent. Do you want to take the call?'

Lilah smiled wanly at Hugo. 'The final act?' she whispered. And then, to Mrs Owen, 'Of course. If you could have it put through. It's someone I've been expecting.'

As usual, Rijnhard van Polen was impeccably correct. 'Lady Samson,' he began, 'I'm sorry to disturb you. I wouldn't have called you at home, but I've been talking to Mr Watson-Smith. He tells me Sir Roger has left for Aspen.'

'Don't apologize. I know you're not just ringing to wish me a happy new year.'

'Which, of course, my dear lady, I do. I also have – how does it go in English? – good tidings of great joy. At least for the purposes of Stam.'

Hugo watched fascinated as the sparkle seemed to return to Lilah's eyes. 'Really?' she said, her cheeks colouring. 'How very interesting.'

In his study at home in Amsterdam, Rijnhard smiled in modest self-congratulation. Over the previous few months, he had taken a fine-toothed comb through Samson International's books. 'Sir Roger has been clever, very clever. But even he has not been able to cover all his tracks. Especially now Mr Hamish is no longer there to help him.'

'Poor George,' murmured Lilah. 'You mustn't think badly of him. I know he was very unhappy. It was the strain of all this that killed him.'

'No doubt. But now the accounts are more transparent. That's why I have been speaking to Mr Watson-Smith.'

Lilah took a deep breath. 'Is it bad?'

'I'm afraid so. Sir Roger had been dealing in Samson International shares during closed periods.'

Hugo saw Lilah shrug her shoulders. 'It doesn't surprise me,' she said. 'He used to say that everybody in the City was up to it.'

Rijnhard gave a crisp, Calvinistic cough. 'The practice is nevertheless illegal.'

The more Rijnhard talked about money, Lilah noted, the more punctilious his English became.

'Besides, Lady Samson, we are not talking about mere trifles.'

'How much did he make?'

'At least a hundred and fifty million.'

Lilah gasped. 'A hundred and fifty million! But why on earth? Why take the risk? Roger was rich enough already.'

Hugo looked up in time to see Lilah biting her lip. Why this? Why the platinum scam? Why anything for that matter? How stupid and irrational could sheer greed possibly be?

'It seems,' said Rijnhard, 'that Sir Roger used these funds to pay for his private power. Some was even used to bribe the institutions to support Samson International.'

'A sort of slush fund?'

Hugo pricked up his ears.

'Yes. As you say, a sort of slush fund. It is now my duty to advise my fellow directors. But of course, Lady Samson, as a major shareholder . . .'

'Of Samson International . . .'

'But naturally of Samson International, I thought it only right to advise you as well.'

Hugo watched as Lilah paced around the room. 'I've got to figure out how to play this,' she said, resting the phone momentarily on one of the Riesner consoles. 'Who else have you told so far?'

'Only your friend, Mr Watson-Smith, who says he will do anything he can to help.'

'Good. In that case, I think it's best if I handle the disclosure of this information . . .' Lilah smiled across at Hugo, 'via the usual channels.'

'So you would like me to remain silent for the time being?'

'Just for a few more weeks.' Lilah searched for a reason. 'You've done an incredible job, Mr van Polen. But if Roger still thinks you're on his side, you might find out even more.'

The idea appealed to Rijnhard. It salved his conscience while massaging his ego. He readily conceded. 'I'll dispatch all the information to you this morning. Do you want me to advise Miss Weiss?'

'No, I don't think so. She's on vacation with her fiancé and besides,' Lilah stood up and stretched to her full, impressive height, 'I think the time has come for me to deal with things alone.'

By the time Rijnhard rang off, Hugo could barely believe the transformation. The miserable lethargic creature of that morning had completely disappeared. Lilah flitted from chair to sofa, filling in Hugo on all the details, unable to contain her excitement. 'Of course, I said alone,' she dropped a kiss on Hugo's cheek, 'but you'll help me again, won't you, Hugo darling? Your friend at the *Courier* is always desperate for scandal.'

'You know I will.' Hugo got up to leave.

'Don't go,' protested Lilah, grabbing him by the arm. 'Let's go somewhere to celebrate our latest coup.'

'I'm sorry. I don't think I'm feeling up to it.'

'Oh come on. Don't be such a kill-joy. I thought you'd come to cheer me up. Well, now I am cheered up. So where shall we go?'

Hugo studied her face for a minute. 'You're really enjoying yourself, aren't you, Lilah? Oh yes, there are still a few residual qualms. But deep down, you're really enjoying yourself.'

Lilah stood in the middle of the drawing room as her eyes followed him to the door. '*Et tu*, Hugo?'

'I'd never betray you, Lilah,' he said, turning to meet her gaze. 'Just make sure you don't betray yourself.'

CHAPTER FORTY-THREE

London, early 1991

THE FINAL year accounts for Samson International were
announced in January 1991 and the shareholders' annual general meeting called for early March. It was decided that the
company's poor results together with the future intentions of
Stam N.V. were to take top priority on the agenda.

Three weeks before the AGM, after a short telephone conversation with Hugo, a large package of documents arrived on
Freddie Higgins's desk. Manna from heaven, thought Freddie.
The *Courier* hadn't had a real humdinger of a scandal for weeks
and Hugo had always proved a most reliable source. Excited,
Freddie phoned through to his secretary. 'No calls, love,' he
ordered as he tore open the brown paper covering. 'From the
look of this little lot, I reckon I'll be busy all morning.'

It took Freddie precisely half an hour to realize that this
information was something very different. So far, the *Courier*'s
revelations, though damaging to Samson International's share
price, had all been more or less deflected by Sir Roger and his
lawyers. But this – this was in an altogether far more serious
league. Freddie shook his head with something bordering on
despair. It broke his newspaperman's heart to admit it, but
this was too hot to handle – even for the *Courier*. Reluctantly,
he dialled a number. For stuff like this, he decided, there was
only one place and one person he could turn to.

Sitting at his immaculately tidy desk at the Serious Fraud

Office, Detective Chief Superintendent Anthony Rawlinson was intrigued to hear that Freddie Higgins was on the line. 'Of course I'll take the call,' he told the switchboard operator. 'You can put him through immediately.'

Rawlinson sat back and smiled as he waited for his old friend to be transferred. At first sight, the two men seemed the strangest of bedfellows: Higgins, the uncrowned king of Britain's tabloid newspapers and Rawlinson, the pride and joy of the British police force. But both had cut their professional teeth together over two decades ago in the Midlands. Indeed, Rawlinson could still remember his days as a bobby on the beat when an earnest young hack named Higgins had come to interview him about a hit-and-run. The two men had taken to one another immediately. Freddie admired Rawlinson's quiet and thorough professionalism. Rawlinson applauded the relentless way in which Freddie attacked and pursued a story. In those days, Rawlinson would have been the first to admit, it was thanks to Freddie that many a criminal was apprehended.

'Freddie, you old rascal,' began Rawlinson, when the call clicked through, 'to what do I owe this pleasure?'

'Tony, old son, today it's all your birthdays on one day. Have I got a bundle of stuff for you.'

Rawlinson's tone became immediately more serious. 'Reliable sources?'

'The best. Or, at least, they've never let me down yet.'

The detective chief superintendent was seated bolt upright in his chair. 'Big players involved?'

'The biggest, sunshine. If you've been reading the *Courier* over the last few months, you'll know who I mean.' Freddie could hear a sharp intake of breath at the other end of the line.

'Have you got enough there to nail a certain person?'

'Nail him? You'll have enough to crucify him. And a few of his mates besides. Believe me, Tony, there's enough here to put him away for a couple of years at least. That's so long as your blokes don't manage to go and cock it up.'

Rawlinson's jaw set hard. By this stage there was no way anyone was going to blow anything. He'd been waiting years to get something substantial on Sir Roger Samson and his friends. 'I'll be over straight away. And, Freddie, I don't need to remind you, do I? *Total* secrecy from now on in. If certain persons got wind of this, they'd start shredding all the evidence.'

'Mum's the word. But just remember one thing, old son, I reckon you owe me one.'

Two days later, four people found themselves seated around the table in the detective chief superintendent's office. After a thorough examination of the contents of Freddie's package, there was no longer any doubt in anyone's mind. At last, Rawlinson turned to Gordon Keays, the accountant co-opted from the Institute of Chartered Accountants to deal with company fraud.

'How do you think we should play it?' asked the super.

Slowly, Gordon lit another cigarette, at least his tenth that morning. 'It's a complicated case,' he replied. 'Very complicated. If you're going to raid the premises, there's no point tipping up with a load of helmets. I'm going to need time to brief the boys so at least they know what they're looking for.'

Rawlinson nodded. 'Don't worry,' he said, making a note. 'I'll get you ten of the best. Some from our own staff and some from the Metropolitan and City Police Fraud Squad. You can have them all to yourself for a day.'

'You're also going to need three or four good exhibit officers,' added Jeremy Gilbert, a brilliant left-wing barrister who often acted for the prosecution in such cases. Rawlinson agreed. There was no need to remind him how important it was to do things according to the book. It had only happened once to him and Gilbert, but it would never happen again: a case dismissed after failure to seal the evidence seized in regulation plastic bags.

Seated at the opposite side of the table, Maureen Butler continued to make notes. Terrifyingly bright and able, this young solicitor had already carved a reputation for herself as the most outspoken feminist in the legal profession. Men like Sir Roger Samson were anathema to her. They represented the phenomenon she hated most in life: the corruption of any male-dominated society.

'When do you think we can move?' asked Rawlinson, turning to face her.

Maureen smiled, almost patronizingly. Boys would be boys, of course. They loved their little raids. 'Not for three weeks,' she replied, shaking her head in frustration. From experience, Maureen knew that the wheels of justice moved all too slowly. The Crown Court, an *ex parte* application for a warrant to seize documentation – all these things took time. All the same, the application for warrant would bear public interest immunity. The whole process would be shrouded in the secrecy necessary for ultimate success.

Still studying the contents of Hugo's package, Gordon lit up another cigarette. 'And about the platinum business?'

Maureen scribbled a memo in her notes. 'We'll need a Red Notice,' she replied. 'Interpol can then contact the individual national police forces who in turn can organize raids to coincide with ours.'

Rawlinson looked on, inordinately pleased. Jim di Pietro *et al* had no idea of what was soon to be winging their way. 'Maximum publicity,' he said enthusiastically.

Maureen looked up from her notes. 'If you really want to make a meal of it,' she said, 'I'll try to get the warrant for the day of Samson International's AGM. *Pour encourager les autres*, perhaps.'

A broad grin spread across the detective chief superintendent's face. 'That would be very helpful, Miss Butler,' he said. 'I owe a story to a certain newspaper editor. This would help settle my debt.'

It was early March, the day before the AGM, and Lilah was working in her office when the phone rang. She picked up the receiver.

'Lilah? Hi, it's Sophie here. Just ringing to wish you all the best for tomorrow.'

Lilah leaned back in her chair happy, as usual, to hear her friend's reassuring voice. 'Thanks, Sophie. I'm going to need it. I'm still here, struggling with my speech.'

'You worry too much. You don't have to convince anyone, you know. It's already in the bag.'

'I know.' Her voice sounded anxious. 'But it's important to me. I want people to understand. I want Roger to understand.'

'However you want to play it. From now on, you're on your

own.' Sophie could have bitten her tongue. 'I'm sorry,' she added immediately. 'I didn't mean . . .'

Lilah stared hard at her notes. 'It's OK, Sophie. Don't apologize. The trouble is, I am.'

Later that evening, Sir Roger Samson sat alone in his study, wrestling with the figures. It was going to be a close call, too close in his view, but it looked as if he just might make it. He had pulled in every conceivable marker to retain control of Samson International. Over the last few months he had fought tooth and nail through the courts, which he loathed, and against the media, which he despised, to keep control of the company he'd created from nothing. Tonight, as a chill March wind whistled unhindered through Regent's Park, Roger felt drained.

Scattered across his desk lay drafts and redrafts of the speech he intended to make at tomorrow's AGM. Public speaking, Roger knew, had never been his strong point. Some, like Lilah, might enjoy the gift of the gab. But Roger had always relied on the sheer force of his personality to draw others along with him. He looked at the silver framed photograph of his wife which he kept on his desk. Between them, they ought to win the day.

Lilah. Roger knew his preoccupation with the company had been putting their relationship under considerable strain. It was hardly surprising that she often seemed distant. Poor darling, she, too, must be worried to death about the future of Samson International. No wonder their sex life had suffered – at the moment it was non-existent. Never mind. Tomorrow, everything would be sorted out. Then he could take her away – a trip down memory lane to Jamaica, perhaps. He would let her decide. Dear Lilah, she really deserved a break.

Roger refilled his Mont Blanc fountain pen – he preferred to draft in long-hand. Bold black decisive copper-plate – he was proud of his handwriting. It was his only real affectation. For a moment, his mind wandered to his mother as she taught him how to write in that large, lined exercise book. How many hours they had spent together, patiently forming the letters of his name. 'R-O-G-E-R S-A-M-S-O-N,' she had read out loud the day he printed it on the front of his book. The small boy at her knee had only just turned four. 'I'm very proud of you, darling,' she'd said, kissing him fondly on the forehead. 'If you continue like this, you're going to go a long, long way.'

Roger returned to his notes. There was no point in dredging up such emotional garbage now. OK, so he'd done things his mother would never have approved of. But what of it? If blame were to be apportioned, where had she been when he'd needed her most in his life? Involuntarily Roger's whole body winced. He was what he was. He'd done what he'd had to do in an effort to feel secure. Sure, on occasions he'd been obliged to sail close to the wind. But there had always been plenty of people happy to jump aboard once the victory buoy was rounded. Roger rubbed his eyes. It was all right for men like Christopher Grafton – they'd always had money delivered to them on a plate. And Charles Watson-Smith – even if he hadn't had a fortune to start with, he'd always had the advantage of family and name. But for Roger life had been a fight from start to finish. And in fights the weak and unsuspecting were bound to end up hurt. Roger shrugged his shoulders. It was the law of the jungle and he hadn't made the rules.

Roger put a line through the first paragraph of his speech. Samson International – the whole thing was his creation. Why the hell should he be explaining and apologizing to anyone? Shareholders' bloody meetings! What a pathetic bunch of wimps they always managed to throw up. What did any of those creeps know about running a successful business? In the good days, these same folk had been falling over themselves to accept the Samson shilling. Roger suppressed a cynical smile. There had never been too many searching questions at shareholders' meetings then.

But now . . . Roger poured himself a large malt whisky. That bastard Freddie Higgins. Where on earth was he getting his information from? He certainly couldn't blame Andrea now. Roger began his first sentence again. 'Over the years, the fortunes of Samson International . . .' He stopped. The fortunes of Samson International, he thought, have been far better than any of you blighters could possibly have hoped for. Roger felt an overwhelming surge of bitterness. Yes, he'd made these people rich before in the past. And he'd make them rich again if they had the sense to stick with him. Roger called up the overnight share price on the screen of his computer. Down to 50p once more. And to think that just over twelve months ago it had been riding high at 240p. Freddie bloody Higgins! Roger crashed his heavy crystal tumbler down on the desk. If ever a man deserved the Queen's Award for Disservice to British Industry it had to be that bastard!

Exasperated, he put another line through what he had just written. 'In this world,' he began again, 'there are those who do and there are those whose task is nothing but to criticize the doers . . .' Roger reread the sentence and decided he quite liked it. Yes, that was the way to play it tomorrow. Sir Roger Samson, doer, builder and creator versus a hoard of niggardly media critics. Roger took another sip of whisky and started to redraft the entire speech. For once, he found, the words seemed to flow. Desperation was perhaps the unsung muse but she was still by far the most powerful.

By the time Roger finished it was well past midnight and his whisky decanter was half empty. Pleased with the results of his endeavour, he picked up the shiny lump of ore which always stood near his ink-well and slid the sheets of foolscap underneath. A piece of the platinum-rich Merensky reef, the rock made a beautiful and unusual paperweight. Roger studied it, glistening iridescent in the lamplight. Meroto – the rock, quite literally, on which Samson International had been built. Right now those early prospecting days seemed far, so very far, away. Suddenly, Roger started. A wayward thought, perhaps, or a trick of light, but somehow tonight the white anorthosites, the grey chromites and the dark pyroxenes of the ore had combined to form a face. Roger shuddered. Sitting there, staring at him from the top of his speech, was his former benefactor, Simon Weiss.

Shaken, Roger poured himself another Scotch. He didn't believe in ghosts or omens but this was quite uncanny. Whichever way he looked the face, worn and rugged, continued to stare at him. 'But surely,' said Roger out loud, without knowing quite to whom, 'equal pay rights for black miners would never have worked. Not even in Meroto. We could never have been competitive. Surely, Simon, you must have understood.

What I did was business, pure and simple. I had to have control.'

Swiftly, Roger pushed the paperweight out of sight behind his computer. He was exhausted, that was all there was to it. Uncertainty was the most debilitating of all emotional conditions. Not that Rijnhard van Polen had mooted anything, that was not his style. But with Samson International languishing in the doldrums, the AGM might force Stam into making a takeover bid. Roger pulled a clean piece of foolscap out of his drawer and, for the hundredth time, did his sums. Stam controlled 29 per cent of Samson International. There was nothing to be done about that. But so far, if no one reneged, Roger had 10 per cent in firm promises and 19 per cent in irrevocables. With the Samson family holding of 22 per cent, currently in Lilah's name, that made a total of 51 per cent – just enough to fend off any possible bid. Roger drew a thick, black line under the column of figures. Fifty-one per cent – it was not ideal. But, in the end, it was all he needed to fight another day.

Lilah lay wide awake in bed unable to fall asleep. Thank God, Roger had said little over dinner that evening. As usual, he was keeping his apprehensions bottled up tightly inside himself. In the darkness of her bedroom, Lilah tossed and turned.

Their Last Supper. At least, before retiring, she had not kissed him on the cheek. That, she felt, would have been going too far. Instead, claiming a headache over pudding, she'd avoided the chance of discussing tomorrow's meeting by retreating to her room.

Thirty pieces of silver. In her case, that meant almost £2 billion so far. What would her dear departed parents have made of it all? The Dooleys had been good, honest, straightforward folk. To her father, winning the office sweepstake on the Grand National had seemed like untold wealth. And her mother had never had more than twenty pounds in a Post Office savings account to call her own. Lilah squirmed uncomfortably among the soft sheets of her antique four-poster bed. No, they wouldn't, couldn't possibly have understood.

Hers was a different world, a world the meek would only inherit if they shafted the wicked first. Lilah stared hard into the darkness, hoping for an answer. She was right, wasn't she? Surely, what she'd done just had to be right?

Judas Iscariot? It had been pointless, perhaps, expecting Sophie to understand. 'Wise up,' she'd remonstrated, the last time Lilah had tried to explain her feelings. 'You can't betray a traitor. And even if you could, two negatives make a positive so you'd still be doing everyone a favour.'

How Lilah envied Sophie the courage of her convictions. No doubt her years as a dealer had left no room for vacillation.

'You've made your decision, now stick with it,' Sophie had told her rather sharply. And then, lightening up a little, 'And I thought the Jewish people had the monopoly on guilt!'

Hot and cold under the bedclothes, Lilah thought long and hard. It was all right for Sophie to talk about following through. Hatred and vengeance were so much easier in the abstract. Lilah felt a dull pain spreading through her chest. Had that last additional twist of the knife really been necessary, after all? Surely the Serious Fraud Office already had enough on Roger without information on the platinum scam? But Rijnhard had insisted and all the details had now been handed over. For Rijnhard, sentiment was out of the question. Roger Samson, as far as he was concerned, was a total crook.

Lilah slipped out from under the sheets and onto her knees beside the bed. It must have been twenty years since she'd knelt to pray. Tonight, however, there seemed nothing much to say. Outside, the wind had dropped and apart from the clock, chiming two in the drawing room, the house was completely silent. Lilah pictured Roger in his study, still agonizing over his speech. Closing her eyes, she made another, more determined effort. But it was hopeless. For some reason, she wanted to pray for Roger, and ended up weeping for herself.

At four o'clock Lilah heard him opening her bedroom door. Moving across to the bed, he bent down to kiss her. 'Sleep well, darling,' he whispered, stopping for a moment to gaze at her face. 'You're going to need it for tomorrow.'

Leaving as quietly as he had entered, Roger returned to his study to rehearse his speech.

*

The next morning, Lilah seemed cheerful enough when he left for Samson Heights. Despite a sleepless night, he looked calm and relaxed, completely in control.

'So you'll be joining me later at the board meeting,' said Roger, kissing her goodbye.

'If you insist,' said Lilah, looking up from her copy of *Le Monde*. Still in bed, she lay surrounded by her usual pile of foreign and English papers.

'Yes, I do.' Roger's voice was confident and even. 'I want you there beside me at the board meeting and at the AGM. It's important, Lilah. Today, it's you and me.'

Lilah said good-bye and returned to her newspapers.

'Any plans for dinner?' he asked, about to leave the room.

'No, no plans at all.'

'Then how about a quiet celebration – just the two of us – at Mosimann's?'

Lilah failed to look up, engrossed, apparently, in some article or other. 'Let's take a raincheck. After all, I'm sure to see you around.'

'I'm sure to see you around.' It was only later in the board-room, with time to reflect, that the words struck Roger as odd. Impatiently he glanced at his watch. Half past twelve! The meeting should have started an hour and a half ago. Where the *hell* was she?

The two panelled doors of the boardroom were flung wide open. A curious hush descended as Lilah finally appeared on the threshold.

'Well, darling,' said Roger, getting up to go and kiss his wife, 'better late than never.' There was something in her face that stopped Roger in his tracks. For the moment he could not pinpoint it. But where else had he seen that look?

Lilah flashed the members of the board her most dazzling smile. 'Gentlemen, I'm so sorry to have kept you waiting.' Gracefully, she moved across the room to the place reserved for her at Roger's right-hand side. The rest of the board swiftly resumed their seats around the mahogany table and Roger called the meeting to order.

'I don't intend to waste the board's time,' he began in a

calm, clear voice, 'with a rehearsal of the speech I shall be delivering to this afternoon's meeting.'

'No, don't,' piped up Mike Patterson in a loud stage whisper. 'This lot are looking dozy enough already.'

Good old Mike, thought Lilah. He never missed a trick.

'The purpose of this get-together,' Roger's eyes moved around the table, stopping briefly on each director in turn and ending up on Lilah, 'is to establish what's best for the future of this company.'

'Hear, hear,' said Sir Howard Anderson automatically.

'You're not at Prime Minister's Question Time now,' snapped Mike.

'Fortunately,' Roger ignored the by-play, 'I've had time this morning and over the last few weeks to discover what most of you are thinking.'

Certain heads around the table nodded. Eagle-eyed, Roger counted them carefully.

'As you know, gentlemen, I've never been a man of many words. I leave that end of the business to the company's major private shareholder.'

A small wave of amusement rolled around the table.

'So I'm sure that you'll all now be interested to hear what Lady Samson has to say. Lilah . . .'

There was a brief round of applause started by Charles Watson-Smith. He looked across at her supportively.

'Gentlemen,' she began, her face slightly pale yet serene, 'I hope I'm not going to disappoint you. But for once, I'm afraid, I have very little to say.'

'Tell it to the marines,' heckled Mike, good-naturedly.

'Certainly,' countered Lilah, 'via their spokesperson at the Marine and Associated Maritime Activities Amalgamated Union.'

Roger started to relax. If Lilah remained in this form, they would walk it this afternoon.

'All I do wish to say,' continued Lilah, 'is that this company deserves to be run by someone who cares for it and the people who work in it. At this afternoon's AGM, I'm sure we're all going to do our utmost to ensure that.'

There was a loud round of applause.

'Thanks, darling,' whispered Roger, looking at her in frank

admiration. 'And thank you, too, gentlemen,' he continued, bringing the meeting to an unexpectedly early close. Roger was pleased with the way things were shaping up. He had anticipated more dissension from his fellow board members. Luckily, they were all there – as he had hardly dared hope – right behind Lilah.

'The AGM starts at three o'clock in the ballroom of the Samson International . . . Ah, yes, Miss Kerwin . . .' Roger held up his hand for silence as his personal assistant appeared beside him.

'Gentlemen, Miss Kerwin has a housekeeping notice for us.'

'A buffet lunch has been arranged for all members of the board,' she announced. 'You'll find it laid out in the Margaret Thatcher Room.'

'Along with the corpse of the British economy,' muttered Patterson, shovelling his documents into a battered old plastic briefcase. Lilah suppressed a smile. She knew he had several, far more expensive, leather models at home. But for grand occasions, such as today, he much preferred to use this one. He'd once told her that he'd had it since his days at comprehensive school.

'Come on,' said Roger, taking Lilah by the arm and guiding her out of the room. 'The last thing I need this morning is that bolshie Patterson's snide remarks.'

'Oh, Lilah.' Charles Watson-Smith pushed his way through the milling throng of directors.

'I'll see you downstairs,' said Lilah to Roger. 'I must have a word with Charles.'

Roger nodded and headed off towards the lift.

'Charles,' said Lilah, kissing him lightly on both cheeks. 'I must say, you're looking younger every day.'

'And you too, my dear,' replied Charles, manoeuvring her into a quiet corner. 'Lilah,' he continued, smiling down at her kindly. 'I just wanted to tell you that whatever you decide to do this afternoon – and I mean *whatever* – you'll have my whole-hearted support.'

The slightest shadow of doubt scudded swiftly across her face. 'Thanks,' she said. 'I only pray I'm doing what's right.'

*

By three o'clock, the atmosphere in the ballroom of the Samson International Hotel was already one of heady excitement and mounting heat. The high profile of the Samsons combined with the never-ending scandals of the last few months had guaranteed a capacity crowd. Dowager aunts and elderly vicars, the sort of shareholders who had never before attended an AGM, now jostled for prime positions. The banks of seats reserved for the press had been snapped up hours ago. City editors, feature writers, gossip columnists, even the odd fashion correspondent, all waited, pens poised, for the business story of the year. For weeks, speculation about a possible Stam takeover bid had been rife in the City and Fleet Street. The press's financial experts were now split fairly evenly as to which way today's meeting would go. The *Courier*, naturally, had weighed in first with a swingeing attack. 'Sir Roger Samson,' the two-page editorial had begun. 'Is this man fit to run a public company?'

The left-wing *Mirror* was determined to gain maximum political mileage from the Samson International débâcle. 'GREED AT SPEED' ran that morning's banner headline. There followed a vituperative attack on Roger's personal wealth, a symbol, ran the piece, of the get-rich-quick mentality fostered by the Tory government during the eighties.

By contrast, the right-wing tabloids had come out against a foreign takeover of one of Britain's most important industrial conglomerates. 'SCRAM, STAM!' was the headline in the previous day's edition of the *Sun*. Even Roger had been moved to smile.

The more serious elements in the broadsheets were far more circumspect. But, on the whole, most pundits felt that, under Sir Roger's inspirational leadership, the company could still be pulled around. There was one point, however, on which everyone was agreed. Everything, but everything, depended on the way things went today.

The ballroom fell silent as Roger called the meeting to order at five minutes past three. At one end of the room a podium had been erected for Samson International's board of directors. Grave and attentive, they were already seated behind the white-cloth-covered table. On Roger's insistence Lilah had again been placed at his right hand. She could feel the dull ache in her chest and the emptiness in the pit of her stomach both fighting for attention.

'Ladies and gentlemen.' Somewhere, it seemed like miles away, Lilah could hear the resonant confidence of Roger's voice. Outside, in function rooms throughout the hotel, extra amplifiers had been set up. The entire hotel, it appeared, was in thrall to Roger's every word. 'In this world, there are those who do . . .' a camera-bulb flashed as Roger turned his steely gaze towards the gaggle of press in the corner '. . . and there are those whose task is nothing but to criticize those doers . . .'

At Samson Heights Clive, the doorman, stared dumbfounded at the warrant. In all his forty years in security, he had never been faced with a PACE order. A warrant to search and seize – it made his blood run cold.

'I think you'll find everything's in order, sir,' said Detective Chief Superintendent Anthony Rawlinson. 'Now, if you don't mind, we'd like to get on with our business with as little fuss as possible.'

Clive nodded slowly as the group of twenty-odd men made their way past him to the lifts.

'The chairman's office,' asked Rawlinson. 'It's on the twentieth floor, sir, isn't it?'

Clive nodded again. What else could he do under the circumstances? Somehow his faculty of speech had just deserted him.

Back at the Samson International, Sir Roger Samson was warming to his theme. 'For almost ten years,' he continued, 'Samson International has been a cruiser many people were happy to take.'

Around the ballroom, there were murmurs of approval. The journalists scribbled furiously.

'During that time, we moved from port to port with seemingly effortless ease.' Roger paused for a second. 'I say *seemingly* because in this world no success is effortless. As my mother used to tell me when I was a small boy, the only things worth having are those things you have to fight for. Well, I have fought, ladies and gentlemen.' Roger brought his fist down on the table. 'I've built Samson International up from nothing. And, in the process, I've created the wealth and jobs from which all of you here have benefited.'

'Hear, hear,' responded Sir Howard Anderson loyally. There was an encouraging round of applause. Roger smiled as he took a sip of water.

'I'm telling you here today that never once in the first ten years of my captaincy, never once did I hear a single word of complaint from any of my passengers.'

There was another burst of applause as Roger smiled confidently into the middle distance.

In the press section, Freddie Higgins was becoming increasingly irritated. 'That bastard's going to swing it,' he whispered to his finance editor, Des. 'These stupid buggers are lapping it up.'

Des nodded, mesmerized like the other stupid buggers by Roger's performance.

'Over the last twelve months,' Roger's eyes scanned the room, as if he could see everyone in it, 'our ship has sailed into some very troubled waters . . .'

'Holed beneath the water-line, if you ask me,' heckled someone from near the back.

'Let the man speak.' A redoubtable, upper-class female voice put paid to the fledgling opposition.

'But I ask you, what do sensible passengers do when their ship hits a squall? Do they talk, at that stage, of throwing their captain overboard?'

A strong chorus of 'No' reverberated loudly. By this stage Freddie Higgins was beginning to wish he'd brought his hip flask. 'I tell you what, Des,' he said, 'that bastard's got this lot eating out of his hand. I've never heard such a load of crap. It's worse than *Listen With Mother*.' Des watched, intrigued, as swiftly Roger wiped his brow with his handkerchief.

'Over the years, many of you have come to know and trust me. Today, I merely ask you to reflect on that before you cast your votes.' Roger sat down to tumultuous applause. Hidden from the audience by the table, Lilah could see his fist, shaking with emotion. But his face betrayed nothing as he waited for Rijnhard to take the floor.

*

At Samson Heights Gordon Keays was scanning Roger's files. All around him, exhibit officers were carefully marking up the plastic bags in which seized documents were being placed.

'Make sure you tie those properly,' Detective Chief Superintendent Rawlinson warned his men. They all nodded. Correctly tied, those bags could only be cut open again. Such measures ensured that evidence could not be tampered with. The super turned his attention to Gordon. 'Found what you're after?'

The accountant looked up from a heap of papers and placed his cigarette in the ashtray. 'We're getting there,' he said, shaking his head. 'But from what I've seen already, it looks like Samson's for the high jump.'

'Des, old son,' said Freddie after the first five minutes of Rijnhard van Polen's speech, 'any chance of a few snifters from the bar?'

Des nodded enthusiastically. 'There was nothing to write home about in this speech. All the guff about 'clarity' and 'transparency', it sounded like a lecture on Waterford cut glass. 'What's yours?' he asked.

'Scotch,' whispered Freddie. 'Make it a couple of doubles. Sounds like the Flying Dutchman could be rabbiting on for hours.'

Des made good his escape to the nearest watering hole just as Rijnhard was moving on to the concept of Christian justice in business dealings. Like Des, many members of the press had already repaired to the bar, ready to file their copy.

'Samson's got it made,' opined Mel, one of Des's oldest Fleet Street friends. 'Have you heard that bloke van Polen talk? I've heard more excitement in the shipping forecast.'

'The boss is furious,' agreed Des, picking up a trayful of drinks. 'He reckons Samson could sell time-share in Beirut. Beats me how he does it.'

By the time Des got back his seat, Rijnhard had started on probity.

'Talk about the Sermon on the Mount,' gasped Freddie, sinking a Scotch in one.

'Our two proud, sea-faring nations . . .' continued Rijnhard.

The longer he spoke, the more pronounced his Dutch accent became.

'Oh, God,' groaned Freddie, 'not more life on the ocean waves stuff. I don't think I can bear it.'

Des fanned his face with his notebook. By now it was intolerably hot.

'. . . which is why . . .' Rijnhard was clearly flagging. He had been on his feet for over fifteen minutes. '. . . I shall continue to ensure the company's continuity and seek to maximize shareholders' value.' The speech was met with muted applause. It had been a difficult one to make. On Lilah's suggestion, he had stuck to underlining the general tenets of good management. The result had been rather tedious. Lilah surveyed the ballroom. Several shareholders had gone to sleep. Roger got to his feet.

'And now, ladies and gentlemen,' he said calmly, 'if anyone else would like to take the floor . . .'

Slowly, deliberately, Lilah raised her hand.

He smiled. 'Lady Samson,' he announced, 'the company's major private shareholder.' He glanced across at his wife with pride. 'I'm sure the AGM is looking forward to hearing what she has to say.'

'At least she'll pep things up a bit,' whispered Freddie, looking lustfully at Lilah as she walked across to the lectern. He turned to the *Courier*'s fashion correspondent, seated in the row behind. 'Got this, have you, Hilary? Fabulous body, unbelievable legs, red, clinging jersey number . . .' Freddie took a large slug of Scotch. 'Jesus, is there no end to that bastard Samson's luck?'

'Odd,' said Des, watching as Lilah adjusted the microphone. 'You'd have thought she'd make her speech from the table. You know, Stand By Your Man, and all that sort of stuff.'

'You've no idea, have you, sunshine?' answered Freddie, shaking his head. This new generation of journos! They might have degrees coming out of their ears, but basically they didn't have a clue. 'Can't you see the effect she's having by standing up there alone? If she told this mob to do the hokey-cokey, there isn't a man in here wouldn't do it.'

'And what about the women?' asked Hilary, busily taking

notes: auburn hair loose; no jewellery to speak of; low-heeled black patent shoes.

'Who cares about the women?' snapped Freddie. 'Since when did women decide the future of major public companies?' Freddie sat back, inordinately pleased with himself.

'Ladies and gentlemen . . .' Scanning the room, Lilah hesitated for a second as the lights of the chandeliers seemed to blind her. Then, taking a deep breath, she began again, her voice well pitched and clear.

Slowly, Gordon Keays inhaled another puff of smoke.

'I thought that was one of your New Year's resolutions,' said Detective Inspector John Mackintosh, pointing an accusing finger at the offending cigarette.

'It was,' replied Gordon, taking another puff. 'At New Year, I reverted to high tar.'

Mackintosh shook his head. An Oxford Rugby blue, he had never smoked in his life.

Anthony Rawlinson laughed. 'Leave the man alone,' he said. 'God knows, it's difficult work keeping track of the criminal mind.'

'You can say that again,' replied Gordon, flicking through a bulging red file. Suddenly something caught his eye.

'Look at this,' he said handing it to the detective chief superintendent.

Rawlinson read for a minute in silence before a smile broke across his face. 'Great,' he said enthusiastically. 'Just what I was hoping for. Gordon, you stay here and keep searching. Mackintosh, go and get three of the lads. We're going down to Park Lane to pick up that bastard.'

'No, ladies and gentlemen,' resumed Lilah, once the laughter in the ballroom had subsided. 'Today is not about control or companies. It is not even about profit and loss. Today is about something which affects us all at a far deeper level. Today we are talking about trust.'

'What a woman!' whispered Freddie. 'Great copy. Make sure you get it all down.'

Des nodded as he wrote. Getting it down would be a darned sight easier if Freddie would stop drooling in his ear.

'Trust . . .' Slowly, Lilah surveyed the room, embracing everyone in her gaze until her eyes met Roger's. That look again! What was it?

'. . . the foundation and cement of every worthwhile relationship. Like the air we breathe, it is so essential to our existence we often take it for granted.'

There was a murmur of general agreement. Confidently, Roger glanced at his board. Even the surly Patterson was staring, spellbound, at the figure in red by the lectern.

'And yet,' continued Lilah, her voice now deeper, more velvety, 'we are right to trust. That is why any betrayal of our trust is a most serious offence.' Lilah paused almost imperceptibly. 'In future, ladies and gentlemen, I can assure you that your faith and trust in Samson International will not be disappointed.'

Roger relaxed once more as Lilah resumed her seat to a standing ovation. He'd known it all along, of course. She was always going to knock them dead.

'Questions from the floor?' he asked, determined now to wrap up this AGM as quickly as possible. Immediately Freddie Higgins put up his hand. His question was a plant, suggested to him by Hugo. By this stage it seemed pointless. Samson had won the day. All the same, thought Freddie, he might as well cause maximum embarrassment. A steward arrived with a floor microphone.

'Freddie Higgins,' he began. 'Editor of the *Courier*.'

The vein on Roger's neck started to pulse. That bastard Higgins! He'd done his level best to cause Samson International's downfall. Well, he'd failed. Now what the fuck did he want?

'Chairman,' Freddie's voice was smooth, 'in view of this company's recent poor performance, has Stam N.V. considered a takeover bid?'

Roger gestured towards van Polen. Blinking behind his half-moon spectacles, Rijnhard rose. 'If the majority of shareholders felt that Stam could do a better job for the company,' he replied, deliberately, 'then we at Stam would have to consider it seriously.'

Roger smiled confidently. There was no way Stam could get a majority now.

'Chairman.'

Roger turned, surprised, to find Lilah already on her feet.

'If Stam were to make an offer,' she said, 'then I would support it.' There! She had done it! Now she felt as if the blood were draining to her feet. Gazing at the sea of bobbing heads, Lilah felt suddenly queasy. For a split second there was total silence before all hell broke loose.

'Together,' shouted Rijnhard above the ensuing pandemonium, 'Lady Samson and Stam do represent a majority. A bid can now be launched.'

But it was hopeless. No one could hear a word as journalists and photographers fought to get onto the podium.

'Quick, Des,' shouted Freddie, elbowing his way through the crowd. 'Over here, lad. Where's that bloody photographer?'

'Coming.' Des was less adept than Freddie at flattening the opposition. Inured to the indignities and scrambles of the Paris collections, Hilary was already neck and neck with Freddie. 'What was it you were saying?' she screeched. 'About women and major public companies?'

'Shut up,' yelled Freddie, 'and give me your tape recorder. I've got to get an interview with Lady Samson.'

Roger was staring at his wife. Frozen next to him, it seemed as if Lilah had lost the strength and the will to move.

Suddenly, she felt a firm hand, taking her by the arm. 'Come on,' said Charles. 'I think I'd better get you out of here.'

Pushing his way across the podium, Rijnhard van Polen arrived to help. 'Well done,' he said, the vaguest hint of a twinkle illuminating his eyes. Lilah looked at him, her own eyes barely focusing. She was very cold. Soon Stam would have control of Samson International. And she had control of Stam. She was one of the richest and most powerful women in the world, but the information meant nothing to her.

'Let's get her away from here,' insisted Charles, concerned.

'I think she could do with a brandy. Tell them there'll be a full press release later today. Anything. Tell them anything to keep them happy.'

Rijnhard nodded his agreement and proceeded to make the announcement.

'No, Lady Samson is making no comment,' said Charles, brushing aside a score of microphones.

'But, please . . .'

'Just one question. Why?'

'Does this mean the end of your marriage?'

Seeing Lilah being pushed and jostled, Mike Patterson hustled his way to her side. 'You never cease to amaze me,' he said, helping Charles to move her forward through the crowd. Lilah watched in a daze as Mike punched one particularly insistent journo in the stomach. Freddie Higgins dropped his microphone as he doubled up in pain.

It was, of course, the picture they had all been waiting for. Photographers fought for pole position as Lilah's eyes met Roger's.

'Why?' he whispered, as Charles and Mike tried to usher her past him.

'Andrea.' Her voice was toneless. Roger buried his head in his hands.

'Oh, my God.'

'And a man named Simon Weiss.'

Roger looked up at her. *Then* it struck him. That look on Lilah's face. It was the same look he had seen on Simon's ghoulish features only the night before. Roger bowed his head again. This was how vengeance looked.

'Simon Weiss? How did you . . . ?'

But it was too late. Already Charles and Mike were steering Lilah down the steps of the podium and out of the nearest exit.

In the hotel manager's office, two men were finishing the afternoon tea Miss Kerwin had so thoughtfully provided. Well groomed in their double-breasted pin-striped suits, Anthony Rawlinson and John Mackintosh looked more like successful merchant bankers than members of the Serious Fraud Office.

'Extraordinary,' said Rawlinson. He and his colleague had followed proceedings via the loudspeaker in the office. 'And to think everyone believed she was besotted with him.'

Mackintosh nodded vaguely. Thirty-five years old next birthday, he had already seen too much at the SFO to be surprised by anything any more.

There was a slight cough as Miss Kerwin announced her arrival. 'I'm sorry, gentlemen,' she said, trying hard to look calm. 'As you've probably heard, the meeting's just broken up.'

'Miss Kerwin.' Rawlinson's voice was kind. In his experience, it was always the innocent who suffered most. Loyal employees, doting wives, impressionable kids – so often these were the hapless victims of other people's misdemeanours. 'I wonder if you'd be so good as to advise Sir Roger that we're here?'

Roger looked up to see his PA fighting her way towards him. The security guards were doing their best to keep the press at bay, but among all the confusion and commotion, it still seemed unwise to leave the podium at this stage.

'Sir Roger,' she whispered as eventually she was escorted to his side.

'Yes?'

For once, Miss Kerwin struggled to find the words. She could see the poor man was already in shock. How on earth could she break this to him now?

'Sir Roger, there are two gentlemen waiting for you in the manager's office. They say they want to interview you.' Miss Kerwin was having the greatest difficulty in fighting back the tears.

'No interviews,' replied Roger, gesturing towards the seething mass of media. 'Tell them all to go to hell.'

'These – these gentlemen are from the Serious Fraud Office. They say they want to see you now.'

'Jesus,' groaned Roger. Lilah! It must have been Lilah. But how?

Downstairs, in the hotel's underground car park, Lilah's chauffeur was waiting as instructed. Since dropping his employer off at Samson Heights that morning, Eamonn O'Reilly had run a few errands for Mrs Owen before making his way to the Samson International. Since then he had been listening to one of the local radio stations. Its half-hourly news flashes had kept him fully informed of developments inside at the AGM. Ten minutes ago, with an unholy din going on in the background, a reporter shouted a hoarse account of Lady Samson's amazing intervention.

'Good on herself,' said Eamonn to the St Christopher medal glistening against the burled mahogany dashboard. Herself had once told him some Pope had decided your man was no longer a saint. Eamonn had never heard such a load of old bollocks, not even from the Vatican. Perhaps one day St Christopher would get even by cashiering the Polish Pope down to a curate back in Cracow. Eamonn smiled. Talk about being cashiered. Eamonn did not know what Sir Roger had done. But whatever it was that blackguard surely had it coming. Not that Lady Samson had ever mentioned anything to him – she didn't even have to. Call it Celtic intuition. But Eamonn knew something had happened to make that woman so bloody miserable.

Two minutes later Lilah and her escorts came hurrying out of the lift. Eamonn jumped out of the car and opened the back door for her. She looked even more banjaxed than this morning.

'Thanks.' Her voice sounded uneasy. 'We're going to have to get a move on.'

Mike Patterson hovered around the car-park lift, ready to deck any importunate pressman who had managed to follow them.

'Are you sure you'll be all right?' asked Charles solicitously.

Lilah kissed him affectionately before stepping into the car. 'Don't worry about me,' she said, as Eamonn closed the door. 'I'm very grateful for everything, Charles. But it looks like I'm a big girl now.'

The two men waved as the car glided up the ramp, out of the car park and into Park Lane's early evening traffic. Eamonn asked no questions. He knew herself well enough by now. She would talk when she was good and ready. Right now, unless she said anything to the contrary, he would simply continue home.

Shivering despite the warmth of the car, Lilah could hear a loud thudding in her head. Roger – oh God, she could hardly bear to think of him. What sort of a future was facing him now? Prison, for sure, and then . . . ? She'd taken away his company. There was no way he'd ever get over that. His eyes! For once they'd shown fear and hurt and – no, she couldn't go on like this.

Dazed, Lilah tried to recall the people who had supported her throughout her struggle. Hugo, dear old Hugo, he'd ended up helping her even against his will. And Charles – darling man – at least *he* was happy again. Then, of course, there was Jonathan. What on earth had got into her? Those last angry words she'd shouted at him. Would he ever speak to her again? Lilah closed her eyes. Had it all been worth it? She'd been right to do what she'd done, of course. But why was being right so painful?

The two policemen stood up as Roger entered the office.

'Sir Roger Samson?' asked the detective chief superintendent.

'Yes.'

'Sir Roger, you are under arrest on suspicion of fraud. You are not obliged to say anything unless you wish to do so. But what you say may be used in evidence . . .'

The lights changed and Lilah's car merged into the crush around Hyde Park Corner. She stared out of the window at Decimus Burton's Wellington Arch. With its bronze group, the *Quadriga*, perched proudly, even arrogantly, on top, she had always loved that monument. Suddenly – the tension was too great – she burst into tears. A terrorist named Jojo Matwetwe. A hard-nosed dealer called Sophie Weiss. And a Lady christened Delilah Dooley. What furore the three of them had managed to create. The sculpture faded into the London gloom.

'Eamonn?' Her voice sounded strangulated.

'Yes?'

'Why would any artist in his right mind portray Peace as a woman?'

Eamonn shrugged his shoulders. His experience of life with Mrs O'Reilly read like an account of the Punic Wars. 'You've got me there, m'lady.' Eamonn studied his employer in the rear-view mirror. Oh dear. Herself was taking it badly. Never mind. She'd feel better in the morning, just as soon as she realized what a favour she'd done herself, ditching that shit of a husband.

The car moved back up the Park Lane one-way system.

'M'lady, I take it we're going home?'

Lilah thought for a minute. A shadow of a smile crept slowly across her face. What the hell? Even at this stage it was worth a try.

'No, Eamonn,' she said at last. 'You can take me to the airport. It may be too late already. But there's someone I've got to go and see.'

Gordon Stevens
Shadowland £4.99

THE EXPLOSIVE NEW THRILLER FROM THE AUTHOR OF *AND ALL THE KING'S MEN*

November 1989 . . .

In the final tense weeks before the fall of the Berlin Wall, from three cities across the world, three men are unleashed on a devastating manhunt . . .

Dispatched by his Washington superiors, Michael Rossini: soldier and politician, now spymaster extraordinaire.

From the heart of the Federal Republic, Hans-Joachim Schiller: once an escape organiser, now an unrivalled spycatcher.

And from East Berlin, Werner Langer: uncompromizing border guard, now risen to State Security General.

For eight long days, as history edges towards the brink, their paths cross, their destinies collide — and a long-buried Cold War secret is dragged to the surface . . .

Success now, for two of them at least, might change the future of the world. But failure could plunge it back into the dark times of the past . . .

Ann Victoria Roberts
Louisa Elliott £5.99

'I am filled with admiration. A great job.' Rosamunde Pilcher, author of
The Shell Seekers

In a passionate world of loyalty and betrayal would true love win the
ultimate victory?

The past was ever present in the ghostly shadows that lay between
the flickering gas lamps of the city of York, binding cousins Louisa and
Edward Elliott with the stigma of their illegitimacy.

Until out of the mists emerged Robert Duncannon, an Irish officer with
the Royal Dragoons. Dashing and impetuous, he is everything that
worthy, steadfast Edward can never be.

Her conflicting loyalties swept aside by an overwhelming love, Louisa
sails to Dublin with Robert. But in Ireland she encounters hostility –
and the mysterious Charlotte who, together with Captain Duncannon,
hides a guilty secret that threatens to shatter Louisa's dreams for ever.

At once an irresistible blend of period detail and passionate love,
Louisa Elliott is classic romance gloriously reborn as a magnificent
novel from the pen of a major new talent, Ann Victoria Roberts.

'A magnificent novel . . . a portrait of an extraordinary woman of her
time – for all time' CATHERINE GASKIN

Barbara Pym
No Fond Return of Love £4.99

'My favourite writer' Jilly Cooper

'"I'm sure things will be better in the morning," she went on, feeling that this was really the coward's way out. "Do you think you will be able to sleep now?" What a pity we can't make a cup of Ovaltine, was her last conscious thought. Life's problems are often eased by hot milky drinks . . .'

As far as Laurel could remember, Aunt Dulcie was a reasonable sort of person and quite young for an aunt, but there was nothing elegant or interesting about her. She wore tweedy clothes and sensible shoes and didn't 'make the most of herself' since (as her mother put it) a love affair had 'gone wrong' long ago.

For her part, Dulcie Manwaring accepts the arrival of her young niece as a not entirely unpleasant family duty. Preoccupied with uncomfortable (and newly discovered) feelings for a married man she has recently met at a conference, Dulcie is content to allow Laurel all the freedom she desires. Regrettably, her heart will not allow her to extend the same privilege to the distinguished editor – and troubled husband – Dr Alwyn Forbes . . .

'I pick up her books with joy, as though I were meeting an old, dear friend who comforts me, extends my vision and makes me roar with laughter. I invariably take one of her books on holiday to remind me of what is true, good, funny and touching about English life'
JILLY COOPER

'A splendid, humorous writer' JOHN BETJEMAN

'Sharp, funny and sad' THE TIMES

Revenge £4.99
A short story collection edited by Kate Stevens

Revenge is the deepest form of justice, which goes beyond any man-made law. Sometimes, not even death can stand in its way.

The stories in this new collection show revenge in all its forms — from bloody, impulsive acts of violence, to the subtlest turning of the tables. All demonstrate that whether revenge is tragic or melodramatic, horrifying or hilarious, it is always sweet.

Including stories by:

MURIEL SPARK	ALICE WALKER
ELLEN GILCHRIST	RUTH RENDELL
ELIZABETH GASKELL	WINIFRED HOLTBY
SHENA MACKAY	EMMA TENNANT
ELIZABETH BOWEN	LOUISA MAY ALCOTT

and new stories by:

CANDIA McWILLIAM	LUCY ELLMAN
MARY FLANAGAN	JOANNA BRISCOE
LISA ST AUBIN DE TERAN	MAUREEN FREELY
KATE SAUNDERS	ANNE ENRIGHT

'A book which offers both catharsis and entertainment' SHE

'Compulsively readable' TATLER

'A cracklingly good collection . . . to be read with relish and pleasure' SUNDAY TIMES

All Pan books are available at your local bookshop or newsagent, or can be ordered direct from the publisher. Indicate the number of copies required and fill in the form below.

Send to: Pan C. S. Dept
            Macmillan Distribution Ltd
            Houndmills Basingstoke RG21 2XS

or phone: 0256 29242, quoting title, author and Credit Card number.

Please enclose a remittance* to the value of the cover price plus: £1.00 for the first book plus 50p per copy for each additional book ordered.

*Payment may be made in sterling by UK personal cheque, postal order, sterling draft or international money order, made payable to Pan Books Ltd.

Alternatively by Barclaycard/Access/Amex/Diners

Card No.

Expiry Date

Signature:

Applicable only in the UK and BFPO addresses

While every effort is made to keep prices low, it is sometimes necessary to increase prices at short notice. Pan Books reserve the right to show on covers and charge new retail prices which may differ from those advertised in the text or elsewhere.

NAME AND ADDRESS IN BLOCK LETTERS PLEASE:

....

Name _____

Address _____

_____

_____

_____

6/92